The Days of Reckoning

Hailey Gosack

Contents

CHAPTER 1

Sarah

October 9, 2025

Nine sweltering hours in the back of the army's packed canvas truck. My lower back aches, my stomach growls. We only took two bathroom breaks from the time we left in the morning. Some people couldn't hold it. Just before our first bathroom break, my neighbor turned to me and apologized sheepishly. Before I could ask why, I felt the dampness seeping into my pants. The memory of the smell still sickens me—a mixture of body odor and urine trapped in the stagnant air and amplified by the heat. Water wasn't passed out until the second bathroom break.

Our treatment thus far has called into question our decision to leave with the army and work in exchange for basic necessities. Ava and I communicated this silently with looks of fear since setting off from the first bathroom break. However, attempting an escape during the second bathroom break was too risky. We were many hours outside of Salt Lake. The landscape had turned. Red mesas and rock spires dotted the increasingly barren landscape. The temperature had risen. We had gone South—of that, I was confident.

Four army trucks had arrived within close proximity of each other. Loads of us piled out of the backs of the vehicles directly into a large, white yurt, where we were instructed to take a number and wait our turn to speak with an entry agent. Before I did this, I went to the water table and helped myself to three glasses. The remainder is still sitting in my stomach. It rolls when I move as the water sloshes around in the otherwise empty interior.

I itch to get a glimpse of where they've taken us. What the heck did we sign up for? I sit on a cold, metal folding chair with a clipboard and paperwork in my hand. I've filled out dozens of similar health questionnaires before and reviewed thousands of these with patients.

Question number 15: *Have you ever had suicidal thoughts? If yes, please explain.*

I hesitate. Technically, no. Not *seriously*, anyway, but sure, they flitted around in my head from time to time like a fantasy. Sometimes, it just seemed like the easiest option compared to the slow death from cancer that awaited me. But I was glorifying it, of course. Back in the day, when I had access to an arsenal of prescription medications, it would have been like a slow dip into the black abyss. Easy, no pain. But today, it would prove more difficult, and I don't have the mettle required. Besides, those thoughts are buried in my mind now that I'm here. I made it here to the army base. There's a kaleidoscope of future possibilities shifting inside my mind.

The monotony of a health questionnaire has me buzzing from this sip of normality. Surely, more will follow. Surely, the treatment we received on the ride here was just a one-off.

I check "no" and move on. At question 29, I squirm in my seat. *Have you ever been diagnosed with cancer? If yes, please explain.*

Breast cancer, I write along with the diagnosis date and a summary of the last scans I had taken. Then, I use the margin on the questionnaire to write out the action plan that I had discussed with my oncologist before the blackout in hopes that it would give the team here a road map of sorts.

I look up at the screen to check the number they are on. I'm waiting for my turn, along with some other arrivals. It displays thirty-nine. Nineteen to go. I stand and stretch for a moment. My rump is still sore from the long ride in the back of the cramped truck with only a thinly padded bench seat.

I've felt hunger many times before and come to normalize the sensation, but this time is different. I know that behind the admittance doors, there's food. The anticipation creates an eager stomach that growls with renewed ferocity. Will there be fresh, crisp vegetables and fruit? I allow myself to fantasize. Perhaps some cheese or warm bread with butter? My mouth waters and my stomach rebukes me with a rumble as I swallow yet another unproductive bite of saliva.

Ava approaches me, evidently finished with her questionnaire. "Why do you think they need to know all this stuff?" she asks.

I shrug. "Seems pretty standard to me. We're army volunteers now. Makes sense."

She nods. We sit next to each other in silence for a minute, taking in the scene. People shuffle up to plastic folding tables manned by gray uniformed individuals who seem to ask more questions and then stamp their paperwork as they direct them toward their door.

"What do you think they mean? The yellow and the green doors?" Ava jerks her chin toward the doors.

"I don't know," I reply. We fall quiet again while I finish my questionnaire. I complete it just as my number displays on the large monitor. I peek at Ava's questionnaire. There's considerably less written on it. Ava's knee bounces as she watches for her number.

"That's me," I announce. Ava gives me a weak smile as I go to the next available uniformed person.

The agent reviews my paperwork with the occasional "hmm." I'm surprised when she stamps my paper with a yellow smiley face, not bothering to ask me more.

"What do the colors mean?" I ask. "Yellow and green?"

"Oh," she looks up at me, "just different occupations. You'll learn more once you're through the doors." She looks back down, apparently finished with me. I scoot the chair back and walk to the yellow door.

As I push open the yellow door, I turn back and give Ava a thumbs-up. She returns the gesture with an encouraging smile. On the other side of the door, I see people grouped together in the center of a room shaped oddly like a train station terminal. The ceiling is half-domed, and the room is long and plain. Concrete walls line either side. There are no train tracks.

It seems we are waiting for one of four doors to open. Each side of the room has two heavy sliding concrete doors with a number above it. I don't have time to ask anyone what we're waiting for. The door with a flaky number four painted in solid white slides open to our left with a piercing screech that echoes throughout the space. A uniformed soldier steps across the threshold. He stands erect, holding a large rifle across a thick, green vest that stands out against the drab gray uniform I've become accustomed to seeing.

"Ladies and Gentlemen, please follow me and listen carefully to instructions." His voice is deep and commanding.

"When do we eat?" someone asks bravely.

The man glowers at the one who dared speak. His broad jaw flexes before answering through gritted teeth, "Soon. This way." He motions us to enter through door number four, where we shuffle into a smaller room with a similar door on the opposite side. When we are all through, the man shuts the door behind us. We stand, crowded together, while the soldier pushes past us gruffly to the opposite door.

The space is dark except for the single light bulb hanging from the concrete ceiling. There are no windows, and it smells of campfire and something else I can't quite put my finger on. As he opens the other door, he slides through quickly. An elderly man is close on his heels, seemingly eager to follow, but he's stopped with a hand placed firmly on his chest by the guard who had just stepped through.

"Just a moment," the officer says as he shoves the man away from the door. The door shuts in his face with a high-pitched squeak followed by a loud *thunk*. I barely have time to feel outraged on the man's behalf when something else sets in: consternation. There's a sound like bolts sliding into place on the other side of the door.

We trade glances that all seem to ask, what's going on? The tension is now palpable. I instinctively move back towards the door closest to me that we had just entered through when I step on something that crunches beneath my sneaker. I kick the gray dirt aside and see something small and white gleaming through the drab gray. I bend down to see what it is just as I hear someone else murmur, "Hey, there's jewelry here." But what I have isn't jewelry. It's a porcelain tooth. Just as my own panic is kicking in, the group seems to sense it, too. I let the tooth fall from my hand. Someone screams. The sound is deafening as it bounces off the walls that entomb us. I rub at the fine gray dirt left behind from the tooth I'd held only seconds ago. It smudges between my fingers.

There's a mad dash for the doors. I'm knocked down and kicked in the side. Someone steps on my leg. I can't hear anything other than my own blood pumping in my ears and the sounds of other's desperate cries, but I can see, and what I see is the single light bulb dangling from the ceiling's center change from its dull yellow glow to an ominous red.

And then, I smell it.

It burns my nostrils. I cover my nose with my shirt, trying to keep it out, but it seems to seep in through my pores. My body screams for escape. Bodies drop around me. With fewer bodies blocking the view above me, I see weighted clouds of fog-like mist rolling down in billows from vents in the ceiling.

And then, it all dawns on me. *The smell. The teeth. The heavy doors. The ash.* We're in a crematorium.

A body falls across me, heavy. I scream, pinned to the floor, watching as a concentrated cloud of gas descends towards me. My lungs are on fire. Tears roll down my cheeks. Everyone is on the floor now. I grab the closest hand I can find of another person. I don't know who it belongs to, but I squeeze it desperately. The hand is warm but unresponsive to my touch. Fear rips through me. Other than the raging panic pitted in my stomach and the burning in my lungs, the last conscious thought I have is, *please make it stop.*

CHAPTER 2

Sam

October 9, 2025

We're leaving Salt Lake. We're lucky that the army's presence there had distracted the citizens. With renewed hopes of aid riding on the army's arrival that morning, we escaped the city without incident. Oddly, people seemed to scatter at the sound of our motors. Not what we expected. We have little to show for our recruitment efforts. A family, two women, and three single men bought our story and agreed to join the resistance.

Miller and Ben are riding ahead on the quiet, electric motorcycles the SEALs had brought with them, scouting for trouble. They'll come back and warn us if there's something alarming up ahead. Having cleared the road on the way down here, I imagine our trip home will go more smoothly. If we do it all in one straight shot, it's a five-hour drive. We may have to stop to charge the motorcycles, but let's hope we make it home.

Thirty minutes into the drive, with the Ogden and Salt Lake metropolises behind us, we relax a little. Everyone but Frank, anyway. Deep lines run between my son's furrowed brows. The skin of his knuckles gripping the steering wheel is stretched white. He's driving the Super Duty, pulling the trailer today. I'm riding shotgun. In the cab is the family we picked up (to my disapproval) and the woman, Carrie. Ted is the dad's name. He has an older boy riding in the back of the truck, and from what I've gathered, the little kids riding with us are Evie and Alex. I imagine that Frank's sour mood has something to do with them. The kids have grown restless. The boy keeps kicking the back of my seat, reminding me that this is far from where we had hoped to be after our attempts to recruit. We picked up stragglers. The men and women could be assets, but these kids? Charity. Pure charity. And possible liabilities.

Carrie sits turned toward the window behind Frank with her forehead pressed against the glass and her eyes closed. Silent tears run down her face. I'm grateful she's not an audible crier. She hasn't said a single word since we left. That's also kind of nice, though I do feel bad for thinking it. She's just been through a traumatic ordeal. The man's body, Cal, I think she said, was easy enough to bury, but I know just because you throw dirt on a grave doesn't mean you've sealed it.

Ted is not nearly as quiet as Carrie. After some awkward attempts at small talk, he tries a different tact. Clearly, he hopes to win our favor—Frank's in particular. "The house we left in Salt Lake has supplies," he announces.

"What kind of supplies?" Frank asks.

"Food, herbs..."

"It's the best hiding place!" Evie chimes in. She has bouncing ringlet blonde hair and large blue eyes. The little girl is a cutie. I'll give her that.

"Oh, yeah. We had a good setup there," Ted says. *Why'd you leave then?* I want to ask. If we're not even picking up a charity case, what's the point here? Someone will be getting a reprimand. I hear it was Crowly who pulled for them. He must have his reasons.

"It's in a secret basement no one can find!" Evie divulges, excited to be part of the conversation.

Frank's expression softens. "Tell me about it," he says.

"You walk into this closet, but it's not a closet!" Evie exclaims.

Ted elaborates, "We were gifted this place, really. It was a lifesaver. The basement entrance is concealed at the back of a coat closet. The house was left in a state that would deter any looters from entering."

Frank rubs his chin pensively. "Where's it located?"

"You know that white 'U' on the hillside above the University?" Ted asks.

"Yeah," Frank responds. I'm following along, wondering where this is all going.

"Follow that West, along the hillside, and the house is located on the uppermost street called Tomahawk Drive," Ted states.

"So, it borders the hillside?"

"Yep, it backs right up to it. There's lots of great hiking back there."

"I'm not interested in hiking," Frank states.

I look at him, "What are you interested in then, Frank?"

"The location, the supplies there, the hidden nature of it. That could make a damn good COP," he says. Before I can ask, he addresses Ted. "What are the views like from the house?"

"Well, you can't see anything from the basement. It has two small windows that look into an interior courtyard, but if you go up to the house's second floor, it has sweeping city views."

"Well, I'll be..." Frank says quietly to himself.

"What's a COP?" I ask.

"Combat Outpost. We could use this place," he says.

"You aren't still thinking about building an army, are you?" I finally say it, unable to hold back on this topic any longer. Building an army of resistors seemed impossible before, but now that we've put forth the initial effort and come away nearly empty-handed, it should be obvious. I want Frank to drop this silly notion.

Frank sighs deeply. The lines between his brows return with renewed depth. I expect Frank to get angry. I expect him to defend his ideas vehemently. But he doesn't. He's silent for a long while. The kids must notice the shift in the mood because they're silent, too.

Finally, Frank clears his throat. "I didn't think it through," he says quietly. It takes me a moment to grasp what he's talking about.

"The army?" I ask.

"Yes, the army," he says, clearly irritated. "They thought of everything."

"So, you're done? Done trying to build an army?" I ask, hopeful.

"Yes and no," he responds. "I think it's time to try a different tact. We've got more weapons than people right now. That's fine. Maybe we don't need to engage in traditional warfare tactics." He's rubbing his chin again, one hand on the wheel. It's his thinking face. He's done it ever since he was a boy trying to construct complex Lego structures.

"There's something else you should know," he says.

I cock an eyebrow.

"Hutchens and Stevens are leaving the Colony once we return. They're ready to get back to their families and off guard dog duty. They've got a comms box if we need to call them back."

"Ok," I say. "I'm assuming they'll be taking their motorcycles with them?"

"Yep," Frank responds. That'll leave us three silent, zippy motorcycles that everyone has come to love so much and three men from the original SEALs team: Crowly, Miller, and Frank. Everyone has come to love them, too. And respect them. They're mascots to the people back at the ranch, but they also represent security and authority. Seeing them watching over us has the same effect as popping a Xanax.

"What did you have in mind?" I ask. "For the different tact?"

"An inside job, maybe." He looks off into the distance. "Besides, to build an army, you have to feed an army. It was never going to work. Winter is coming. We'll have a hard enough time feeding ourselves. If we had enough food, it'd be an easy sell. I should have stored food *and* weapons. It was short-sighted. It was a stupid oversight. Incredibly stupid."

I look out the window and watch the yellow hillsides bordering the highway whiz by. I'm unused to hearing Frank being self-deprecating. "Don't be too hard on yourself," I say. "No one could have predicted this with perfect clarity."

"It ran out so much faster than I expected," he says quietly as if to himself, and I reckon he means the food.

"You and me both," Ted pipes up. Frank gives him a look in the rearview mirror. The truck falls silent again.

"What's next then?" I ask.

"We focus on our own survival," Frank replies, "and we make an attempt to gather intel from our mole within the Metal City. There has to be another way. A weakness we can exploit. Of course, this means someone has to infiltrate their city and look for him. The question now is *who*?"

I nod. This news allows an incredible lightness to settle in me. Frank is talking reasonably. Intelligently. And better yet, he's dropped the idea of building an army. Anxiety I wasn't aware I was holding onto has leeched from my bones.

The kids begin a game of 'I Spy.' I find myself smiling at their game when Evie attempts to cheat, clearly changing her objects to ones that she couldn't have been thinking of when she started because they've just come into view. I would let something like that go, but Alex won't. Ted attempts to mediate. It's all so normal. Maybe everything is going to be ok after all. And then, we see the motorcycles coming back towards us, flashing their lights.

We pull over. The other two vehicles following us roll to a stop. Frank lowers his window and leans out, waiting for Miller and Ben to dismount and make their way over to him. I see Tom and Crowly in my sideview mirror coming to join them. Tom is among the first to reach Frank's window, and the two brothers' differences strike me. Frank is still well-kempt, with a buzzed haircut and a clean-shaven face. He has a broader build, evident in his square face and boxy shoulders. Tom has a slighter frame, with shaggy brown hair sticking out beneath a bleached ballcap and a full beard he hasn't bothered shaving in months. Both have my blue eyes, sure, but that's where the resemblance ends. Frank looks more like Rose. Tom and Lilly look more like me. None of the kids was lucky enough to get Rose's hazel eyes. I wonder if this is where the favoritism started—how I've categorized the two boys. Or was it later when Tom took an interest in ranch work? Frank always had other plans.

As Miller approaches our vehicle with Ben close behind, he says, "There are people camped out on the road ahead."

"How many?" Frank asks.

"Hard to say. Maybe twenty," he replies as he shades his eyes with his hand.

"Shit. Do you think they heard us on the way down and are waiting for us?" Tom asks.

"It's possible," Miller responds.

Frank sits back in the truck and turns to me. "What do you make of this, Dad?"

I lean closer toward Frank, resting my forearm on the center console. "Did they see you?" I ask, looking at Ben and Miller. They exchange a look.

"The bikes aren't completely silent, but I don't think so. Why?" Miller asks.

"Can we go around?" I ask.

"Maybe, but you know they'll be able to hear you guys coming from miles away," Miller responds.

"What are you thinking, Dad?" Tom places his hands on the truck above Frank's window and peers down at me.

I think back to what happened to Justin outside of Challis. This is why we were never going to be able to build an army. This is why the EMP was the perfect weapon. This is why we'll always be at a disadvantage. "We go around them," I respond. "If that's not possible, we go through them. Let's prepare for the worst."

CHAPTER 3

Carrie

October 16, 2025 One Week Later

Is this what my life has been reduced to? Backaches from sleeping on a thin camping pad, bathroom breaks with only leaves for wiping, weekly cold baths in the icy water of the creek, and hairy armpits? To my dismay, toilet paper was one of the first things to run out. It's one of the only things I miss about the office—toilet paper stocked for hundreds, but only myself there to use it. Well, that and the warmth the building offered. But that had been a different time of year. It'll be cold in Salt Lake by now, too. Wishing for anything I had back at the office building is an exercise in frustration and futility. I'm here now—the Idaho ranch. We've been calling it the Colony.

I unzip my tent flap and crawl out. Last night was damn cold. I feel as if a permanent chill has taken residence in my bones. Last night was the first night I slept without the tarp covering my tent. They took those to protect the crops. I zip up my tent and stand, looking forlorn at the naked tent before me. I can't sleep like that again. Sleep is a generous word for what I did last night. The cold at least keeps the heavy fog of sleep deprivation from consuming me completely. Regardless, I head towards the fire as I rack my brain for solutions. I peer into the sleeping quarters of the other tenties (that's what we call those of us who are waiting on a real roof to rest our heads beneath). In other tents, some people sleep under mountains of blankets. Some have animal skins. A few tents hardly resemble tents anymore. They're covered in a patchwork of duct-taped cardboard or a pallet structure that's been topped with mounds of dirt.

As I weave through the settlement and toward the large community fire, I notice other things. Pots occupy every square inch of free space within the tents, and piles of gathered goods have begun to spill out alongside them. The pots and the disturbed earth directly around the tent sites are all attempts at people trying to grow a little bit of their food. Either to supplement what's handed out or to use for trade and barter. It's fascinating how quickly a sub-economy has bloomed here. People trade mainly in food, ammo, alcohol, and cigarettes. I have none of these—demonstrated nicely by my plain tent and meager possessions.

I pass old man Kirk, who winds his handcrank radio every morning. The never-ending static fades behind me as I approach the fire.

While warming my hands by the fire, I ponder ways I can insulate my shelter. I think of the sleeping pad beneath me. I could tear it apart and duct tape it to the top of the tent. But then, I'm stuck sleeping on the cold, hard ground, and they may take my creation anyway. They're desperately trying to keep the fall crop from freezing. I sigh. I can hardly blame them; besides, I stand to benefit from their success. But still, I'll have to do something.

I should be at work soon, but with my fingers toasty and my core beginning to hold some heat, I go to the evergreen forest that rings the small valley floor we've claimed as our settlement site. I pull on my gloves and jump up to pull down broad branches using my weight. If they don't snap right away, I move on. I've collected six good-sized evergreen branches with a decent canopy of pine needles spreading from the branch's core. This should help cover my tent and protect me from the cold. Despite the gloves I'm wearing, the needles occasionally bite into my skin. Prickly bastards. Shit—will they rip my tent? ...Probably not. That material is sturdy. I toss a branch on top of the tent and watch it bow slightly beneath the weight. I lean more branches against the sides to support the branches I lay across for a roof. I stand back to admire my handiwork. I think I'm on to something here. I'll need to gather more branches to cover the gaps, but I'm out of time. Everyone is up now, rustling about. Most grumble about something. No one offers to help me, but I'm used to this. It's time to head to work.

Laundry. This is the job I've been assigned. I did laundry for Cal, too. Is this what I'm destined for now? From the youngest Associate Vice President at a prestigious financial firm to a Launderer, not the money kind. There's never-ending laundry, *Little House on the Prairie* style, with a makeshift washboard and a bucket filled with lukewarm water heated over a fire. If I'm lucky, that is. Some days, it's ice cold. But the water temperature doesn't matter much towards the end of the pile. My hands are stiff from exertion either way.

To make matters worse, I'm an outcast here. I didn't mean for it to happen. My discontent with this place seeped through and displayed itself for everyone to see. The other women here seem to have decided that the discontent extends to them as well. They must assume I think I'm better than them. It doesn't matter how much I try to fake a smile or start a conversation. They can smell it on me, and they slowly inch away. I've stopped trying to hide it. Fuck pleasantries. I'm here due to a lack of options. I couldn't stay at Cal's house without Cal. I knew I'd be ostracized, and that would be as good as dead. Sam took pity on me and said that I could come to the ranch if I could find a way to contribute. I told him about the stockpile of food at Cal's house, hoping that offering would be enough to convince him that I had value. But I don't think it was vital.

Sam is a big softy who doesn't realize what a teddy bear he really is. He carries authority, too. And it's a good thing, or I would have been denied entrance immediately. Early on, the Colony was being picky about who could squat here. I can't blame them. It was smart.

Sam didn't want to risk a scene at Cal's house once he heard the neighborhood had developed its own kind of 'clan' mentality. "Let them have it," he had said to me, but I was stubborn. After we buried Cal by the lake, I walked back to the house alone and filled as many bags as I could carry back to the lake where Sam and the others waited. I felt watchful, curious eyes on my back as I left, or perhaps it was just the guilt. Either way, I made it back with those bags, and it's the reason why I can look at these women today with my nose turned up. *I earned my entrance*, I want to say to them. I should really be grateful to be here, but I can't help longing for something more than constant hunger pangs and frozen fingers. Something more than always being slightly smelly, dirty, and tired. But most of all, something more than the crushing loneliness.

I have one person I've talked to on multiple occasions, one person to whom I can semi-relate. His name is Ted. We arrived together as outsiders. With Sam behind us, we were allowed in, but Ted managed a slightly less hostile welcome, in large part to the three kids he brought with him. The little girl, Evie, is incredibly adorable with a little bit of a Shirley Temple vibe. Alex is cute, too. The teenager was welcomed because he's an able-bodied worker. Ted's also seen as someone of value because his home, or the home he was *borrowing*, can be used as some kind of base for any additional trips to Salt Lake. It was discussed at length during the long ride from Utah to Idaho.

Still, Ted and I share the same hollowed-out expression of someone who thinks they're in a bad dream. Like any moment, we'll blink and wake up. But Ted is a man. I don't want a repeat of what happened with Cal. And I know he's hurting because he recently lost his wife, and he has three kids to look after. Plus, he's old. Too old for me. It's too bad he isn't closer to grandfather status. Then, a romantic relationship would be out of bounds entirely. But no. It still falls within the realm of possibility. I'll have to try harder to find a female friend.

I look up from my wash bucket and wrinkle my nose at the candidates. The other women I launder with like to whistle while they work. One sings.

Sometimes, I don't mind, so as long as she doesn't try any alto. Her voice is meant for baritone, but she gets adventurous at times, and I have to resist putting my hands over my ears.

I'm annoyed that only women do the laundry. I want badly to believe that I can keep up with the men. It was a lie I fell into easily in the corporate world where there were anti-discrimination laws, but out here, we've fallen more or less into old-fashioned roles. It feels like a thorn in my side to witness it, but I've been toying with the thorn lately, debating on pulling it out and not letting it bother me anymore. I've had to face the reality of things: I'm not as strong as the men. I can't build, and I can't hunt. My job possibilities are limited here. The best jobs, in my view, are those of teachers, but those have been reserved for the elderly or those with teaching backgrounds. My corporate finance background is useless. So, I have to fall back on the only thing I have to offer: manual labor that doesn't require a lot of strength. My options are gardening, laundry, or cooking. The gardeners are filthy at the end of the day, and cooks have to gut and skin animals, a task I find repulsive. So, here I am. Laundry. Again.

My stomach rumbles, and for about the thousandth time today, I glance at the supply shed. There's food in there. I don't know how much, but definitely enough to gorge myself on. I haven't been full in weeks. With winter approaching, the rationing has gotten intense. We all feel the longing for more. Many glances become gazes, entranced by the lure of the supply shed. This is probably why two people are armed to guard the shed at all times. It hurts morale a bit, but it was explained in a way that we all agreed was in our best interest. That conversation might not go over as well these days with our stomachs constantly talking to us—whispering about the spoils hidden inside that shed.

The hunger pangs felt across the Colony have also created a sort of ambient hostility toward newcomers. And there seems to be a newcomer every other day. Sometimes multiple. Most are turned away, but I couldn't say what tells them apart from the ones who are accepted. Possibly, it's about who you know that's already here. I've learned that tribalism runs deep in these small communities.

They're supposed to have a meeting to address the issue of newcomers soon. I assume they'll have to start requiring an entrance fee of food or something, but the people who come to us now are coming out of desperation. What could they possibly have to give at this point? I'm not sure, but I'm glad I'm already in, even though sometimes I wish I were out. I think about the alternate possibilities. I could have stayed in the office complex and scavenged the increasingly dangerous city for food. No, that was an option I nixed early on when I decided to head to Cal's house. Maybe I should have stayed in Cal's home and explained what had happened to the neighbors. Wishful thinking. I was an outsider there, too, and returning without Cal would have only contributed to their reservations about me. Plus, I'm kidding myself if I think they're safer there. The city is the worst place to be when resources are scarce. Like it or not, it's time to admit that this is the best place to be.

***

The community leaders have called a meeting for tonight. Finally, something exciting. These are the highlights of my days. Once, someone was brought forth for trial. His crime? Stealing from the supply shed. His sentence? Exile from the Colony. One of the fancy men they call a SEAL had put him on his motorcycle, driven him far away, and returned without him. We stopped glancing at the supply shed so much after that. Tonight, to my disappointment, the meeting doesn't involve a trial.

We've all gathered below the large ranch house on the lawn as the council members stand above us on the dwelling's expansive deck. The house is built into a hillside, and the deck juts out towards the field in which we all now live. It serves itself nicely as a sort of throne, I think. Or a rock-like

Mufasa used to hold Simba up and address the other animals of the Pride Lands.

"By our calculations, we will not have enough food to sustain everyone until crops can be harvested without jeopardizing the integrity of the herd," the voice booms. We've all come to know this voice well. It belongs to Tom, and it's his land we're on and his cattle we're consuming. Some folks around here still refer to it as Sam's Ranch, but that's just the old-timers. Sam told me about the ranch on the way here and how he had sold it to his son Tom the year prior. We're all aware that we need to keep enough cattle to reproduce and sustain us. If we eat them all, we won't have milk, and we won't have any more meat.

Tom stands near the railing as he addresses us. Several others occupy the deck with Tom. There's Sam and his daughter Lilly and a handful of other people that make up the council. The SEALs are nowhere to be seen tonight. They seem to make frequent disappearing acts. Frank, I know from what Ted told me, is taking Bodin to an army volunteer site in Salt Lake. That kid has balls. I'm aware that his son's volunteering has further added to Ted's value at the Colony. The gap separating us as equals here grows wider.

The other SEALs, though? Again, I don't know where they go—not my pay grade.

"Before we discuss any radical next steps, we have a proposal." I assume the "next steps" have to do with newcomers. We are all silent, anxiously awaiting what Tom will suggest. "We'd like to propose a recon mission. We need to exhaust all of our options by exploring closer to town and on the other side to see if there's anything left and what kind of state the people are in. We need supplies—fishing gear, nails, food, tools, ammo... those kinds of things. We don't expect to find much. Anyone who volunteers will be risking their lives. We must operate with a level of secrecy. We do not want to invite any more people to join the Colony. We are at capacity." I feel a few shift their gazes to me, and I wonder whether Ted feels their eyes, too. We are outsiders—"city folk" who have taken valuable places within the Colony that could be extended to locals.

"We'd like to ask for volunteers to venture into town and the areas beyond. You'll largely be responsible for your own food and water once you leave. The time horizon is unknown. You could be out there for weeks. You'll also be on your own. Our SEALs have other matters to attend to." He pauses, looking around. Chatter rises amongst the people.

Someone shouts out, "What matters?" but receives no response.

Tom's voice rings out, "Please raise your hand if you want to volunteer. We need a maximum of ten people." I look around. Some hands shoot up immediately. Others extend tentatively. I count eight. Then, one more. Nine. Before I can stop myself, I raise my hand high.

"That's ten," Tom confirms. "Volunteers stick around after tonight's meeting for further instruction."

The council members disappear from the deck to inside the house. The crowd disperses, some bumping my shoulders as they divert around me like water moving past a stone. I swallow.

What did I agree to?

CHAPTER 4

Bodin

October 16, 2025 One Week Later

I close my eyes and hit replay again.

Evie clinging to my leg. Evie crying. I promised her I'd come back.

There's this feeling that won't go away. I'd rather be punched in the stomach. And there's this thought that won't leave either. *How could you do this to her? She just lost her mom. We just lost our mom.*

The thing is, I would have chosen to stay. I would have picked her up and shut the door on my Ava fantasy for good, but it wasn't just about Ava anymore. The "rescue" mission I had carefully pined for had morphed and gained momentum. I couldn't stop it. I had to go for the sake of every single person still fighting to live. At least, that's how they made me feel.

I was told that I could make an impact with the intel I could glean. I hold onto that. It will be worth it if I can accomplish that. Of course, it's a long shot. And if I fail... well, I just hope I can keep my promise to Evie.

It all happened so fast. I was only at the ranch for three days before it was time to go. Frank didn't want me to miss the opportunity to be recruited from Salt Lake because we didn't know where the army was going next. Ron flew us in his Cessna and dropped us in the Wasatch Mountain range that lines the Eastern side of the Salt Lake Valley and runs north. We were dropped north so we could come down from the hills behind our old house. Ted's house. Our aim was Edith's house, the house we moved into after Mom died. If we had hidden it well enough, it would provide food and shelter, and our entrance from the hills behind it would shield us from detection.

Things went smoothly enough. The house was there as we had left it just a handful of days before. I do have a couple of complaints, though. The first is that it was humiliating to be strapped to Frank tandem-style as we jumped from 6,000 feet in the Cessna, but he insisted that we stay together, and without proper parachute training, I was apt to crash-land. Maybe he had a point, but I'm starting to loathe the guy and his commander complex. Secondly, we were dropped so far from the city that it took us an entire day of hiking to reach the house. Third, Frank made me wait at the house while he did some "scouting" in the valley to try to determine if anyone knew where the next recruitment would take place.

It didn't take him long to figure out that they recruit from four consistent locations. One is the same place Ava and Sarah were picked up. A fifteen-minute walk from the house. All we had to do was wait. And wait. Finally, three days later, we were in business.

"Remember what I've told you," Frank said as I pulled my backpack onto my shoulders. "You have to find our inside guy. He's got a port wine stain birthmark that runs just past his hairline on the right side of his face."

"Yeah, yeah," I said. We'd been over it. He placed his hand on my shoulder.

"We have to know their weak spots," he added.

"I know!" I shrugged him off and began walking away.

"Crowly and I will be waiting for you in one week. Don't attempt escape before then because we might not be there. If you make it out, we'll see you. Just get as far away as you can as fast as you can," he called after me. I threw my hand up in a curt good riddance without turning around, but he wasn't finished. "And Bodin," he said. I stop, caught by the seriousness of his tone. "We won't wait forever," he added. I didn't look back. I took a deep breath, and I kept walking.

I can't believe that conversation occurred just this morning. Seems like the hours in this truck have stretched across days. I'm going nuts. I know from what Frank told me that it'll probably be about a nine-hour drive to make it to the Metal City in Arizona. We've had two breaks. The light that appears briefly through the flap on the canvas tied together at the back of the truck is dimming. It shouldn't be long now.

The truck is stuffy. The lady next to me needs like a million Tic Tacs, and she just fell asleep with her mouth agape. I look at the poor sucker whose shoulder she slumped back on, but he's also deep in slumber with his mouth hanging wide, too. I wince at the exchange of air going on between the two. I lean back with my head pressing into the cold canvas and think of what Evie might be doing. It's hard to believe our lives consisted of school drop-offs and six o'clock dinners just two months ago. Now Evie, Ted, and Alex live in a camp in Idaho, and I'm on an army caravan heading for the secret city of the elites in hopes of bringing back Ava. Oh, and getting intel. I can't forget that.

The same thoughts have sloshed around in my head for the past two hours. Mercifully, the truck begins to slow. I've gotten my hopes up before, but when two slaps can be heard coming from the cab, I know it's the real deal. We all begin to stir with angst. The guard sitting at the back, like a pencil was shoved up his ass, stands. His commitment to that upright seated position the entire drive here is impressive. My legs need to move. My ass is numb from the constant cajoling from the last hour. That's when we left a paved road for a dirt road. I could smell it, and I could sense it when the speed was reduced, and the truck jumped and swayed in a way that only a back road could confer. The truck comes to a stop but then turns around and reverses. It backs up and reaches its final resting place, signified by a hiss of the breaks and a silenced engine. I stand with eager anticipation, along with just about everyone else.

The tailgate drops and a flap of the canvas is pulled back. I squint against the bright, invading artificial light and watch my foot placement as I climb out of the truck. Two soldiers flank the rear of the truck, offering hands to anyone who needs help down. I decline but watch my feet as I move from the truck. I need a minute to catch my bearings. When I look around, I notice that we've been backed into a giant white yurt that has chairs lined in neat rows in the center, two long tables at the front with two individuals seated with clipboards at each one, a black screen up high in the middle of them and behind them are two more armed guards standing straight with guns held across their chests. My eyes flicker across two sets of double doors on opposite sides of the yurt. One is outlined in green, and one is outlined in yellow. There's a blue port-a-potty close to us at the back and a table with water on it. One of the individuals sitting behind a table rises and addresses our group as the last of us hops from the back of the truck.

"There's water on the far table and a bathroom in the rear," she says, pointing like she's directing air traffic. A small microphone clipped to her gray jacket amplifies her soft voice. "Once you've taken care of your business, have a seat, and we will be with each one of you shortly. The chairs are numbered. Please advance to an open individual with a clipboard when your number is displayed on the screen." She gestures to the screen and then to the four of them waiting patiently behind the tables.

For a few moments, everyone stands around, blinking against the light as if dazed. I move to get a glass of water, and the spell is broken. The group splits like pool balls during the initial break. After getting my water, I walk to the chairs and pick a seat in the second row. The chair's seat has a spray-painted number eight. Numbers one, two, three, and four flashes on the screen one after the other. I watch the interaction between the officials and the recruits sitting at the tables. The officials have laptops opened in front of them and type things out, occasionally nodding in response to dialogue I can't hear. The gaunt woman with the rank breath who sat next to me on the truck is directed to the yellow door after about three minutes. She shuffles over slowly with her back arched in a pronounced stoop. The number five flashes on the screen. The others take longer. One more moves to yellow, and two move through the green door. It's my turn. When eight flashes on the screen, I approach the first available official. She's thin, with perfectly straight brown hair cut sharply at the chin line. Her nose is bird-like, and her thin lips are bright red, but her smile is kind. I feel at ease when I sit across from her.

"Hello," she says.

"Hello," I reply.

"Name and date of birth please."

"Bodin Weiss. March 10, 2008."

"Almost eighteen," she says as her fingers peck away at the keyboard. I shift in my seat, not wanting to get into small talk. "Let's jump right into it, shall we?"

I nod.

"Alright then, tell me about your health history, Bodin. Have you ever been diagnosed with anything?"

"No."

"Hospitalized for anything?"

"Um, I broke my arm once." Her fingernails clack as she makes a note on the computer.

"And how would you describe your level of physical fitness?"

"I dunno," I shrug. "Good."

"Did you play any sports?"

"Football for two years." I was kicked off the team my junior year, but I wasn't about to tell her that.

She nods. "And what do you like to do?"

I blink at her. "Like..." I deadpan.

"Like hobbies," she prompts.

"Um, I played video games, and sometimes I put together model cars." This all seems so stupid to me.

"Video games. Are you afraid of heights?" she asks.

I remember jumping from the Cessna just days ago and the exhilaration.

"No," I answer.

"What's your height and weight?"

"Six foot one. And I dunno... maybe 165." Her fingers dance across the keyboard.

When she's finished, she looks up at me and asks, "Uh-huh, and where's your family?" Her face is sympathetic and quizzical. I swallow.

"I don't know," I say as I look away. When I look back, her eyes are still on me. I shift again. "My mom and sister never made it home, and when Ted went out to look for them, he never returned either." I swallow hard. It's still challenging to mutter the simplest of words: Mom. It packs a punch. I swallow and look away again, hoping she doesn't call my bluff. She types out some more things while she mutters to herself about how much she likes the new paperless system and hits a button on the keyboard hard, with finality.

"You may continue through the green door." She gestures in that direction as she leans back in her chair. I stand but hesitate before moving away from the table.

"What do the different colors mean?" I ask.

"Just different vocations." She smiles again, but the sweetness disappears. I nod and push the chair back up to the table, but before I turn to go, I act on a feeling of curiosity.

"How many people have been through here?"

Her eyes widen and her mouth pulls to the side. She chews on her cheek before answering, "Well, I don't know."

"Just guess," I prod as I eye the next person approaching.

She flicks her wrist through the air. "Maybe 50,000," she responds.

"Hello," she says as she smiles and greets the next person in the same practiced manner she did for me. I turn and walk to the green door.

I push through the double doors outlined with deep green paint, eager anticipation winding up my spine. And then unwinding. A long hallway with fluorescent lighting and white-out walls is on the other side. The walls are lined with closed doors and windows whose secret interiors remain cloaked in mystery behind bland, gray interior curtains.

The floors remind me of Grandma's kitchen linoleum with checkered black and white squares. The drop-down ceiling looks like the ceiling at my high school, where I spent so many hours suffering from boredom.

The familiar has diverged into foreign terrain. It's unsettling.

"Hello?" I call.

The door directly to the right of me clicks open. I jump instinctively and attempt to pass it off. From the door, a tiny woman squeezes through the opening, not allowing the gap to be any wider than what is necessary for her short, stout body to maneuver around. Her behavior piques my interest, and I steal a glance inside before it clicks shut behind her. I saw a standard, boring wood desk and a bookshelf-lined wall containing mostly white binders. I give her a look. *What's the big deal, lady?* But she only smiles and begins to talk.

It comes out fast and squeaky like a mouse on Adderall. "Sorry. So Sorry. Last-minute task. Hi, I'm Natalie, your liaison." She holds out a tiny hand, which I shake without enthusiasm. I notice her eyes take in my height. She gulps.

"My what?" I ask.

"Your liaison. I'll show you where to go, how to do your job, and answer any questions you may have." Her hands move like tiny dancers enunciating her words. "This way, we can walk and talk."

She takes off down the hall at a surprising speed for the length of her legs.

"Right, right, left, right," she mutters before addressing me again. "I hope you're happy to be here. We're happy to have you. Of course, there are rules to follow." She makes a right turn down another identical hallway. "You'll have a color-coded uniform issued for your line of work. You'll wear this every day. The uniform will be waiting in your room upon arrival. Lights out at ten o'clock. In your room by nine o'clock. PM, that is." She chuckles to herself and pauses at the next intersection. The choices are left, right, or straight.

"Right, right, left, right," she mutters again. "Right," she says confidently as she turns for the second time down another identical hallway. "Sorry, new here," she offers with a dismissive wave.

"And what is my line of work?" I ask, but she continues to prattle on, either ignoring me or not hearing me.

"Meals come to your room morning and night. A small dispensary near the sink will administer supplements daily in the AM. Don't forget to take them. You must take them. It's one of the rules," she says cheerily.

"What happens—" but she cuts me off. This mousy lady is starting to get under my skin. We turn left, down another hallway.

"When the toll sounds after breakfast, your door will open, and you will have two minutes to exit. Always follow the green arrow illuminated on the floor when it's time to exit the building. Once in the Arena, you'll find the color assigned to you and join your group before beginning your daily work duties. Your work color arrow will take you out and bring you home but don't worry about it. There's always an agent escort, but we find the color-coordinated arrows still useful to keep an orderly line. You'll catch on quickly, and there will be further instructions once you've entered your room. Showers are limited to three minutes. We have to preserve water. Clean clothes are delivered to your room on Fridays." She stops at another hallway intersection. I want to tell her right, but I watch as her hands and head bob to her quiet, rhythmic, *right, right, left, right* chant. We turn right.

At the end of this hallway are two double doors and some equipment.

She continues, "You'll be scanned in and out every time you leave your room and likewise when you leave the dormitory building and enter the city. Oh, and when you get to work and leave work. You may also be subject to random check-ins. If probation is warranted..."

I zone out for a second. A sickening sense of unease has lodged itself firmly in the pit of my stomach.

"And here we are." She stops abruptly at the double doors and turns to a machine backed against the left-hand side of the wall. The machine looks an awful lot like a dog tag engraving kiosk.

"Right or left?" she asks with innocent blinking eyes and a smile that seems increasingly forced.

"Excuse me?" I say. Like, I'm supposed to know what the fuck is going on here.

"Which wrist do you prefer?"

I want this lady out of my sight before I lose it. "Left. What about...?" She yanks my sleeve up unexpectedly and thrusts my arm into a hole in the machine. She is stronger than she looks. I'm temporarily stunned by her aggression until I feel a cuff inflate like the ones on blood pressure monitors, only way faster. I try to pull back, but it's too late. My arm is firmly stuck in the machine and throbbing from the hold. The machine whirs to life. She must see my eyes widen in panic.

"Don't worry, it won't hurt a bit. Oh, and once you get to your room, there will be further instruction..." she turns her back to me, still talking. She already said that, but I'm mostly stuck on *won't hurt.* "...that'll contain everything I've said and more..."

Holy shit. I jerk away as a burning sensation ignites in my wrist. It's like a lighter is being held to it. I grit my teeth and let a pained, angry growl escape as I watch through the glass viewing window on the machine. A blinding blue light moves across my skin.

I punch the machine with my right fist repeatedly as the burning sensation moves along the entire surface of my wrist. Then, a hissing noise interrupts the pain, and a blue mist concentrates onto my wrist before clouding the viewing window. I feel some relief instantly. The hissing noise stops, and the pressure releases on the cuff securing my arm. I rip my arm away and cradle my injured hand.

I blink, horrified at the number 31186 etched across my wrist.

"You fucking branded me?" I snarl. I see her cower away before the double doors are opened from the outside. Two armed soldiers tower in the doorway like mouse lady's guardian angels.

"Sorry. So sorry. They'll take it from here," she says as she scuttles back down the hallway from which we came. "Welcome to Eyth!" she calls over her shoulder.

Eyth? What happened to Metal City?

I look at my wrist again. The smell of burnt flesh assaults my nose. *My* flesh. 31186. The numbers are black. The skin surrounding them glows an angry pink.

Armed or not, I glare at the soldiers. They don't so much as flinch. Their mass and the direct sunlight coming into the hall block the view behind them.

I take a deep breath and mouth silently to myself the only words that can offer me a modicum of comfort right now: *right, right, left, right.* What's that in reverse? Left, left, right, left? Then, the soldiers step aside, and I see the city behind them.

CHAPTER 5

Sam

October 16, 2025 One Week Later

I stand upright with my hand on my heart before I catch myself. My heart does that loop-de-loop it's been doing lately. It's like the rhythm gets thrown off just a moment, and it takes my breath away. I don't want to worry Rose. So, I haven't mentioned it. Luckily, she isn't around now, or I might have given myself away. But the men don't notice. They're men. And Rose is off with the women. Most men and women reverted to traditional roles rather naturally. Women on cooking, cleaning, and gathering. Men on building and hunting. Only a few women have griped at the injustice of it, but when offered building duty, they'd acquiesced.

All but one, anyway. She was a "buff chick," as I heard one of the guys call her. She's a harder worker than half the men on the team. But being old-fashioned myself, I have caught myself thinking she's the exception, not the rule. I stand firmly in the camp that men's work is not for women—most women. The only job positions where they will mingle are those of the recon crew, who are tasked with combing through nearby houses and bringing back things we need—mattresses, pots, pans, silverware, wood, fertilizer, and that kind of thing.

Still, due to the lifting component, mostly men take it on, and they almost always go with a heavily armed SEAL for protection. They don't pass out weapons to just anyone. They have to prove themselves. Until they've earned one, it's Frank, Crowly, or Miller on babysitting duty.

I've been steeped in a strange feeling lately. I can't put my finger on it, but it has to do with being back on the ranch. Only it isn't the ranch anymore; it's the Colony. At least that's what some folks started calling it, and it just stuck. We have almost two hundred heads now—not cattle, people. That's two hundred mouths to feed and bodies to shelter. But I still feel like I should be able to walk into the old house, bark orders to the ranch hands, and sit down for Rose's home-cooked dinner at five-thirty. But no. This isn't the ranch I remember. It's a corpse of its former glory. Almost unrecognizable. Every piece of spare wood possible has been stripped to build more housing. Every building, barn, hay shed, or garage becomes another dwelling or community resource. The fields are littered with tents, makeshift log homes, and shacks thrown hastily together with tarps and pallets. We're doing our best to keep up with demand, but word is spreading quickly about what we're doing here. We work harder than ever these days from sunup to sundown. God has mercifully held off the snow, but it's coming. I can feel it. And I know my heart is telling me to back down, but with so much to be done, I can't admit defeat to old age just yet. Plus, the elderly are given jobs I have no interest in, like teaching, reading, and babysitting, so the parents can work.

Tom wants to have a conversation before the fireside chat tonight. He said he had some ideas he wanted to toy around with and use me as a sounding board or whatever. Walking up the steps to the main house, it hits me again—the peculiarity of walking up to one's former home and knocking on the door. We were offered a room in the house when we arrived, but we declined. Instead, the single-car garage that sits just next to the house was partitioned into two rooms, and we have assumed one of the rooms. We were given a real bed from inside the house at Tom and Lily's insistence. While I was grateful, I couldn't say it for fear if I opened my mouth, I'd refuse the bed. Luckily, Rose saved the day and accepted the bed for the both of us.

It's also strange being in the garage, with its familiar smells of motor oil and metal. There are still tools that line the one wall and cabinets I installed myself years ago that have been re-purposed to hold our meager possessions. We've attempted to insulate the garage door and have mostly been successful, but there's still a permanent chill in the air. Rose spends most of her time in the main house tending to the grandchildren and doing whatever else she can find to be helpful. I wonder what it's like for her to be back here under such different conditions, but most nights, we're so exhausted that sleep wins out over conversation.

I rap lightly on the large red door. I hear a shout, "Come in!" from the interior. I open the door slowly and peek through. "Come on in, Dad. No need to knock." Tom watches me with amusement as he leans against the kitchen counter, drinking from a mug.

I nod a greeting and remove my cap as I step inside the house. It's an open floor plan with large expansive windows looking over the valley on the far wall. The kitchen is immediately on the right, and a small office is on the left when you walk in. The office is a bedroom now. Whose, I'm not entirely sure. The door is shut. Past the kitchen is the large dining table I was so fond of before, and past that, below the floor-to-ceiling windows, is the living area.

"What did you want to talk about?" I ask, ready to get down to business.

"Here, let's sit." He gestures towards the kitchen table and pours a second mug of coffee. He doesn't bother asking. He sets the mug down on the table across from him and scoots it towards me. I drink as he talks. It's watered down—which still hasn't ceased to be disappointing. The coffee is running low.

"I know no one wants to talk about this, but we're going to have to draw the line somewhere. We can't be a charity for everyone. We don't have the resources. Instead of turning everyone away, maybe we can screen them somehow. Accept the useful ones or the ones that have brought something useful for us. We've got two hundred and sixteen people down there now, and almost daily, we have newcomers trying to enter. The more we ration food, the more tensions rise. We can't sustain this."

I sigh. "And how do you propose we keep them out? We have natural barriers, but those are easily overcome if you're desperate, and everyone who comes to us is desperate."

"We'll beef up the guard surrounding the west and south sides," Tom says. "The mountains border the other two sides and aren't easily surmounted."

"So, are you prepared to shoot people then?" I feel my blood pressure rise.

Tom looks down into his mug. "We might have to. Do you have a better idea?" he asks.

"No, but I know that I can't shoot anyone for trying to survive or protect their family. What if it's a mom and her children?"

"It'll be tough for sure, but it's looking clearer to me every day. It's them or us. Plus, after a few are shot, word will spread, and people will stop coming."

"Or they'll come ready for a fight," I add.

Tom's brows knit together. He runs his hands through his hair and blows out a breath. His foot begins to tap. It's a stress response he's had since he was a boy. "What the fuck do we do then, Dad?"

"When I am afraid, I put my trust in you. Psalm 56:3," I say.

Tom ignores the reference to God, the problem at hand clearly consuming every ounce of his conscious thought. "If the ground wasn't already freezing and winter approaching, we may have a chance, but that's not where we are. We have some tough choices to make." His knee still bounces away, and his gaze is far off, looking out of the windows and down on the Colony.

"You should be proud of yourself," I say, following his gaze. There are people milling about hard at work. "They've got a real shot of making it through the winter because of you."

"Hah," he scoffs dismissively. "Not if we don't stop the influx."

"Have you talked to Frank about this? Maybe he can help," I say.

Tom is silent. Tension has grown between them since Frank's arrival. There's a power struggle wedging itself firmly between the two. Frank's confident demeanor, his entourage, his soldier-like appearance, and insider information have pulled a lot of respect, but Tom's ownership and initial cunning also receive high regard. The two could be a powerful force leading together, but I sense confusion among the colonists, who often wonder why their allegiances are spread in two different directions.

"I can't shoot a member of this community. I know that," I say. Tom bangs his fist on the counter.

"Dammit! I know that, but what the hell else are we supposed to do?"

"Is this a democracy or a dictatorship?" I ask.

Tom looks at me with his head cocked.

"Put it to a vote," I say. "Bring everyone in on the decision. You don't have to carry this alone." Tom considers this. He nods. I continue, "It might also be nice to know what we can expect first. What else is out there? How desperate are the people in the community? Are there other places we could direct people to who show up?"

He rubs his chin and paces the kitchen. "Let's find out," he says, still walking as he mulls it over. "We'll ask for volunteers tonight to go out into the community." He stops abruptly and snaps his fingers. "Yeah! We'll start there. We'll put it into motion tonight."

I give him a curt nod and head towards the door. My job here is done.

"See you tonight," he calls after me.

I acknowledge this with a grunt as I close the door behind me. My mind is still plagued by images of us shooting other members of the community—people we used to smile at in the grocery store aisle. People we used to arrange playdates for our kids with. People we used to sit with on the bleachers as we cheered on our home team. But I don't see any way around it. There can't be anything good out there. The suggestion was just a way to stall to see if I could come up with a better solution in the meantime. One that doesn't involve killing people we know.

CHAPTER 6

Bodin

October 16, 2025

W hen I first heard 'Metal City,' I pictured a lifeless urban construct. I imagined futuristic, gleaming buildings reaching toward the skies. Those are here, but what strikes me most is the green. Nature embellishes the space. It climbs up the walls of massive skyscrapers. It adorns the sidewalks. It juts from every angle. It's breathtaking. The second marvel that's immediately apparent is the streets. They're narrower, allowing for only one car and a sidewalk. This makes it feel like the buildings are encroaching on you with towering authority. The narrow streets between the buildings lend to the appearance of an intimidating maze. The only source to orient myself is what appears to be a tentacle shooting up from the center of the city. It reaches up and splays out its fingers as if holding up the sky. It's at least a third taller than the second-highest building.

My eyes linger on the red lights at the top of the tentacle column. They seem to scan the city below with a circling spotlight motion. The sight of them is unsettling, like a centurion guarding the city. There are flashes of red lights in the sky as well. Wait, no, they're just reflections of the lights from the column as they move. They *are* holding up something. The sky is glass.

Squinting, I can make out the vague outline of a pattern encasing the city under a dome. As my eyes travel from the center of the dome to the outer wall of the dome just behind me, a pattern emerges. It's easier to see from up close. The dome looks like a honeycomb pattern made up of interlocking glass hexagons.

One of the guards breaks my trance. "Follow me," he says. I do as he says, observing where we're going and doing my best to map the way in a place that's so completely foreign to me that it feels like I've stepped into a Sci-Fi movie.

The buildings vary in height but appear mostly the same other than that. Beneath the greenery, they shine like dark water. They remind me of Ted's titanium wedding ring, which, as of late, he twists obsessively as if trying to unscrew the memory of Mom. A car that looks like a white pod with a glowing blue light emanating from a single window glides by smoothly and silently.

Moments later, another identical one appears, and it's heading straight for the other car sharing the single lane. I watch, transfixed. I hold up my arm instinctively, intending to yell in hopes of preventing the collision, but one of the cars lifts up into the air and glides above the other car as they pass. I lower my hand, feeling stupid. This answers my questions about why the street is only one car wide. They can move vertically. I try to glimpse inside as the car whirs past me, but the window that runs like a stripe through the center of it is too tinted to see if anyone is inside. I look behind me as it disappears and see another car cut behind it on a cross street. It's then that I realize there are no stoplights or stop signs here either. It must all be... coordinated. Automated.

As we walk into the belly of the city, the map I had been dutifully attempting to sear into my brain disappears like a helium balloon I can no longer hold onto. I try to grab it, but it's no use. The best I can do is look behind me and hope something is distinguishing about the skyline. My eyes search desperately. A tree on top of a building is slightly out of place. It appears to be leaning to the left as if peering over the edge and gaging the drop below. That's it. That's all I've got. The base where I was processed and admitted is behind that building with the crooked tree.

After several blocks, the guard stops at what looks like a covered bus stop. Two others are sitting on the bench, staring absently into the space before them. I stare at them and wave hesitantly, but neither one looks at me. Their trance-like appearance is alarming. In my fascination, I miss the guard placing a large headset over his ears. I'm about to ask what those are for, but he grabs my arm abruptly and pulls me towards the bench. There's an obnoxious noise. I move my hands to my ears to block it out, but then suddenly, it's calm.

The bus is waiting the next time I blink. It appears out of nowhere as if by magic. I stand, surprised to feel my ass throb from the newly restored blood flow. When did I sit down? I'm curious about this but don't have the mental energy to ponder it. I walk stiffly to the bus. Or a bus limo hybrid thing, anyway. It looks a little bit like a hovering bullet train. There are twelve of us now. This registers as odd to me, but I can't place why.

Once seated, a fog slowly begins to lift. It must also be happening for the others because many concerned glances dart around the bus's interior. The bus ride is smooth, with no lurches or squelching of brakes like the buses I remember. We seem to float along. I quickly realize there is another peculiarity about this bus. No windows. There's only an illuminated image of a beach passing by, though I know it's not real. This can only mean they don't want us to know where we're going. Goosebumps rise on my arms as puzzle pieces assemble in my head. Somehow, at that bus stop, they put us into a trance. This city is not what I was expecting. So many mysteries and advancements... Maybe it was a mistake coming here.

The bus comes to a stop. The right side of the vehicle lifts with a whoosh, like a fluid and fast garage door.

"Follow," a guard says. Not the same one that deposited me at the bus stop. I linger behind as the others follow the guard. I look up at the tall building we're about to enter before running to catch up. We enter what appears to be a hotel lobby. It's a vast space with travertine floors and a large ring of lights hanging above a black emblem on the floor. There's nothing else in the space except for rows of elevators lining the back wall. Our footsteps echo as we follow the guard to an elevator. He punches in some numbers and scans his wrist. The door slides open, revealing a large elevator behind him. He gestures for us to enter as if holding the door for us. We file in. There's plenty of space for the twelve of us. He steps in after us, and the doors shut.

To my surprise, we don't go up. We go down. Down, down, down. My armpits begin to sweat. When we stop, we're ushered out into another ample space. The size of it is awe-inducing. It's like a football stadium in here. More guards, just standing by. Most don't acknowledge our arrival. Four women step forward, each wearing a different color blouse beneath the same black pantsuit: purple, green, brown, and gray.

The lady in brown calls out three numbers, "31185, 31188, and 31189. Report to me, please." I glance at my number again: 31186. Not brown, then. I remember what the woman said about the colors indicating different work vocations. The ladies in green and gray claim their people. That leaves one other guy and me for purple. He's slightly overweight, with a thick pair of glasses perched on a nose that seems smashed into his face. My face drops. What could we possibly have in common?

The woman in purple steps forward at last. "That leaves you two with me. It's your lucky day." She smiles brightly, and I almost believe her. Almost. "Follow me, please," she says. I'm getting sick of hearing that. She leads us to another elevator, where we go up for a few seconds before stopping. It opens into a hallway with shiny floors and many, many gray doors stretching as far as I can see. They're numbered in black. I gulp. She walks. The chub and I follow, exchanging wary glances.

"Due to the hour, you will retire to your rooms for the evening. In the morning, you will see green arrows illuminated on the floors. Follow the arrows until you see purple. Then follow the purple arrows, and you'll get to the appropriate gathering area in the Arena. That's what we call that large space we just came from. It's where we all gather before work." She stops in front of a door. She scans her wrist, and the door opens automatically by sliding to the left. "31186, this is you. Don't forget your room numbers, please." She smiles, but it doesn't reach her eyes. I shiver involuntarily.

I step through and turn back to ask her a question, but my mouth hangs open when I see the smile on her face, watching me, mocking me. The door shuts quickly behind me without my intervention. My hand falls through the air as I attempt to grab a knob that doesn't exist. I look down. There isn't an inside handle on the door. My stomach lurches. I turn back to the tiny room and take a deep breath to avoid the panic rising in my chest.

I look around. There's a tiny corner shower to my left that lacks a door or a curtain. The water falls into a drain on the floor, which is just a continuation of the plain concrete floor throughout the rest of the room. Opposite the shower on my right is a closet where I notice two gray jumpsuits with purple patches around the sleeves. There's a small twin-sized bed slightly elevated off the floor that runs along the entire remainder of the wall on my right side. It has white sheets, a white pillow, and a thin gray comforter tucked tightly beneath the thin mattress. There's a sink opposite the bed, along the wall with the shower. Between the sink and the mirror on the wall directly across from the door is a silver toilet bowl jutting from the wall. The mirror above the sink looks more like shiny, reflective metal than glass. This completes the room. Shower, sink, toilet, closet, bed.

I take two long steps and confirm that I can reach the far wall with two small strides. I hold my arms out wide and find I can't touch either wall simultaneously, but I'm pretty close. I huff as I sit on the bed and kick my legs up, testing the length of it. I just barely fit. As I rest my hands behind my head on the pillow, I notice a small flat-screen TV attached to the closet wall at the foot of the bed. It was just out of view when standing at the door. I look around for a remote but see none. Instead, I see something else in the corner of the bedroom. *A spider?* I pull my foot up to remove my shoe to squish it, then put it back down. The environment looks entirely too pristine for a spider. So, I stand on the bed and peer closer. It's a small glassy object like a black marble. A camera, most likely. I slump back down onto the bed.

What am I supposed to do now? I lie back. My thoughts wander towards comparisons with prison life. This seems worse, somehow. More enclosed. At least in prison, you can see out of bars, and sometimes you have cellmates. This is more like solitary confinement but with a TV.

I glance at the TV again, wondering where the remote is. I get up, intending to drink water from the sink by cupping my hands, and notice a white toothbrush next to it. When I turn the handle, no water comes out. *What the hell?*

Before panic can take root, I notice a white glow in the mirror. I turn and see the television illuminated. I step closer. There's a message on the screen in plain black type with a white background that reads, "Please stand by. Your program will be available shortly." I climb onto the bed, stick the pillow behind my back, and sit against the wall at the head of the bed. I pull my knees into my chest and wait, eyes transfixed on the screen.

A woman appears on the screen with a familiar red, white, and blue backdrop like she's broadcasting from the White House. *Where is the president?* I wonder. The spokeswoman's light brown hair is pulled back into a bun. Her brown eyes and simple makeup make her somewhat unremarkable. She's about Mom's age. She smiles sweetly, but I already want to punch her in the face the second I hear, "Welcome! We're glad you're here." She pauses. "You probably have some questions. I'm here to acquaint you with your new job responsibilities and the expectations we have of you while you enjoy our facilities." *Christ, lady, this isn't the fucking Mariott.*

"Let's begin with your schedule. Each morning, an alarm will sound promptly at five fifty-five. The shower will then turn on for three minutes at six a.m. After the shower has commenced, you have ten minutes before breakfast is delivered to your room. We suggest you use this time to get dressed and brush your teeth. All personal hygiene products can be found in dispensers mounted on the wall." Her hands are clasped in front of her, and the fake smile never falters. This video isn't far from the informational videos they used to play before a flight.

"Next, the door will open, and you are expected to calmly follow the green arrows to your respective color in the Arena to join your group. Your color is located on your jumpsuit for reference. You may be wondering what the colors represent. Each color is associated with a specific job task." To my disappointment, she doesn't elaborate further. I hope purple is something cool. "Please follow your color closely and comply with a single file line formation." I salute the screen and glance guiltily at the camera. She continues, "You might like to know more about our beautiful city. We are a state-of-the-art, 100% sustainable city. There are other cities like ours throughout the world." Images of other cities flick on the screen, one after another. I furrow my brow as I stare at all the images moving across the screen. There are so many cities across the world. This is not just a United States problem; this is a world problem. The walls of my "room" seem to inch towards me, eliciting a brief panic from claustrophobia. I breathe deeply and try to distract myself by returning my attention to the television.

"Our public transportation system includes shared, autonomous electric vehicles on demand for easy and fast passenger mobility. The transit system includes air mobility as well as high-speed underground trains."

The camera zooms through the streets, highlighting the coordinated and effortless movement of hundreds of vehicles simultaneously.

She continues, "Our food system is completely regenerative. Fish feed the plants growing in the aquaponic warehouses. The warehouses are designed to imitate perfect growing conditions." As she talks, the screen pans over walls and walls of plants growing higher than the camera can span. At the bottom of each row is a water tank, highlighting the fish. I see tomatoes growing abundantly, distinguishable only by the bright red sticking out against a carpeted green expanse. Then, another warehouse cuts in, and I spot lemons and oranges—my mouth waters. *At least the food here will be good.* "We use recycled plant matter, leftovers, and water from the fish tanks to fertilize the soil for our traditionally grown crops such as potatoes, beets, and carrots." The camera highlights a seemingly endless field plowed and tilled in neat rows. "Traditional crops and livestock are maintained off-site. As you can see, we waste nothing in Eyth. Everything is integrated seamlessly into the architecture of the city. We hope you'll come to be as proud of our city as we are. Once again, welcome."

The television screen changes to a panoramic view of the city, Eyth. I'm impressed. There's something else crowding out the awe, though: fear. With a city this advanced, any hope I had harbored of escaping dwindles by the minute. And any hope I had that we would one day, as a rag-tag bunch of disgruntled citizens, attack or control this city vanishes.

CHAPTER 7

Carrie

October 17, 2025

We're on our way bright and early the following day—faster than most of us had expected to start our recon mission. Hoping to trap some heat, I hold my arms tightly around my body. I peek up at the sun, which has just barely shown itself over the mountaintops. I will it to move higher. My body shivers violently.

"Best thing to do is to keep movin'." It's someone behind me. I don't look to see, just nod. I met everyone last night but only remember the names of a few. There was Pax, with a trimmed beard and soft brown curls. I remember him because he was cute and about my age, and he made a point of introducing himself to me. Hammer, I remember, too. He's middle-aged with eyes so lightly colored that I stared, transfixed. And, of course, with a nickname like Hammer, I wasn't about to forget him. Caroline, I remember, too, unfortunately. Her refusal to shake my hand during introductions seared her pretty face with a contorted sneer of contempt directed at me into my brain. I don't know what her problem is.

I look down at my boots. The toes are wet from the frost, but my feet remain dry at least. Cal gave me these boots. Everything I'm wearing was given to me by the kindness of others. Everything except my bra. This last reminder of where I've come from and the normalcy my life used to represent is hidden beneath layers of thin sweaters and a puffy coat. I haven't seen it in days.

Despite the layers, the cold finds ways to seep in. I tuck my chin down into the collar of the coat and keep my thinly gloved hands held beneath my arms. I have a small list of things I hope to find out here. Warmer gloves just moved to the top of that list.

Not for the first time since setting out early for the town, I doubt whether I should have volunteered. It would have been so easy to just stay in bed this morning. I had finally slept well last night. My insulation efforts paid off. Admittedly, it is not very comfortable, and the sleeping bag is not for temperatures below freezing. I desperately need supplies for the winter. *That's why you're here*, I remind myself, but I let those words vibrate in my head. *That's why you're here?*

The words take on a different meaning. Deeper. Why *am* I here? Why not Cal? I've never been religious or even spiritual, but something is changing within me. I search for meaning in places higher up. Maybe it's Sam's prayers after every meal or the small makeshift chapel that is frequented often by just about everyone else. Or maybe it's because nothing else makes sense.

We walk in silence for a long time, chasing the puffs of hot air that we push out in front of us with our breaths. I see a soggy, cardboard pizza box off to the side of the road. The sight of it is jarring. How normal that pizza box was just months ago. Now, it's a feat of impossible manufacturing. It was so insignificant before. Now, I feel as if it should be picked up and preserved. Put on display. It takes a great deal of effort to peel my eyes away from the pizza box disappearing behind me.

There are ten of us. Seven men and three women. I'm the odd one out, I know it, but I try to brush off the furtive glances. I should be used to it by now.

After a while of walking, the ground becomes softer beneath the sun, and our tongues must also thaw because the group starts to strategize.

"We'll cross at Shoup Bridge and follow Highway 93 towards town," Pax says.

"Couldn't we just feed the colony by fishing?" someone asks.

"Of course. We've tried that. We don't have large enough hooks for Steelhead and no bait. Plus, there aren't enough fish to feed this town. It's what everyone's trying," Pax responds.

"Oh, what about traps?" I ask as I think back to listening to Cal's fishing success stories. He would have found a way to catch fish.

"Traps? You got one hiding somewhere in your tent up there?" The speaker is the young blonde, Caroline.

Some of the group snickers. I turn my gaze to the road in front of me.

I bet the library would have a book on making fish traps or survival in general. Surely the town of Salmon has a library? But I don't ask it. They've already moved on. I can see a few houses now scattered throughout the hillsides, concentrating more towards the highway in the distance. I suddenly feel vulnerable.

"Do we check every house we pass?" Hammer asks.

"Too risky. Let's not forget that compliance was low around here," Pax responds. He's referring to the gun surrender laws they put into place a few years ago. It didn't impact me because I never owned a gun, but I remember Ed and I complaining about "red states" and their resistance to give up their firearms.

"Does anyone know people who live around here? Elderly, perhaps?" one of the women asks. We all know what she's implying.

"I know a couple of families but not elderly. Most folks around here have ended up at the Colony with us. That's why we're going farther out," an older man answers her.

"Can't we just look for signs of life and then barge in if there are none?" Caroline asks.

"And what does that look like?" Pax asks her.

"Boarded up windows...smoke..." Too many people are trying to talk for me to keep it straight now. Most of the group seems opposed to entering homes, but I can't help but wonder, what other option is there? It's not like we can visit the mall for a quick shopping trip.

"Tray lived down here. Said everything's been pretty well picked over. That's why they ended up with us. Nothing left down here," Pax says, attempting to end the discussion.

"Surely, we can still find things like blankets, gloves, hats?" I chime in.

"Possibly. We haven't been prioritizing those things." I look behind me at the respondent, Pax. Our eyes meet briefly. I notice Caroline, who is walking next to him, rolling her eyes. I return my gaze to the road in front of me, feeling his eyes still watching me.

"We're looking for fishing supplies, tools, water filters, matches, and lighters. Food and water for ourselves. Tom gave us some ammo to trade if the opportunity arises," one of the men states.

"We'll start with the businesses in town," Pax asserts. His voice, along with Hammer's and Caroline's, are still the only voices I can put a name to. I keep my eyes trained ahead of me, outpacing the group.

"There's gotta be some hoarders out there holding onto supplies that they don't need. We just gotta find 'em," someone adds.

"Who's packing here?" Hammer asks. I look behind me, curious. A few hands go in the air. Well, that's a relief at least. Guess I wasn't one of the trusted few to receive a gun. Or maybe the guns are their own. The indignation is short-lived. I wouldn't know how to use one anyway.

I let their chatter fall into the background. I only tune in when something interesting catches my attention. Hammer is not from around here, I glean. I wouldn't have guessed based on the ease with which he seems to melt into the group's open arms. I would have put my dinner on him being a local. I try not to be bitter about it. Maybe there's something I can learn from him.

I feel the weight of the near-empty backpack resting on my shoulders. We were only given enough rations to last us a couple of days. The rest we need to find. We must all feel it now, our survival instincts kicking into high gear. I almost forgot what this felt like, being solely responsible for my next meal. *When I come back, I'll have new gratitude for the Colony.*

There's a smell that has come to signify people. I remember it from Salt Lake. Rotting trash and human feces. Without the ability to make new purchases, the trash hasn't grown in size, but it has gotten more putrid from hours of exposure to the elements. The stench was muted this morning, but as we get closer to town and the sun warms the garbage, it's more noticeable.

We've been walking for hours with hardly a moment of silence. Whether it's nerves or some sense of self-importance, the group feels compelled to fill in any moments of silence with prattle. They talk mostly about things they miss, like Burger King Whoppers and Alfredo from Junk Yard Bistro. I wish they'd shut up. Unlike the rest of them, I'm on edge. I investigate every sound and constantly scan the area around us. These guys have been on the ranch for too long. I move farther and farther ahead of the group. I feel like a scout leading a troop of kids or something, but it feels safe to put distance between myself and their noise. And even though I'm not familiar with the town, we're on the highway now, and all we have to do is follow it.

The air carries the warning of winter in its bite. I can see snow dusting the tops of the deep blue mountains that encompass the valley. It's a beautiful contrast. If someone had shown me a glimpse of this future just a few months ago, I wouldn't have believed it. No makeup, dark roots peeking out from my blonde hair, clothes that hang loosely from my frame, and a landscape unlike anywhere I've ever been. I'm a city girl. For me, this place is a place from National Geographic magazines. Its quiet, natural beauty is something I would have admired from the comfort of my city apartment while sipping a latte and scrolling through my social media feed. Perhaps none of these things would have surprised me the most, though.

The biggest change has been intangible. I can feel it in my mind and body, just as I'm sure it's evident on my face. A metamorphosis has taken place. There are two Carries. The old Carrie, who I'm beginning to despise more and more due to her whining and complaining about unfair circumstances, and the new Carrie, who I'm starting to respect and appreciate for her acceptance and perseverance. Was she there all along? This is the persona I need to embody to survive here. Allowing the old Carrie to live is just punishing. This is my reality now, and arguing against reality just breeds malcontent.

The sun has peaked in the sky. It's past noon now. I take off my coat and tie it around my waist. I can feel the heat bouncing back at me from the pavement beneath my feet. My cheeks glow with warmth. It's a happy reminder that there's still time before winter, but the peace the thought brings me is wiped away when I remember something Sam had said to me while we made our way up here from Salt Lake. "The weather in the mountains is fickle. One day, it's summer. The next day, it's winter. You can't trust it." We were fortunate to have had a conversation as mundane as the weather after being shot at by a group camped along the highway outside of Malad. Aside from some broken windows, we made it through and back to the ranch without incident. There was return fire from our side. Who knows how the Malad group faired? But unlike us, they were exposed.

As the houses become more concentrated and businesses begin to dot along the highway, I know we're close. I should slow down and take a minute to regroup with the others, but it's been a more peaceful walk the last hour. I pass an auction house and a car dealership. A few people look at me from front yards or out from behind windows, but no one seems remotely threatening. I'm beginning to understand why the group seems so at ease. Maybe small towns are different. Maybe because most people know each other, they treat each other with more compassion.

There's a large, plain yellow building on my right. Dark paint that was once protected from fading in the sun by large letters leaves behind the ghost of a sign "Shopko." The building must have been abandoned before the blackout, but I keep my eye on it because I hear people inside. Whatever it was before, now it's some kind of shelter. There are a series of blue and brown tarps laid on top of pallets and other haphazard contraptions in the parking lot. The tarps are pulled taut at an angle, and buckets are set out beneath them. They're an attempt to collect water, no doubt. I wonder if they get enough. It only rained once in the past two weeks.

The familiar tingle invoked by the sound of strangers crawls up my spine. I slow my pace. I should really let the group catch up. We're on the outskirts of town. It's time to go over the plan. I turn back, but the road is empty. When did it get so quiet? My pulse quickens. I don't see them anywhere. I curse under my breath. I wasn't that far ahead of them. My panic quickly turns to anger. *Assholes.*

I start walking back in the direction we came from when a gunshot nearby causes me to duck instinctively and freeze in place. Where did it come from? It's impossible to tell, but it was close. I shouldn't be walking on the open road like this.

Luckily, there's a borrow pit that sinks below the road on either side. As I crawl into the borrow pit, I still have to duck behind the road for cover as I retrace my steps in a hunched position. Mud sticks to my shoes and weighs down my feet. My nerves are revving higher by the minute. I don't make it far before I have to rest. My quads and back demand it. I sit and debate stashing my backpack somewhere, but I don't want to risk it.

As I wait, another gunshot shatters the silence. It's closer this time—across the road from me, I think. I lie on the incline that reaches up to the road, cursing at the dampness that's soaking into my shirt while

I peek up over the road. I see the large auction house I passed not too long ago. It's just up the road, set back a few hundred feet by a wide, dirt-packed parking lot. Large double doors hang wide open. Were they like that before?

I lie still with my eyes trained on the doors. I think I see movement inside, but it's too dark to tell. Moments later, I spot them. They're exiting the auction house with their hands raised. Someone follows them with a gun pointed at their backs. I curse under my breath. They're barefoot without coats or backpacks. Those idiots. All of their provisions are gone. Our ammo for trading and their guns, gone.

They're led a few hundred yards toward the road before the man following them backs up and disappears into the auction house. The large double doors swing shut behind him. The group is close to me now. I count them. They're all there. I watch them for a minute, debating. Some look dazed. Some look angry. I could leave them. They're liabilities. It might be safer to move on my own, but how would I explain that if I returned to the ranch alone? Maybe they've learned their lesson. Eventually, their feet start moving, and they're coming closer to my location. I can hear them talking, "Should we go back?" "Will we make it before nightfall?" "Where the fuck is Carrie?"

I sigh and stand up. "I'm right here," I hiss. Most of the group jumps at the interruption to their pity party.

"What the fuck, Carrie?!" a woman barks.

I shoot her a death glare as I hold my fingers up to my lips. I jerk my head towards a large, green building just a few blocks down the road. Looks like a tractor yard or something. I remember passing it on the way. The building had a massive garage door on one side and a normal-sized door for entry on the other side. The building is a large, metal square surrounded by tractors that were displayed along the road. I can't say why I chose that building. A feeling, I guess. The only thing I remember noting about it was how clean it looked. Untouched maybe. They all turn to look. Some nod. Some shrug. Others just trudge along with heads heavy from embarrassment.

I walk around the building when we get there. There are two windows on the side facing away from the road and a small window next to the regular size door facing the highway. I try the only door. Locked. I look back over my shoulder and notice the others watching me. Their faces reveal nothing but curiosity. There's been a noticeable shift. Either they've decided to trust my judgment, or I just became the boss—or both.

I don't want to be their boss, and I don't like their expectant eyes on me. I distract myself by looking for a hide-a-key. I search under the mat that reads "welcome" and then under a couple of rocks close to the door. There's nothing there.

Pax walks over. I had never noticed the definition in his arms before. His muscles flex beneath a forest green t-shirt.

"Can I see your flashlight?" he asks. I eye him. Pax was paying attention when we were handed supplies this morning.

I sling off my backpack and hand him the large black flashlight. He begins to pull his t-shirt up. A trail of dark hair reaches up from his pants and spreads out along his toned abs. I look away, but not before I feel a blush betray me. He wraps his hand with his shirt, grips the flashlight, and produces two sharp blows to the small window next to the door.

The noise sends my nerves firing. The others now have the good sense instilled in them to care, too. We glance around nervously.

"Could I borrow your coat?" Pax asks as he's slipping back on his t-shirt. This time, he definitely catches me looking.

I narrow my eyes at him. He holds his hands up. "Just for a sec. I don't want to cut my arm reaching in."

"Ok, but don't rip it," I say as I untie it from my waste and toss it in his direction. It's a bad throw, but his long arm swoops low and catches it before hitting the ground.

"Thanks," he mutters as he slips one arm into the sleeve and reaches through the hole he created in the bottom right corner of the window. He strains to reach the knob on the inside and says a few choice words as he smashes his face against the glass in an attempt to reach the handle. Just as I think he can't stretch any further, there's a click, and Pax extracts himself. He winces and tries another angle.

"Sorry," he mumbles as he hands my coat back.

"For wh..." there's a rip in the upper bicep area of the coat. "Great," I grumble as I tie it back around my waist.

Pax steps through the door first, and I'm close behind. It's a small, unorganized office. Papers litter the desk, and there are boxes stacked in random places throughout the small space and two mismatching metal file cabinets. I have the strange compulsion to clean the area, but I resist. How ridiculous. But it does make me think back to my office in Phili. I can't stop the brief comparison that's now so meaningless but still manages to make me feel superior to whomever this office belonged.

The others file in behind us. The space is cramped, so we open one of the two interior doors on the opposite walls. One is a small bathroom with a toilet, a pedestal sink with a roll of paper towels, a wire wastebasket in the corner, and a basic, unframed mirror. Pax tries the other door. It leads into an expansive space that smells of dirt and motor oil. There are two tractors inside and tools lining the walls, among other pieces of machinery. Everyone shuffles through the office door and into the expansive workspace. We poke around, exploring.

I'm not sure there's much of anything useful here, but I take note of two pairs of gray, oil-stained coveralls, work gloves, three cans of an off-brand cola (one was opened, though), possibly some beef jerky, and a bag of half-eaten chips someone else found. Some of the tools could be taken for weapons, perhaps. After our exploration turns into milling about, someone finally asks what we all must be thinking, "What now?"

CHAPTER 8

Bodin

October 17, 2025

I wake abruptly. My eyes squint against the bright lights flooding my room. The shower turns on. Shit, I have three minutes, and I *need* that shower. I throw the blanket off of me and sit on the edge of the bed, attempting to rub the sleep from my eyes. My stomach feels like it's eating itself. I had packed provisions in my backpack, but it was confiscated when I attempted to get in the back of the army caravan yesterday. I ate a good breakfast yesterday morning, which is more than anyone else could have said on that truck, I'm sure, but that was my last meal.

Suffice it to say, I'm famished. Thankfully, breakfast is soon after showering. That's what the TV lady said. I swallow the saliva gathering in my mouth at the thought of tomatoes and eggs. I don't know what we're really getting, but the food here has to be good after what I saw last night.

I remove the boxers I slept in and step into the shower. I gasp and jump back out. The water is cold. "Fuck!" I stand outside the shower and hold my hand out under the stream. The water doesn't warm any. Knowing the seconds are ticking by, I take a deep breath and hop in. I pump blue soap from the dispenser on the wall into my palm and quickly scrub beneath my armpits and my gonads, holding my breath. Next, I quickly scrub my hair. The cold water on my head is the most jarring, but I'm getting used to it. Still, I jump out; my heart rate is rapid from the cold exposure. I catch my breath as I towel off, feeling oddly invigorated. I tie the towel around

my waist and head over to the sink, where three brown pills have fallen
into the basin below a dispenser. I take the toothbrush on the counter
and use another dispenser on the wall to squirt a thick line of white,
minty toothpaste onto the brush. As I brush, I eye the pills. It's a "rule,"
I remember my liaison saying yesterday. I begin to dress when I hear a slat
open on the door, and something shiny is tossed into my room before the
slat slams closed again, nearly hitting me. I stare down at what appears to
be a large protein bar in silver metallic wrapping. In black letters, it says,
"Meal Bar."

Shut the fuck up. This is breakfast? I almost laugh, my hysteria bordering
on tears. I finish dressing quickly and reach over and grab the brown pills.
I fill a paper cup by the sink with water. I have seconds to make a decision.
I'm aware of the camera. I stand up, throw the pills into my mouth, and
take a big gulp of water as I walk over to the closet, the only corner out of
view from the camera. I fish the pills out of my cheek with my finger and
place them in my fist. Then, I sit on the toilet and drop them quietly behind
me into the water. I do my business and flush. Then, I pick up the meal bar
and sit on my bed. I hold it in my hands, looking it over. It's heavy for a
bar. I sigh and rip open the package. It's brown. I sniff it. It doesn't smell
that different from other protein bars I've eaten in my life. I take a bite. It's
chewy. Interestingly, it tastes like Berry Kool-Aid. I eat the bar, surprised to
find that I feel full.

The door slides open, and I see the glassy hallway floor illuminated with
a green arrow before it disappears behind shoes and bodies, all dressed like
me except for the different colored bands around our sleeves. Hoards of
people crowd the hallways. I step into the thick of it.

Once in the Arena, I see neat lines of people and more people filling in
behind them. There are thousands of people here—tens of thousands. I
curse under my breath. How am I supposed to find Ava? I spot the purple
arrow on the floor and follow it to the far side of the Arena. Some colors

have more people than others. Purple is the lightest-populated color, with only two lines. A quick headcount by tens, and I would guess it represents three hundred people. There are a lot of Green and Brown. Yellow and Purple have the least. Blue, Pink, Orange, and Red fall somewhere in the middle. The first Purple line appears complete, so I walk up the second Purple line and wait behind a short girl with a low ponytail. Everyone stares straight ahead.

"So, what now?" I ask.

Three or four people "shush" me in unison.

"Well, okay then. Be that way," I say.

I scan the Arena, a plan forming in my head. It might take a while, but if I wait long enough to be one of the last ones walking in, I can pick a line and scan it for Ava. Then another one. Trying to move through a color each day. Of course, I've been scanning the Purple lines, and even though their backs are turned, I know Ava isn't a Purple worker. No one in these lines has her long, jet-black hair.

Armed soldiers are scattered throughout the Arena. Their eyes sweep the space in practiced patterns. I wonder what they're looking for. A man appears at the front of our line. He's in a black, tailored suit with a purple silk undershirt. Without a word, he turns, and the rest of the purple ahead of me follows. I look around and notice similarly dressed personnel, each with a different color silk shirt beneath form-fitting dark suits. In my head, I've already nicknamed these guys "the Suits." So, the Suits take us to our work assignment, like a crosswalk guard at school or something. I snort. I guess no one else finds it funny. Their complete lack of interaction with each other has me on edge. I take one last glance at the guards dotted around the Arena and think I know what they're there for now.

We move up an elevator. Cross a street. Get into another elevator in another building. Go up briefly. We're split into groups of forty. When my group files through the door in front of us, I hear a quiet "ping" as each of us enters the room. I hear my "ping." My tattooed wrist has a slight tingle, but I'm too distracted by the room to care much. I'm surprised to see that it looks a lot like a movie theater. It's dark and windowless, with rows of reclining chairs and equipment dangling from the ceiling in front of each one. There's another Suit waiting for us at the front of the room. She looks bored as hell or maybe angry.

I follow everyone else and find a seat, wondering what comes next. Everyone else pulls down the equipment. There are eye goggles and remote controls. It looks like we're about to enter into a gaming tournament. Finally, something good here. I like video games. The woman looks down at a tablet in her hand and then looks up at me, frowning. "31186," she shouts as she walks towards me. "Welcome to the Crawlers," she says as she approaches.

"Number 24461," she says. The kid next to me pulls off his goggles, looking terrified at having been addressed. The Suit has eyes like ice. "Show number 31186 the ropes." 24461 gulps and nods. The woman walks away, assuming her position at the front of the room again, her eyes remaining on us.

I look over at 24461. He's short with glasses and a freckled nose. He's a serious tub, though I can tell from cheeks hanging loosely around his face that he's lost significant weight recently. He appears to be about my age, but he's not the kind of kid I'd hang with in school, and that might be putting it lightly.

"What's your name?" I ask.

His eyes shift to the woman in the front of the room. She's not looking at us anymore. "Sean," he whispers. "But best not to call me that."

Fine. "What do we do here?" I ask.

"We're Crawlers," he states. "We man small robots around the city. When you pull on your goggles, your assignment for the day is waiting for you. Each robot has an area of the city they clean up. We prune plants, pick up trash, wash windows, and occasionally make deliveries of special request items."

"Cool," I say, reaching up for my goggles.

"Before you put those on, this is the remote." He goes on to explain to me how it moves. Apparently, he's enjoying this moment of authority. It seems pretty standard to me.

"Where's the bathroom?" I ask, feeling that meal bar working its way through me.

He nods towards a door at the right. "Two minutes, tops. Don't try to stretch it out." His eyes are full of warning.

"That's a quick dump," I say, leaning back and reaching for the goggles once more.

"And don't try to venture anywhere your robot hasn't been assigned to go," he hisses as he pulls on his own goggles.

Once I strap the goggles onto my face, I look around. I'm on the side of a building, clinging to it like a spider. I don't know what the robot looks like except for what I can see out in front of me. My legs are spindly and appear to be aluminum or something shiny like that. The feet are harder to discern. They look like a blob. Something about them allows the tiny robot to cling to the side of the building. It doesn't take me long to become fluid with the movements. I click into my "assignment" box and read. Today, I'm pruning and picking up leaf debris from building forty-two. The debris goes into a compartment inside the robot. At first, I thought it was funny to stuff leaves in the robot's "mouth." The robot has a mechanism that compresses the debris, giving it a high carrying capacity. I laugh to myself again, thinking of one of Evie's favorite movies, Wall-E. I sigh deeply. I'm here while Evie is back at the ranch without her brother and mom. I've got to get out of here. My mind shifts gears.

I could use this robot to search for the Mole. I brighten at the idea. Maybe it won't take me as long as I thought it would. I move my goggles to the top of my head.

"Hey, Sean," I whisper, leaning towards him.

"What?" he responds with his fingers moving across the remote.

"When's lunch?" I ask.

"Ha. There's no lunch."

"What?" I ask, incredulous.

He sighs, his fingers pausing momentarily, but the large oculars remain on his face. "Look, save your meal bar from the morning and nibble on it throughout the day. It helps."

I lean back into my chair and notice the Suit's eyes lowered at me. I pull back on my goggles to resume work.

It's been a long day. I'm not having fun anymore. My ass is sore from sitting. I want to get up and move. Finally, the screen indicates quitting time, and I can hang up my equipment. As I pull off the goggles, I blink, trying to adjust to the room's darkness while I flex my fingers. At some point, the woman Suit was traded out for a man.

"Let's go," his deep voice penetrates the room. I follow Sean, whispering behind him.

"This is what we do all day?"

"Yeah," he says without looking at me. "Somedays, you get different duties. So, try to sit in different spots." He sounds sad.

We follow the lines back to our rooms. It's only Purple right now, making for a much less chaotic walk back to the Cells. It's another one of my apt nicknames. We're escorted every step of the way. How am I ever going to find the Mole when everything I do is monitored? I swallow my panic. The robot might give me a chance, but it's still as if I'm drowning in the middle of the ocean and I've been thrown a single water wing. When I enter my room, there's another meal bar waiting for me.

CHAPTER 9

Carrie

October 17, 2025

T he group discusses our predicament, everyone vying for some air time to be heard. Nerves are still running high. I lean back against a workbench and watch without trying to look smug.

"There's nothing out here for us. It was dumb to think not everything had been picked over," Caroline grumbles.

"We did find a few things," someone counters.

"We're so fucked," a man states.

"We don't even have shoes anymore," someone else adds.

"Tom is going to be so pissed we lost two of Frank's handguns," Hammer says.

Aha, so two of the guns were loaners from Tom. Why wasn't I given a gun? Because I'm a woman? I scold this version of Carrie. *It's probably because you have no* experience *with a gun... not everything is because you're a woman*, I chide myself.

"We could turn back and still make it before dark," Hammer suggests.

"Empty-handed with our tail tucked between our legs?" a woman scoffs.

The group members decide to spare themselves the embarrassment by sticking it out for one night and using our tractor garage as a home base while we explore the immediate surrounding areas. They're just residential homes, and after the wake-up call the group just got, no one explores very enthusiastically, and they exert more caution than is probably necessary. We come back empty-handed as darkness begins to settle in the Salmon Valley.

***

Most of the group huddled together for warmth last night. It was quite the poignant reminder of the situation their stupidity got them into yesterday. They spent their time this morning fashioning grease-stained rags around their feet for makeshift shoes that would carry the heavy weight of their defeat back to the ranch.

I'm staying. I thought I'd be alone in my plight to see this thing through, given I'm the only one with any water or sensible clothing left, but there were two other volunteers: Pax and Caroline. Pax volunteered first. And, with a look of disgust directed towards me, Caroline announced she'd also be staying. So, those two were given the two pairs of gray work coveralls that we found last night. They also have work gloves, a few empty soda bottles to hold water, and one shoulder bag that we saw in the office to share between them. Their needs have now become priority number one, and I'm finding it hard not to resent them for it.

I'd be lying if I said my heart didn't skip a little when Pax volunteered. His gray coveralls barely fit. The fabric is pulled tight across his chest and biceps. It doesn't look entirely comfortable, but he hasn't complained. He's really the only guy in the group I find tolerable. Caroline is at the bottom of that list with her sharp, often upturned nose, ropy muscles, and tanned skin. She's the kind of girl who brags about running as fast as the boys and bagging trophy-winning game during hunting season. I've heard her talk. She's the girl who hangs with the boys and watches football and drinks beer, but she's pretty enough that she gets more attention than just "one of the guys," and I bet she thrives off that attention. From what I gather, she's not married, probably in her late twenties. I don't know what her deal is, but she made her disapproval of me evident from the moment we met. I threaten her in some way. I take satisfaction in that.

So, here we are. We've geared up with what little we have, and we're heading out. Pax wants to take a route that skirts around town and back towards the river with a pitstop at his apartment. He says there isn't much left there, but there might be a pot for boiling river water and some clothes for him. I have a few matches for fires, at least. After we get out of town, we'll look for a safe, sheltered place to hole up for the night.

When Caroline suggests we stay at Pax's apartment for the night, he shoots her a look. "I was living in the office at the gym. There are no windows and one exit point. I don't want to risk it just for a futon," he says. If any homes farther away from the town look deserted, we'll investigate, but personally, I see that as a long shot.

As I watch the sun sag in the sky, I'm reminded that we don't have the luxury of time on our side. Instead, it consumes our every decision and will ultimately decide our fate. If we don't find food, clothing, shoes, and other supplies today, we'll have to go back to the ranch tomorrow. I look up at the non-threatening blue sky. At least the likelihood of snow trapping us down here is close to nil.

Pax's pitstop at his office/apartment has me irked, but he's in and out with clothes, shoes, and a pot in under a few minutes, and we successfully manage to avoid the central area of town. He tosses Caroline a few clothing items that she absolutely swims in, but they'll provide her with more warmth than the coveralls. Still, they both need coats.

"How'd you cook in there?" I ask, referring to his apartment.

"You can do a lot with a hot plate, mini fridge, and microwave." He winks at me.

"And protein shakes?" I guess.

Pax grins. "You know me so well already."

Towards the end of the day, just before debating on whether to camp in the open, we get lucky. There's a house close to the river with enough trees to give us cover. We feel safe investigating it. The inside is in complete disarray and has been picked through. Not a morsel of food remains, but there is bedding, two ancient sleeping bags, and more appropriate clothing for Caroline. The house has a fire ring in the backyard with some large logs placed around it for seating.

"We'll stay here for the night," Pax declares. "The river is close enough that we can gather water, and we can start a fire here." He points to the fire ring.

I nod, grateful that he's taken charge, and note that my skin doesn't prickle as it would have at the thought of a male taking the boss role.

"I saw mattresses inside. Should we sleep there?" Caroline asks.

Pax looks at the house and frowns. "Sleep where you want," he says. Caroline glowers at him. Pax has been taking these small jabs at her all day. Apparently, they have a history. I don't know the extent of it, but I take satisfaction in witnessing these rebukes. Pax is funny, and Caroline's obvious affection for him has affected me, too. I know it's human nature to want what others want, but knowing that intellectually doesn't change the feeling. I smile when Caroline purses her lips as Pax flirts in his not-too-obvious way with me or when he asks me questions, intentionally leaving Caroline out of the conversation.

I share what little food I have even though I wish I could tell Caroline to find her own food. That means that after a really scant breakfast, we'll have nothing.

It's late now. We're sitting side by side on the thick trunk of a fallen tree that was rolled near the fire for seating. I smell like campfire smoke, and my hair must look greasy in a slicked-back ponytail, but regardless, I sense the mood. Pax nudges my knee with his, vying for my attention. When I look over at him, his eyes lock onto mine until I turn away, embarrassed. Opting to sleep in the house with her blankets, Caroline has left us alone. Pax and I won the two archaic sleeping bags we found in the attic after a game of Rock, Paper, Scissors. They're heavy with a strong fabric and soft cotton interior, but they're not made from the lightweight, slick, waterproof material that they made sleeping bags out of recently.

"Carrie, you're killing me," he says with a frustrated groan.

"What?" I feign innocence as I attempt to buy some time. His goal here seems obvious, and my options are clear: either I give in to his advances or shut this down now. A thought occurs to me with sharp clarity: I could have sex with this man. The thought is thrilling.

There's a part of me that feels insecure. Is that why I'm hesitating? Because my legs are hairy, I have a wild bush going on in my panties, and I smell like a cavewoman. I look at him. He must not care. He has to know I haven't been visiting the spa lately. I push those insecurities to the back of my mind because, in a way, I feel as if I've been permitted to do this looking and smelling like an animal. There's something exhilarating about this. I could just give in to instincts and leave all of the toxic culture-permeating messaging from the past behind. I'm not perfect, but it's okay. I could just choose to set the programming that clouds my brain down neatly next to me like a purse carrying a snake. Then there are all of these unwritten rules that keep coming to mind: you haven't met his parents, he hasn't even taken you out on a proper date, you still technically have a boyfriend, or even you don't know his last name. Fuck rules. The former rules of society no longer apply.

But despite this knowledge, they don't just melt away. I still feel them weighing in on my decision like flies circling a corpse. I swat at these proverbial flies in my head, but they act just as I expect. There's really only one way to rid myself of these pests. I turn towards Pax and do something I might regret.

"Fine," I say.

His eyebrows arch in amusement. "Fine?"

"Why the hell not?" I ask quietly as I lean towards him.

At first, we share an awkward, closed-mouth kiss. His stiff, cold lips touch mine, and we stay like that momentarily. Then his hands find the back of my neck, and he pulls me in closer. That does the trick. Desire takes over, and we can't remove each other's clothes fast enough.

Ed and I had never had sex on the hardwood floors in our townhome, but I imagine this is what it would feel like. Despite the rocks digging into my back, the experience is exhilarating. I feel as if I've been unleashed. I'm running wild now, feeling raw freedom unlike anything I've encountered before. We do our best to stay quiet, but by the end, I wonder how Caroline could have slept through it. We should have been quieter, but once the delirium of what we were doing set in, it couldn't be stopped. It's possible that she didn't hear us. I suppose we'll know in the morning.

After we dress, we fall asleep, spooning to the sound of the crackling fire. Best sleep I've had since everything went to shit.

***

When I wake in the morning, I discover Caroline is gone. I'm not worried about it. I think she heard us last night, and she's heading back to the ranch. My sense of victory is short-lived as Pax stretches along the ground, groaning as he arches his back. I know the feeling. He opens his eyes and looks at me, then smiles sweetly. I return the gesture shyly. More than knowing what we shared last night, it's the feeling of intimacy now that is the most oppressive.

"How'd you sleep?" he asks.

"Fine," I answer. "Caroline isn't in the house. Must have left."

Pax looks around and says with a yawn, "Guess it's just me and you today."

"Guess so." We both share a knowing smile.

Pax wears a flannel shirt-jacket over a white tee shirt, a pair of jeans, socks, and sneakers that he took from his apartment yesterday. We're going to venture downtown today. With nothing worthy to steal and a local such as

Pax by my side, I feel bolder today. He secures the sleeping bags we found on his back by rigging a cinch strap he located in the garage. He takes a blanket, too, and wears it around his shoulders for added warmth this morning. I put a pot in my backpack along with the full water bottles that we filled with river water this morning after boiling it.

Downtown turns out to be non-threatening. Pax does the talking when we come across people. If he doesn't know them immediately, he finds a way to connect to them through some common thread—people they both know, usually, or the high school sports teams. He's always successful. It seems people here are only separated by one or two people. I'm beginning to understand what he meant by the small-town thing, and I feel the tension I tend to hold in my shoulders melting away.

We've explored downtown. Pax was able to trade one of the heavy sleeping bags for a can of beans. We opened it by borrowing the man's can opener and ate it on the spot by bending the lid and using it as a spoon, careful not to cut our lips on the edges of the thin metal lid as we tipped the black beans into our mouths. Pax asked around about shelters or supplies. People have indeed begun to band together. Some are known for their ammo. Some for toiletries. All seem to struggle for food.

My only spoils for the day are two novels from the library and a toothbrush, deodorant, and hair dye from the local grocery store. The toothbrush I found kicked beneath shelving, and the deodorant had a shattered plastic lid but was otherwise functional. Found two boxes of hair dye in blonde—my color. They're in my backpack for now, knowing they'll get tossed if something better comes along. To my disappointment, I had no luck finding toothpaste, sanitary pads, or tampons. Food, of course, I didn't expect.

We decide to camp in a small park near the river. There's a firepit with logs that still have a little life to them. We light the fire, knowing the warmth will be short-lived. As we sit around it, boiling water in the pot for tomorrow's rations, we agree that we'll head back to the ranch tomorrow if we can't find any food in the morning. Today was all business between Pax and me. I was beginning to wonder if he intended to pretend last night never happened. The only indication I got that he was still thinking about it was the way he traded that sleeping bag and suggested we'd have to cozy up together tonight with a wink. But now, with just the two of us around the fire, I see his demeanor change.

"So..." Pax pulls me in close.

"So," I say, feigning indifference to his suggestive move.

"Last night was fun."

"Uh, huh," I say flatly. Last night *was* fun, but one time, you can brush it off. Two times feels like more than just a mistake. It's intentional. But was last night a mistake? The nervous energy gathering in my chest would suggest that Pax has more of an effect on me than I'd like to admit.

Pax sighs and lays his head on my shoulder. It's an oddly personal, vulnerable gesture, and my resolve begins to melt. We sit like that as the glow of the fire weakens. Its warmth retreats from a relentless affront from the cold. I feel it at my back.

Pax sits up straight. "Let's take a walk," he says as he stands and extends his hand to me. I allow him to help me up, but his hand doesn't release mine after I'm up. I don't struggle with it. I let myself go along with it. We walk, holding hands, until we reach the river's edge. The sound of the fluid water rolling softly over rocks is melodic, and I feel oddly at peace despite the chill in the air that packs a warning.

"It's strange being in the mountains. The temperature fluctuations are a lot more drastic than what I'm used to," I say to break the silence.

"Yeah, I used to hate living here. Not because of the temperature but because I thought small-town living wasn't for me. Then I went to college and couldn't wait to get back here," he chuckles.

"Why did you change your mind?" I ask.

"Guess I figured it was better to be a somebody in a small town than a nobody in the big city."

"Huh." I mull over his words for a moment before asking, "So you're a 'somebody' here? What does that mean? I've only ever known city living."

"Well, people know who you are. It's hard to do anything in town without running into someone you know. I like that. I also like that, for the most part, we have each other's backs here. Like, there's a real sense of community and belonging. Not like rotary clubs or college towns where the people always seem transitory."

I squeeze his hand, unsure of what to say.

He turns to me, his eyes serious. "I like you," he states. I feel myself blush and look away. He continues, "I know that our circumstances aren't remotely traditional, and I can't take you to dinner or a movie, but we could still... date. In a sense."

"In what sense?" It sounds more bitter than I had intended. I let go of his hand, unsure of why I'm feeling defensive.

He looks at me with eyebrows drawn together and his mouth pulled down. "I know," he says and leaves it at that. I don't engage him. I just cross my arms and stare out at the river. The last few inches of sun are descending behind the mountain.

"Everything just seems so much harder now. Pointless even," I say as a way of explaining myself.

"Our way of life changed. Suddenly. But basic needs still exist. Food, water, shelter, and companionship. Same as always, we just have to work harder for it," he says.

"I don't want this life," I say as I turn and walk back to our firepit, where I hope to shake the chill creeping into my skin. Pax follows me but doesn't say anything. When we return, we work silently to bring the fire back to life. It's only after we manage to revive the fire a tad by rolling a log over and we're holding our hands up to it that he speaks again.

"Nobody asked for this life, Carrie."

"You're not going to give me some kind of 'make lemonade out of lemons' bullshit are you?" I ask.

"Naw. Or maybe yes," he says quietly, looking off into the distance. "You're my lemonade," he says.

I suppress the urge to roll my eyes. "That's a line if I've ever heard one."

"It's not a line, Carrie. I'm not just trying to pick you up or sleep with you. I like you." His expression is sincere. Vulnerable.

I turn my face away from him. "It's not like there are a lot of other choices."

"Oh, stop it." His abruptness makes my eyes widen. "You're not some consolation prize. Seriously, I know this whole situation is shitty, but I still can't help but feel lucky because it brought you to me."

I blink, unsure of how to respond or how I feel.

"Look, I don't want to sound creepy, but I've had my eye on you since the day you arrived. I tried to talk to you that first day. Do you remember?" I think back to that day. It was all such a blur. Everything was new.

"No," I answer, but I doubt myself as his face appears in my mind's eye with the backdrop of that first day.

"I didn't think so," he says. "You seemed kind of shell-shocked."

I snort. "I was."

Pax moves next to me and puts his arm around me, drawing me into him. He's warm, and his plaid jacket is soft. I let myself sink into him. I don't know how I feel about Pax, but he was right about human nature still being the same. His arms around me feel safe. Being a part of someone's circle feels safe. I'm not wanted back at the Colony, but Pax wants me. For the reason of survival alone, maybe I should go with this. Survival seems to be all that's on anyone's mind anymore, anyway. If the game was making money before the EMP attack, now it's not starving, and if I want to play it smart, I'll let Pax feel like I'm his. But there's still a part of my pride that doesn't want to allow a man to protect me. I sit up and move his arm from around me as I scoot a little farther away from him. He doesn't protest.

After looking into the dying embers of the fire for a few minutes, Pax breaks the silence. "Do you ever think about bananas?"

"Bananas?"

"Yeah, like they were this fruit I would always buy, but I swear I was always throwing them away after they rotted on my counter. I don't know why I'd keep buying them. They were... expendable. Sometimes, I'd eat one or just a half of one and throw the other half away like it was nothing."

"And now, you'd give anything for a banana?" I guess.

He nods his head solemnly. "I know what we've lost here. The security. But I also feel like we've gained so much."

I grab the sleeping bag propped on the log beside us and unroll it on the ground. I remove my shoes, unzip the bag, and climb in, hugging my knees to my chest. I hope he takes the hint that I'm done with this conversation. I'm not in the mood for any philosophical bullshit. All I see is loss and tragedy when I think of our current situation. I close my eyes and shiver, already feeling the cold on my back. A moment later, Pax lies behind me, wrapping his arms around me, cocooning me in warmth.

"Is this ok?" he whispers. It's then that I decide my pride can go to hell. It feels good to have someone looking out for me.

"Why don't you unzip the bag and come inside, silly?" I say as I stretch out, making room. He does. The sleeping bag stretches around us. Pax isn't able to zip it all the way up behind him, leaving his back exposed. "We can take turns being next to the cold," I suggest.

"Naw," Pax says. "I won't allow it."

We lay next to each other. His breath is in my ear. He may be sleeping now, but I'm not. I feel electrified by his proximity. I inch closer to him. Pax responds by crushing me into him and then releasing me. We're as close as we can be. He kisses my neck softly.

"I could get used to this," he whispers, letting out a contented sigh.
I fall asleep with a smile still on my face and his arms around me.

CHAPTER 10

Bodin

October 20, 2025

My body aches today. We had PT (physical training) yesterday. A welcome break, even after just two days of "crawling." PT is apparently every seventh day for Purples and Yellows. There are no days of rest. Guess these are not the religious types. Or, they just don't give a shit if we are. Which, I'm not, but I would definitely have played that card if it came with any benefits. But no. Six days of crawling and one day of PT. Repeat. If I didn't have an escape to look forward to, I'd go mental. Clearly, that's what PT day is for: to prevent us from going mental.

It felt good to shine in the athletic sphere again. However, a comment was directed at me that if I kept it up, my number would be thrown in the hat for Private status with the army. It was meant to be a compliment but I don't want to join the army. I think I'll tone it down next time. Training took place in the Arena. We shared the space with Yellow. We were split into groups of fifteen. There were circuits, which we set up that morning after all the other colors left for their work duties while the guards barked orders. I've now confirmed that Ava is not a Yellow. Disappointing, but one step closer.

I scanned the Browns the day before PT, my second day of crawling. I got halfway through—which was really shitty since the order changes every day. I have to be faster tomorrow. But I have this feeling, watching the Browns, that Ava is not a Brown. I don't know. They all just looked so... haggard. So unkempt and uncared for. They had brown, suntanned faces—apropos for their color. Ava is remarkable in her beauty. Not just to me, either. I can't see her being thrown into a Brown. Something about it just doesn't fit. Admittedly, Purples fit nicely into the "gamer" stereotype. I'm an exception, obviously.

I crack my neck as I sit up in bed, feeling the muscles down my back respond with a sensation I remember well from two-a-day football practices. I liked PT day, and I like this feeling. It's the feeling of accomplishment and growth. The best part, though, wasn't my impressive number of push-ups or my time on the rope climb. The best part was dinner. Finally, we got an authentic meal last night. Potatoes, broccoli, and chicken with gravy. To top it off, we each got a square two-inch by two-inch piece of vanilla sponge cake. Positively divine. The best meal I've had in ages. I'll be dreaming about that meal on PT Day every day that I'm crawling. Another deliberate intention, probably, but it's something, and I'll gladly take it.

The shower turns on, and my morning routine commences. When the doors open, I decide to be the first one out so that I can scan the Greens as they get in line. That was my other mistake the first couple of days—being last in and thinking it gave me an advantage. No, I want to be first and watch the faces from the front of the Purple line. I sprint down the hallway, knocking people aside as I go.

"Sorry, sorry," I mutter.

I'm close to one of the first in line for Purple. I turn and watch the Greens file in. They line up on the other side of Brown, and given the sheer number of lines, I have to squint to really see their features, but I think I'm close enough.

As my eyes scan the Greens, my pulse quickens. This is a color of beautiful, groomed people. This is a color that would suit Ava. After getting my hopes up a couple of times already, I cautiously scrutinize another girl with jet-black hair pulled into a tight bun at the top of her head. Unaccustomed to seeing her put together like this, I almost wrote her off. *Almost.* I stare for a moment. *Holy shit, it's her.*

I push my way through lines, barreling toward her like a maniac until I realize at the last moment that my desperate display to reach her is uncool. I slow down, only saying her name once I'm close enough to use a normal range of voice—definitely not yelling from across the room as I had wanted to do.

"Ava?" I think it sounds cool and casual, like 'fancy meeting you here,' but I'm a bit out of breath. She turns. Her face is puzzled until her eyes find me. Surprise lights up her face.

"Bodin?!" she exclaims.

I smile, I can't help it, but it falls from my face immediately when she says, "What the fuck are you doing here?" Her eyes are angry as they scan the room, looking for what I'm unsure. She glares at me, her lips pulled into a tight line. "Why. Are. You. Here?" she demands, annunciating each word. I blink at her, stunned. Her words sting, but her face is arresting up close. There's something different about her. She's wearing some make-up—which is odd because no other color I've noticed wears makeup or does their hair like this. The thought doesn't hold long. There's something else about her. It's an unsettling feeling—like the person I've come for no longer exists.

"I came to get you out," I whisper. Her head snaps back like she's been slapped. "Among other things," I add defensively. She looks around again, searching for something. She's on edge. Her facial expressions shift faster than a frightened octopus.

"I need your help finding someone," I say, hoping that this will cement the fact that I didn't just come for her. Stupid thing to say. She looks at me quizzically. "He has information I need. He has a port wine birthmark that's just visible on his face. By his hairline."

"Bodin," she whispers. I'm immediately hypnotized by her soft words. I lean in. "Do you know what this place is?" she asks.

I nod. She blinks long and slow as though trying to compute this.

I attempt to break the spell. "Where's Sarah?" I ask.

Ava seems to come back to herself. She frowns. "I haven't seen her since we arrived."

I can't help it. My eyes travel up and down her body. "What's your job?" I ask. She swallows hard, and a bright red crimson flashes up her neck and settles in her cheeks.

"Maid," she says, looking down at the floor before adding, "basically." When she looks back up, she scans the room again. Her face changes in an instant. "Shit, you've been spotted. You have to go." She begins pushing me away when I don't move. "Say it's your first day," she says quickly. "Say you didn't know." I turn to see what she sees—a security guard marching purposefully towards me as the people around him part like the Red Sea for Moses. I gulp, but I turn back to Ava, unsure if I'll have another chance.

"What door did Sarah go through?" I ask.

Ava blinks and scrunches her eyebrows together, unsure of the relevancy of this question but trying to find the meaning and then failing. "Yellow. Why?" she responds through the corner of her mouth as she turns away from me, trying to dissociate before the guard reaches us.

I square up to him, intending to state my case, but before I get the chance, I'm knocked to the floor. Winded and stunned, I try to stand, but I'm held down by his boot, heavy on my shoulder. My blood freezes as I hear a gun cock. I'm left with very few choices. So, I grovel.

"I'm new here. It's my first day," I say, squeezing my eyes shut and waiting for the bullet.

I breathe in. A breath. A single, precious breath I didn't think I'd have a second ago.

Nothing is said, but his boot comes off of my shoulder. I look up to see him holstering his gun, a scowl still on his face. "Don't let it happen again," he says through gritted teeth.

"Yes, sir," I say without a hint of sarcasm.

With my heart still pounding wildly, I make my way back to Purple. I don't dare sneak a look back at Ava. My armpits are sweating. When I get in line, there are a few curious glances. I take a deep breath in, recognizing and appreciating its precarious existence. *Holy fuck, this place is whack.*

My workday is totally uninspiring. I've sat in a different seat each day, and it has kept things somewhat interesting. I finished my work assignment early today, and I've been given another one, which the next person who sits here will resume tomorrow. The best part about this is that I get to crawl to another building, and it isn't another skyscraper. It's an interesting, glossy, black, stubby building visible below the ten stories I'm currently at. As I descend, making my way to my target, I take the opportunity to look around. I don't think this is suspicious behavior. It's normal behavior to be curious. It'd be more suspicious not to look around, I convince myself. To my disappointment, my robot has limited optic capabilities. No, it's not my robot. It's the software. My destination building is clear as day, but the surrounding areas are blurry. Frustrating—but smart on their part. Another reminder I'm out of my league here. Still, I have to keep holding out hope. I won't be trapped here. I can't. I'd rather be fending for myself, constantly on the verge of starvation, than be here as an easily expendable servant. At least out there, my life has some value. There are still some people who love me and depend on me. People who would miss me. Here, it's all just so... empty—this existence. They probably dump you in a pit when you die and leave you to rot. I shudder.

When I reach the building, I find the wash port along the far side. I enter the code supplied to me and open the compartment. My assignment is to wash both the exterior and the interior windows after filling a water canister, securing an empty one for the dirty water, and fitting two of the robot's arms with washing attachments. This is the most exciting job I've had yet. Something new anyway. I fumble a bit with the attachments and have to open the help icon in the upper right-hand corner of the screen for instructions on how to operate them. After this, something unexpected happens—I'm given a choice. 'Interior or Exterior first?' Appears on my screen. I've never been given access to the interior of a building. In fact, the windows were blurred out during my tree pruning days. I couldn't even look inside. I've always just assumed the interiors were off-limits. So, naturally, I select 'interior.'

Instructions pop up on the screen. I crawl to the building entrance. The double doors slide apart for the tiny robot, and I enter. Whether they opened from some sort of wireless communication, or they're just motion detecting, I couldn't say. Upon entering, I take a moment to take it all in. It's a factory of some kind. Brown workers mill about like bees in a hive. My presence draws curious glances from a few of them. There's a low hum that comes from five large vats on the far wall and a shrill whir from machinery directly in front of me. I look at the equipment and the layout. I begin to make out the production line. It starts with the vats. They empty their contents into what is probably a grinder. The pasty results of that, which look completely unappetizing, are squirted into a massive mixing bowl that turns slowly. A worker pours a bucket of some kind of clear liquid into the bowl. Further down the line, a large conveyor belt dumps the molded contents into a red, glowing oven, and those items fall into neat rows on the other side, where they're moved to a freezer that has billows of cold, icy air rolling from the entrance. Further down the line, I see the packaging machine. It picks up and neatly wraps a brown brick of food into a shiny, silver package and then stamps the package before the final product rides the belt and falls off the edge into a massive bin. Full now, the blue plastic bin is wheeled to a holding area. There are dozens of bins full of the finished product: meal bars.

I scope out the nearest window and get to work. A couple of hours later, I make my way to the nearby vats; the hum emanating from them is now loud enough to be thoroughly irritating. These windows above the vats are particularly dirty. I swipe away a thick layer of grime, letting in more light with each pass. The tops of the vats contain a finely meshed lid. Once, I caught a fine mist of water being sprayed from the ceiling into the vats.

I'm nearly on top of them now. I peer down into the first vat, but it's dark in there. Nothing but the top foot or two is illuminated by the light from the windows. They appear empty. I've nearly passed the vats now, and I'm glad about that. The hum is obnoxious.

I've cleaned the worst of the windows when I see a man approaching in my periphery. I turn the robot's eyes to watch him. There's a small bucket held to him by a belt around his waist. It has what looks like a spray attachment tied to the bucket's handle. He climbs up the ladder that leads to the top of the vat closest to me. I scuttle closer to see what he's up to. I'm standing directly above the vat now. I peer down into the blackness just as he reaches the top. He works to loosen the bucket and secures it on a nearby hook. Then he unwinds the nozzle and twists it. He leans away from the tank and fans a fine, brownish-green powder over the vat's mesh topper. I think he must be trying not to inhale the powder, but then I see it. There's movement from within the vat. The man turns his head away, a look of repulsion on his face. I crawl a little closer, but it's hard to see anything. Then, I slam back in my chair. My stomach heaves. Insects. The vats are full of insects. They undulate like a blanket waving in the breeze as they crawl over each other in their frenzy to reach the top of the vat. My stomach heaves at the revelation of this. I rip the goggles from my face, unable to watch anymore. My skin crawls, and I brush away frantically as if they're on me. I swallow back bile as I think back to the meal bar I ate this morning and the meal bar that'll be waiting for me at dinner.

Bastards.

CHAPTER 11

Ava

October 20, 2025

That stupid boy. Sarah was right. I made him believe he had a chance. That's assuming he came here because of me. Was that person he asked me to find even real? Or is it just a way for him to offload his embarrassment? I don't want to believe it because I don't want to be responsible, but I can't help feeling like that's precisely what his teenage hormones told him to do. I'm a bit flattered but mostly angry at myself. And where the hell is Sarah? It's been eleven days since we arrived, and I haven't seen her once. Why did Bodin ask which door she went through? I try to picture other faces that went through that door, but they don't come. That day was such a blur, and there were so many people being filed in and out of that area.

My muscles squeeze my heart a little with the memory. So many people volunteered. People who, like me, thought they were being saved. I wonder if, like me, that gratitude quickly turned to resentment and fantasies of revenge. This is no refuge. We're fed enough and provided just enough comforts that we don't revolt but not enough to be genuinely content. Worse than the realization that we're slaves is the hopelessness of wishing for anything different. I bet Sarah works in a hospital somewhere. I try not to think mean thoughts, but I can't help it. For once, Sarah's fat, ugly face landed her a better job. My looks have turned out to be a curse. Oh, what a sick alternate reality I've landed in.

I choke back a sob, thinking of Bodin's Purple designation. I don't know why I'm crying. Is it because Bodin isn't a Green, or because I am? The first night as a Green recruit is unique. I can tell from Bodin's youthful, hopeful face that he wasn't subjected to what I was. I can see it on all their faces: the other colors. Boredom, anger, and maybe even shyness, but I don't see the look of Greens. Dejection and shame are reserved for Greens.

I will never forget my first night as a Green. We were paraded through a large space, like a warehouse, with temporary walls creating different paths we were ushered through. First, we were bathed, and our inner cheeks and underwear were swabbed by medical personnel. I remember thinking, *these are my people. This* could be my job. I was a PA. I tried to chat with them like we were equals—colleagues. Like I was interviewing for their position, and I needed them to like me, but they said very little except to give me instructions, and they did not smile. I think that's when the feeling of dread started to solidify, but it wasn't until I reached Cee that it was confirmed.

Cee, unlike the others, was loose-lipped and eager to talk. She was my makeup and wardrobe artist—the last step in the assembly line. She had sparkling green eyes encircled with thick, dark makeup. Her curly hair was tied loosely behind her. Heavy, gold earrings tugged on her earlobes. When I asked why I needed makeup and wardrobe, she told me it was for tonight's Trade Party, like I should have known. She informed me that she was a Green recruit up until four weeks ago. She was picked up in Phoenix one week after the EMP.

"Oh girl, shit was already getting crazy in Phoenix. People were dying of heat stroke, and the water was gone. It was ugly," she had said as she painted my lips scarlet red. I could feel her bubble gum breath on my face. Then, she told me all about the Trade Party.

"It's important that you act like you belong. That you hold your head high. Some like the timid, scared animal look, but not many. It's possible a woman may pick you up, but not likely. You'll be paraded around the party like a prize. This is the one and only time you will see so many of the elites in one room. Oh girl, (Ava, is it?) wait until you see the extravagance..." She paused the application of my eyeliner to make an explosive gesture. "You'll be taken to the VIPs first for their consideration. I think you've got a shot at being picked up by one of them. You've got an exotic look to you. What is it? Iranian? Indian?"

"My dad is Indian. Mom is Caucasian," I answered through parted, frozen lips as she applied a gloss on top of the red lipstick. She stood back to admire her handiwork on my face.

"Gorgeous," she had whispered and then looked me in the eye. "Remember not to eat the food. It's everywhere, but it's not for you." Having clearly read the look on my face, she crouched before me and said in a soothing voice, "Hey, it's not all bad. Just do your time. When they get tired of you, and they will, you'll be moved to another position where you'll have more freedom and downtime. You could be like me." She smiles brightly. "Or you could go to the clubs." She wasn't as enthusiastic about that option for me. "But tonight, I bet you go for a pretty penny." She had turned around and was putting the makeup back into her case. "I don't know if they really trade in money. I think it must be more like favors and secrets." She shut her case with a loud click and told me to dress. There was a long, shiny emerald dress hung on a rolling coat rack. The silk hugged my sharp curves. "Too skinny." She frowned and then sighed. "Like all the ones we've seen recently."

I do remember that food. The extravagance of that classical music serenaded ballroom was dizzying. The glow of yellow light cast fragments of gold from the chandeliers. Tables with food piled high. Chefs stood behind stations, ready to prepare food fresh to order. The dessert table resembled more of a colorful work of art. The size of the jewels that hung from the necks and ears of the women was jaw-dropping. I twirled for some people. I opened my mouth for others. The man who paraded me through the hordes of people would pause me before an interested buyer and ask, "What do you think?"

I shake myself from my reverie. The green arrows illuminate on the floor beneath my feet, and we all shuffle after them. How ridiculous that they think we can't move forward in a line without stupid green arrows. It's humiliating. All of it: my job, my outfit, my existence. A joke. But is this really any worse than being out there? We couldn't live off Bodin's food forever. It was not sustainable. But even so, depending on Lane's mood for the day, my answer changes.

Lane is my... boss. Apparently, he was the highest bidder that first night. Calling him Master would be more appropriate. He told me I was to clean his house. Which I do, but the job title feels tentative. He couldn't have purchased me for that. There is another color that does the house-work—Yellow. I feel like a mouse that's being batted around between a cat's paw.

Green is the color of beauty. Not green itself but the people working in Green. We're the attractive ones. This can't be coincidental. I look around while we're waiting to start the day and see other girls like me. Men, too, but they're fewer. The girls' hair is pulled back in tight buns to start the day. Their beautiful faces, light makeup, and eyes that used to look forward proudly have steadily fallen under the weight of the humiliation. Some contain bruising poorly disguised under thick makeup. I hate Lane, but it seems like it could be worse.

Once outside, I follow the green arrows towards the city centers. There are other color arrows present out here. I don't know what every color does, but I know that Brown workers follow arrows out to buses that take them to the fields where they harvest food, milk cows, or whatever. I hear some of them get to leave the city and go to offsite farms. When the green arrow ends, I feel normal for just a moment—walking on ordinary sidewalks toward my building. Greens, Yellows, Pinks, and Reds work all over the city, but we all take large metal elevators explicitly designated for employees. The only period I can pretend I'm living a normal life is that brief sidewalk jaunt from when the colored arrows end until the moment I step foot onto the plain, metal elevators. The charade ends after that. I've seen the inside of an elevator for residents with patterned walls and thickly framed mirrors—nothing like ours.

Other Greens work in my building. We each scan the numbers etched onto our wrists as we enter the elevator. I've inspected the ink, wondering where it could be hidden: the computer chip. But there's no indication. Still, I fantasize about ripping it out of me. Maybe I can figure out a way to ask Lane how it works. He loves to boast, and so he tells me things—bits of information that inflate his ego and make him look important. I have to be careful not to overstep, though. It'll have to come up naturally. Lane has a temper. Once, when I pushed his hand away, he threatened me. His hot breath on my cheek as he spat with rage about sending me to the sick ward. I remember wondering why a sick ward would be such a bad place, but I know from the way he said it that that's exactly what it is: a bad place.

The elevator stops at each floor as it makes its way up. I'm the second to last stop. We scan our wrists as we exit onto our assigned floors. I notice that one girl's arm shakes as she holds it out to the scanner. When the elevator stops for me, I take a deep breath, scan, and step onto the landing, which is nothing more than a small, empty hallway leading to another door. Another scan. A green light illuminates and the door opens. I screw a smile on my face and enter.

First, I unzip my coveralls and step out of them. I place them on a hanger in the small closet and grab my outfit for the day. Sometimes, it's different, but most of the time, it resembles a French maid's Halloween costume. I suppress a scowl as I see it's the pantsuit and fake glasses. I can guess Lane's mood by the outfits waiting for me. Today will not be a day unchaperoned.

Once the suit is on and I've slipped into the black pumps, I smooth the front of the blazer while steeling myself for the day ahead with two deep breaths.

"Girl? Is that you?" Lane calls from the kitchen.

I hold back an eye roll and the urge to reply hotly. *Who else?* He's always called me "girl". I'm not sure he even knows my name. I prefer it this way. It separates us somehow. It allows me to hold onto something dear—some small part of me that he can't have.

Instead, I infuse my voice with feigned delight as I round the corner towards the kitchen, where I know he'll be, "Hello, Lane. How are you today?"

He takes a look at me and lets out a whistle. "You look hot."

"Thanks." I force a smile.

"Coffee?" he asks.

I look for a hint that he's joking. He never offers me coffee. He's either creating an opportunity to be cruel, or he's in an exceptional mood today. Either way, I have to play his game.

"That would be lovely," I respond.

"Cream? Sugar?"

"Yes, please." I try hard not to feel any sort of excitement about the prospect of coffee, knowing that this could all be part of his plan: work me up so the letdown is greater, but I can't help it. I reach for the carrot. He pours a full glass of the deep, dark liquid into a clear glass mug and tops it off with cream and sugar. My mouth is watering. He catches me looking longingly at it and smiles.

"You want this, don't you?"

I nod, waiting for the catch.

"Well, if I give this to you," he passes the coffee underneath my nose, "then you have to do something for me."

"Which is?" I hold my breath.

He reaches behind my head and pulls the pin from my bun. I feel my hair tumble down my back.

"Now, shake it out. In slow motion," he demands.

I clench my jaw and watch as he takes a sip of his own coffee, his eyes peering at me with amusement from under his thick lashes. I might think Lane was attractive for an older man if not for his hideous, cruel nature. He's in his mid-fifties, I would guess, with peppered white and dark hair. He wears thin-rimmed, rectangular glasses around his light blue eyes. He has a plump lower lip, a strong jaw, and a thin nose. Sometimes, his lips shine like he's wearing lip gloss. Naturally, he does it just because he likes to catch me staring at them. Thinking I actually desire him is a critical component to the success of this ruse. I don't doubt he can send me to the "sick ward." It's just a good thing I thought I wanted to be an actress before I went to school to become a Physician's Assistant. I learned a few things about acting.

I do as he says, pretending I'm trying out for a hair commercial. He squints at me and begins to pour the coffee down the drain.

"Not good enough." He sighs as he sets the empty cup on the counter and leaves the kitchen.

I get to work cleaning the kitchen, but I keep my ears and eyes open for any sign of his return so I can screw that fake ass smile back onto my face because right now, I'm scowling. As I mop the floor, I can see him sitting through the open office doorway at his desk in front of the massive windows that display multiple screens. Any glass in this apartment can be used as a touchscreen computer as well, it seems. When the phone rings, a green light flashes on all of the glass surfaces. Even the bathroom mirror. He only has to say "answer," and whichever screen is closest displays the person calling. I guess there's no such thing as physical phones anymore. They're just built in. I was in such awe when I came to this place. I marveled at the technology and the ease. Everything seemed to run seamlessly, and everything seemed to be a surface with smart features, but now I see this technology differently. It's the barrier between us, the thing that keeps me in check.

The phone rings. I move to his bedroom, where I'll be out of sight once he takes the call from the office, but I can still hear him. It's the same call every morning.

"Sir, your morning status report," the man on the other end announces.

"Please continue," Lane says.

"Energy storage is at 60%, water levels at 40%, food production running with 93% efficiency, barracks at 96% capacity, employee housing at 86% capacity..."

The man continues, but my thoughts drift to Bodin. I hope he's ok. They didn't shoot him right away, so I take that as a positive sign. Lane clears his throat, and I jump in surprise. He's standing in the doorway to his bedroom, looking pleased with himself.

"Daydreaming?" he asks as he closes the space between us. "Tell me, what do you daydream about, girl?" He runs his fingers across my cheek.

He's being playful, but I pretend not to pick up on that. Instead, I wonder if he'd answer me seriously.

"What's the sick ward?" I ask.

He frowns. "Why do you want to know that?"

"Perhaps my daydreams are really nightmares. Tell me, Lane, what should I be scared of?" I blink innocently up at him from under my lashes.

"Oh, you don't need to concern yourself with that." He adds, "So long as you're obedient."

"And if I'm not?" I tease.

He sighs and begins to walk away. "You're boring me today."

Before he can exit the door, I take a chance. I don't want to waste Lane's good mood today. "Where does the yellow door lead? When we first arrived."

He stops with his back to me. "That's enough, girl."

I push just once more. "It's alright if you don't know," I mumble. A little ego poke. I continue to sweep the floor, moving the white, sheepskin rug aside at the foot of his massive bed.

"Of course, I know," he growls, turning towards me. "It goes to the sick ward."

I pause and look up from my task. "Like a hospital?" I ask with genuine interest. He can't mean the same place he threatened to send me to, could he? Sarah had breast cancer. If it goes to the sick ward, that could be why she went through the yellow door. I allow myself to feel hopeful. Maybe Sarah has been getting treatments this whole time. Perhaps it's not such a bad place.

Lane smirks. It's a wicked expression. "No, they're deemed unfit to work, so they're... *disposed* of." He flicks his hand in the air like he's swatting at a fly. I lose my composure for a moment as his words sink in. Then, with annoyance as he exits the room, he adds, "Stop asking questions."

I hear him walk into the living room and plop down on the leather sofa. I feel faint, so I sit on the edge of his bed with my hand on my chest as I attempt to control the roiling emotions inside me. *Motherfuckers,* I curse over and over again. I try not to picture Sarah's kind face with the smile that pushed her cheeks up and crinkled the corners of her eyes. I try not to think of how she may have been "disposed of." How could they do... *that* to her?

I hear Lane get up, and I stand up quickly, wiping furiously at the tears that won't stop falling. I turn my back to the door and hide my face. Luckily, he goes to the kitchen. I sniff and take a deep breath. *Fucking compose yourself until tonight.* Save it for then when I'm alone and free to feel again. I have to tell Bodin somehow, but there's also a tiny part of me that wonders if he already knows.

Chapter 12

Lane

October 20, 2025

She'll be here in five minutes. Does she even realize I own her? The power I feel when she flinches away from my touch is like a drug I can't get enough of. I dream of letting the world see that power. Of course, the other elites know, but outside of them, I'm not sure these peons like Ava grasp their new reality. But she must? Maybe I'll tell her again in a subtle way. Offer her coffee only to pour it down the drain.

She is beautiful, but what I like most about her is her demeanor. She's so obvious with her emotions. She's fun to toy with. Especially since she thinks they're so well hidden. She'd make a terrible poker player. I found this out later, though. I chose her initially for her resemblance to a nanny I had as a boy. A nanny who made my life a living hell. There were and have been plenty of beautiful women to select at the Trade Party. Ava is my first, and she's here only because of that uncanny likeness and some deep, irrational desire to settle an old score.

Speaking of poker, I'll have to let the boys know I'm not coming to the Basement tomorrow afternoon for our Texas Hold 'Em tournament. I've got a meeting with Hosh. I'm not sure if that's his real name, and I don't care. The hierarchy here is arcane. Since the president was assassinated and a new order was established, we're mostly all on the same level, save a select few that operate like a Board of Directors. Hosh is one of those select few.

I'm not sure if it's even a he or a she, and I'm doubly unsure of why they put a meeting on my calendar.

I gaze out my window at the single barren, black tower that holds up the dome and patrols the city, but I'm not looking at it for its sharp contrast to the rest of the buildings. I'm wondering who's behind the dark glass in the highest penthouses just above the engineer's deck and whether they have any privileges or things I don't. It's intriguing and also irritating.

I worked my ass off my entire life and had enough to secure my spot at the table with some of the world's richest and brightest minds. And, of course, I had to prove my loyalty with "the favor," but that was easy enough. I've never been squeamish when it comes to killing people, and the orders were easy enough to follow once I knew what the prize was. Well, sort of. I knew it got me into the most exclusive club in the world—the inner circle to the inner circle. I had no idea what they had planned until I was admitted. Then, the thought of an EMP blast causing mass destruction and a population brought to its knees begging for help and worshiping people like me was... intoxicating. My only regret is that we don't have hidden cameras filming their struggles. An oversight, clearly. That would make for some pretty entertaining reality TV around here.

The most frustrating part of this whole Eyth business was just how long it took to come to fruition. The painstaking process of purchasing patents, building a city undetected, implementing new technology, *agreeing* on the new technology, hiding money, constructing a narrative to hide things that did come to light, and laying the groundwork for the population to fall into line, proved almost too much. When I lament back on these days with the guys, I'm reminded that what was accomplished here was warp speed in terms of traditional construction timeframes. Most parts were manufactured offsite and shipped here, where they were assembled. There were many times the plan almost unraveled. Small truths, or versions of the truth, would often creep up on the web. If they gained traction, tactics were deployed to dissemble. It was easy, really.

Step one: call something a conspiracy theory, and you're halfway there. Step two: produce false evidence and experts to counter the argument and spread it widely among prominent media sources, and you've nearly wrapped up the other half of it. And then, finally, step three: mop up dissenters by limiting their reach—censorship, basically. It's all so easy, and people are all so predictable. I found myself rooting for the truth sometimes, just to keep things interesting. But, no. I suppose it's best that never came to fruition because here we are, basking in the glory. Victorious.

I'm fifty-four years old with crow's feet at the corners of my eyes and gray hair concentrated at my temples now. I was forty-two when I was first admitted into the club. I never did marry or have children. I thought the process too... domestic. It all seemed incredibly dull to me, and I find children exceedingly disagreeable. However, there have been times when I've wondered to whom I will leave my legacy. Who might I tell about my successes, and who might I pass the knowledge down to? But no, children are still not worth it. There's no guarantee they won't despise me because of it instead of imparting the "awe" and respect I rightly deserve. However, I hear the re-education camp here is quite effective at molding children into anything desired. I could always use Ava as my breeding stock. I hear there are ways to accomplish this. She could do all of the hard work of raising a child. She'd get a better living arrangement. I wouldn't have to see her or the child. I'm too impatient to wait for that, and that could change the dynamics of everything for me. I'd still have to see the child. "This is your daddy," I can imagine Ava saying as she points and kneels down next to a cherub-cheeked boy with wide, frightened eyes. The thought is unsettling. No, I won't bother.

As I sip my coffee, I smile to myself, thinking again about how I'm going to offer Ava coffee this morning. I glance down at my Rolex. She'll be here in ten minutes. I walk from the kitchen to the living room with my coffee mug in hand.

"Schedule, please," I say to the room. The large windows that display the city beyond just barely remain translucent, and an image races from the upper left corner and shows brightly in front of me. I view the schedule again. My eyes fall on the meeting with Hosh. It's still there. I shake my head a little. Curiosity will eat me alive before I make it to that meeting tomorrow. I'll check that schedule at least another ten times before then, wondering if it will disappear just as quickly as it appeared and if it was a mistake after all.

I wave the schedule away with my free hand. It races back to the corner, where it disappears. The windows lighten so that they're pellucid once more. I watch below as recruits move like ants in neat formation to their work assignments. The streets are quiet. We don't usually venture out during this time or during the conclusion of the work assignments. It's too busy, and besides, not much is open until the help arrives.

The underground clubs, however, are always open—a good thing because they're my favorite. I frequent them often. The women, the booze, and the drugs allow me to live in bliss. Of course, there are still tasks that I must complete. We can't let this place be run by the servants alone. Someone has to be in charge; part of the deal is that we are all in charge. Except, of course, for those select few. I draw my eyebrows together. I cannot say for sure, but I'm rather looking forward to scrutinizing my superior tomorrow. Discreetly, of course. I've been told that my cunning and good looks are unmatched in this world. Though I'm not sure anyone would deem it wise enough to say otherwise to me, I tend to believe them.

The service elevator dings to signal an arrival. I hear the whoosh of the doors opening behind me. I smile to myself as I hear Ava open the closet. She'll look at the outfit I have picked out for her today with secret scorn. I can't wait to see the look of humiliation on her face. I catch my reflection in the glass of the windows and note the devilish grin. It's not a smile that anything good comes from, and if you're unlucky enough to see it, it likely will mean there's something special in store for you. Will today be the day I break Ava? No, I don't think so. The buildup is still there. The longer I wait, the stronger and more secure she feels. This makes the moment of total domination all the sweeter. I'm waiting for this peek moment to use her name. Drag it through the mud. I will destroy her.

Chapter 13

Carrie

October 20, 2025

After we wake, we drink from our water bottles. I rifle around in my backpack, but I already know. Our rations are spent. Pax and I exchange a look. Today, we head back to the Colony.

"There's someone I want to check in on before we leave. He lives up on the bar. Not a long walk." He nods towards a hillside on the opposite side of the river littered with homes.

I shrug. Why not? I sling the light backpack onto my shoulders and follow Pax in silence. We walk across the only bridge that provides access to the town for the residents living on the bar. The bridge has become a memorial of sorts. There are framed photos, wooden crosses, and the occasional article of clothing tied to the railing. Many people are fishing from the banks of the river, desperately hoping to catch a meal. I follow in silence until we come to a small white house with a chain-link fence and a red door with peeling paint. The grass is yellow and dry, the yard littered with dirt patches where it seems they tried to start a garden. *Too little, too late*. Like many of the other homes in the area, the yards look wild, as almost everyone tried to work their land to bear food to some degree.

One house has a large, established garden surrounded by a tall fence. There are many people working throughout the garden, and I marvel at their collaboration. I want to believe what Pax said about people in small towns, but I also can't help but feel as if it's a shaky alliance not yet challenged fully by the threat of starvation. My mind wanders to the Colony. Wouldn't the same rules apply? There's something different about us, though: we're exclusive and protected. We don't trust everyone to collaborate or respect what isn't theirs. We have people in positions of authority, and we'll carry out punishments if the rules aren't respected.

Pax knocks softly. Non-threatening. I come up behind him and stand on the steps leading up to the door. I hear feet shuffling from inside. They're yelling at someone or something to quiet down. A man answers the door. A small child peeks out from behind his pant leg at us. I can't tell if it's a girl or a boy. They're both filthy—their clothes, their hair, and their faces. They're also both skinny. The man has sunken eyes and pasty skin. His eyes widen and his eyebrows shoot up when he sees Pax. He extends his hand as he shakes his head in disbelief. They do some fancy handshake.

Pax speaks first. "Cole, it's been a while. How you holdin' up, brother?"

"Pax. Didn't think I'd see the likes of you again."

"How about we let bygones be bygones? We've got bigger problems now."

Cole shakes his head in agreement.

Pax asks again, his voice laced with concern, "How you holdin' up?"

"Hardest six weeks of my life once my stash was gone, but I made it through the withdrawals. But hey, finally got sober," he says in an attempt to make a joke. Pax doesn't laugh.

"Silver lining," Pax says as he looks at the kid who shrinks farther behind Cole, away from Pax's gaze. Cole still hasn't opened the door any wider in an invitation, but I'm not sure I'd want to enter anyway. I can smell the musty air from inside, and I can see the mess in the kitchen just behind him. I guess this guy's mentality is, why clean up when the world is going to shit? I shift my eyes from the kitchen back to Cole, only to find that he's watching me appraisingly. His eyes travel up and down my body. I shiver involuntarily.

He looks back at Pax, "We don't got no food, man. If that's what you're after."

"Naw, man. Just checking in. Wondering if you've heard of any good news."

Cole snorts. "Right. Good news. We'll be lucky if we survive the winter."

"But you will, right?" asks Pax, dropping his gaze to the kid still clinging to Cole's pants.

Cole brushes him off. "Yeah, man." Then he eyes Pax suspiciously. "Where you holdin' up?"

"At the cabin." He nods to the mountains on the right, and I note how coolly he lies. "Just came to town to see if there was anything left."

"Shit, no," Cole scoffs at Pax's apparent stupidity. "Long gone. The only thing is that the Armory has got a bunch of protection. They're doling out ammo in trade. Likely only looking for food, though."

"Where's Rugor?" Pax asks.

"Have you noticed any dogs around here?" Cole's tone is cold. He's right. I haven't seen any dogs. It hadn't registered for me until just now.

"Around here, if you don't eat your own dog, someone else will," he says. My eyes go wide.

Pax scratches his neck. "Maybe we'll go check out the Armory," he says by way of parting as he begins to back up.

Cole nods towards me, seeing his window of opportunity closing. "Who's the girl?"

"Oh, found her wandering around the old Boulder campground near the cabin."

Cole eyes me and wets his lips before looking back at Pax. "Any game up that high?"

"Not really," answers Pax. I can sense his eagerness to leave now, and I begin to lead the way so that Cole gets the message loud and clear.

"Alright then," Cole says. "Ya'll take care." He half-smiles, and I can't tell if it's a hostile gesture or a sweet one.

I wave out of politeness, and we turn towards the street. I breathe deeply, hearing the door close behind us.

"What was that all about?" I ask once we're out of earshot.

"Cole and I were good buds back in high school. We got into some stuff. I pulled myself out of it, but Cole never did. I always felt guilty about that. Sometimes, the withdrawals will kill you. I just wanted to know if he made it. I knew he had a kid now but thought she was living with his grandma." So, it was a girl. Poor thing. "The grandma must be there, though. I saw her empty jars of canned goods on the counter. She used to tie a burlap ribbon around all of her jars. I suspect that's how they're surviving. That gave me an idea, though."

"I'm all ears," I say, curious.

"My paps used to live across from our old house. He died when I was ten. My grandma died long before that. I remember a cellar he used to have under his pantry in the back, though."

"How is the cellar of your long-since dead *paps* a point of interest?" If he noticed my slight teasing at the nickname he uses for his grandpa, he doesn't comment.

Pax kicks at a crumpled-up soda can in the road. "Because someone bought the house after he died, but about three years ago, it burned down. Those people moved away, and it's been an empty lot ever since."

"Ok..." I say, unsure of where he's going with this. I put my hands in my coat pockets and scan the area as we walk.

"Well, maybe the cellar is still there. Under the ground," he says.

"Huh, sounds like a long shot, and perhaps now is a good time to remind you that we're out of food and can't be messing around." A few heads turn towards us from the large garden we passed earlier. Deeming us safe, they return to the task of weeding and laying out ground cover like straw and mulch around some of the tiny, budding plants.

"Well, here's the best part: it's on our route back towards the Colony. Can't hurt to check it out," he says.

"Fine."

"Just keep your eyes peeled for a shovel or two." But even as he says it, we both know we can't attempt to take anything from such a populated area. Maybe farther out of town, we'll have some luck.

We walk for over an hour. The sun is high overhead, and I shed my coat and tie it around my waist to savor the lingering warmth. Pax found a hoe, but we didn't find a shovel. I found a thick stick that would have to do.

Pax turns off the highway, opens a rusty gate that creeks in protest, and leads us down a dirt road that's barely distinguishable from the rest of the pasture. A single strip of gravel holds the weeds back. We follow it until we reach an area shaded by large trees.

"The house was here," he says, but I can already tell by the outline of a foundation and various other debris lying around. Pax begins pacing the ground, muttering to himself until he stops and says, "Here." He begins raking the dirt and weeds back with his hoe. I bring my stick over but soon learn it's of little help. So, I watch. Pax peels back dirt, chunks of concrete, and decaying wood, but it only looks like more dirt underneath until a *ping* rings out from the hoe striking something metal. He begins pulling the dirt back more eagerly, and then I see it: a metal latch of some kind and dark wood that's barely distinguishable from the dirt.

I get to my knees and help Pax by brushing the dirt off, excitement building. We unearth the door, which has decayed and caved in in a spot. Pax pulls on the latch, but the door protests. He yanks harder, once, twice, and finally, the door gives and pulls open, revealing a dark cavity beneath. I fumble for my flashlight in my backpack, click it on, and shine it below. There are rotting stairs and a pile of dirt that's covered a third of the staircase, but we could still hop over it. I bend down and shine my light deeper into the cavity. The smell of mildew and earth hits my nostrils. I hold my breath. I can't see much, but I can tell there's something down there.

I look up at Pax, "you first."

He nods and takes my flashlight. "Take this too." I hand him the stick. "For the cobwebs," I elaborate when he arcs an eyebrow.

He knocks down most of the cobwebs. I sit at the opening and peer inside after him. My breath catches as I see his light fall over cardboard boxes. I'm disappointed not to see food, but I still hope the boxes might contain something useful. Pax takes down a box and coughs.

"Shit," he curses.

"What is it?!" I yell after him, hating the sound of that word.

"Books!" He yells back.

"Shit," I mirror Pax's reaction. I hear another box fall to the ground and listen as Pax rummages through more boxes. My heart sinks with every passing second that I don't hear Pax yell out in victory.

Then he shouts, "Whoo-eee! We've got something here."

I perk up. "What is it?"

"Survival food!"

"Hell, yes! How much?"

"One of those 72-hour buckets," he says.

Not much, but something. I wait patiently as Pax continues his inventory. Ten minutes later, he makes his way back up the stairs. I stand to get out of his way. Before he's reached the top step, he pauses and gives me a huge grin. I'm wiping the dirt off my pants when I stop. "What?" I ask, alarmed and excited by his evident delight.

"Honey," he says.

I wrinkle my nose and flush for a minute before I realize he's not ad-dressing me with a term of endearment. He means *honey*—the sweet, sticky stuff.

"Buckets of it!" he adds.

I clasp my hands together, giddy with the news. Having paused at the top of the steps, he disappears back down into the cellar. He comes back to the top with a white five-gallon bucket. I take it from him, surprised by its weight, and heft it aside. He goes back down and reappears with another. And another. And another. There are four white five-gallon buckets of honey and one red bucket with a peeling and aged label that I can still read. It says "72-Hour Emergency Food Kit. 3-Person Kit." This is better than I expected.

Once Pax is out of the cellar and has brushed himself off, I hug him. I'm so happy. It was meant to be a quick embrace of victory, but Pax holds me close to him for a beat longer than I feel comfortable before kissing the top of my head and releasing me.

"What should we eat first?" he asks with wild animation.

"Honey!" We both say at the same time. We pry the lid off the bucket that Pax had already broken the seal on and dig our fingers in. It's hard, but we still manage to scoop some onto our fingers and pop it into our mouths. I about die from pleasure. We dig our fingers in again and again, completely drunk off of the sugar and the abundance of it.

When we finally stop, Pax looks at me thoughtfully, still licking his fingers. I know I shouldn't let the circumstances of our good fortune fuel this wild excitement, but I'm so happy at this moment that I let my guard down and continue this wild indulgence we've been on. I walk over to him, take the finger he was licking, and put it in my own mouth while I watch him. Pax's eyes go wide. I move my hand over his crotch. He sucks in a breath through his teeth. We can hardly get our clothes off fast enough.

For the second time, we do it on the ground. Tired of feeling small rocks digging into my back, I push Pax off of me and straddle him. I move my hips back and forth as Pax closes his eyes in utter bliss, but before I really get into it, he pushes me off of him quickly.

"Sorry," he says sheepishly once he's finished and caught his breath.

I brush myself off and smile, liking that I had that effect on him. "It's alright," I say as I pull my underwear up and resituate my clothes. He dresses, too. Then we both stare at our haul.

"How are we going to get this all back?" I ask, already feeling the weight of the buckets.

"Farmers carry," he says. I frown, unsure of what that means. Pax walks over and takes the handle of a bucket in each of his hands. He lets them hang heavy at his sides while he walks. It even looks heavy for him. I cock an eyebrow. He sets the buckets down.

"Maybe you just carry the 72-hour kit?" he suggests.

I salute him and walk over to grab my bucket.

"I think we should hide these other two buckets of honey and cover the door to the cellar back up. Just in case."

I nod. Even though it's unlikely, I'm unwilling to take a chance our loot could be stolen.

"I'll come back later today to get them," he says.

We walk at a slow pace. Pax makes an impressive distance before setting the buckets down to rest. The handles digging into his palms seem to give him the most grief. I offer him my gloves, which he takes gratefully. We're almost to the bridge and are about two miles from the ranch. Pax sits down with his legs outstretched in front of him, his face to the sky with closed eyes. I let him rest for a minute. When he gets up, he looks around.

"What is it?" I ask.

"How would you feel about keeping a tiny bit of this for ourselves?"

I feign shock. "What? Mr. Small Town doesn't want to share?"

"I know, I know," he says, holding his hands up in defense. "It's just... it would be reeeaally comforting to know that if shit hits the fan at the Colony, like hard, we'd have a private stash out here. Just for us. Just in case."

I'm 100% on board with this and don't feel the need to communicate anything else to save face or whatever. Plus, I'm touched that he'd suggest sharing this with me. It'll be our little secret.

"What'd you have in my mind?" I ask.

"Let's stash the kit somewhere." He nods towards my 72-hour bucket.

I smile. "Let's do it."

CHAPTER 14

Lane

October 21, 2025

My only source of comparison thus far, this elevator, has already confirmed my suspicions: there are more luxurious living arrangements in this city. This rubs me. I'll have to tamp down the feeling if I hope to hide it. But then again, I don't think there's anyone as good at reading people as I am. Still, even though I'm sure I'm being watched in this elevator, I allow myself to look around and feel indignant. There are no buttons in the elevator. I stand wondering what to do for a second before the door closes and the elevator begins its silent ascent. The only indication that it's moving is the heaviness that grows at the bottom of my stomach as it picks up speed.

The walls of the elevator are a velvet purple, with artwork displayed in a case in the back that appears to be a Van Gogh. Though, not particularly well preserved. Still, if this is elevator art, what treasures do the actual living quarters contain?

The doors in front of me appear sleek and black, like obsidian. My reflection in this black material is mirrored back to me with crisp clarity. I study myself. My suit is a perfectly tailored blue that matches my eyes. My jaw is strong and broad, my features are cut as if from stone, and my hair is perfectly combed into place. I know I'm good-looking, but still, I frown.

It smells of lavender in here. I throw my head back and take a deep breath. I stare up at the ceiling with incredulity. It's dome-shaped with a small crystal chandelier and is significantly higher up than most elevator ceilings I've encountered in my life.

The elevator arrives, and the doors glide open without making a sound. I step inside Hosh's apartment. It's not what I expect. That is to say, it's not like my place. For one thing, I thought it would be dark, given how opaque the windows appear from the outside. But no, the inside radiates bright and sunny. The air hangs heavy with humidity. The source is a large wall of water that cascades to my right, separating the combined open space of the kitchen and living area to my left from another room off to the right. The water falls in one large sheet and disappears quietly into the floor below without a splash. A large, glossy wooden island that appears to have been cut from a single tree stands in the middle of the kitchen. Above the island, plants hang from the ceiling, growing upside down. I recognize a few culinary herbs. The space is massive, with expansive ceiling heights and large, oversized furniture. The ceiling slopes upwards without linear limitations.

I look back at the wall of water and attempt to discern the shapes behind it. A bed, maybe? With a red bedspread. A blurry shape appears and comes closer. The water parts like curtains being pulled aside from a stage, and out steps a small Chinese woman with a sharp bob cut so precisely above her eyebrows and down to just below her chin that she appears almost doll-like with painted red lips, pink cheeks, and small black eyes. She is not who I expected, and I find it impossible to say just how old she is. She could be thirty-five or fifty-five. It's funny how people of a different ethnicity than mine are harder to discern. Or is it ethnocentric?

Despite her delicate appearance, her voice is rough and intense. "*Nihao*, Mr. Lane Font."

I recognize the Mandarin greeting. Unsure if my rusty Mandarin would only end up offending her, I extend my hand to her.

"You must be Hosh." Should I have addressed her as my boss or inserted some kind of formality? But then, how could I if I don't know her last name?

She nods once sharply, not bothering to take my hand. Her eyes travel down to my shoes, and her lips turn down into a tight line.

I notice she is wearing a kind of soft, oriental slipper. I suppose I've managed to offend her all the same.

"My apologies," I say as I slip my shoes off and scoot them with my foot off to the side.

"You must be wondering why you're here. Please, follow me." She turns on her heels and glides towards the living room. She sits on a small cushion near a low table and gestures for me to do the same opposite of her. I copy her folded legs and straight-back posture. Once seated, I'm surprised to see someone working in the kitchen. Their movements are fluid, and despite handling a tray and preparing what appears to be tea, they are mouse-quiet. Suddenly, I'm desperate for a distraction—anything to break the penetrating stare from Hosh. I clear my throat, but before I can speak, she intervenes and spares me the awkward icebreaker.

"You can tell a lot about someone from these moments of silence. Their soul reveals itself, if only fleetingly," she says.

I blink. Her eyes never break from mine, and despite her statuesque manner, I hold her gaze. I know what's in my soul, and I'm not ashamed.

"I know you," she says in a hushed voice. "Someone who believes their post in the world is secure. Someone who needs constant dopamine and adrenaline to stimulate an otherwise dull existence." Her features pull into hard lines. So, the feeling is mutual, I suppose. Anger boils in my belly, and I consider relaxing into a more comfortable position that's sure to offend her, but I suppress the urge to antagonize this person. I didn't come to be in my current position by making choices based on emotion. To control a situation, one must control their reactions.

"I'm sure you didn't ask me here to pass judgment on my character," I say.

She sighs, apparently bored that this string of dialog has ended. Perhaps she was looking forward to a heated exchange.

"No, I suppose not." Her eyes close as if suddenly heavy. They stay closed while she takes a deep breath, exaggerating the rise and fall of her chest. When she opens them, her dark eyes hold a new look—one of determination.

"I believe we've had a breach," she says. "Correct me if I'm wrong, but you helped pioneer blockchain technology and then used that knowledge to exploit the system and steal millions of dollars."

I sit up taller, my body suddenly on alert. It's no secret to the world that I helped develop software that changed how information was passed and stored over the internet, making transaction times mere seconds instead of minutes and cutting costs considerably. Still, I believed my side project of exploitation to be known only to me until now. During development, I inserted a code that allowed me to shave just fractions of a penny off of each transaction when cryptocurrencies were exchanged. No one would notice such a small amount, but when millions of transactions occur every day, the sum is substantial. The code was built as part of the framework. So ingeniously disguised that it was undetectable.

Or, *nearly* undetectable.

She smiles in triumph at the effect her divulgence has had on me. "Of course, we knew," she sneers. "Only those with secrets refuse the implant." She's referring to Metalink. Knowing that many refused that implant allows me some comfort. There are a lot of secrets in this city.

I consider her words. I'd like to ask who *we* are, but I feel my place in this establishment has been called into question. I could not have afforded the entry fee without that code. If it's a matter that must be voted on, there's a possibility that the surreptitious source of my funds may be enough to give me the boot. I don't allow myself to get carried away with the what-ifs and imaginings of being out in the world alone during this time because it's obvious she didn't come here just to tease me. She wants something. She must.

"What kind of breach?" I ask, bringing the conversation back to safer ground.

"We've identified a code that doesn't appear to belong in the software for the air purification and de-humidification system. However, we're not sure what it's designed to accomplish or who put it there. You've been tasked with identifying this threat before we experience any... disruption of service," she informs me.

I nod. So, there it is. "And how will I be granted access to the source code?"

"You'll report to Engineering in one hour, where you'll be escorted to the top deck with the hardware and given the highest level of security clearance."

I wait for more, but she stands gracefully and smooths the front of her lined slacks down with her hands. I stand as well. "I believe you know the way out," she says as she nods slightly as a parting gesture. I make my way back to my shoes, where I slip them on. I hop off balance as I attempt to pull on the left shoe. "Oh, and Lane?" I look up, only now realizing that she's still watching me.

"Yes?"

Her voice is low and menacing, "Don't fuck this up." I hesitate for a moment. The words sounded like they should have come from someone else's mouth. With my shoes intact, I turn my back to her and attempt to walk calmly to the elevator, showing that I'm unrattled. I'm unsure if I will succeed. As I enter the elevator and turn back towards the door, her gaze follows me until she finally disappears behind the silent closure of the elevator door. I'm left staring at myself on the black, reflective surface. My face appears unreadable, but I know what's roiling inside.

Fear.

After exiting the building and taking to the street, something odd occurs to me. Security—everywhere. I'm acutely conscious that I must present myself in a particular manner now. Otherwise, I give myself away. What I'd really like to do is punch a wall. Every nerve in my body is wired, and my desire to yell *FUCK* has never been stronger. This feels infinitely worse than the other worst moment of my entire life: an IRS audit. But I managed to weasel myself out of that one. After all, money does buy favors. But no, this is different. Different because I see no way out. Everything I do is too closely monitored, and there really are no people in positions of power here who would accept a bribe. They already have everything.

While Hosh may have known a delicate secret of mine, she did not know my most coveted secret of all. For if she did, she wouldn't have tasked me with this. The ingenious code that provided so many opportunities for me wasn't even my brainchild. I stole it. My coding skills are mediocre at best and subpar at worst. Plus, they're rusty. I rose up to the top through cunning and conniving. Skills that don't translate to much once you've reached the top. Eyth is the top.

I am, without a doubt, fucked.

CHAPTER 15

Lane

October 21, 2025

I have fifty-six minutes until I have to check in at the Engineer's tower. I look at the black building rising from the city's center with a different feeling now—my earlier childish concerns about equality have long since vanished. I could be doing a thousand things, but what I find myself doing is moving towards the Basement. I want to quiet the panic bouncing around in my head. Drown it out with sex and alcohol. I reach the discreet, plain door labeled "service" and descend down a dark stairwell to the bottom, where another door marked The Basement sits unobtrusive at the bottom of the dimly lit stairwell. The disguised entrance is, of course, only part of the fun. It draws you in with the false ambiance of exclusivity when, in reality, every inhabitant knows about the clubs and has access to them. There are three—each is slightly different, but all offer the same temptations and escapes.

When I reach the door, I knock three times. After a mechanical *click,* the door swings open. A large man nods at me and says in a deep voice, "Boss."

I nod back and walk the long hallway where there are large, heavy velvet curtains of a deep purple that sweep the floor as I push them aside. The resounding rhythmic thump of bass can be heard behind them now. The last curtain parts to reveal the lobby. The noise explodes. This is The Lobby where you mainly go to drink and socialize. Very PG here. Then there's level two, which is confusingly labeled Six. Six is a poorly disguised way of landing you on the floor for sex with the prostitutes. Though, we like to refer to them as 'the help' since too many negative connotations are associated with the former term. I find this floor particularly fun due to the numerous fantasy-themed rooms and the vast catalog of women to choose from. Or men, if you're into that. I'm not. The final floor is level three. While alcohol and drugs are available on every floor, level three is where you go for the hard stuff. When you're really trying to escape, you could be there for days. There are medical professionals on staff, themed rooms, and rooms for sleeping it off.

I hit level two. I really don't have the luxury of time for drinking, and I have to keep my wits intact for my assignment. So, that really only leaves a quick jaunt to two.

***

I had numerous variations of the same dream last night. I battled with it all night. The first thing I remember is feeling the desert heat and the way it penetrated my skin. Then, I remember watching the dust plume fade into the distance behind the army truck that dropped me off. And lastly, I looked around and could see nothing but miles and miles of sand and desert air waving in the sun's heat. A death sentence to be left there.

I swing my legs off the side of the bed. The bed sheets peel away from the sweat on my back. My feet hit the cool floor and slide into sheepskin sleepers.

"Draw curtains," I say stiffly as I swipe my hand across my damp forehead. The tint on the windows begins to fade, and I squint against the intrusion of the sun. "Display systems," I command. My mailbox indicates thirteen unread emails, the temperature inside the room is a perfect seventy-two, and the time is 7:49 am. An entire hour later than I usually wake up. I won't be working out this morning. The mental exertion from yesterday must have worn me out.

I was able to make it look as if I knew what I was doing yesterday after checking into the tower. I do know how to code, after all, but this task is, as predicted, beyond my skill set. Perhaps Clark would have been able to do it. He did build some of the most ingenious code the world has ever known. The very code I took the credit for in front of Hosh. But no, we will never know what Clark was capable of because Clark is at the bottom of the ocean.

How long can I pull this off, and what is the end game? I don't even know who runs in the same circle as Hosh and who knows about this assignment. There's no one to... *take care of* like Clark. There's no way to make this problem go away. The only people who stand a chance of understanding the bit of inserted code are the very team that Hosh doesn't trust—the existing software engineering team. Surely there has to be a better way to narrow it down. How many of them can have the same access? How many of them are smart enough? Of course, we're talking about the best the United States had to offer, but how good are they really? Only one answer really matters: better than me.

I don't allow myself to dwell on the consequences of not following through, but it's obviously surfacing in my dreams. Like a mountain lion quietly stocking its prey.

I pad to the bathroom with considerably less enthusiasm for life than most mornings. I peel my clothes off my body and step into the shower, which turns on automatically. The perfectly heated water sprays my back. Something so simple, a shower, could go away forever. A horrible thought invades my brain. What if this is my last shower? I tip my head back into the spray and let the water run over my face and down into the drain, where I let the pessimistic musings follow. Today, I will figure this shit out.

I step out of the shower and reach for a warm towel. I pause at the sound of footsteps clicking against the travertine tile of the floor before I remember that Ava arrives at eight o'clock. I let out a breath of relief and hurry to finish, eager to see her for reasons I haven't yet pinpointed.

I'm pulling on my shirt as I come around the corner and find her there. She averts her eyes, but not before a slight tinge of rose flashes across her cheeks. With the shirt secured, I head for the living room. I need to know the scale of what I'm faced with.

"Pull up directory for the software engineering staff," I say. The windows darken to create sufficient backlighting as files flow from the right corner of the windows into neatly organized cards in front of me. The list is three rows deep and ten across. Thirty possibilities. Shit.

Faces appear like mug shots. I scan them. It has to be someone with level three access. "Sort by level three access," I dictate. Cards fly off the screen, and the rest are consolidated in front of me in a neat, manageable row of six people. "Discard results with Metalink," I command. There's a buzzing noise, and a dialogue box pops up on the screen that reads, 'Information Not Available.' I stand with hands on my hips as I survey the faces of the remaining six in front of me. They're unnoteworthy—typical software guys with some brown hair variation. The two standouts are the bald one and the one with a maroon birthmark still visible despite his unkempt, wiry brown hair falling in his face. "It's one of you bastards. It has to be," I say to myself. I whirl around when the sound of a broom clattering to the floor behind me startles me.

"Sorry," Ava mutters, averting my eyes as she gathers the broom and walks from the room. I glare at her but turn back to the work in front of me.

I'll have to figure out which one has Metalink because it can't be someone with the implant. That'd be too obvious. Hosh would know in that case. I don't recognize any of the men from my visit to the Engineering tower yesterday. It strikes me as odd that I reported to a level two software tech on floor nineteen, not twenty, for intros and access codes, but I let it go. I need to clear my head.

I walk to the kitchen. "Start dark roast," I say. The wall hums to life as the built-in coffee panel lights up and gets to work. I run my hands through my damp hair. I have a refrigerator, but the only things in it are grapes, a few mandarin oranges, and a few condiments, which are all handmade and stored in mason jars like so many products these days. The freezer is even more sparse with ice and a bottle of half-drunk vodka. I would typically order a veggie omelet, but this morning, I feel like indulging. I go to the panel above the food port on the wall and browse the breakfast offerings. I order waffles with whipped cream and strawberries, a side of bacon, one fried egg, milk, and orange juice. A timer has started to countdown on the food port panel, indicating the food will arrive in five minutes.

I make my way to the coffee machine, where I reach for the coffee before hesitating. "Add vanilla syrup and cream, please," I instruct. I watch as things are squirted into the cup, and then the mug develops a whirlpool as it's mixed using frequencies undetectable to my eye. I pull the mug from the panel and ask for another black coffee.

"Ava, come in here," I call. "Please," I add rather awkwardly. It came out as more of a question. She appears hesitantly at the entrance of the kitchen. I watch as her eyes spy the two cups of coffee, and her mouth turns down in the corners as if to say, "Not this again." But this time, I hand her the mug. She doesn't take it right away. Probably waiting for the part where I pull it away. Like a dog who's tired of being teased with a hidden jalapeno in a delectable piece of turkey, she looks into the cup and eyes it with suspicion.

"I wasn't sure how you liked your coffee, so I took the liberty of adding vanilla and sugar." She continues to stare at it, wary. "Oh, come on, it's not poisoned," I say, losing patience, but I feel myself grinning despite my best efforts. For some reason, it thrills me that she thinks I may have put something into her cup. Like a roofie? Please. I could have her in a second if I wanted. I don't need to roofie her for that, and we both know it. She takes the cup, sniffs it, and then sips. I can see the dopamine centers in her brain light up the second the liquid hits her tongue. Her eyes give her away. I turn away from her to grab my own coffee.

She's drinking rather quickly now. I see her internal struggle—trying not to look too eager but unable to help herself. I'm suddenly curious about a few things. "When was the last time you had coffee?"

"Coffee like this?" Her gaze looks far off. "Since before. I was always getting lattes from The Coffee Corner at the hospital." She smiles shyly, wondering if she said too much. It's interesting to watch such a poignant response addictive substances such as sugar and caffeine have on someone. The effect is almost as if she just did a line of coke. Immediate. If I were to take it away from her now, I wonder how disappointed she'd be. Tempting to find out, but I have one more question.

"What's it like out there?"

She gulps audibly and then coughs a little.

"Out there. Like, what do you want to know?" she asks. It must be exhausting, I think, to always be trying to figure out what someone else is up to. Then it hits me. We're not that different, Ava and me. Not anymore. This thought irks me.

"Just tell me what it's like," I say. Just then, the food panel dings, announcing an arrival. The plates of food are stacked neatly inside the delivery box. I slide them out and place them on the counter along with the milk and juice glasses.

My stomach growls, and I cut a massive bite of waffle with my fork. I maneuver it into my mouth and savor the taste. It's light and crisp on the outside with a hint of butter and soft and fluffy on the inside. I take another large bite. I can't believe I've never had these before. I begin to motion for Ava to start talking, but the way she's looking at my waffle temporarily stops me in my tracks. I slow down my chewing, and she looks away, embarrassed.

"Another plate of waffles," I say aloud after I've successfully swallowed the second massive bite. I walk over to the glowing food panel and hit "confirm" on the prompt for the waffles. I keep eating.

"Am I excused?" Ava asks.

"No, tell me what it was like for you outside of this city, and you can have the waffles," I say. The food panel dings with the arrival. That was fast. I set it next to my plate and slide it across the counter toward her.

She picks the waffle section up with her hand and begins to eat. I realize then that I didn't get her a fork, but she's figuring it out.

"Talk," I say after she's had a couple of bites. She sets the waffle down, disappointed.

"I never thought I'd have a coffee like this again," she says as she picks up the mug and stares into it. "There was coffee at first, but the bigger problem was water. We figured we'd better conserve water and stop consuming a diuretic anyway. The gravity of the situation wasn't fully understood at first. We were so busy triaging that we forgot to think about ourselves, about the future. We were just putting out fires, and there were a lot of those. Loads of hurt people coming into the hospital, and many existing patients in crisis. Then there were robberies." Her index finger circles the edges of the mug as if it were a crystal wineglass she's trying to make sing. She takes a deep breath. "Pretty much every day after the first was spent thinking about food and water. The hospital staff disappeared one by one. It was just Sarah and me in the end. Just a week into the blackout, things that you never would have considered important before started to consume us. Things like the quality of our shoes, the sounds outside, securing a safe place to sleep. We were always hungry, never satisfied, and then one day, you realize you're out of toothpaste now, too, because you ate it the day before. That was more like week three stuff." She looks up at me with a smile, attempting humor, but her eyes are sad. We hold each other's gaze for a moment before she looks back into her near-empty coffee.

I clear my throat. "I better get going," I say as I place my mug near the sink and walk away from two pieces of bacon and a quarter of a waffle. I wonder if she'll finish mine too while I'm gone.

As I slip on shoes I've stored in the hallway closet, what she said sticks with me like a marking I can't wash off. A new determination sets in. That will not be my reality. I won't eat fucking toothpaste. I stride towards the elevator and punch the down button. It has to be one of those six. That narrows the possibilities down considerably. I need only to figure out which of the six has Metalink, eliminate those possibilities, and find a unique identifier for each of the others—a digital signature of sorts. Every coder has a style that gives away their work. If I can distinguish these, I've got it. I interlock my fingers and stretch them out in front of me. If I'm no closer to finding an identifier in the malware code by the end of the day today than I was yesterday, I'll go about this a different way—a more *physical* route. That, I'm damn good at.

CHAPTER 16

Lane

October 22, 2025

I'm close. I can feel the excitement of the chase narrowing down. My nerves hum with vigor. There are three possibilities. Three of the six are without Metalink implants. I found this out by observing them throughout the day. I deduced a Metalink implant on a short, fat man who walked by a food portal just as it dinged with a steaming cup of coffee and a donut that he didn't scan for. He took both without any surprise and kept walking.

The next step would be to identify their unique coding signatures, but day two has already drawn to a close, and I feel as though I'm running out of time. Besides, it may not even be possible to flush out these hackers. People specialize in this kind of thing. It takes years of experience to hone a talent for deciphering coding signatures. This is as far as my computer skills take me.

Now it's time to do what Lane does best. The talent that catapulted me to the level of success I see today is data extraction. Violent, physical data extraction methods, to clarify. But I need somewhere private. The only places where eyes and ears are forbidden are the rooms on levels two and three of the Basement.

I wonder if Hosh knows about my data extraction hobbies from before. Of course, it can be assumed by the level of adoption surrounding Metalink that most of Eyth's elite inhabitants harbor some secrets. In drunken musings with other inhabitants while lounging around the Basement, a slip of the tongue let it be known that the adoption rate sat at a disappointing 26% of elites. The middle class (as we like to call them), known as "essential workers" officially, are closer to an 80% adoption rate. There have been talks of mandating it for the other 20%. We'll have to address that carefully as the essential workers are just that—essential. How disgruntled can we make them before they revolt? Keeping them in line while allowing them enough freedom to be grateful and loyal to Eyth is a delicate act.

Metalink did not appeal to me for several reasons. First off, I don't go under the knife unless necessary. Being completely vulnerable and at the hands of someone else while under anesthesia is highly unsavory. The second reason is the unknown limitations to which Metalink can access one's thoughts. Some secrets I'd like to take to my grave. The third reason for my refusal is the weak value proposition. With Metalink, people can access their home's control systems with mere thoughts. It's said that Metalink can learn from your habits and predict your desires, making changes to lighting, music, temperature, order food, etc., all before you even think of them. Well, I can use my voice and my hands. The fourth reason, again, something I would never admit aloud, is a distrust of the technology inventors. Similar products were tested years ago for the purpose of control. While all alpha predators are concentrated here at Eyth, I was never too naive to think that I couldn't be the target of some bigger fish.

Of the three remaining candidates, there's a tall, lanky man named Joseph Knudson. His hair is buzzed to a quarter inch, and his glasses are perched atop a rather large, offensive nose held in place by rather large, offensive ears. The second is a man named Paul Sadino with a plump face and straight brown hair that looks as if his mom still cuts it for him using a bowl. The third is Mark Bird. Mark is memorable because of a red birthmark that extends from his scalp line onto his face about an inch poorly disguised by wild, brown hair—poor bastard.

I climb into bed, exhausted from the exertion and stress of the h... strategize about how I'll get the three into the Basement. Elaborate schemes are cooked up in my head before I finally settle on something much more straightforward—I'll ask my first target if he wants to hang out. I'll start with Paul. Gut feeling, can't say why. If I get this right the first time, it will undoubtedly make my life easier.

And with the plan hatched in my mind, I fall asleep.

***

Today is not going as planned.

I stand momentarily stunned, with my arm still holding a position similar to that at the end of a golf swing, as I look down at Paul. The beat of my heart begins to settle as it comes down from the high energy demands a moment of blind fury creates. I study the man. I watch his chest. There's no sign of breath. The side of his head near his temple is indented, like the time I backed the Ferrari into a fire hydrant, trying to get a good parking spot.

I slowly lower my arm.

"Well, shit," I say out loud. I guess it was Lane with a wrench in the Playboy room. What the fuck was I thinking? I wasn't. I lost control. It's happened before. But this time, it feels different.

On the one hand, I feel I did the loser a favor. I had asked, "Why didn't you plug into Metalink?" He hadn't wanted to reply, which only added to my angst. I made a move to extract another fingernail from his left hand. The threat of the action alone was enough.

He blubbered, "Because I'm a zoophile."

With complete composure, I stood in front of him and asked, "And what is that?" Snot ran down his upper lip, and his body was wracked with giant, heaving sobs.

"I'm attracted to animals," he finally said.

wasn't even aware that I had brought my arms back with the pipe wrench and swung them forward using an unstoppable force. There was a crack as it made contact with the side of his head, which now leaned over his right shoulder, unblinking eyes looking down at the ground.

It felt right in the moment. The only real friends I've ever had in this world were canines. What he said hit me like a personal assault. Sick fuck. But now, I'm left to face the consequences. The strange thing is, I've never been in this position before. The world before the EMP was different for me. I had felt untouchable, but now... my mind visualizes the glass dome that protects the city and harnesses energy. I see another purpose for the dome now—to keep the inhabitants inside. I'm a rat in a cage. What favors do people owe me here? None. Everyone here is like me in one way or another. Well, almost everyone. As an engineer, Paul was considered a second-class citizen, though they're never called that directly to their face. His accommodations and food provisions were far above those provided to the recruits. Recruits are expendable. They're required to run the day-to-day operations and maintenance of Eyth, but anyone can do their job, and the list of desperate people willing to sign up for that gig is lengthy. These second-class citizens had been hand-selected for their unique skills—software developers and technicians are needed for their knowledge and experience. Eyth isn't perfect. There are still glitches, and there are still operations that need to be started and stopped by hand or reprogrammed. One dead second-classer may still put me in hot water.

I look down at the body. "What the fuck do I do with you now?" I walked in with him. That'll be on the street and elevator cams. How long after I walk out alone until someone starts asking questions? Hosh might let this slide if I can produce what she wants. It's either Joseph Knudson or Mark Bird. It has to be. It wasn't this sorry sap. But still, I'd like to be sure. I watch as blood trickles from one of Paul's fingertips and drips down. The quiet, dull kerplunks as the droplets hit the carpet is the only sound interrupting my thoughts. The blood blends in with the dark carpet quite well, and the bash on the side of his head, while purple and bulging now, has surprisingly bled very little.

"I suppose I'll just have to stash you away for a bit, Paul," I say. I move to the large, four-post bed and pull a soft brown blanket from beneath the comforter. I roll Paul up and then clean up the scene. I roll his body towards the bed and use my legs to position him beneath it. He'll have to stay here for a while. I push him as far towards the middle as I can manage before he snags, his thick shoulders wedging him stuck.

***

I've managed to coax another one, Joseph, into the Basement with me. These people are so gullible to think that an elite would be interested in befriending them, but they can't seem to resist. I have a Mickey in my pocket that was obtained from the Basement's level three drug stores. No one asks questions down there. All I had to do was drop it in his drink if he showed any reservations and then take him stumbling down to level two, but once we chatted a bit in the lobby and had a drink, all I had to say was that I had something to show him and he followed like a lost puppy. I hope this is my guy. The day is coming to an end, and I'm growing tired of this. Two guys left: Joseph and Mark.

I used the Mickey on him after all to get him tied to the chair. Once we were in the room, awaiting the surprise I had promised, I slipped it in his water. He sipped at the water as a way to pass off his nervousness. Joseph is a bit bigger than Paul and has a bit more sense. When he's finally shaken off the drugged-out stupor, I get right to work.

He spits blood on the carpet. Red spittle speckles his chin. "You think people like you are immune? Like you're not next? You fucking idiot. You're already caught in their fucking web, and you don't even know it." It starts as a sputter but then turns into a full-blown cackle. His lunatic laugh would normally infuriate me, but I'm stuck in the calm before the storm, and I pull patience from an infinite pool. So, I wait.

After a few minutes, the spell passes, and he sits still with his eyes turned to the floor, the look of the forlorn etched on his face. *That's more like it,* I smile, but he's not looking.

I have some witty last-word kind of remark to make, but he speaks first, and my blood freezes. "Once you're called to Hosh's house," he begins with a far-off look, "that's as good as having your death cert signed."

I stare. He may be tied up, but somehow, I feel the power has shifted.

"How do you know?" I applaud myself internally for the even way I could convey the words because, on the inside, my body feels as if it's crawling with fire ants.

"Because I'm smarter than you. You've allowed hubris to cloud your perception of reality. Only five people hold real power in this country anymore, and you are not one of them."

"Neither are you," I say as I pick at my fingernails, attempting nonchalance.

He cocks his head up at me, considering. "True, but we're not the same."

I lower my eyes at him. "You're right. We are not the same."

He smiles at me, and I backhand him to wipe the smug look off his ugly face. His face jerks to the side, but his smile remains plastered. I know now, without a doubt, that I will enjoy killing this man. I only hope to hold out long enough to extract more information, but then I catch myself. I can't kill him. I might have to deliver him to Hosh.

I kneel down in front of him so that we're at eye level. "What you said earlier about Hosh. How do you know who she and the other leaders are?"

"I'm an Information Assurance Systems Engineer," he replies, cracking his neck like he's recovering from an awkward sleeping position.

I frown at him. "Elaborate," I bark as I hold the wrench back in a ready-to-strike position.

"Security, man. Security. I see everything."

Hmm, I rub my chin thoughtfully as I stand up.

"What have you seen?" I attempt, though I don't expect it to be this easy. He's been more tightlipped than Paul.

"Think about it, Lane. You're more expendable here than me. You've already paid. You no longer contribute meaningfully. What are you other than another elite to please? Another mouth to feed? Are there even people here who would miss you?"

A tight cord pulls through my torso. I sit up straighter. He's struck a nerve, and he knows it—a wicked grin spreads across his face and pulls at his cracked lip. Still, he smiles wider.

"Think about. I mean realllly think about it," he says. He's enjoying himself now. "Hosh could have found out who did this. You think you're special? What did you do? Use the directory to narrow us down and then figure out who didn't have Metalink? You're doing her dirty work, and then you'll be a liability."

For once, I don't know what to do here. Kill him? Yes, I'd love that, but right now, I still have the upper hand. He's the one tied up. What he said rings true with the clarity of a noon bell pulling me from a lazy summer slumber. I feel stuck, but then it dawns on me. I may have one more trick up my sleeve. I could use Ava here. Couldn't I? She's at my disposal. Why not leverage that? Make her take the fall. I'm grasping, maybe. I need more time to think this through. I gag Joseph. He kicks at the restraints I've used to tie him to the chair, but they look secure. Unable to talk and only able to manage muffled screams that'll never be heard in these level two rooms, designed to hide the noise of unscrupulous activities, I leave the room.

He could be my guy. Mark could be my guy. Either way, what Joseph said eats at me. I've got to come up with a contingency plan in case he's right, and I need to clear my head. I go down to the third floor.

I sit down in one of the plush, oversized armchairs that populate the main area. I won't be needing a private room today. An attendant approaches, holding a silver tray with a cocktail of goodies. "Something to calm my nerves," I tell him before he can greet me. "And then something to sharpen my mind. And make the turnaround quick."

The attendant nods as he sets the tray down on a small table next to me and prepares something in a needle. I roll up my sleeve as he does this and look around. There isn't much going on down here at the moment. There's one other person, a woman, dozing in another armchair. A dozen other oversized, velvety chairs in the vast, dark main area are empty today. The man ties my arm off and swipes an alcohol swab across the inside fold of my elbow. I feel the cooling effect of that and then the needle prick. I'm flooded with sweet relief. I lie back.

The man arranges things on the small table next to me. He raises his goodie tray and gestures to the table. "For when you're ready to come back." A thin line of white powder on a small, mirrored tray, and a small tube like half a straw rests beside it.

I nod and close my eyes as I sink further into the plush comfort of the armchair.

The escape is blissful. It's unclear how long I'm influenced, but thoughts of Joseph upstairs flutter back, and I reluctantly snort the powder. A raging bull of reality storms back. I'm ready to get to work.

I climb into the elevator and hit level two. Once it lets out, I stride purposefully toward the Playboy room I have reserved. I punch in my code and push the door open. I stop, frozen midstep. The chair that held Joseph is lying on its side, and Joseph is nowhere in sight.

CHAPTER 17

Ava

October 24, 2025

It's been two days since I found out about the man Bodin is searching for, but I haven't been able to tell him. Now, however, I see Bodin up ahead of me. He's a Purple, and that knowledge helped immensely because there are so few. We're still a chaotic bunch, just exiting the main doors leading into the Arena. We're not yet in nice, neat, color-coordinated rows. This is my chance. I push my way through the crowd and grab Bodin by the shoulder, holding him back and allowing the people filing in around us to camouflage us.

"What the..." he begins, but I break him off.

"Shh! It's me," I whisper into his ear, but he already knows this, having whipped around immediately to assess the threat. He blushes.

"Hey..." he begins again, but we don't have time for pleasantries.

"I saw your man," I interrupt in a hurried hiss. I wait for him to grasp the implications of this, but he looks confused. "Birthmark, man," I clarify, annoyed.

"Oh!" he exclaims.

"His name is Mark Bird. He's a software engineer, which means he works in the center tower. The big one."

"Can you talk to him?" Bodin asks, glancing around nervously. I can't blame him after what happened the other day.

I contemplate this. "Doubt it," I say. "But my employer was looking into him two days ago. I don't know why."

"Shit. That doesn't sound good."

"It can't be," I agree. I look around. We've got to go. The crowd around us is thinning out. "What would I say if I could talk to him?" I hurry.

"Tell him the code phrase. Start by saying, 'as a reminder,' then, make sure he looks at you and say 'sorry, thought you were another chap.'"

I try to commit that to memory. It's easy enough. "Then what?" I ask.

"Hear what he has to say and see if he can get us the fuck out of here," Bodin says.

I nod, and we both scamper off. I look around, breathing a sigh of relief when I'm not followed by any suspicious eyes. That was exhilarating. I have no idea how I'll ever make contact with this Mark fellow, but just knowing there's someone out there who may be able to help us escape is like taking a shot of morphine. And yes, I tried morphine once at the hospital. It felt too good ever to do it again.

When I arrive at Lane's, he's not waiting for me and my outfit hasn't changed from yesterday's—French Maid. It's hanging just as I left it. After dressing, I poke my head into the various rooms, searching for him. When I look into his bedroom, I hear the soft patter of the shower running. He's been getting up later and later. It's unlike him to be so undisciplined. I'm used to him standing there waiting for me, having already eaten and exercised.

I also see his clothes in a lazy pile near the foot of his bed. I never usually have to pick up his clothes. I walk over and figure my first order of business will be to deposit them into the hamper. When I pick up his shirt, I freeze. It's stained with blood. I know blood. I've seen it on the scrubs of nurses and doctors for years. I drop the shirt and step out of his room, hoping he never learns I was here.

I go to the kitchen and begin to sweep; though Lane is so tidy anyway, there are hardly any crumbs. Still, every day, I wipe already clean counters, wipe down already clean furniture, and sweep and mop already clean floors in hopes that the illusion of being busy keeps Lane from thinking of things I can do for him. Flawed thinking, but if nothing else, it fools me into believing I'm here just for cleaning.

When Lane emerges, I immediately know he's in a sour mood. His eyes are sunken and tired looking, his face gloomy. He opens a cupboard to take out a coffee mug. I attempt to exit the kitchen and put some distance between us, but then the mug smashes against the wall next to me.

I jump.

"Going somewhere?" he snarls. I turn around reluctantly. His eyes are piercing. "I need you to do an errand for me." He walks quickly from the kitchen. Despite having just showered, I notice a small bloom of darkness spreading beneath his armpits. Lane is stressed. Really stressed. This puts me on edge. "Come in here!" he bellows. I hurry into the living room. "I need you to find this man," he says as he puts the picture onto the screen.

It's him, it's Bodin's guy.

Shocked recognition must register on my face because he demands, "Do you know this person?" When I don't answer immediately, he takes a step closer to me and screams with the fury of a man who is quickly losing his sanity, "*Do you know this person?*" Spit hits my face. I shrink away.

"Yes," I say and then immediately regret it.

"How?" he demands.

I'm shaking. "He might be someone who could help me," I squeak out. I've stepped in it. I've really stepped in it. I know that, but I can't take it back. I can at least leave Bodin out of this. I can at least be vague. I don't know anything, really, but at this moment, I hate myself. I can't believe I may have just given up the identity of our only chance to escape.

"Explain," he says. He's tuned his voice down a few octaves.

"I think he knows how to help recruits escape. I don't know. It might just be a rumor. I don't know," I repeat.

Lane appears to consider this. "Bring him to the level two Playboy Room in the Basement."

I blink at him. "Where is that?"

"Pull up directions to the Basement," Lane projects into the room. A map pulls up on the screen behind him with a green arrow delineating the way. "It's there," he says. His voice has changed. He sounds tired, dejected even.

We're silent for a moment.

"What if he won't come?" I ask in a hushed voice.

"Make him," Lane growls.

I swallow. "How?"

Lane lets out an exasperated sigh. "You're fucking useless, aren't you?" I don't answer. Lane crosses his arms and hangs his head deep in thought. He looks up. "I'll put a lunch meeting on his calendar at a populated place. He shouldn't expect anything. Then, you'll show up." He turns towards his windows. "Scheduler, request a meeting at The Eating Establishment at Noon today with Mark Bird." There's a soft pinging noise as the computer does some thinking or whatever. I wait. And then it comes—a bell and a popup dialogue box that states, "Meeting Confirmed."

Lane looks at me. "Don't fuck this up." He brushes past me and shuts his bedroom door behind him. I relax. My stomach swirls. Nausea overtakes me. What just happened? I busy myself with cleaning, glancing at the clock every few minutes. Lane doesn't reappear until 11:30. When he walks out, he looks more composed. More sure of himself.

"You'll need to convince him to go to the Playboy room with you," he says. "I don't care how you do it. Use your girly charms. Threaten him. Just make it happen. Don't say anything that would implicate you or me. Keep it simple." He tells the room to pull up a map showing the way to

The Eating Establishment. I study it. "Show up at 12:05. He's expecting me, but it'll be you that sits down next to him." I nod, nerves humming as I swallow. I have no idea how I'm going to do this.

"What do you want from him?" I ask.

"Maybe the same thing you do," he states.

My eyes widen. "Why?" I ask. "Why would you want to escape this?"

"Because I might not have a fucking choice," he says through gritted teeth.

I look at the clock.

"You can start walking," Lane says. "I'll meet you in the Playboy room. Mark can probably help get you there."

"Ok." I turn to go. I feel his eyes on me. When I turn around in the elevator and hit the lobby button, his intense blue eyes are still lingering. The doors close, blocking Lane from my view. I let out a breath. I don't know how it happened, but somehow, this day has turned out to be one of the most important days of my life.

Finally, I'm standing outside of The Eating Establishment. It's 12:08—I had trouble finding the place. I cross the threshold, and the sound of cutlery and conversation fills the space. I scan the room.

"Can I help you?" The hostess steps forward, her eyes dragging up and down my body. I'm still in my maid's attire. She knows I don't belong here. I can see it in her eyes. And then, I spot him. Sitting alone at a small table with an empty seat across from him. He, too, is scanning the room, a half-empty glass before him.

"No, thanks," I respond. "I see him." I push my way past her. She lets me go. When I plop down across from him, he looks up, confused.

"As a reminder," I venture. His expression changes from confused to curious. "Oh, sorry. Thought you were someone else, chap." I hope I got that right. He narrows his eyes at me and opens his mouth to say something, only to close it again.

He stands. "I don't like this," he says and goes to leave, but I grab him by his wrist.

"Stay. Please," I plead.

He considers me and then sits back down. He leans across the table and whispers. "You made an appointment using an elite's scheduler. You have sixty seconds to explain yourself."

Panic rises within. I'm not good at this kind of thing. I would have made a terrible spy. My nerves seem to choke off my brain. I can't think of anything clever, so I revert to the only thing I know: the truth.

"Lane wants out, too," I say.

Mark hides his face behind his menu. "I need a better explanation. How did you hear the code phrase?" I glance around and spot a camera in the corner of the dining room, distinguishable by its gleaming glass lens. They're not even attempting to hide it. There could be more, but I don't risk making myself even more obvious. I copy Mark.

"A boy named Bodin. He just arrived as a new recruit. He was told to look for you. Told me to watch for you, too."

"And the elite?" he asks.

"I don't know," I respond, as I choke back a sob. I feel like this is the part where I'll lose him. "He's acting strange. All stressed out and stuff. He's looking for you. Guessed by my face that I might be, too. Seemed to sense I recognized you." I sound desperate. I'm trying to hold back tears, but the effort is evident in my voice.

Mark sighs. "This can't be good. What does he want from me?"

"I don't know," I repeat. "He wants us to meet him in the Playboy Room at The Basement now."

Mark lets out a huff. "Christ," he says. "Follow me. I might have a plan. Something that could buy us more time. But first, is there any way to get to this Bodin kid?"

I don't respond because I realize I know really nothing about his whereabouts.

"I don't know," I say again. I hate that I sound helpless.

"You said he was a recruit. What's his color?"

"Um, purple," I respond, happy I could give him some helpful information.

"Ok," he says. "Follow my lead."

Mark drops his menu on the table. "Let's skip right to dessert," he says as he eyes me mischievously. "That's what you came here for, isn't it?"

I blink.

"Let's blow this joint and head to The Basement." He gets up and takes my hand.

I nod and put my hand in his, following him out. Happy to play this part that he's handed me. Once we're out on the street, he releases my hand. "I have to stop by my place of work first," he says. "Grab a few things."

"Ok," I say as I follow him deeper into the city's heart. After five minutes of walking, he stops in front of the black tower. It's the one we all know so well because it sits at the heart of the city and reaches higher than any other building. It's the only building that touches the dome.

"Wait for me here," he instructs.

I nod and lean against the building just outside the entrance. I feel that every minute that ticks by, Lane must be growing increasingly anxious, wondering when we'll pop through the door. Wondering if I succeeded. Ten minutes pass. I begin to fidget.

Mark exits the building, walking fast. "I called a car," he says as I come up alongside him. "We've got to hurry." I want to ask what his plan is, but I don't. I feel too exposed here. Like everything I do could get Mark or Bodin or me into trouble. I have to trust him.

A car comes and whisks us away. Mark gives directions to a numbered building. It means nothing to me.

We pull up outside a building that looks like every other building but closer to the outskirts of town. We get out. Mark walks fast. I hobble behind him, cursing the heels still on my feet biting into my cramped toes.

Mark stops outside large double doors and checks his watch. His forehead sheens with sweat. He looks up at me. His nervousness puts me on edge. Then, an alarm blares. Loud and ominous. It's like an air-raid siren in old war movies.

I must look terrified because Mark pulls me aside. "It's fine," he says. "Just a drill." Before I can answer, the doors swing open, and people begin to file out in an orderly fashion, walking toward their muster point. "Find Bodin and bring him here," he demands. I look around, confused, until I see the people spilling out are Purple recruits.

My eyes search desperately for him. Then, he's there. I push through the first line and grab his arm, yanking him through the crowd. I catch him off guard, and he stumbles, but he follows fast once he sees it's me. I hop as I remove my heels. Then I run as if we're being chased, shoes in hand. Someone is going to notice that a recruit just stepped out of line. The siren in the background amplifies my fear.

Mark no longer stands by the entrance of the building. I follow him as he rounds the corner, looking over my shoulder the entire time. Eyes follow us. I can see this, but no one is in pursuit so far. Once around the corner, I freeze. Mark has disappeared.

"Down here!" he yells.

"There!" Bodin points to a hole in the ground. We scramble to follow. Mark's head pokes out like a gopher, scanning the area around us. He stands aside on the ladder to make room for us. Other people are making their way towards us. I don't know what this is or where we are, but Mark shouts at us to hurry. Once I reach the manhole, I climb down a ladder with a dim, red light providing enough illumination to see where I'm going. Bodin hovers above me, nearly stepping on my hands on the rungs below him in his haste to climb down. I hit the landing and move out of the way just in time to avoid a collision with Bodin, who stumbles down the last quarter of the ladder and scrambles not to fall once hitting the landing. I look around at the concrete walls that entomb us.

Where are we?

CHAPTER 18

Bodin

October 24, 2025

The man yanks me down into the dark chamber, and I nearly fall down the ladder. I hear the echo of the trapdoor slamming above me. Angry fists pummel the outside of the door in dull thuds of protest, but it's so thick, they sound underwater.

I look around. The walls curl up around us. A dull, red light provides enough light for me to see that we're standing in a concrete tube of some sort. It's about twelve feet deep if I had to guess. I could reach up and touch the ceiling, which puts it at about nine feet high. Benches and long rectangular shapes above them line the dull, gray walls. There's shelving at the back, with a few items stacked neatly among them.

The guy who had shut the door behind us jumps down. "That was close," he says, running his hand through his hair.

I squint through the darkness and use the red light from the exit sign to make out his features. It's *the* guy. It's the Mole. I look at Ava, stunned.

He seems to register that I recognize him now.

"This is the safest place to talk. No cameras and a lot of moving bodies to hide our movements. We've got at least an hour before they figure out it was a false alarm."

"A false...did you...?"

"Tell me who sent you and what you're doing here." He addresses only me. I look at Ava, but she looks down at the floor away from me.

"I'm Bodin," I put out my hand, but his arms remain crossed as he watches me through shaded eyes. The red light seems brighter now that my eyes have adjusted. It gives him a sinister look. "Uh, Frank sent me," I add.

He doesn't give any indication that he knows Frank. His expression does not change. "And what is it that Frank told you about me?"

I don't answer him right away. "What is this place?" I ask, looking around.

"Bomb shelter," he says. "There are hundreds of them throughout the city." I think back to the dull, persistent thudding against the door that has since ceased—no doubt they left to find another shelter, unaware it was a false alarm and scared shitless. The thought is oddly satisfying.

"He gave me your description. Said you'd help me. ...Er, us, " I say, answering his previous question. I keep my eyes on Ava, who is exploring the space with her back to me. "He said I should get as much information as possible from you and bring it back to him," I add, looking at the Mole.

"He did, huh?" The man turns around and motions to a cold, hard bench. "Sit down. We're going to be here a while." Ava and I sit on the same bench across from him. I keep glancing at her, but she avoids my gaze. The room seems to become narrower and shallower by the minute. I try not to dwell too much on the cramped quarters. I'm not normally claustrophobic, but an underground bunker pushes my comfort limits. Only Ava's presence is keeping me cool.

"Where is Frank now?" he asks.

"I'm not at liberty to say," I reply, returning his composed gaze with effort.

"Uh-huh. Maybe you're not as dumb as you look." I try not to react to the dig.

"So, do you think you can help us get out of this city?" I ask.

"Maybe," he says with a frown, shifting his gaze to Ava. She's leaning over with her face in her hands. I resist the urge to rub her back.

"Ava?" I nudge her. "What's going on?"

"Everything just seems so out of control," she sobs. I hardly recognize her voice. "Lane knows about Mark and says he wants out, too, but he was looking into Mark before that."

"Mark?" I ask. Ava sniffs and gestures half-heartedly to the Mole. So, his name is Mark. Got it.

Ava sniffs and continues, "And Lane has been acting unhinged. He's super stressed about something. And he knows that I know who Mark is." She turns her head to peek up at me through her hands. I see her clumped eyelashes and smeared mascara through her fingers. "Everything is just so fucked up, Bodin. I'm so sorry. I don't know what's going on, but I feel like this is it for me. Lane is going to kill me. I think Lane killed someone else, too," Ava says.

Mark and I look at her.

"What?" we say in unison.

"He had blood on his clothes this morning. His behavior... erratic, furious... maybe even scared. He's been looking into guys in the Software Engineering Department."

"Holy fuck," Mark says. Now, we turn our attention to him. "Paul left work yesterday. Said he was meeting someone. He never came back. It was really unlike him, but I still didn't think much about it until Joseph went MIA, too." He and Ava stare wordlessly at each other. Then Mark ventures, "If Lane did something to them, he's in deeper shit than he knows. He'll be desperate." He clasps his hands in front of him and brings them up to his mouth, breathes through them. He addresses Ava, his voice muffled by his hands. "Explain it to us. From the beginning. Everything you've seen and know about Lane," Mark requests. I notice his tone is considerably gentler with Ava.

Ava sniffles and wipes at her nose with the back of her sleeve. She starts telling us from the beginning. When she finishes, Mark leans back on the bench and crosses his ankles.

"Someone suspects something, and somehow, that led Lane to me. That's not good. But I'd venture a guess and say Lane is caught in someone's crosshairs, too." He bites his lip and looks up at the shallow ceiling. We're all quiet, searching for answers in the recesses of our brains. Mark seems to snap out of it first.

He fixes his gaze on me. "What has it been like since the EMP?"

"The real world, you mean?" He doesn't indulge me with a response but shoots me a look like "duh."

I sigh. "A lot of people have died." My throat constricts, thinking of Mom, but I push through it. "The rest of us fight over everything. Food and water mostly. We found a few good people, and we've banded together somewhere safe. We have weapons, thanks to Frank. They're working on building homes for everyone. We're taking mattresses, rugs, doors, glass, and stuff from the nearby houses that are abandoned. Some of the owners are with us at the ranch. Seems like everything gets repurposed now. Most nights, we're lucky if we're warm enough and there's food in our stomachs." I have no idea why I keep talking, but I can't stop. It's helping me diffuse some of my nervous energy, I guess. "The ranch is in this small valley that's pretty defensible. That's what they say, anyway. But no one has more guns than us. What we really need is food, though, especially with winter coming. Everyone pitches in, but it wasn't like that in Salt Lake."

Ava wipes at her face and sits up. "You made it to a ranch? What happened to the house?"

"Long story." I give her a meaningful glance, not wanting to say too much in front of Mark.

"Is it... good there?" she asks.

"Yeah. Sort of," I say. "There are other kids for Evie to play with. We don't have to hide. I wasn't there long, but it seemed like they looked out for each other. And it just felt good to be around people again. People who don't want to kill you, anyway."

"That sounds nice," Ava says quietly before returning her face to her hands.

"You'd like it," I say. I look back at Mark. "It's not like rainbows and unicorns, though," I say. "It's scary out there."

Ava scoffs into her hands. "It's scary in here."

"Yeah," I agree. "Guess the world is forever different now for people like us. Well," I say, shooting Mark a look, "not you."

Mark looks at me, considering. "True, but I still know people out there." We look at each other for a moment, and then he says, "I could die helping you. I want to know why I should."

I fidget on the bench. "Frank said you'd help," I say. I'm annoyed at the petulance that betrays me. I wasn't told more. I thought this would be easy. I thought he was supposed to be "one of us."

"Frank is not here. The rules are different now. Tell me how Frank will make my death meaningful if I help you."

I'm taken aback. I don't know what to say to this guy. I hadn't realized I was asking him to risk his life, but what did I expect? I've seen the lock and key of this city. Everything seems controlled or monitored in some way. It makes sense that Mark wouldn't be untouchable. I realize, at this moment, that I had put the guy on a fictitious pedestal. And now, I'm taking him down, and it's unsettling like the ground is shaking beneath my feet again, threatening to swallow me. There are no superheroes here. I stand and begin poking around the room. I look at the rectangular shapes on the walls and realize they're sleeping cots that can be folded down. Then I go to the shelving. I run my hand across a tightly folded wool blanket and ask Mark, "Can't you just come with us? Escape, I mean?"

"I'm not sure," he responds.

"That's a lot like maybe," I retort.

He sighs and changes the subject. "What do you think of this place?" he asks with childlike wonder. "It's magnificent, isn't it?"

"Yeah, I guess," I venture. "But like I said..."

He cuts me off. "You guess? You clearly don't appreciate what it took to build this place or what it's capable of. This place has a glass dome equipped with Intelligent Glass Control to project images for camouflage or change the level of UV exposure, all while doubling as solar panels that capture enough energy to run this city twice over." I open my mouth to comment, but he doesn't give me the chance. He keeps going, more animated than ever, "The air from the outside goes through dehumidification to remove the moisture for water. Crops and livestock get watered in an environment with systems that recapture runoff and condensation and recycle urine—making our food system extremely efficient with very little water expenditure. Nothing here gets wasted. There's technology here that no one has ever seen before. All the cars are smart driving and run off a sustainable energy grid. There will never be any car accidents. There is no exhaust. It's the perfect temperature inside, always."

"I get it. I get it," I say, plopping back on the bench across from him.

"It's fucking beautiful," he says, relaxing against the wall.

"Do you know they feed the recruits *bugs*?" I ask.

He peers up at me, his look sheepish. So, he knows. He tries to explain, "They're an excellent source of protein, and they proliferate so quickly. It's the perfect food source to feed a crowd, really." I wrinkle my nose and look at Ava, who has the expected reaction. Despite fresh tears running down her cheeks, she sits up with a horrified expression. Mark continues to make his case. "You know they eat bugs in other cultures, right? It's just your programming that has you guys so squeamish."

I cock an eyebrow. "Do *you* eat the meal bars?"

"Well, no..."

I hold up a hand to stop him. "Enough said." He closes his mouth.

Ava wipes at the wetness on her cheeks and says to Mark, "As great as this place is, you have to realize that from our perspective, it's a special kind of hell."

Mark considers this. "I know."

"So... let's get back to figuring out how to get us out of here," I say.

"If I can get you two out of here, there's something I'd like you to tell Frank. Something more personal," he says.

"Alright..." I say hesitantly.

He blows out a long breath. "I know it's not good for recruits here. I know that. Just hear me out." Ava and I exchange a look. He charges ahead, "I don't think it's all that bad here. Maybe I've been drinking the Kool-Aid for too long, but this Era Unveiling? Maybe it's for the best."

We sit silently for a minute while I chew on the words that just came out of his mouth. A reflex begins to take hold.

"How can you say that?" I say through gritted teeth. "My mom fucking died because of these assholes. My little sister..." I choke on the words and swallow hard. "My little sister no longer has a mom, and we're hungry nearly every day. How the fuck can you think this is for the best?"

"No, no, no. I know. It's not like that. I just mean from now on. This moment right now. What they did was fucked. There should have been more collaboration and effort put into finding a solution that didn't involve so much suffering but..."

I cut him off. "No one here has suffered one fucking bit."

He rubs his hand down his face. "I know, I know. But listen. We don't have a time machine. It happened. People died. A lot of people. But what if now, we can somehow start over?"

"Start over?! These people murdered my friend! How's that for starting over? They're still murderers!" Ava spits, a vein protruding from her forehead.

Mark frowns. "That's not exactly what I meant," he says quietly.

Ava sputters and stands as if outraged. Mark holds up his hands to fend off Ava's rebukes. This gesture seems to take some of the wind from her sails. She sits back down with an angry huff.

I wonder who Ava's friend is, but I don't want to risk provoking her further. Instead, I look at Mark. "Frank would say you're fantasizing. That people in power only want more power. That fewer people more reliant on a single authoritative force, cannot be a good thing." I've heard a version of this from Frank many times in the days we stayed holed up in Salt Lake together, waiting for the army to pick up new recruits. I've heard it enough to know that what I'm saying is pretty close to his words. He told me about the Era Unveiling, and there's nothing about it that sits well with me or with him. The Era Unveiling is their plan for the world. Mark has hit a nerve. I'll never trust these people to rule us, and I'm beginning to question whether I can trust him.

"I know I'm reaching for a silver lining, and if there is one, it's that maybe, just maybe, we can save this planet. Make it sustainable again," Mark says.

"At what cost? What good is that if we don't have freedom?" I ask.

"I think any other living organism on the planet would think this was a good thing. Maybe it's time to stop living so selfishly," he says.

We sit in silence for a long time. Ava returns to the same state she was in previously, her face resting in her hands. I don't know what to say to this guy, but he's starting to make me nervous. Is he one of us or one of them?

I break the silence and return to the same pressing question that keeps sloshing around in my head. "So, what's the plan for getting us out of here?"

He snorts. "I'm still trying to figure that out without implicating myself. There might be hope," he says as he pats down the sides of his pants until he successfully locates his prize. He takes a pack of cigarettes and a lighter from his pocket. After thwacking the back of the pack, he holds a single cigarette between two fingers and lays the pack on the bench beside him.

I watch him. Although I've pretended to like cigarettes many times before, I'm not too fond of the smell and can't help but scrunch up my face preemptively.

"You don't mind, do you?" he asks around the cigarette now held between his lips. He doesn't wait for a reply before flicking the lighter and holding it to the end of the cigarette. He takes a deep breath in and exhales a long, drawn-out puff of smoke. "Just a puff. I know this isn't the best place to light up." With that, he leans over towards me with the cigarette outstretched. I hesitate before taking it and bringing it to my lips. Cigarettes are one of those things the adults have placed great value on since the whole blackout. The thought of indulging in something so sacred to some is irresistible even despite knowing it's not my favorite. As I inhale, the taste hits my tongue, and I hope I can hide the look of disgust on my face. I feel lightheaded as I exhale and do my best to suppress a cough as I reach across the aisle to return it to him. He looks at Ava, whose face is still in her hands like he might offer her a drag but thinks better of it.

My mouth feels as if it's filled with dirty cotton balls. I stand and go to the shelving where I spotted water canteens during my earlier assessment. I turn back to him as I unscrew the lid and take a swig. The water has a heavy mineral taste. I drink enough to wash the taste from my mouth. Mark takes one more drag and delicately snuffs the end on the bench before placing it back in the pack.

"Have you heard of the Era Unveiling?" he asks.

"Sort of. Just what Frank has told me," I answer.

He harumphs. "I don't think Frank knows this version. Most people would say they'd heard of it. It wasn't exactly a secret before all of this went down, but the real plan for the Era Unveiling is not what they sold to the public."

"So, what is it?" I ask irritably. I don't know how much longer we have down here, but the pressing issue of our escape has yet to be addressed.

"A reset. A do-over for the hierarchy of the world which will give them more control and preserve the planet."

"Ok..."

"It's not all bad, but here's what it means for people like you." He looks at me. I narrow my eyes at him. "You won't be able to take a shit without them knowing about it. Forgive my bluntness. Put practically, everything you do will be tracked and controlled."

"How?" I ask.

"Simple. A computer chip. The people surviving right now are desperate. So, once the population has been sufficiently pruned, the new government comes in with an olive branch. Food, water, even electricity, but there are two conditions. One, you have to move to one of the five cities they indicate, and two, you must accept an implanted chip. This chip can read some biomarkers like your heartbeat and your blood pressure. These vitals won't be used to assess your health but rather your state of mind—whether a revolt has your heart pounding or a certain image invokes a specific response in your body. They'll probably know who is at risk of revolting before they do. And it'll be used to track you with the satellite system, and it'll be where your money is stored, which will be Digital Global Currency. All other forms of money will be useless."

"Is that what this is?" I roll up my sleeve and turn my wrist so he can see the numbers. "A chip?"

"Naw," he says. "That's just graphene oxide. It's useful for keeping tabs on you by storing just enough information to identify you when you scan, but that's it. A chip would be wasted on you here. You're already fully controlled without one."

"Oh. So, what happens if the people accept this chip?" I ask with renewed interest.

"Isn't it obvious?" He sighs. "Why did they send some kid?" he mutters under his breath.

"So, explain it to me then!" I snap.

"Fine. So, you're forced to move to one of five cities if you want any hint as to what life was like before—hot food, running toilets, electricity, that kind of thing. And these cities have been prepared for this purpose. Hardware and power grids were hardened beforehand. At the flick of a switch, certain power plants and city blocks will have working electricity again. These will be the housing sectors where everyone will basically live in an apartment. They have just enough housing for 200,000 people (give or take) in each city, and that's how many they need to work to get the economy back up and running. The cities are Portland, Cleveland, Salt Lake, Austin, and New York. Portland, Cleveland, and Austin will largely be agriculturist cities where the bulk of work will be done in fields tending to cattle or growing food. The other two cities are the factory cities where those folks will work to produce textiles and other goods. Following so far?"

I roll my eyes. "Yes."

"Once you're there and you've been chipped, they own you. You'll work twelve-hour days with one day off per week and minimal compensation, which will automatically load onto your chip at a specified time. You can then purchase what's available in stores for food and other goods. There will be no access to information. No smartphones and no internet. This will ensure that the masses are never informed enough to rally or feel indignant about their circumstances. Televisions will be provided with pre-approved programming. They have to keep these people just happy enough that a revolution isn't tempting. So, you know, they still get their TV. There may even be newspapers that circulate. Again, pre-approved information. Strictly entertainment value stuff."

"It doesn't sound that bad…" I venture. Ava looks up at Mark with wide, concerned eyes.

"Oh fuck, dude. You really are clueless," he says.

"Fuck you!" I stand to leave before realizing that's impossible.

He runs his hands through his hair. His purple birthmark becomes visible before his hair falls into place again. "Look, do you want to own a car someday? Have a girlfriend? Maybe even have kids?"

I shrug and intentionally avoid looking at Ava. "I guess."

"Well, fucking forget it. You'll need to apply for a permit to have kids, and likely, you won't even have the freedom to choose your partner. If they allow you to have a partner at all, it'll likely be a match based on genetic compatibility, and they may not even let you raise the kid together. They'll probably have centers for that, so they have full control over brainwashing the little rug rat. A nuclear family with strong family bonds is a threat. And a car? Forget ever driving one of those unless it's deemed necessary for your job."

I scratch nervously at my collarbone.

"Feeling the noose tighten?" he muses.

"Why wouldn't some other country just swoop in and take over the United States right now? I mean, it's just this city now, isn't it?" I ask.

"We still have our army positioned around the country and the backing of multiple other countries who are part of the Era Unveiling and now reside under the One World Order. Other countries aren't likely to defy a country that's part of the new One World Order. Combined, we're too great of an adversary. Besides, it's likely that those countries who haven't joined yet will be beaten into submission soon enough once they feel the pinch from the absence of trade deals."

"Frank wants to destroy this city. Make the leaders pay somehow. Say we succeed in taking it for ourselves or just destroying it. What happens then?" I ask.

Mark lets out a low whistle. "Depends, but I'd say the United States is up for grabs at that point. Your only hope then would be that a country that's not part of the One World Order comes to your aid and that our army cooperates in aiding your plight."

"Which countries are not a part of that?" I ask.

"Quiet a few, but there's only a couple worth mentioning. Canada, for starters, was a surprise last-minute withdrawal. Given their proximity and size, they're your best bet. And, of course, China, who is trying to rally the remaining countries into joining their own version of the Order. I guess then they'd have to change their name from One World Order to Two World Orders." Mark chuckles to himself.

We're all quiet for a moment before Ava speaks up, "Bodin, did you know about Sarah?"

I look at her and blink. The abrupt conversation shift has given me whiplash. "What about Sarah?" I ask.

"The yellow door," she states.

"Your friend went through the yellow door?" Mark asks Ava.

She nods. "Tell me it's not what Lane said it is." Her eyes are pleading, but Mark's look gives it away.

"Sorry, doll. There's no charity here." He says it gently, but Ava still wails.

I look quizzically at Mark and mouth, "Yellow door?" Mark puts two fingers to his temple and mimes a gunshot to the head. Well, fuck.

"Ava?" I ask gently. "Is Sarah the friend you were talking about earlier? The one that was murdered?"

"Yes," she whispers through her hands covering her face.

My stomach does a flip. Sarah. It's not like she was my favorite, but still, the news is jarring. No wonder Ava is distraught. I was curious about the yellow door, but I never expected this.

Ava's cries die down quickly, and she looks up. Her eyes focus on Mark, a steely determination etched across her features. "We wouldn't be here under a bomb threat rouse unless you thought there was some hope. Tell us what you're thinking and how we're going to get out of this mess," she demands. Thank god Ava seems to have snapped out of her stupor.

"Yeah, how the hell do we get out of here?" I ask again, feeling overwhelm kicking in. I want to get back to simple. To the ranch. To my family. And I want to offload this information onto someone else. Make it their problem. At this moment, I'm happy to play the kid card.

"I'm working on it," he snaps.

I kick at the floor. "This is so fucked. I never thought this would be the world Evie would have to grow up in. No Saturday morning cartoons or birthday dinners at her favorite restaurant..." Tears prick at my eyes, but I swallow them back, hoping they don't notice. Ava stares expectantly at Mark, whose eyes are glued to the ceiling.

"There might be a long shot," he says quietly.

I wait, but he doesn't elaborate. Instead, he reaches for his cigarettes again.

"I wish you wouldn't," I say. My head is still cloudy from being stuck in this cramped space with secondhand smoke from his previous light-up.

He sighs. "Fine."

"Are you going to tell us about this long shot, Mark?" I ask.

He takes a deep breath. "A few very lucky recruits with special skillsets get promoted to Essential Worker upon entry. It gives you more freedom to roam and security access levels that could open up possibilities. I suggest you find someone who knows software. Someone in good health," he adds, glancing at Ava. *Right*, I think. Green door people. He eyes me. "With that person, you hit one of their weak spots, and you decide—either take the city or destroy it. My vote is for taking the city. Why not use it?" he says this last part to himself mostly as his hands slap his thighs before standing.

"Isn't it all moot if either option leaves us at the mercy of China?" I ask.

Mark shrugs and mutters, "Better hope Canada is game for an alliance."

"But what are their weak points?" I ask, wondering if I'd missed something from earlier.

Mark settles himself back on the bench and answers, "Ah, yes. I was getting there. I just hadn't decided if I was going to help you yet."

"And have you decided?" Ava asks.

He sighs deeply and speaks clearly, "I don't have all the answers, but I don't like what they're planning for my friends out there. Whatever you decide, just make it count."

CHAPTER 19

Bodin

"The way I see it, this city has three weaknesses: the air intake valves, reliance on technology, and the army. The only thing this city still needs from the outside is fresh air. The intake valves are a point of weakness. If you take those out, the city will run off of recycled, filtered air for a while, but eventually, the oxygen will get too low, and the residents will either need to vacate or they'll need to fix the valves."

"How long before they run out of air?"

He shrugs. "It could be weeks. I'd have to calculate based on CO_2 output, plant conversion rates, and cubic air space."

"Why is the army a weak point? Seems like that's their strong suit," I point out.

"That one is interesting. The army was forced into compliance. They were inoculated with annual shots, but they were unaware that a few years ago, the shots contained a gene-altering messenger RNA sequence. It turned on the 'Obedience' gene and turned down the 'Critical Thinking' gene. The interesting part is that they knew they needed to establish a source of authority before turning the obedience gene on so that the target knew who to listen to. The army was easy because they already identify the U.S. government as their authority figure. The problem they didn't anticipate was just how esoteric the U.S. Government was to the army and that the chain of command would be broken. The army had to hear direct orders from the U.S. President to act. You can imagine how cumbersome that became. They assassinated the president after the EMP, hoping that would solve their problem."

"So, the president's dead?" I ask.

"Yeah, not sure why or how it went down, but I know he's not here, and a new order was established so fast that it must have been preemptive."

"So, who's in charge of the army now?" I ask.

"You know the woman from the orientation video you watched when you arrived?" Mark asks.

"Yeahhhh..." I picture the woman with the slicked-back hair and thin, red lips. I ball my fists involuntarily at the thought of her.

"Well, she did many training videos for the army. They knew they needed a consistent message drilled into each soldier's head so they'd all have similar programming and they'd see similar results from the gene-altering shot. They didn't anticipate that that woman would become the face of the Government, which translated to her being the source of authority. *The* source after the president was announced dead." His eyes go wide with excitement.

"So, *she's* their leader?" I ask incredulously.

"Exactly." He sits back and folds his arms like he's finished with his explanation.

I'm trying to follow, but I'm going to have to swallow my pride and ask. "How is that a weakness?"

He reacts, as I suspected, with a condescending eye roll. "Without her, they have no leader. *Comprende*?"

"Ok. Wouldn't they default to the next person in line?" I ask.

"There's no one else that has anywhere near enough face time to become their new leader. It's got the new government sweating bullets. Plus, the effects wear off quickly and they have to keep getting reinoculated," he answers. "It's a real drag."

I guess I know what he's saying, but I decide just to catalog our conversation and let Frank work it out later.

He leans forward conspiratorially. "There's something else you need to know."

I raise my eyebrows. "Is it the brown pills they tell us to take?" I ask.

Mark's mouth forms an 'O'. His eyebrows pull together. Then he throws his head back and roars in laughter. I feel my face heat up. He takes a lot longer than is really necessary to stop laughing. "No," he says, attempting to reign in another chuckle. "Those are vitamins. What I was going to say is that they have a deadline of December first to bring in new recruits. They recruit from Salt Lake, Denver, and Reno."

"Why those places?" Ava asks.

"It's just about efficiency. They're the closest cities with the highest survival rates. The major cities south of those were hit with deadly heatwaves early on. Not pretty. Water ran out fast." I stare at him, trying not to picture the people who lived in those places. He continues, "If you plan on planting more from the outside, you'll have to act fast." With that, he looks me over, assessing me. "And I do suggest you and your little group do that. Just blowing up the intake valve from the outside won't be enough to bring them to their knees."

"Ok, but..." Ava interjects with an exasperated air. "How do we get out of Eyth?" Mark estimated we'd have an hour down here. We've got to be drawing near to that. It's clear both Ava and I feel it—the crunch of the clock.

"I think I've got a plan," he says. Ava and I exchange a hopeful look. "But you have to do me a favor," he adds.

"What's that?" I ask, suspicious.

"Take Lane with you," he says.

Ava bolts to her feet. "Why?" she challenges.

"It's only a matter of time before someone comes for him, and he gives up my name as a suspect. If he hasn't already. It's just better if he's gone. Makes things less complicated. Plus, you said he wanted out anyway. Win, win."

"Hardly," Ava says under her breath.

Mark leans forward, nodding his head to some thought that popped into his head. "Yeah, he could be useful. Lane can leave. He can walk out. No one cares if an elite leaves. They can go where they please. But you two...you two are trackable." He rubs his chin, deep in thought. "I'll have to deactivate your numbers, but that's so obvious..." I can practically see the wheels turning in his head. I'm hoping they click at some point. "This has to happen as soon as the door releases," he says, jumping to his feet.

Ava's face mirrors my own panic.

I feel the walls of anxiety closing in on me.

"When we're out of here, you guys go talk to Lane," Mark says.

"Without you?" Ava asks.

"I'm not going near that guy," he says.

Ava whimpers. "What am I supposed to say to him when Bodin and I show up alone?"

"He wants you to meet him in the Playboy room, right?" Mark asks.

I look over at Ava, unsure of what he's talking about. "Yeah," she responds.

"Tell him you'll get him out. The three of you will walk out."

"Just... walk out?" I ask.

"I'll go back to the office after this. Instead of deactivating your numbers, I'll reassign you to brown. Most of them work outside the city. You should be allowed to pass through the exit."

"Mid-day? When the rest are already working?" Ava asks, skeptical.

Mark takes a giant step in my direction, grabs the purple armband from my sleeve, and yanks. It rips. Mark pulls at it again and again until he rips it off. Ava is not in her standard recruit coveralls, so there's no patch to pull from her sleeve. There's still so much I want to ask her about.

"I know it's not perfect, but if you have Lane with you, sure, it'll be weird, but no one would dare try to stop you. They're all essential workers who guard and provide oversight to the recruits. In their eyes, Lane is above them. Should be easy. Just make sure you're long gone by the time they figure out you didn't return for the night with the rest of the Browns. I'm assuming Frank has a plan for when you're out?"

"Yeah," I answer. "He'll be waiting for us."

Ava looks at me, surprised, and then turns back to Mark to ask, "What if we're stopped?"

Mark runs his tongue along the inside of his lower lip as he plops back down on the bench. "Don't know," he says.

I let out a breath. "Fuck, this doesn't sound promising. Is there a Plan B?"

"Plan B will take considerably longer. By then, we may all be swinging. If there's any suspicion, they won't hesitate to exterminate us. They'll probably look into me a little more since I'm a Software Engineer and not as easily expendable, but still. It won't end well."

"Humor me," I say. "What's Plan B?"

He looks at me seriously. "There really is no Plan B. Not for me, anyway. You use Lane. This is the only way I can deflect suspicion."

With time running out, I have one more question that doubles nicely as a distraction from what's about to go down. "Why do the guys on the outside call it the Metal City when it's actually called Eyth?"

"The Metal City was just a nickname. They used it in the early days. Likely, that's all your guys on the outside know it as since that's what was used in the classified documents and the patent documents. Naming the city Eyth came after everyone moved in. We all voted. It was the first act of solidarity. Really, it was just a big show to make it seem like we were all equals here. The Metal City came from the fact that everything in here is hardened against EMP attacks. This city is like one big Faraday cage."

"Faraday cage?"

"Never mind," he says pointedly, brushing me off.

"Why don't you come with us?" Ava asks. I look at her, shocked.

Mark responds, "Not yet. You still need me here if you want a chance at succeeding and I've got code I need to bury. The dirty work falls to you guys now. Which is fate intervening. I wasn't sure I wanted to see this place shut down anymore." He looks far off, deep in his thoughts. Then, the muted siren from outside stops, and the dim red light turns to green. Mark jumps up, clapping his hands together. "It's go time," he says.

CHAPTER 20

Bodin

"Follow me, and don't talk," Mark tells us as we climb the ladder behind him. We squint against the sunlight as we make it onto the street. Many others also look disoriented, shading their eyes with their hands as they look around.

We follow Mark, who is walking at a brisk pace. He takes Ava and me to an unmarked door down an unmarked, dimly lit stairwell and knocks three times at the door at the bottom. A slat slides open to reveal the dark eyes of someone with a deep voice behind it. Mark holds his badge near where a door handle should be but is not.

From behind the doors, a chime comes through the slat that must signify his credentials have been verified because then the eyes say, "Sir."

"I have a delivery for the Playboy room," Mark answers and steps aside. He uses a sweep of his arm to indicate that it's us. If this is a strange request, the man doesn't let on. "You got it," he says as the door swings open to admit Ava and me. She looks behind us at Mark with terrified eyes. I see him give her one firm nod. His hands are placed in his pants pockets. Then the door slams shut, and Mark is gone.

"Follow me," the gruff voice commands.

I take this moment to grab Ava's damp hand and give it a reassuring squeeze. *I'm not going to let anything happen to you*, is the message I'm attempting to convey. She smiles gratefully at me and keeps hold of my hand. My heart skips a beat.

A reverberation causes a vibration in my chest every time the bass hits. A few curious eyes follow us. Our escort is just the kind of burly, bald man I expected to be behind the deep voice at the door. The bartender gives him a look, and he nods, passing along some silent communication. The bartender returns to drying wine glasses. He holds one up to the dim light, looking for imperfections.

Once we've entered the elevator in the lobby and gone down to level two, we step out onto the thick carpet and pad silently down a dark hallway with padded walls. There's a light above each door. Some are different colors. Each illuminates a room name: I read 'Nurse,' 'Massage,' and 'BDMN.' I look at Ava, who has eyes round as quarters. She gulps. We exchange knowing looks. We reach the Playboy room. Ava's hand is positively wet now. It takes all of my self-control not to release her tight grip to wipe my hand on my pants. The man knocks twice with authority and then turns to leave, not bothering to wait for an answer.

When the door swings open, Ava releases my hand immediately.

So, this is Lane. He looks manic right now with his wild, desperate eyes and messy hair, but he's ultimately disappointing. I pictured someone meaner-looking, I guess. This guy is what I'd call a pretty boy. Though, he's old. Maybe Ted's age? So, pretty man? He could be on the cover of some billionaire romance novel—Fifty Shades-type stuff. Or maybe I'm just thinking that because of where we are. Sex toys are hanging on a wall behind Lane, and a vast, oval bed with a Red Velvet comforter is in the back of the room.

His eyes barely register me. "Where the fuck have you been?" he growls at Ava. I step forward, protectively. This guy looks like he's got some muscle, but I still have him in height. He turns a menacing glare on me.

"We had to hunker down for the bomb drill," Ava says, moving around me. He steps aside, and I follow Ava inside. He closes the door behind us.

"Where's Mark?" he asks quickly. Then he gives me a more thorough look over. "And who the fuck is this?"

I glare at this man. He needs to know that I won't take his shit and that I already don't like him. Lane glares back.

"This is Bodin," Ava explains. "I knew him from before, and Mark wouldn't come, but we did talk to him."

"We?" Lane looks between the two of us, trying to figure out how we fit together.

"Bodin was looking for Mark, too."

"Why?" His tone is sharp.

"Long story," I respond as I fold my arms across my chest. Ava frowns at me like she disapproves of my bravado. I wonder what this dude has over her. He doesn't look that scary to me.

Ava breaks our stare-down. "He says we need to leave. Now. All of us."

Lane narrows his eyes at her but seems to be considering this. "How?" he asks.

I'm shocked that this guy is entertaining the idea, but I'm also relieved because up until now, I had forgotten just how badly we need him to get out of here. The other Crawlers will be wondering where I am by now. Who else is wondering? Or will Mark take care of this when he changes us to Brown?

"He said to just leave with you. He said he'd reassign our numbers to Brown and that we'd be allowed to walk out."

"Just, walk out?" Lane asks as if we've requested he strip naked.

"Yeah," Ava says, less sure of herself now.

Lane scoffs. "Some plan," he says under his breath.

"Mark said they'd never question an elite," Ava adds. I notice how Lane stands a little taller upon hearing that.

"No, maybe not," he says as he eyes us. "I've got an idea. Follow me." He exits the room and walks deeper into the hallway away from the elevators. He stops in front of a door with a white light above it. It reads, "Office."

"Good, it's vacant," Lane says as he punches in some codes and answers some prompts on a small screen set into the door above the handle. The door opens. Lane strides in like he knows the place and begins opening drawers. He pulls out a suit, eyeballs me, and then puts it back before grabbing another one. He throws it across a chair that sits in front of a vanity like a star's dressing room prop. Then he pulls out a skirt suit for Ava. Ava shakes her head, apparently thinking further ahead than I am.

"I may need to run," she says. "Is there a women's pant suit? And different shoes?"

"Good thinking," Lane says and pulls something else out. I notice Ava perk up at the compliment. I hate the kind of pull this guy has on her. Lane is watching us. "Well, what are you waiting for?"

"For you to turn around," I say.

Lane rolls his eyes and turns around. Once we've dressed, he stands back and assesses us. He looks at Ava and frowns. He strides over and releases her hair from her bun. It falls in a dark cascade down her back. He begins pulling strands out and arranging them along her face. My breathing is shallow. The way he looks at her and touches her has my fists balled at my side. It's like she's his possession.

"Right, then," he says. "I guess we'll need provisions. Someone is waiting for us on the other side, right?"

He's asking Ava, but I answer, "Yes." It's been exactly one week. They should be waiting for us now. Lane turns to me and frowns before walking toward what looks like a metal trap door on the wall and an electric panel next to it. He pats it like it's a favorite pet. I give Ava a look. "What's up with this guy?" I mouth.

"Any last meal requests?" Lane asks without deigning to look at us.

"Pizza," Ava responds. I look at her, confused. Is she for real? Is Lane for real? Playing along couldn't hurt, I suppose.

"Burger and fries," I say. "And a milkshake."

Lane types into the keypad, and a countdown begins on the display.

"What is that thing?" I ask.

"Food panel," Lane responds. I raise my eyebrows, astonished, and look at Ava. She nods, confirming what Lane has said.

"Wait, so do I really get a burger and fries?" I ask, unable to keep eager anticipation from my voice.

"And a milkshake," Lane says. My mouth begins watering immediately. I shake my head in disbelief. We're eating goddamn insect meal bars, and these guys have a food panel in every room where anything they could ever want is delivered in minutes? I go to war in my head at hating Lane for this and being grateful to Lane for this.

"I also got us bottled waters and meal bars for the road," he says. I wrinkle my nose at this. Lane sighs. "I know, but they come packaged, they're shelf-stable, and they're packed with calories and nutrition. It's just the most practical choice," he says, resigned.

Lane seems more subdued and less angry since the reality of our escape is setting in. I don't blame him. Why would you ever leave a food panel, water, and a bed? He's running for his life here. There's no other explanation. I guess elites are known to eat their own occasionally, too.

The food comes, and it is heaven on a tray. I do my best to savor it. I share my milkshake with Ava, who lacked the foresight to get one for herself. What did Lane mean about this being "the last meal"? Maybe not the *last* last meal, but the last meal that'll ever resemble a meal from before the EMP. It's so weird watching it disappear. I want to make it linger, but it's a matter of seconds before it disappears. And infuriatingly, my obsession over this last meal shit is taking away some of the enjoyment. Still, I try to commit it to memory so I can revisit this moment at a future time. Maybe then, I can enjoy the hot, crispy fries and the melted, gooey cheese that oozes from the burger. Oh, and the bun. The soft, bread bun that smashes beneath my grip. It's divine.

Lane has a backpack filled with water bottles and meal bars. He places a ballcap on his head and gives us a nod. Ava tips the last of the milkshake into her mouth and searches the bottom for more. She must sense it, too. That this is it for the decadent food items we took for granted just months ago.

"We can exit one of two ways: the new recruit entrance or the exit for the field workers. I'll make a gameday decision as we approach and go with the one my gut is telling me," Lane says.

We nod. I feel my nerves kick up the burger in my stomach. Maybe it wasn't such a good idea to eat so much. It sits like a brick in my belly. We follow Lane out into the sunlit streets, where I have to shield my eyes from the onslaught of it. Lane moves at a brisk walk. We keep up, a pace behind. We round corner after corner, the gap between Lane and us is growing. As we turn another and Lane comes back into view, he's taken off running. Ava and I exchange worried looks before we break into a run after him. What the fuck is he playing at?

I'm out of breath. Ava is, too. She's fallen behind me a little. I can still barely make out Lane. The dudes in shape. Finally, a landmark I recognize looms above us. It's the crooked tree that hangs over the building, just a block or two in front of the new recruit building.

I yell back to Ava, "Almost there!" Some people are milling about. Most look at us with bewilderment and annoyance, but no one cries for help or pursues us. We must look like spoiled elite kids now or young business professionals in our ridiculous suits.

I see the building. Recognize the double doors. No guards stand outside of them today. Lane has long disappeared from my view. I slow up to let Ava catch me. We bend over our knees and suck in rapid breaths.

"We did it," I say through huffs.

"Not yet," Ava says. And I know what she means. We still have to try opening the door and walking through it. I place my hands behind my head like we used to do in football practice when we were winded.

"Come on," I encourage Ava. "Before someone gets suspicious."

She stands back up and mimics the hand-lock behind her head. We walk towards the door. Once in front of it, I take in a deep breath and yank. It opens. Now, we just have to step through the threshold. I close my eyes and step inside. There's a ping registering a scan, but then nothing. Ava steps in behind me. Our eyes lock, wide with the thrill of it.

I look in front of us. No artificial lights. The sun filters in through the covered office windows lining the hallway. They must not be expecting new recruits today. We take a few steps. Our footsteps echo loudly. I place a finger up to my lips and remove my shoes. Ava does the same. We tip-toe through the hallways as I repeat what I hope is an accurate retrace of my steps that day—left, left, right, left.

Then, the green door is in front of us. I push it open, and we enter the seating area we had used the first day. It's deserted. It's warmer, too, and the smell is different. The floor is packed earth. The rows of metal chairs in the emptiness look like gravestones. The back of the area where we were unloaded from the truck has a long line of sunshine illuminating the flap that gets pulled back to allow trucks to back up when they've got recruits to offload. That's all that's standing between us and freedom now, a flap of heavy fabric.

I move quickly in that direction, but I realize Ava isn't following. I turn back and see her staring at the yellow door on the opposing wall. I shake my head slowly, still afraid to pierce the silence with my voice. She takes in a breath and looks down at the floor. She closes her eyes almost as if she's saying a prayer for Sarah or talking herself out of whatever she is considering. Then she follows me out.

We squint against the barren, naked landscape before us. The sun is already hot on our heads. We turn to each other and smile.

Then, we run.

I look behind us frequently, but no one is pursuing. After a minute, I hold Ava back and remove the blazer I was given. I hold it up above my head and use it as a shield from the sun. Ava does the same with hers. Thank you, business professional attire. I don't know when Frank will spot us or when they'll be here, but I hope soon. Lane took our water, and I'm quickly losing my body's reserves through my pores and down my back and forehead. It's hot out here. Really hot. And then, Ava points to something. I narrow my eyes. It looks like a tiny dark speck that could be anything, but we walk towards it anyway. As we get closer and the dark speck comes into view, we exchange looks. It's Lane, and he's walking towards us.

"What the fuck?" I snarl as I push Lane back hard. He holds his hands up in defense.

"I just had to distance myself from you guys in case you tripped the alarms." He looks at the black numbers on our wrists. "I was waiting for you out here."

I don't know what to believe right now, but as Lane takes off the backpack and tosses each of us a water, my anger diffuses. I can't say I would have done anything differently. It was smart.

"You might want to slow down," Lane says to us. "We don't know how long we'll have to conserve water." Ava screws the lid back on and then stops mid-action, her attention snagged by something on the horizon. I follow her eyes and see a trail of dust.

"A vehicle?" I ask.

"I think so," says Ava. We walk toward it.

Twenty minutes later, a beautiful sight comes to a stop before us. It's Frank and Crowly on their two dusty electric motorcycles. The two images, the motorcycles and the SEALs, have begun to fuse as one in my head. Those are their babies or an extension of themselves, like an extra appendage.

I watch Frank remove his helmet and hold it in the crook of his arm while he assesses us. His blue eyes are steely, his expression stern. "We weren't expecting three," he says, eyeing Lane.

"I know," I say. "We'll explain later. Can we just get out of the sun?"

Frank nods at me and barks out orders. Ava, Crowly, and Lane smash together on one bike, Frank and I on the other. The wind in my face is a welcome respite, but I'm aware that my skin is still burning. My lips feel as if they've been dipped in boiling water. It isn't long before we reach a rocky outcropping. Strewn-up tarps, the color of the desert sand amplify the shade. I dive under it when we arrive. Once I'm comfortable, Frank comes over and ducks beneath the tarp, joining me on the ground. I watch as Crowly, Lane, and Ava have a private conversation once they dismount from their bike. Lane extends his hand to Crowly who lets it linger before giving it a quick shake. I look away. Frank and I stare silently at the image of the domed city in the distance. The sun glints off of its surface. The dark outlines of tall buildings are just visible from this distance.

"You did it, kid," Frank says quietly, jerking his head towards Ava. I try not to, but I can't help it—I smile.

Ava, Crowly, and Lane join us beneath the shade.

"Why did you leave the city?" Frank asks Lane as he leans back, propped on one elbow. All of us shift our eyes to the city in the distance.

"Eyth wasn't for me," Lane responds. "Too many rules. Plus, it wasn't fair what they did to you all. I never agreed with it." I see Ava squirm from her position towards the back of our group. Lane keeps his eyes on the city, but Ava and I watch him like he's a crouched tiger.

"How do you all know Lane?" Frank asks as he looks behind him at Ava and me.

Ava shifts positions and then changes again as she tries to get comfortable.

Lane answers for her, "Ava was my employee. She cleaned house for me."

Frank and Crowly look between Ava and Lane and then at each other. It happens so quickly that I almost don't catch it, but I do. Lane glowers at Ava, who's still silent.

"Yep," she responds finally in a high-pitched tone.

We lounge the rest of the hot afternoon away as we catch up on everything that's happened and, of most interest to Frank and Crowly, the story behind Lane's jailbreak.

We never venture from beneath the canopy that Crowly and Frank had strung between two cacti on a bluff. Crowly and Frank kept an eye on the exit points out of the city, but nothing happened. No pursuit.

Night begins to fall. The colors it throws across the desert sky are mesmerizing, but those aren't the best part. The stars that follow them are. I never noticed the stars under the dome because I was always locked away in my quarters by nightfall, but out here, they blanket the night sky. I've never seen so many before.

Crowly and Frank have two bunk cots to keep us off the ground. Ava will sleep above Crowly, and I'll sleep above Frank. Since we're the lightest, we get the top bunks. I figure the cots are to elevate us from the snakes and other creepy crawlies, but I'm too tired to ask, and I know it'll be more unnerving to hear the reasons why out loud. Lane is tossed a jacket to sleep in. He takes it with a scowl. Frank and Crowly have made their disapproval of him evident from the start, but I think Lane has managed to ingratiate himself somewhat. I can tell it's hard for him to put on that face, but what choice does he have? We're his best shot at survival now. Still, the fall from his ivory tower was a painful one, I'm sure.

We leave before the sun makes an appearance, but its glow in the distance is perceptible as it intrudes on the deep purple night sky—backlighting the behemoth silhouettes of rock formations on the horizon. There are still thousands of stars illuminated in the center of the sky. I pass out the meal bars for breakfast. Lane looks disdainfully at the offering but wisely chooses to keep his remarks to himself as he takes a tentative bite. Even though it was an intelligent choice, I can tell by his hesitation that he knows what they're made from, and he wishes he'd brought something else. I smile at his discomfort and take a big bite of mine. Ava eats unbothered, too. I wonder if I should tell Frank and Crowly what they're made of.

I watch them chew and mutter, "Not bad," and "Mmm, hmm." A smile spreads across my face. I think I'll keep this knowledge in my back pocket for another time.

We drink from canteens. Crowly and Frank exchange glances as Ava passes the canteen to Lane, who gulps greedily despite having additional water bottles in his backpack.

Lane and I end up on the back of Frank's bike, and Ava is with Crowly. I don't like the sight of them. Frank is probably forty—too old for Ava, but Crowly is younger. Hard to say how much younger, but he doesn't have the same forehead lines and streaks of gray along his temples as Frank does. A couple of hours into the ride, Frank and Crowly stop the bikes.

"Pee break," we're informed. We all shed a layer of clothing as the sun becomes increasingly intense. Frank and Crowly remove the seats from the bikes, revealing shiny black solar panels.

"Bike at forty percent," Frank tells Crowly.

I step away to do my business and stretch my legs. I do some jumping jacks to loosen my stiff body.

"Can I try driving?" I ask when I've rejoined the group.

"Hell no," Frank grunts.

I shrug my shoulders. Worth a shot.

Frank digs into a compartment on the bike and tosses a white tube in my direction. I snatch it out of the air deftly, hoping Ava saw. I look at it. It's sunscreen.

"Lather up," Frank commands. We take turns passing it around.

"I think if we consider the weight distribution, Ava and Bodin should ride with Frank. I'll take Lane for the rest of the day," Crowly states as he smooths the white paste over his muscular arms.

I want to make the comment that Lane and I probably weigh the same, but I hold it back because it means Ava will probably have her arms wrapped around me on the bike.

Frank agrees with a head jerk, and we mount the bikes. I have to make a snap decision. Either Ava puts her arms around me or Frank. I get in behind Frank, leaving the rear to Ava. I'm acutely aware that my crotch is too close to Frank, and Ava's arms around me might arouse me. I squirm uncomfortably to try to get some space between Frank and me, but it only puts friction on my junk. I swallow hard. I didn't think this through. I could have had my arms around Ava. Too late now.

We zip along at high speeds. At first, it made me nervous, but now I have supreme confidence in their driving skills. Plus, it helps that there's no one else on the road. We've run over a rodent, and I'm pretty sure we flattened a snake too. It's been a few hours, and the skin on my arms is definitely burning despite the sunscreen. The terrain all looks the same to me. Hills, sand, dirt, rocks, a few scraggly trees here and there, and cacti. Lots of cacti.

I tap on Frank's shoulder and yell over the wind, "Can we take a break soon?"

"Just a few more minutes," he shouts over his shoulder. I squirm. My ass is starting to throb.

I watch a shape in the distance start out small but then get more prominent as we approach. I kept guessing what it was right up until we pulled up next to it, and Frank parked in its shade—the carcass of a Boeing 757.

Sand has blown up against the shattered cabin, burying half of it beneath its golden weight. The tailfin is nowhere in sight. One wing is intact, pointing at an upward angle and casting a long shadow, which we are currently taking advantage of.

"Don't look inside," Frank says as he dismounts after us and wheels the bike a few feet into the sun, where he exposes their panels for charging again and kicks the kickstand out. I turn to look at the looming plane and gulp at the size of it. A queasy feeling pits in my stomach. I used to hate flying. I hear the second bike pull up beside us and turn to see Crowly parking the bike. Alone.

"Dude, where's Lane?!" I shout unnecessarily loud over the quiet hum of the engine. Crowly turns the key, and the bike elevates slightly as he swings his leg over, relieving the shocks of the burden. Crowly removes his helmet and runs his hands through his hair with all the coolness of a cucumber.

"Where's Lane?"

He shrugs. "Must have fallen off."

"Wait, what? What do you mean?" I ask.

He shrugs again, and now I'm starting to get it. "What did you do to him?" It sounds harsher than I intended. I'm surprised by my tone. I don't particularly like Lane, but this is getting me worked up.

Crowly's calmness is pierced momentarily as he makes an ugly face and says, "Prick deserved it."

I huff indignantly. "We have to go back for him," I say, looking back into the endless sea of sand. Frank puts a hand on my shoulder.

"Crowly is right. Let it go, Bodin," he says. Although his deep voice is laden with finality, I find myself storming internally. I rake my hand through my hair, flustered. I turn around wildly and look at Ava, but I'm at a loss for words, so I just raise my arm in a "Can you believe this?" gesture. Then, she does what Crowly did—she shrugs.

"Oh, come on!" I shout at no one in particular. "This is a *person*. A human being. You can't just leave him in the desert!"

No one responds, but Ava moves closer.

"Bodin," she says in a gentle voice. "I knew him better than anyone. He would have done the same to you or me in an instant. He is not one of us. He only cares about us if it means he gets something in return. When that dynamic ends, his loyalties will shift. He was a... *liability*."

I feel the fight evaporating from me as I look into her pleading eyes. I know she's right. They all are. My shoulders relax as a tension I didn't realize I was holding is released. I scratch awkwardly at my right ear.

"Alright," I say quietly. I'm a bit embarrassed by my outburst, but I still feel the grip of indignation on behalf of Lane holding me.

"Drink, pee, and let's get moving," Frank says as he tosses a water bottle my way. I catch it deftly and hold it out towards Ava to drink first. I notice it has a Delta label on it.

"Did you get this from in there?" I ask, gesturing towards the plane.

"Yep," Frank says. "This aircraft is what's been sustaining us out here."

I look at the plane again with renewed interest and see the figure of a person through one of the windows. Despite the heat, I feel my cheeks blaze further. From the corner of my eye, I catch Frank watching me. I turn around and look out to the horizon as I wait for my turn to drink. *So long, Lane.* Guess it's true what they say, Karma is a real bitch. If I'm honest with myself, I feel a weight has lifted. My mind has been freed up like an internet browser running in the background, slowing down my computer, has been turned off.

I shift my thoughts and feel myself yearning to return to the ranch to see Evie. I want to hear her squeal when she sees me. I want to watch her blonde curls bounce as she runs towards me. I want to feel the weight of her in my arms as I scoop her up. I want to feel the softness of her body still clinging to the last remnants of baby fat as I squeeze her tight.

Ava bumps my arm with the water bottle, and I take it as I shrug off the daydream. I drink fast.

"Let's go," I say as I screw the cap on.

"Woah there, tiger. Use the bathroom."

"Yes, sir," I say as I salute Frank, who returns my gaiety with a scowl. I do as he says and find a spot slightly hidden behind the bike to unzip with my back to the others. The sound of my urine hitting the dirt cuts through the silence.

CHAPTER 21

Ava

October 25, 2025

The fire crackles, and I scoot back as I wave away the smoke. Frank, Crowly, and Bodin laugh, but I can see Bodin is uncomfortable with the line of dialogue. I don't much care for the backslaps of men boasting about their female conquests, either. I've been largely quiet, but I decide a subject change is warranted.

I clear my throat. "What's your guys' stories?" I ask Crowly and Frank. They exchange a glance. Crowly shrugs, and Frank pokes at the fire with a stick.

"Oh, come on," I prod. "How'd you guys get here and assume the role of vigilantes?"

Crowly sighs with resignation. "Someone leaked a classified document. Long story short, Frank was one of the recipients. He met with me shortly thereafter to discuss it. I checked with one of my sources and found some interesting things. Or didn't find some interesting things. Both were equally as important. Anyway, we prepared for the possibility that it was all true."

I squint at Crowly. "You know you can say more things now, right? I don't think old rules apply. Why not divulge the details a little?"

He does another one of his iconic shrugs and says, "It's not that interesting."

"Ok, so, here. How did you get *here?*" I point to the earth beneath my feet.

"Motorcycle," he says as he jerks his head towards the bikes we rode in on. I roll my eyes. He grins at his wit, and it's not the first time I've noticed his smile. He's not someone who would stop me on the street with his looks, but when his smiles break through his usually serious demeanor, something inside me stirs.

"Ha ha," I demure as I look away, hoping I'm not blushing.

Frank decides to jump in at this point. "I grew up near here. My whole family lives close by. It also just happens to be an ideal strategic location, given the absence of civilians. We stashed weapons in an abandoned mine in the area. We came back to retrieve them. There can't be an uprising without weapons."

"So, your family lives here, and you decided it was a good place to stage a rebellion?"

"Pretty much," he says.

"Huh. What did that classified document say?" I ask.

Crowly scratches his nose, and Frank waits out the silence until Crowly speaks. "It was basically an outline of a large-scale water reclamation project."

Bodin chimes in, "What? How was that relevant?"

Crowly elaborates, as though feeling more verbose like he's hit a stride. He's probably been so used to keeping it tight-lipped that the feeling of release must be soothing. "A *classified* water reclamation project in and of itself is interesting, but what grabbed our attention was the location. It was in the middle of a desert, and the city's name was unfamiliar to us. They called it the Metal City. Anyway, it was a breadcrumb. Frank started looking into other large purchase contracts and found tons of money and resources being pulled from other projects throughout the years. Purchase orders for raw materials, manufactured goods, labor, etc... It all suggested extensive infrastructure was being built in a concentrated area, but there weren't any projects like it that were known in the public sphere. I knew... *someone...*" he clears his throat. "...in satellite surveillance at Homeland Security, and I had her scout the Sonoran Desert. She found it. A massive, high-tech city was nearly complete. She found several others around the world, too."

Woah. I wait for them to continue. Crowly shifts nervously and looks at Frank, who stares down at his feet.

"Then another document was sent," Frank adds. "This one was an order for an EMP attack on the United States signed by United States officials, sent through Homeland Security."

Crowly takes a deep breath. "The woman who helped us, Sal. She was found dead two days later. They called it a kayaking accident, but we know it wasn't an accident. That's when we knew for sure that there was no turning back. We had to lay low and plan carefully."

Frank picks up the story again. "We found Project Metal City stamped on all kinds of patents. The picture became pretty clear after that. There would be an EMP attack on the unsuspecting public, and high-up officials and others with exclusive invitations had a safe place to go while the world crumbled around them, and I guess now we know why."

I nod. Bodin had imparted the latest version of the Era Unveiling that Mark bestowed upon us and the elite's plans for the five cities last night. Lane was still around. He pretended not to know much about it, but I noticed the slightest smirk on his face.

"Who is Mark to you guys?" I ask.

"Mark Bird. A private security contractor for the government who was far smarter than they gave him credit. That's who leaked those initial documents. He found us one night. Tucked in the corner of a bar. Said if he could find us, so could they. He covered our digital tracks for us, filled in most of the blanks, and together we formed a plan. Only, we didn't know their full end game. But those details hardly matter. The response was always going to be the same: armed citizens putting up a fight and taking back power."

"Ok..." The thought of an armed resistance sends shivers down my spine. We told Frank and Crowly most of what Mark told us, but I still get the feeling they're not grasping the impossibility of attacking that city. They have a bomb shield for crying out loud, and technology far more advanced than anyone here has ever operated. I avoid the subject.

"So, how did you two meet?" I ask, nodding to indicate Crowly and Frank.

"How did you all meet?" Bodin adds. "And why does everyone call you the SEALs? Are you really SEALs?"

"SEALs?" I ask, not following.

"There are three more just like these two here," Bodin says. "They dress the same, walk the same, talk the same. They're like their own little pack. Yeah, what's the story?"

Frank picks at his teeth with his fingernail, and I cringe, knowing the kind of bacteria he must be introducing into his body. "We served together," he says.

"Frank was my sergeant during my second tour," Crowly says. "I follow Frank because I respect him. After I left the army, I went into personal training. Frank tapped me on the shoulder early on and brought me into the loop. It felt good to get back into it."

"What about the other SEALs?" Bodin asks.

Crowly looks at Frank and, when he doesn't answer, says, "Frank's the thread here."

"Hutchins and Stevens went home. It's just Miller, Crowly, and me now," Frank states. He squirms on his log. "They're all guys I knew I could trust—all former military. None of us is a Navy SEAL. We were all Army, but if Miller were here, he'd make sure you knew he was Special Forces."

"Why them?" I ask Frank.

"I'm the only one who stayed in the military, but I left infantry for a desk job about seven years ago. I chose them because they were all defectors in some way," he glances at Crowly. "They all had their reasons, but at the root of it was trust—or lack thereof—for our country's leadership."

Crowly nods. "It's a good thing, too. A civilian came in handy when trying to move massive weapon reserves around."

"That too." Frank smiles one of his rare lopsided smiles.

"If you were in the army, how'd you avoid the gene-altering jab you told me about?" Bodin asks.

"They weren't pushing it on personnel like they were for active members in the infantry. I was slotted for it. Had an appointment on my calendar, but I never made it. I just kept kicking the can down the road, and I'm not sure why."

"I do," Crowly says. "Because you're smarter than that."

"Maybe. Or maybe it was just dumb luck, but I will say this: if I hadn't missed that first appointment by accident, I would have gotten it. It was something about their persistence in pursuing the issue that flagged something in me."

We're all quiet for a moment. Then, I figured enough time had passed to take the opening. "So, if you were on your second tour when Frank was your sergeant, that would make you how old?" I ask Crowly, averting my eyes. When I look up, he's looking at me with amusement.

"That would make me thirty-one," he says, smiling broadly. I look away. *Please don't blush. Please don't blush.* I do the mental calculation of the age difference quickly. Nine years. That's not so bad.

Bodin, clearly unaware of the loaded exchange between us, chimes in, "So why do you all dress like that all the time?"

Frank leans back and kicks his feet out in front of him. "It commands respect, that's why."

"Oh," he says.

"Worked on you, didn't it?" Frank asks playfully.

"I guess so," he mutters.

The conversation fizzles out. Frank gets our cots and instructs us to insulate below us with whatever we can find so the air doesn't steal as much of our body heat. We see grass in the direct proximity of the camp and layer it on top of the cots beneath our sleeping sacks. Frank and Crowly use their spare clothing. It's strange that it comes to me just now, but I'm aware of just how few possessions I have now, and it's unsettling. The pantsuit I'm still wearing is obviously not made from quality material. For its costume purposes, it's stiff and scratchy. We leave the fire burning low and pull the cot bunks around it. Crowly and Frank take the lower bunks. I sleep above Crowly, and Bodin rests above Frank.

In the morning, Crowly tells us he has an assignment and asks us to go to the ranch without him. He says he'll meet us there tomorrow. Of course, Frank knows what's going on, but neither one wants to tell us. I feel disappointment and curiosity as I watch him ride away.

After a breakfast of oatmeal, we break camp. The cot bunks unfold into a surprisingly small square that fits into one of the two built-in compartments on the motorbikes. As I attempt to finagle the deconstructed cot into the designated compartment, I realize just how light Frank and Crowly have to pack when they're on these trips. Evidently, the bikes are built for stealth and speed, not carrying capacity.

"Ava is the lightest. It helps if she's on the back," Frank says to Bodin. They both look displeased at this prospect.

I'm careful to hold onto Bodin in the most "friend-like" manner I can muster, but I don't want to fall off, and I don't think Bodin can distinguish between the two touches. He just knows that I'm touching him. I can feel him tense when my hands grab his waist.

The back of the motorcycle is incredibly peaceful, but during the long stretches where landscapes blur together in one seemingly long reel, my mind wanders. I wonder how I can communicate to Bodin that he's nothing more than a brother-type to me. I don't want to hurt him, but I don't want to string him along, either. He's a good kid. I wonder what he's feeling right now as he gets closer and closer to his people. His family.

Sarah is gone. She was my closest tie to my past life. I feel adrift in a world that seems to change by the minute. I used to suffer from anxiety when I worked at the hospital, and I'm surprised that ever since walking out of that city, it's disappeared completely. I would have expected it to get worse with so much uncertainty and constant threats to my life, but it's done the opposite. Life is different now. It's like the noise in the background has finally been unplugged, and I can focus on the simple, important matter of surviving. There are no workplace relationship dynamics to navigate or money problems to bear on my shoulders. There's no lingering expectation to behave a certain way or achieve something great. There's no pressure to receive likes on Facebook or followers on Instagram. I had a boyfriend before, but I didn't think that was going to end up in marriage anyway. It was pure fun. Almost nothing was worth keeping from my life before the EMP, and it's only now that I realize how shallow my existence really was.

Of course, my parents and my sister are the exceptions. I would give almost anything to be able to talk to them again. To know they're ok. But they're not here. It's just me. Right here, right now. Sure, there are times I torture myself with the what-ifs, but they don't leave a taste in my mouth. Not like before when the weight of my thoughts would linger and disrupt my peace. Being completely cut loose and knowing that everyone is in the same situation is somehow freeing.

Although, I imagine Ted, Bodin's stepdad, would think of life now differently with a dead wife and a little girl to look after in an uncertain world.

***

It's been three days since we left Eyth. After the first day, the motorcycles ran out of charge, and we had to take significant chunks of our daylight hours to charge them. Frank does not like the idea of riding at night. So, it was out of the question.

The landscape is beautiful—high, snow-covered peaks approach from the distance. We pass over rivers and ride alongside their raging white-capped rapids. The air has gotten progressively cooler, and I imagine my cheeks are now a deep rose. The cold always makes me look like a painted doll. Every now and then, I catch the scent of pine, and it reminds me of Christmas. My family lives in Minnesota. Every year, I'd go home for Christmas, though this year hospital admin informed me I'd have to work Christmas, but I could have Thanksgiving off because last year was my Christmas year. One of the downfalls of working in a place that never shuts down, I guess.

All of that is moot now. I hope my family doesn't worry too much about me. I don't worry too much about them. I can't explain it, but I know I'll see them again one day. They've got each other, and they're brilliant. They also live in the country, away from a major city. Mom is an active community member and has many friends. Dad is more reserved, but he's resourceful. My younger sister, Clair, started her senior year of high school this year. She can be a snot, but she's strong. That's also why Bodin will never resemble a romantic prospect to me. He's too much like my little sister. They'd probably be friends. Or hey, maybe even date. If only she were here, I could be like, *sorry, Bodin, I'm too old for you, but have you met my little sister*? She would slug me so hard if that ever happened in real life. She is beautiful, though. Like me, she has long dark hair, milky brown eyes surrounded by thick lashes, and our signature long pointed nose Mom gave us. Once, in an attempt to flirt, a plastic surgeon at the hospital told me I had the kind of nose he sculpts for his patients.

I begin to notice more housing and other signs of life. Frank drives slower now, weaving around the occasional vehicle carcass with deftness. His presence comforts me. It's his appearance, big, strong, and capable, but it's also his demeanor. His confidence never wavers.

Frank has a square face, and his hair is cut too close to his scalp, military-style, but he's still an attractive man. He has a slight cleft to his chin and the stubble of a beard that's only recently been neglected. I imagine the prickle of his beard on my skin before I shake it off, embarrassed. He's too old for me. Crowly is the better prospect, but I'm not sure I'm ready to explore these thoughts.

I still think of my boyfriend, Kyle, sometimes. Since we never officially broke it off, I find I still associate my relationship status with him even though I'll probably never see him again. I feel differently about him than I do my family. He feels... *farther* somehow. Gone maybe. He chose the wrong time to travel. I feel my chest tighten and take a deep breath before I start to cry. I've been so lucky, but I know for most people, they've been on the opposite end of that stick.

I look up and notice a Welcome to Challis sign. The population is listed at close to 1,000. Somehow, the triple digits signifying inhabitants revs my nerves a bit. I see numerous plumes of smoke rising nearby. I hold onto Bodin a little tighter.

We pass through the town largely unnoticed, thanks to the fact that the highway doesn't bisect it, and the motorcycles have an engine that sounds more like the whir of a microwave than a motor on a Harley.

I know we're getting close now. We've been following the Salmon River for about thirty minutes. A sign announced it as we passed over a bridge that towered over the water. We've been riding alongside it ever since. Bodin told me about the river and the ranch last night. He didn't know much about the town but said we'd reach the ranch before the town. I'm getting anxious to see the place I will likely call home for the foreseeable future.

But then again, with a possible attack on Eyth looming, I suppose all of that could be part of a fantasy—a desire to protect some notion of normalcy. The thought of attempting revenge is the only thing that penetrates my newfound resignation and leaves a lingering stink.

CHAPTER 22

Bodin

October 27, 2025

I can hardly sit still. I want the bike to go faster. We follow a dirt road up a gulch as we approach the mountains. We reach the familiar blockade they made using dynamite to secure the small valley the ranch occupies. I jump off the bike and run the second my feet hit the dirt.

I hear Frank behind me. "Someone's eager to be home," he says, but it fades behind me as I use my long legs to climb the dirt wall like a gazelle.

Lookouts announce our arrival with shouts of, "They're back!"

I stop for a moment on top of the blockade and look out at the familiar valley below. It's only been two weeks, but I can tell there are building additions. Or skeletons of ones, anyway. I push off again, half-running, half-sliding down the back of the blockade and towards the home site that was assigned to Ted, Evie, Alex, and me.

I pass people who provide various greetings and questions, but I'm only paying them enough attention to take note that they're not Evie or Ted. Out of breath, I finally reach the hut. I put my hands on my knees for a second, take a deep breath, and then straighten as I push aside the fabric shower curtain that poses as the door. My mood plunges when I stare into the empty space.

I look around. It hasn't changed much, but there are a few additions to the basic, one-room hut we've been calling home. For one thing, the log jams have been filled. There's also a curtain adorning the previously naked window. The three mismatched wooden chairs and small kitchen table are in one corner. On top of the table are some crayons and a coloring book. Around the fire, there are a couple of new pots. There are a few things stacked on a shelf: two books, some dishes, a frame for the family picture I'm used to seeing, and a couple of candles. There's still the queen mattress on the floor that Ted and I carried on our backs for miles. To my disappointment, he still hasn't managed to secure another one, but I guess he probably needed my help for that. There also isn't much room for one. Maybe a twin in the last corner. The bed is a mess, piled with blankets and a few articles of clothing that also double as blankets in the night. Ted was never good about picking up after himself, and, at four years old, Evie certainly isn't going to make the bed for him.

I take one last glance at the life we live now before pushing the curtain aside and stepping back outside. I shield the sun from my eyes, wishing I had sunglasses.

"They're not here," someone says with a voice that shakes with age.

I look over at an old man who carries a bucket and a spackle. His hands and clothes are splattered with a thick gray material.

"Evie is at school," he says, then turns and points to the big house. "They've been hosting classes in the basement there Monday through Friday. Trying to give the kids some sense of normalcy, I guess." He has a slight accent and seems far too eager to keep chatting. My legs itch to carry me up to the house, but he keeps going. "And Ted is with the logging crew today, securing more firewood up in those parts." He points to the tall mountain behind him. It always felt like these mountains stood guard around this ranch. "We figured we'd better start using the lumber around these parts for firewood and start stripping abandoned houses for the treated wood to continue our building efforts. I've been chinking the logs as best I can to seal the joints so the bugs and the cold can't get through." He holds up his bucket for me to see.

I know he'd like to keep talking, but I have to get to Evie. "Thank you. I'm going to check on my sister now. I'll see you later!" I yell over my shoulder as I propel myself towards the ranch house.

I don't bother knocking. I just walk in the front door. Sam and Tom are in the kitchen. They jump, and then Sam's surprised face settles on me. "Bodin, it's good to see you."

"Is Frank back too?" Tom asks.

"Yeah, he's here. Just behind me, I think. I ran the whole way," I say.

Sam nods. "Go on downstairs. She's in the room labeled Bees. When you've had a chance to say hello, come on back, and let's have a discussion."

"Yes, sir," I say as I bound down the stairs two at a time. I can hear soft voices from behind closed doors. I see doors with white pieces of paper prettily decorated and boldly displaying classroom names such as Butterflies and Bears. I spot my target: Bees. I don't bother knocking. I pull the door open. Everyone stares, and then I see her sitting cross-legged on the floor, sandwiched between other children.

"Bodee!" she squeals as she hops to her feet. Her clothes are a little dirty, but her hair and her face look clean. I squat down and lift her into my arms. She laughs in a child's nervous yet excited kind of way. "You came back," she says.

"Of course I did," I say. "We'll be right back," I say to the teacher, who nods patiently. I shut the door behind us and squeeze Evie before I set her down and kneel so we can talk face-to-face.

"How have you been, Evie Bee?" I ask.

"Good," she says without elaborating.

"What's new here?"

"Nothing."

Our dialogue continues like this for a few minutes before I tell her I'll see her after school. I promise to wait for her outside the house so we can walk home together. I kiss her forehead and let her back into the classroom.

I watch her sit down and wave goodbye with an animated hand movement before I head back upstairs.

Frank is there when I'm back upstairs, having just arrived, judging by the way Sam and Tom slap his back in a half-hug welcome. I stride over to them, feeling nerves pit themselves in my stomach. It's a strange sensation to be regarded as a source of valuable intel.

Frank makes a 'go ahead' gesture at me. "Time to spill the beans, small fry. Don't be shy," he says with a hint of a smile.

"I don't know where to start," I confess, scratching my head.

"Start by describing the city," Sam suggests.

I look off through a window as images of Eyth flood my mind. "It's beautiful," I say before I snap out of it. I clear my throat and begin again. "Ava was there, too. She should be here."

Tom looks questioningly at Frank, who confirms, "Yeah, we picked up another plus one dead weight that we dealt with along the way."

"Alright," Sam draws out. "Let's get Ava, too, then."

To my surprise, Frank walks to the door and opens it, revealing Ava sitting patiently on the front steps. Clearly, she is unsure of what she should be doing with herself. I see her face relax when her eyes find me.

"Ava," Frank says. "Come meet Sam and Tom. They'd like to hear about your time in the Metal City."

"Eyth," I remind Frank.

"Right," he says, muttering, "stupid name."

The others turn to look at me. "Metal City was just a placeholder," I say, addressing them all. "They call it Eyth."

"What else can you tell us?" Sam asks, looking between Ava and me once we've all sat around the dining table. Sam holds a small notepad that he took from his breast pocket and clicks the back of the pen, keeping it poised for note-taking. Ava remains quiet, so I begin.

"It's advanced, automated, and self-sustaining. They grow their own food, recycle all the water, use an underground aquifer and dehumidification process to gather more. Solar powers everything. A dome over the city acts as a shield and collects power from the sun." I scratch my head, wondering why everything I say seems inadequate and pointless.

"Tell them about our inside man, Mark," Frank prods.

I light up, "Right! We have until December first to plant more people in the city. After that, they'll stop recruiting. The mole, er, Mark, thought that was a necessary step or we didn't have a chance."

While looking down into her lap, Ava adds, without being addressed, "They kill people." Everyone turns to her. She continues in a subdued tone. "There are no old people working there. Or sick people. They'll let them volunteer and load them on the truck, but we never see them again after that. I worked for a man who told me they were *disposed* of."

"Sarah was Ava's friend. She had breast cancer," I explain. "Ava never saw her again."

Ava sniffs. She sits up taller, her voice steadier. "They're not good people, but I don't see how we possibly have a chance of taking them down," she says. I'm glad she was the one to say precisely what I've been thinking. And avoiding.

We field questions from Tom, Sam, and Frank for the next hour. I tell them more about what Mark conveyed about the army following one leader, the intake system for fresh air, and their reliance on technology. Ava tells them about Lane and what she knows about the elites and the systems.

Despite being early evening, we're exhausted. Seems everyone can sense our fatigue.

Frank stands up and addresses Ava. "I'll show you where you can stay tonight, and I can connect you with a couple of women in the community. They'll take you under their wings. There's no free lunch here. You'll be expected to work."

Ava nods in understanding. I guess it's time I went to see Ted and Alex. Guilt flashes in me. I should have asked about Alex when I arrived. He must be in one of the school rooms downstairs, too. I don't mean to think it, but it surfaces anyway. A part of me wonders if there's another family here that might adopt Alex. Or help raise him. I don't know what kind of interest Ted has taken in the kid after I left, but I know he wasn't thrilled I brought him home to begin with.

Everyone, except Sam, spills out of the house to resume the workday. As I walk out into the sunshine and take in the view of the valley, a thought occurs to me. *It's good to be back here.* I wasn't here long before, but I finally feel vindicated. Like I made the right choice about leaving Salt Lake and going after Ava. She made it here, and it's a better place for Evie and Ted. There's community here. And equality. Evie gets to act like a normal kid again. She gets to attend school—a luxury I didn't know I'd miss.

Chapter 23

Ava

October 27, 2025

Frank is walking me to my new digs. I take it all in, all of the people living here in this small valley. The mountains surrounding us seem to cup the valley in the palm of its hand. The densely wooded forest that borders the back half of the ranch appears like soldiers ready on the front line. Dirt paths have already begun to forge themselves between the various huts, cabins, and tents. It's such a hodgepodge of living quarters around here. I wonder where my spin will land.

"You'll be given a job tomorrow," Frank states.

"Ok," I say and leave it at that. I didn't expect a free ride, and he already said that.

Frank stops in front of a small log hut. The chinks appear to have been filled with mud and straw. The front door is a loosely hung, black and white cowhide. Two women crouch outside on the ground with a shallow basin of water between them. They dip into the basin and splash their faces, rubbing at the day's accumulation of dirt and grime.

"Ladies, this is Ava," he says, addressing them. They stand when they recognize Frank's voice. Both wear a surly expression and are likely in their forties. "She'll be staying with you here. In the morning, you'll need to show her the ropes." They eye me with contempt but nod. If Frank notices their warm welcome, he doesn't say anything. I also take note that he doesn't introduce them to me. He turns to me and nods before leaving—his duty done.

The last remnants of light have begun their retreat, signaling shorter days. The two women push aside the cowhide and enter the tiny house. I begin to follow, expecting them to hold back the hide for me, but it drops in front of me and sways in the doorway. I take in a deep breath and enter.

The inside is barebones. There are two twin mattresses flanking either side of the entry door with blankets folded at the foot of them on the floor, flanking either side of the entry door. There's a small table beneath a two-foot by two-foot window with potted plants covering most of its surface. There are some pots, a water basin, and a corner stacked with odds and ends.

"What are your names?" I ask.

They ignore me. I notice there isn't a fireplace.

"How do we stay warm?" I try again.

The older of the two answers this time as she pulls off her coat and boots and pulls on a sweatshirt. "*We* insulated it well." They brush their teeth by pouring water from a plastic water bottle over the pot onto their toothbrushes and then spitting back into it when finished. Then, one of them tips a small splash of the water into each of the pots crowded beneath the small window. When she's finished, she fishes a piece of cardboard from behind the table and fits it into the window before releasing a flap of cloth over the blocked window that was held aside by an ornate tassel.

I feel as if I've intruded on an intimate affair here. I have the urge to walk out, but I know that if I do that, I risk having nowhere to sleep tonight. If it hadn't been Frank delivering the orders to these women, they indeed would have refused to house me. I noticed the moment I got here that people revered Frank. When he walked, they parted. When he stopped, they waited for him to speak.

I'm tired. I long for a toothbrush. I'd ask if I thought there was even the slightest chance they'd offer one. Their icy demeanor towards me has not thawed. I eye the two mattresses. With my addition, that leaves the uncomfortable situation of deciding who must now share a bed. "Where can I sleep?" I ask quietly.

I'm ignored again. Each woman lays down in the middle of a bed and turns away from me, pulling the blankets up to cover themselves. Luckily, Frank found a blanket for me. I tug on it, wrapping it around my shoulders tightly.

I think of sleeping on the floor, but I also don't want to set that precedence. I've always followed orders. Back in Eyth, I was an object. A maid. Lane's pet. Before that, I was a lowly PA, following doctors' and nurses' orders in the hospital, which always seemed to be unnecessarily rude. Resentment bubbles up inside of me. Just because they were here before me doesn't mean they deserve the beds any more than I do. I have the chance to stand up for myself now—to reinvent myself. I don't have to be somebody's bitch again, and I'm tired as hell of being treated like a rat. I clench my fists at my side. One woman reaches up and pinches out the candle lying on the floor a few feet from the bed so that I'm standing in total darkness. That's when I decide.

I grab the light snuffer by the ankles and yank her out of the bed. She yelps in surprise.

"You will share your bed," I growl. "I'm sick of your rude behavior."

"Bitch," the other woman says.

"Bitch? Who's the bitch!? I didn't ask for this! But I am demanding a modicum of basic human decency. If that makes me a bitch, then fine." I'm shaking, but I'm determined to seize this opportunity and exploit my rare show of boldness. I crawl into the now empty bed and scoot towards the wall to make room for the woman I just ousted. My heart hammers in my chest from the exhilaration.

I hear the short, angry whispers of the two women piercing the dark. "Oh, shut up," I say. "I made room to share the bed."

I hear a scoff, but then it's silent. I lay awake staring at the ceiling for a long time, allowing my body time to recover from the stress of conflict. I can't believe I just did that. No one comes to share my bed. The soft mattress below me feels heavenly after sleeping on the stiff cot for the last few nights. A victory smile spreads across my face.

Then, I fall asleep.

***

I wake in the morning to the sounds of the colony coming alive. Pan's clank and the low hum of chatter filter into the cabin. I turn my head and see that the two women are already gone. I sigh deeply, remembering last night and feeling like the morning is already off to another rocky start. I have to pee. I also need a drink of water, but I don't see any in the cabin. They probably did that on purpose. There's a chamber pot in the corner, but I'm unsure what to do once I've filled it. So, I'll choose a nice, quiet spot in the woods. I pull back the cowhide and feel the pinch of crisp autumn air on my cheeks. The cabin is insulated well—I'll give them that. Even complimenting those two women silently feels distasteful. I narrow my eyes at no one in particular and walk towards the woods.

I pass an open, circular area with a large fire pit in the center and tables lining the outside. There are many stumps and various folding chairs for seating around the fire. There are dozens of people milling about this area. Pots sit in the fire, and the smell of something savory simmering makes my mouth water. People are working by filling water basins, chopping vegetables, and cleaning up the area. I decide I'll return to this spot and see if I can help here after I've peed. The thought of seeking out those women to ask for direction is unbearable.

I enter the forest. With each step I take, the trees act as a sound barrier to the colony just beyond, and the quiet invades. Birdsong replaces human sounds. The smell of pine and mud invades the smell of broth. Hiding in the woods would be a decent way to pass the day, but I dismiss the idea immediately. I know I have to pull my weight or risk being evicted. Those women would love that. Besides, I'm thirsty and hungry. I leave the woods' solace and step back into the valley.

I startle a woman when I exit and step on a branch. She puts a hand on her chest. "What were you doing in there?" She doesn't look much older than me. She has her hair pulled back in a tight, blonde ponytail. Her question isn't exactly unfriendly, but it does sound accusatory. Out of nowhere, I feel like crying. The task of fitting in here seems herculean. I swallow it down and muster my courage.

"Peeing," I say defensively.

She squints at me. "Are you new here?"

"Yes."

"Don't pee in the woods," she says, walking away.

I'm frozen for a moment before deciding to follow her. "Wait," I say as I follow her. She slows to allow me to catch up.

"Where do I pee then?" I ask, coming up alongside her.

"In your chamber pot. You empty the pot into the shit pits." She points to the far side of the valley.

"Shit pits?" I ask.

She shrugs. "Tasteful name, isn't it?" I blink at her. She sighs in what seems like resignation. "Where do you work?" she asks.

"I don't know. I don't have a job yet. My two roommates were supposed to help me with that, but they haven't exactly been welcoming."

She stops walking and looks at me thoughtfully. "That sounds a lot like the greeting I got. You're not from here, are you?"

"Nope. That obvious?"

"They're kind of cliquey here. For a long time, I felt like an outsider, too. Still do, sort of."

"So, it gets better?" I ask hopefully. She smiles at me with perfect white teeth, and I return the smile. She stretches her hand out to me. I take it gratefully.

"I'm Carrie," she says.

"Ava," I respond.

"Come on, Ava, I'll show you around. You can shadow me today until they figure out where to put you."

I grin, happy to have met someone willing to help me.

Carrie takes me to an area with several large, empty metal troughs and several fires burning. There are clothing lines strung between cabins in a zig zap pattern above the open area.

"We do the laundry here," she says. "First, we gather the water." She points to several buckets. "Then, we warm it up." She nudges her chin at the fires that several other women are tending. None of them say hi to Carrie or me. "Then we begin washing." She indicates a large pile of linens and clothes. My eyes widen at the size of the pile. "Lastly, we hang it and then fold it when dried." She gestures to the lines running above us. I nod. "Soap is here, and some clothes pins are here." She points to a few buckets scattered on the ground. Some are filled with white powder, and some are half full of clothes pins and binder clips. "We have a limited number of clips, so we save them for the smaller garments."

"Do people just dump their laundry here?" I ask, referring to the pile.

"Yep, first thing in the morning. They're only allowed linens once per month if they're lucky enough to have them in the first place. And other articles of clothing once per week, but there isn't really anyone monitoring this. I suspect some people drop things off more often than they should."

"That's a big pile," I note.

"Job security," she says as she picks up some buckets.

I follow suit and find my own empty buckets to carry. I follow Carrie to the creek that runs along the western border of the valley.

"So, where are you from?" I ask.

"Philadelphia," she says. "You?"

"Well, I was living in Salt Lake when all this happened, and then I volunteered with the army and went to Eyth, but I'm originally from..."

Carrie has stopped and turned to gape at me.

"What?" I ask, alarmed.

"You lived in Eyth? As in the super city?"

"Uh, huh."

"Holy. Shit," she says as she shakes her head and continues walking towards the creek. "They told us about it some last night around the fire. What was that like?" she asks with her back towards me.

"Um... horrible but also amazing," I say.

Carrie stops at the creek and dips a bucket in. "How can it be horrible *and* amazing?"

"The city was amazing. The cars, the buildings, the technology. The way they treated the recruits was the horrible part."

Carrie and I work together for the entire day. We got one meal break at midday. Apparently, what I smelled earlier wasn't breakfast. It was lunch. There is no breakfast. They stopped serving one weeks ago. Carrie secured a water bottle for me to drink from throughout the day and showed me the location of the potable water dispenser. She explained to me that there's a bell that tolls when the sun starts to go down, and that signifies "closing time." Though smaller, we get another meal at this time, and we all gather around the large fire pit. This is where people gossip, catch up, play cards, listen to a guitar on occasion, or relax before bedtime. Sometimes, town meetings are held during this time to vote on issues or share information.

I lost track of time while working alongside Carrie. I learned she was also working in Salt Lake when the EMP blast hit. I haven't had a real friend since Sarah, but even my friendship with Sarah didn't feel as authentic as this. Sarah was my superior. Carrie and I feel more like sisters. To my surprise, I'm looking forward to another day of laundry with her tomorrow.

When I return "home" to turn in after dinner, the two women are already next to each other on one mattress. The other mattress is gloriously vacant and inviting.

CHAPTER 24

Sam

October 27, 2025

There's a commotion outside. I can hear the muffled shouting from the dining room table where I sit, still pouring over the garden plans and notes I jotted down while listening to Ava and Bodin. Frank is home. That's a relief. And Bodin even brought the girl back. I should have a talk with him about that. Even I can tell that union is never going to happen. While he's been through quite a bit, he's still just a kid—a teenager. In contrast, she is a young woman.

I stand, glancing at the drawing of the proposed crop pattern for the garden in the north pasture, before heading to the window to see what's going on. A crowd has gathered in the Colony. I didn't choose that name, but it buzzed around enough until it finally stuck. I stand up straighter. There's a girl draped across the arms of a man running. She flops as he bounds through the housing that litters the valley floor. Her right arm is loose and hanging down. They're going to the barn, where we converted a tack room into a nursing station. We call it the Med Shed. Other men are pointing towards the woods. They break off abruptly like a play was called in a football game. I walk outside, heading toward the Med Shed, which is considerably closer to my location, so I get there first and wait at the door. When the man approaches, he's huffing from the effort of carrying her. She must be eight or nine. My hand goes to my heart when I realize I missed something watching from the window because of the dark clothes both the man and the girl wear. Blood. Lots of it. The girl's face is pale, and her eyes blink up at the far-off sky.

I push open the door to the nursing station. "Incoming!" I yell. "We've got blood."

Two women spring into action and hurry to help the man inside. They lay the little girl down on the plastic folding table and begin removing her clothes rapidly while they fire off orders to each other and questions to the man. Flaps of skin hang loosely from a gaping wound in her neck. There are other wounds, but this appears to be the source of the most blood. I swallow and look away.

"What happened?!" Their words are tight with stress.

"Dog," the man says, out of breath. "She tried to pet it. I could tell something wasn't right with it." His voice cracks. "I screamed at her not to touch it, but I scared it, and it lashed out at her," he sobs. "I just didn't want her to touch it," he repeats in agony. He must be her father.

Knowing I'm no good here, I think I know where the men who broke off from the group in a hurry are going—hunting. I run back to the house to get my own rifle.

As I approach the house, my jog looking more like a hobble, Rose exits the front door, still holding a pair of pants she's mending. "What is it?" she asks, alarmed.

"Dog attack."

"No! What happened?"

"A girl was attacked when she went to pet it. I don't know her name. Doesn't look good. The thing went right for her throat," I say.

Rose's face drains of color, and she rushes for the Med Shed, but I grab her arm to stop her. "Nothing you can do for her," I say, trying to spare Rose the mental image of the little girl torn up and bloody. I haven't heard a scream yet from that direction, which means she must not have made it. Rose's face is pulled tight with worry. I only shake my head at her. Then

Rose begins to sob. I pull her in for an embrace and hold her a moment until she pushes me away, already knowing why I was hurrying towards the house.

"Go get it," she says through gritted teeth. I don't have to be told twice. I retrieve my rifle.

I saw the men enter the forest from farther down in the valley, likely where the girl was attacked. There's a handful of them. Maybe seven or eight. I decide to enter the woods closest to the house and see if I can head it off. Rose watches me go.

Being in the forest alone provides solace as of late. There's nowhere else to get some peace. Every inch of the house is used. The work never ends. But out here, I can settle my nerves by telling myself I'm working. Hunting *is* work. But I can also relax. Hunting is about stealth, which means slow, quiet progress through the trees. I decide to go to a small clearing not quite a mile away. It's as good a place to start as any.

I make it to the valley without seeing anything other than squirrels and chipmunks, still trying to secure the last remnants of food before they hunker down for the winter. I step into the clearing and look up at the unobstructed sky. Dark clouds gather in the distance, and I wonder if we'll finally see the first snow today.

I pull the gun into position against my shoulder and use the scope to survey the valley. It's hard to tell through the tall grasses. Their stalks have begun to sway slightly with the oncoming breeze, but nothing about the pattern of their bend raises alarms. I put the strap back into place with the gun slung across my chest as I walk through the dry, golden stalks of the grasses lining the valley floor.

There's a *crack* as a gunshot rings out.

Startled, I fall to my knees. It takes a second to set in, but when it comes, it slams into me.

I'm in excruciating pain. I must be having a heart attack, but then I pull my hand away from the left shoulder to see that it's covered in blood. I pull in ragged, shallow breaths. It hurts too much to breathe deeply. It's unclear how long I sit crouched over like this. Then, there's someone standing above me. With the sun behind him, maybe it's an angel coming to take me home. I squint and begin to make out his features. He's a boy with a thin, patchwork beard and even thinner mustache. Acne dots his cheeks.

A wide-brimmed hat shades his eyes, but his dark eyebrows are drawn together. He kneels beside me. His face is full of fear.

"Shit, shit, shit," he says. Then he stands and runs off.

The pain isn't getting any better, but my tolerance is. I attempt to stand. It takes me two times. All I can picture is Rose as I stumble back towards the ranch, clutching my pulsing shoulder. Time is a funny thing when you think you're dying. My time struggling towards the ranch seemed to stretch for days, but once I arrived and looked down at the big house, it felt as if I had blinked myself there.

I'm crossing the driveway, just a few paces from the front door, when Tom spots me from the barn. He comes sprinting like a bat out of hell. Another man follows him. When Tom reaches me, my knees collapse. He reaches down, wraps an arm around me, and hoists me up.

"Get Rose!" he shouts at the man who has just caught up.

"What happened?" Tom asks, breathless, as he walks me toward the Med Shed. I don't protest.

"Gunshot," I say.

"Who shot you?" he asks.

"Boy. Don't know," I say through gritted teeth. "Accident," I add after taking another shallow breath. Tom curses under his breath. I hear the door to the house slam behind us. It must be Rose.

"We can't stop now, Dad. She'll catch up," Tom says as he feels my feet hesitate, waiting for Rose. I don't say anything. I keep shuffling my feet forward, most of my weight supported by Tom.

"Almost there," he huffs. As we reach the door, so does Rose.

"What happened?" she demands of Tom, out of breath. The nurses open the door and usher us inside.

"Gunshot. It was an accident," Tom states so the nurses can hear him, too.

The nurses look exhausted. Their faces sag. There's a sheen of sweat on their brows. I know one of them. She's the head nurse, and her name is Marie. Blood has dried to the color of dark crimson on their clothing. As they lay me down, I want to ask about the girl attacked by the dog, but I don't get the chance. Once my shirt has been cut away, I scream, unable to hold it back as alcohol is poured over the wound. They're talking to me, but everything is spinning. My heart begins beating erratically, and I think this time, for sure, I'm having a heart attack. It's failing me, I can tell. My ears are ringing.

The nurses sound like they're trying to talk to me underwater. "Sam? Sam!" With the worst bite of the pain over, I come back to the room.

"The bleeding is slight. That's lucky, but we have to get it out, Sam," Marie says. She's holding up what looks like a giant pair of tweezers.

"No," I say, but she either doesn't hear me or ignores me because she draws the tweezers closer. "No!" I shout. Everyone in the room freezes. I've never felt so much satisfaction in having a voice that holds authority.

"My heart can't take it," I say. "It'll kill me." Without anesthesia, I do believe that. I don't know how long I have, but I know my heart has been weakening. It can't handle the same level of strain it could even two weeks ago. I feel the constant sputter as it loses its rhythm temporarily whenever I attempt to push it. This event has been stressful enough. I'm lucky it's still sustaining me through this whole ordeal. Rose blinks at me with questioning eyes. I'm about to explain when Frank enters. The door bangs loudly as it's thrown open and slams into the wall behind it. Lilly follows in close steps behind him. Both are out of breath.

"What's happened?!" Frank demands.

Frank, Tom, Lilly, and Rose are all here. I feel a peace settle over me. I can die now. It'd be ok.

The story gets rehashed again. I provide more details now that my grasp is returning.

"Don't remove the bullet," Frank says. Marie throws him an exasperated look. "It's a myth," he says. "Most of the time, it's better to leave them. It'll cause more damage trying to get it out."

"What about infection?" she shoots back.

"Rare," he says back pointedly.

She lets out a breath of resignation.

The second girl, though clearly not in charge here, asks in a quiet, unsure voice, "What about lead poisoning?"

"They're both unlikely possibilities," he responds curtly.

"It's not coming out," I growl. I hop off the table and look at my kids. "Come on, we've got things to discuss."

Lilly gaps at me. "At least let them clean you up and put a bandage on your shoulder."

The room begins to spin. I feel lightheaded. I sit back down. "Fine. Make it quick," I murmur before adding, "Please."

My shirt is cut away and discarded. Lilly is sent back to the house to grab me a clean one while I'm patched up. I'm offered three generic ibuprofen and a Tylenol and told to take them together.

"It's the closest we can get to an opioid effect," Marie tells me when she hands me the pills.

I take them gratefully. It's hard to say whether the painful throb is getting better or if I'm getting accustomed to it, but the pills are a welcome treatment that I hope will dull the ache further. I need a clear head to discuss the next steps with Tom, Lilly, and Frank as I plan to take advantage of this rare moment when we're all together as a family, alone.

With the lightheadedness over, I brush off my kids' attempts to help me walk to the house. Rose knows me well enough not to offer. Once we're inside, we gather around the kitchen island. Rose dolls out water, the only thing we have to offer. They sip while waiting for me to explain why I've called us together like this at such a time. I can't say why but maybe it's the reminder I just received about my mortality that propels me toward action.

"What are we going to do?" I ask. Confused faces stare back at me. "How do we use the information we learned from Bodin and Ava today?"

"We use it to revolt," Frank says, an edge to his voice. It's the same conversation about retaliation he's been feeding us since the beginning.

"And what have you done to accomplish this? You and your crew go out *recruiting* but always return with tight lips. What is happening?"

Frank scowls. "You know what's happening. The people are too preoccupied about their survival to be interested in joining a revolt. If we could feed them, we could build a proper army, but we can't. We've been over this."

"So, that's it? We're all going to starve, and your weapons cache was useless?" I ask. Frank lowers his eyes at me.

"That's not fair, Dad," Lilly says. "We're all doing the best we can. Frank's weapons have come in handy protecting our people."

I slam my fist on the table. "From other victims!" The pain shooting through to my other arm gives my words more punch than I would have normally intended. Everyone stares at me, stunned. I take a few deep breaths to quell the pain. "They did this to us," I say, more subdued. "Our window of opportunity is closing. Our people are starving. We will not last the winter unless we make a stand."

Tom rubs his forehead. "So, what should we do about it?" He sounds tired.

"An attack from the outside is out of the question. We don't have the numbers. But we could still do some damage from the inside," Frank says.

I nod.

"Dad," Frank addresses me. "It's a death sentence." This, however, takes me aback.

"And the war you hoped to start initially, wasn't?" I retort. Frank draws his mouth into a tight line.

"We blow up the air intake valves, and then we get out of there. Clean, quick," Franks says.

"I'm surprised to hear such a proposition from you, Frank. What'll that do besides poke the hornet's nest?" I ask.

Fank glowers. "These are not my people. I have little faith they'll be able to accomplish anything from within the city," he says.

"We have to give them a chance. We ask for volunteers," I say. "We're clear about the risks. We use Ava and Bodin's knowledge to devise a plan."

"We could try," Tom suggests. "It's just that we know they have to be healthy. They have to be younger. We'll be asking for volunteers from our best asset base to risk their lives. This could put us in a bad situation if they don't come back. We need all the help we can get right now."

"What's the end goal?" Rose asks. Everyone looks at her. "It has to be worth the sacrifice," she says. "What are we hoping to accomplish here?"

"Destruction of their technological grid. Cripple their operations," I say. "We know they lost a software engineer to that Lane fellow. It's a long shot, but if we could get one of our people in their software department, we could do a lot of damage."

"Kill the army's commander," Frank chimes in. We all look to him. We know from what Bodin has told him that she is a woman. "It'll cripple the army. Leave them scrambling. At least temporarily. Who knows what kind of contingency plans they have in place." I look down to the floor and take a deep breath before agreeing.

"How does this help us?" Rose asks. "Revenge is not going to get us closer to feeding our people."

Lilly speaks up first. "We'll pack out food and get our people out of there." We look at her. She continues, "The meal bars that Bodin mentioned are packed with calories and prepackaged. So, easy to transport and shelf-stable. If we could find a way to take enough of those, they could tide us over for winter without us having to kill our entire herd. Or we take generators to build our own aquaponic system. So, it's simple. We take food. We take things to grow food."

"It's a long shot," says Frank. "But I like it. Let's take our time here, though. Come up with a solid plan. I'll call Hutchins and Stevens in to confer."

"We've got time," I agree. My energy drains by the second. The adrenaline high I was riding is dumping me in the dirt. I look at Rose. "So, there we have it. Goals. Damage their software systems beyond repair, kill the head of the army, steal food, and escape." We all exchange glances. No one says what we're likely all thinking. We may as well be asking any volunteers to build a rocket to the moon.

CHAPTER 25

Carrie

November 14, 2025 Two Weeks Later

There's a new girl in the Colony, Ava. I like her. It feels good to have a friend again and someone to whom I can relate. We're both city girls. Both have no idea where our boyfriends are, and neither of us has ever been to Salmon, Idaho, before the Colony, and we both have new love interests here.

Pax comes to the laundry station daily unless he's out on overnighters scavenging for supplies or lumber with the recon crew. It's sweet the way he checks in on me. Twice, we've met at the fire ring and enjoyed our dinner of watered-down soup, watching the last fire embers smolder while we talked about our days.

I like Pax. He's trying hard to be my boyfriend. Had I met him in Phili, would I have been tempted? Of course, hypothetically, I would have been attracted to him, sure. He's thinning out, but his muscles are still defined. His curly brown hair, strong jaw, and straight white teeth are a draw, too. However, he is undoubtedly a country boy. He has a full beard now, which Ed could never accomplish. I wonder if Ed is still trying to shave or if he's just let it go like every other man I've met since the EMP, except the SEALs, of course. They seem to be anomalies in nearly every way. I wonder if Ed is... *alive.*

I picture Ed in his business suit, clean-shaven, with his travel mug of coffee in his hand as he walks out the door to start his morning commute to work. It seems like a movie I used to watch instead of what was my real life. I'm not that Carrie anymore. I don't lament that fact. I just sit with it: Carrie, the country girl, the homesteader. I wouldn't have chosen this life. I would have looked down on any woman who did, but now that I've been forced to live it, I don't think I was being fair to those women. This is the more challenging life to live—the more primitive. And I'm beginning to think it's more like the life we were designed to live. There is an odd satisfaction in relying on each other and your own two hands for survival. And something liberating about the obsolescence of the bank account.

I've heard it repeated often enough as a way to console hungry people, but I'm starting to believe it: next year will be better. We have to get through this winter. We didn't have enough time to grow and store our food this year, but next year, we can prepare. The entire north pasture has been designated the garden area. It has already undergone some work to prepare it and the soil. Still, our efforts are mainly concentrated on building structures that can withstand the cold of winter, gathering firewood, and working the fall crops of squash, potatoes, and onions. We will need all the tents and tarps currently serving as makeshift housing for a few unlucky people to cover the expanse of the north pasture garden in early spring to protect it from frost. The growing season is short in Salmon, but there are things we can do to stretch it and increase the yield. I'm just glad some people know what they're doing and are planning out the garden because I've never been a green thumb and had no idea there was so much to it until I attended a town hall meeting where they discussed their plans. The talks of soil quality, composting, crop rotation, early planting crops versus late planting crops, and consecutive planting had my head spinning. I've never so much as glanced at a Farmer's Almanac.

Ava finds me early in the morning, just as I head towards the laundry station, to help the ladies gather and heat the water needed for the day's washing. She holds up a bag and smiles shyly. "Time to wash the lady garments," she says.

I nod in understanding.

"Where can I do that? In private?" she asks.

"I'll show you," I say, leading her to the spot at the creek just before it dives underneath the culvert. This way, no one is downstream from us. The creek has become more of a stream, but we're lucky we still get some water year-round. "Wash here and then rinse your bag out. Once your wet garments are gathered, hang them in your hut. This time of year, you'll need a fire to dry them."

"Well, shoot," she says.

"What?" I ask before I remember that Ava is in a hut awaiting a fireplace buildout. "You can hang them in my hut," I say. I was upgraded from the tent the day Pax and I returned with the honey. I wish we could share housing, but my log hut is packed with three other women and eight-year-old Clara. The hut is only twelve by twelve. We sleep there, that's pretty much it, but it does have a fireplace and a line we've strung across the top bunks to hang our wet clothes to dry. I couldn't ask any of the women there to switch since a hut without a fireplace is considered a downgrade, and I'm also too selfish to give up my place to be with Ava. The low-burning fire at night provides so much comfort. It'd be too painful to relinquish that.

"Thank you," she says.

"Any word on when you'll receive a hearth?" I worry for her with the way the weather is beginning to turn.

Ava blushes. "Well, actually..."

I raise my eyebrows at her, waiting for her news.

"I've been invited to share a bed with Miller," she says.

My eyes go wide at this admission. I know that Miller and the rest of the SEALs sleep on beds inside the ranch house. She'd be warm at night and probably comfortable. I'm happy for her. Her sudden elevation in status has me curious, though. I wonder, briefly, if their union is another one that's more forced due to the drive to survive and be protected, but I let the thought go before it can niggle at me. Besides, does it even matter what her intentions are? There's more and more that seems pointless these days as the need to survive and to thrive dwarfs everything.

I sigh.

"What?" she asks. "We like each other."

"No, no, it's not that," I say as I search for my next words. Luckily, Ava has come to know me and anticipates what's holding me up.

"Pax is a good guy, Carrie. Give him a chance." We're facing each other by the side of the creek, our breath blowing billows into the frosty air. Her hands will be frozen stiff by the time she's finished washing.

"I know," I say firmly. "It's just..." To my surprise, my eyes threaten to tear up. I stop talking before my voice breaks and gives me away.

"It's just what? It's not that hard."

I tilt my head towards her bag. "You better get started. The community fire's going. I'd stop there and warm your hands after you've finished."

She lowers her eyes at me, acknowledging that I've side-stepped the conversation.

"I'll see you at laundry," I say as I turn away and return to the hustle and bustle of the early morning colony life.

"See ya," she calls from behind me.

Dry leaves crunch beneath my feet as I reach the end of the tree line that borders the creek. When was the last time that I washed my menstruation garments? I stop dead in my tracks while I do the mental math. It was weeks before we left for our town mission—the realization strikes me. I washed my lady garments nearly six weeks ago? Dread pits itself into my stomach, and I feel it do a flip.

"No," I say out loud to myself. I force my feet forward and walk into the town while talking myself down. I haven't been eating much. It could just be late. But I'm never late. Yeah, but things aren't normal. Maybe I've lost too much weight, and it's not coming anymore. I did have sex. But he pulled out. Besides, I haven't been sick in the mornings. Don't women get sick in the mornings when they're pregnant? But I have been a little more emotional than usual. Or have I? Why had I just been on the verge of tears when Ava asked me about Pax?

My hand goes unbidden to my abdomen. The truth is, I have been feeling a little...*off* in the mornings. Not enough that I haven't been able to ignore it, but now, when pitted next to my fear, it seems so amplified and obvious. I force my feet to take me to my hut, where I know I'll be alone while the other women are out doing morning chores. I pull back the animal hide that covers the otherwise open doorway and crawl up onto my bed, curling myself into the fetal position. Tears stream down my face as I hold myself. "No, no, no," I repeat over and over.

***

I'm sitting by the fire, swirling the last dregs of dinner broth in my bowl as Frank approaches Ava and me, looking stern, per usual.

He looks at Ava and says, "Your presence has been requested in the ranch house."

"Hi to you, too," I say to Frank. "You know, it wouldn't kill you to smile a little."

Frank weakly attempts to smile. "Hi, Carrie."

Ava turns to me, her eyes questioning or asking for permission. I'm not her mother. "Go," I say impatiently.

Ava frowns. "See you tomorrow?" she asks.

"Of course," I respond.

Ava walks away towards the house with Frank. Eyes around the fire follow Frank and now Ava. Frank has a commanding presence here. We all know it. I don't know why I spoke to him like I did. I'm just tired. My earlier emotional divulgence in my hut over the silly notion that I could be pregnant has worn me out. I'm not pregnant. Just late.

I scan the crowd gathered around the fire. Pax is walking toward me. Caroline is sitting amongst a group of women. Her eyes narrow as she notices Pax's trajectory. To say we haven't smoothed things over would be an understatement. I avoid Caroline as much as possible these days, but unfortunately, it's not just her I have to worry about. It's her posse, too, who have all internalized Caroline's grievances as their own. Whatever the story she told them, it must have been a good one. I tear my eyes away from the group just as Caroline bumps another girl on the shoulder to point out Pax and me.

"May I?"

I look up at Pax standing over me, gesturing towards the empty seat Ava left behind. I sigh. "Yeah, of course." I haven't strictly been avoiding Pax, but we haven't found time to hang out much. It's all work and no play around here these days. Plus, I'm embarrassed that I was immediately assigned a bed in one of the log huts once we returned from our supply run. I know it had everything to do with Pax. He gave me the credit for our honey find, and I saw him talking animatedly with Tom after our return. Soon after, someone found me and said Tom had requested a new living situation for me. With my meager possessions on my back and tucked beneath my arm, I was shown to a log hut with two bunk beds inside. I was given a naked mattress on a top bunk. I spread my sleeping bag out, avoiding the curious stares from the other women inside. A woman and a girl share one bed. The other two beds are solo women. All are on the gardening crew, and none are on Team Caroline. That was a relief, but still, only the child has spoken to me. She informed me her name is Clara, and she's ten. I mostly ignore her because her mother hisses at her disapprovingly when she attempts to initiate conversation. Luckily, work leaves little idle time in the hut to avoid such awkward moments. I should swallow my pride and thank Pax, but something is holding me back. What is wrong with me?

"What was that all about?" He jerks his head toward the direction Ava and Frank just headed.

"No idea, but I'm sure I'll hear about it in the morning." I throw back the last of my soup and wipe the little bit of dribble from the corner of my mouth.

"You two seem to be two peas in a pod," he says.

"I like her," I say.

"I can tell," he responds. We sit looking into the crackling fire. "Can I ask you something?"

I respond with something Ed used to say that would bother me. I'm not sure why it comes out of my mouth now. "You just did."

"Ha," he says without humor. "Seriously, when can we hang out?" He leans over and bumps my shoulder. I blush, wondering if "hang out" is code for something else.

"Is the honey going to good use?" I ask, avoiding his question.

"Dunno. I haven't had any, I know that." He's smiling at me.

"Uh, Pax," I begin. I swallow the nerves clawing at my insides and look down at the ground. "Thanks for getting me into a hut." There, I did it.

"Oh, don't mention it," he brushes it off. I feel relief wash over me. Why was that so hard for me? "What do you say you and I go on a little recon mission tomorrow? Just a day trip. We can stop by the bridge. Maybe fish," he says.

"I'll have to talk to Marlene," I say, trying to hide the excitement in my voice. He means we should have a proper meal from our secret stash. Maybe we should save it for more challenging times, but the temptation of a full belly blinds me to rational thought. I've been ravenous lately. Perhaps it's the work. Marlene has been incredibly bossy with us lately, pushing us to make faster trips with the water buckets and scrub faster to get through it all—the joints in my fingers and the muscles running up my forearms constantly ache.

"Alright," Pax says. I yawn. He puts a hand on my knee. "You look like you could use some sleep. I'll see you tomorrow then. I'll meet you outside your place."

Maybe I should be annoyed at his confidence, but I don't care about that now. I nod, a small smile tugging up one corner of my mouth.

CHAPTER 26

Ava

November 14, 2025

I follow Frank into the living room of the big house. Most seats are taken. I scan the room for him but am disappointed. Miller is not here. Though, I don't call him Miller when we're alone. He's Landon to me and only me. When Crowly introduced me to Miller on my second day while seated around the community fire for dinner, I was almost offended. Until then, I had thought Crowly a plausible prospect, but the way he introduced me to Miller had a clear purpose. He thought we would make a better couple. The sting of rejection didn't last long. Miller was taller than Crowly. His face was serious, but he had a Jake Gyllenhaal vibe to him. The attraction was immediate. And when I get to see one of his rare smiles, my heart stops beating for a second. I might spend the rest of my days trying to earn those smiles.

There are about five people I recognize as council members in the living room—two women and three men. The others I know are Frank, Sam, Lilly, Tom, and even Bodin. Given his presence, I can assume we will be rehashing more of our time in Eyth. A tiresome topic for me.

Sam is wearing a sling around his left arm. I look away, not wanting to be caught staring. There are large glass windows that look out over the valley. The valley is now shrouded in darkness, but multiple fires are burning to keep it illuminated. I sit cross-legged on the floor next to Bodin to complete the circle.

"Welcome, everyone," Sam says as he looks around the room. His eyes linger on Bodin and then me. "This is the council we've appointed to oversee the affairs of the Colony," he explains. I nod, having already heard one of their addresses over a dinner fire. "Everyone, this is Ava and Bodin. They were in Eyth. That's why they're here tonight." He goes around and gives brief introductions for Bodin and me, "Paul, Marjory, Kim, Finn, Dan, and I believe you've been introduced to Tom and Lilly, and, of course, you three know each other." He gestures between Frank, Bodin, and me. He jumps into business next. "I'd like to open it up to the floor first. What do you all have to report or discuss tonight?"

Paul speaks first. "The game keeps getting pushed farther and farther. We're going to have to extend the hunting trips to overnighters." Sam frowns at this.

"How's your shoulder, Sam?" Marjory asks.

He brushes her off. "Never mind that. I'll live." He turns to Paul. "What kind of animals are you seeing out there?" Paul, I gather, oversees the hunting around here.

"Nothing much that's worth a bullet, and our archers aren't quick enough to get a rabbit," he says. "We did get that dog that attacked Camille in the woods, though. Did the starving thing a favor. The news didn't seem to lighten her old man's load, though. He still blames himself for her death." There are murmurs. The undercurrent is subdued. I guess it's still fresh for them.

"Temperatures are consistently below freezing at night," Kim says. Everyone seems grateful for the subject change. "We're keeping the plants covered, but we won't be able to prolong the harvest much longer. The ground is freezing."

"Do we have enough?" Sam asks, concern evident in the thick lines of his furrowed brows.

Kim frowns. "No," she says. That shuts everyone up. They all look at her as if she might give them a different answer, but she doesn't.

"What'll we do?" Marjory asks quietly, breaking the spell.

Sam scratches the top of his head. Frank shifts. Tom wrings a beanie in his hands.

Lilly talks. Her voice is soft and sweet, like a flower. "Perhaps this is where our plan comes into play." She looks at her dad and gives him a nod of encouragement. I look at the Downing family, who seem to more or less call the shots around here. How much input does the council really have?

"Before we get into that, is there anything else you all want to cover?" Sam asks, looking around the group.

"Have you come up with any other way to address newcomers?" Finn asks, his voice quiet. "We've had four kids dropped off this last week. Their parents can't feed them."

Goosebumps rise on my flesh. How can we ever turn away kids? Images of parents pleading for us to take in their kids, to give them a chance to avoid starvation, are heart-wrenching. Looking around at the faces of the others, I know we're all feeling the same.

The room falls quiet. "We've eaten enough cattle that the remaining heads will have plenty of hay. We can eat their cob," Finn says.

I look at Bodin and mouth, "Cob?"

He shrugs.

Sam catches this exchange and tells me, "Cob stands for corn, oats, and barley. It's livestock-grade feed, but if we get desperate, it might work for us."

"Unless it gives us diarrhea," Kim adds.

"True," Sam says, considering. "Someone will just have to try it first. Cook it down."

Finn looks resigned. "I'll try it."

"Thank you," Sam says. "As for the newcomers, I propose an exchange system." Everyone looks at him. "We allow people to trade places with a newcomer, should they choose." My eyebrows shoot up. Everyone seems to like the idea. The group begins to hash out the details.

When it falls silent again, Tom looks at Sam. "It's time to tell them the plan, Dad."

Sam sighs deeply. "Alright then. I don't see any reason to beat around the bush here. We're obviously hurting. Maybe next year we'll be self-sustaining. Maybe the year after that. But one thing is certain: it won't be this year. They didn't leave us with enough time to prepare." I lean forward. Everyone has his eyes on Sam. Sam squeezes his eyes shut as if in pain. "Frank, why don't you take it from here?"

He nods, looking at his father with concern. "We're never going to be able to live happily ever after out here. We'll always be seen as a feeding source for the people of Eyth. Bodin told us that they'll stop taking in new recruits on December first." Bodin shifts when he's mentioned.

"Why?" Kim asks. "Why can't we live happily ever after out here? Eventually."

"Because they'll always need recruits," Frank says. "If it's not us. It'll be our children. Ava," he says, looking at me. "How old were the recruits in Eyth?"

I swallow hard, thinking of Sarah. "Not old," I say. "They only keep healthy, able-bodied people."

He turns to the group. "And what happens when they get old? And what happens when they see colonies of considerable size coming together and surviving out here? Will they let that fly?" He looks around. No one says anything. "As long as they're out there, they're a threat. The sooner we address the threat, the greater our chances of success."

"What are you saying? That we need to fight them?" Paul scoffs at the idea. "Us and what army?"

I find myself nodding before I can stop myself.

"We don't need an army," Frank states. "We need to be smart. How many of you would like to see them pay?" He looks around. Everyone nods apprehensively. "We do this by planting a few people on the inside. We only need to sabotage some of their software systems to bring the city to its knees. To give them a taste of what it's like."

"How?" Finn asks.

"And how does this solve our food shortage issues?" Marjory tacks on. I was wondering the same thing myself.

"Bodin," Frank says. Something tells me I'm about to discover why we've been invited here. "Tell the group about their food systems."

Bodin relays information he gleaned from the orientation video that all recruits are played upon entrance about their food systems. I fill in here and there with tidbits I had gathered from Lane. They have traditional crops, but their advantage comes from their highly efficient and space-saving aquaponics systems. The systems are easy enough. We need fish, which we can get from the river. Trout are some of the best options, and those swim in the Salmon River. We need seeds, which we have. We need equipment, but this is mostly PVC piping and basins to hold water. That shouldn't be an issue. All of this can be managed. It's water circulation and growing lamps that have us at gunpoint. We need a power source.

"If we could get some of their generators, we could build our own aquaponic systems. We could use the barn or this house. Then, we could grow food year-round. Aquaponic systems aren't rocket science. We could figure that part out. Hell, Bodin could probably draw us up plans," Frank says. I see Bodin change position from the corner of my eye. "But we do need power."

"What about the pumps?" Kim asks. "Will existing pumps work?"

"I believe so," Frank says. "It's the more advanced gadgets that use micro-processors that are never coming back. Things like cars, cellphones, computers, and kitchen appliances. We haven't found a generator that works either. Though, an older gas-powered one should work but that wouldn't be a long-term solution with the looming gas shortage. Besides, if anyone had one of those around here, we would have heard about it."

"What if you're wrong about our pumps working?" Kim asks.

"I'm not," Frank says. Kim purses her lips. "They just need to be plugged into a power source."

"Could the bikes be rigged to power the system?" Paul asks, hopeful. We all know he's referring to Frank's babies: the electric, solar-powered motorcycles.

Frank cracks his neck. "Possibly, but they're too valuable to us right now to be tinkering with them."

"More valuable than starving?" Kim mutters.

"No," Frank agrees. "If there's someone in this colony that we feel has a good shot of rigging some kind of power system using the bikes, I'm all ears." Blank faces stare back at him. Salmon doesn't exactly attract your Silicon Valley tech gurus. This is a specialized task.

"Ok..." says Marjory. "So, we steal power. Somehow. Then what?"

"Then, we disable some of their systems. Send them scurrying into the desert for refuge," Tom says.

Bodin says, "They used to feed us these meal bars in the mornings and at night. Most days, it was all we got. They weren't...terrible," Bodin looks at me, and we exchange a look. "But they kept us full for most of the day. They had to have been loaded with calories."

I jump in. "Yeah, and vitamins. Probably shelf-stable, too, since they were packaged and processed. We should try to get our hands on some of those." Bodin reaches over for knucks. I tap his fist, but my face falls. I start out looking at Bodin as I speak but then drop my eyes to the floor. "How are we supposed to steal things? Let alone sabotage anything? I just don't see how it's possible. They've got everything on their side. Plus, what if they

retaliate? Have we forgotten that the entire US Army stands behind them?"
I raise my eyes and scan the group.

"Well, for now," Bodin says. I look over at him, curious. "We only have
to," he makes a gesture of moving an invisible knife across his throat, "one
woman. The head of the army."

"That's it," Frank says in an atta-boy way. "We cut off their hold on the
army, and they'll be scrambling to regroup. In the meantime, we make our
getaway."

I feel a sliver of hope opening. This might work, but it's still a lot to ask
of anyone. *Hey, go risk your lives by being spies and recon agents. Oh, and
while you're at it, kill this person.*

"Who will do it?" I ask.

"Volunteers," Frank says. "It can't be Ava or Bodin. It can't be anyone
old." He points at Sam. "And it can't be me or anyone on my team because
of our ties to the old government."

"Volunteers?" I raise my eyebrows. Suddenly feeling exhausted, I draw
my knees into my chest and bury my face in them.

"It's a long shot," Frank agrees. "I thought we'd be able to assemble an
army, but I didn't anticipate how divided the people would be as they
entered into scarcity mindsets. We're fighting ourselves out here just as
much as they're fighting us. They counted on that, I'm sure."

The group begins to murmur amongst themselves. Bodin bumps me
with his knee. I turn my head to peek at him.

"We have to try," he says quietly. "Sure, it's intimidating, and it's a long
shot, but it's a chance. Besides, we're here, aren't we?"

Frank interrupts us. "Ava, Bodin." We look at him. "We have what I
believe is a solid plan, but we'll need you to prep the volunteers on what
they can expect and draw out maps of Eyth as best you can remember.
The most important thing is to get our people through the green doors.
The second most important thing will be getting one of our people into an

elevated social status. We need someone on the inside that's higher up than a recruit." I open my mouth in disbelief, but Frank anticipates my protests and asks, "Remember how Lane killed that software engineer?"

I nod, my mind attempting to leap to conclusions but coming up with only air.

"Well, maybe there's a job opening."

"You can't be serious," I interject. "How could you possibly...."

"We'll take care of that part. You don't need to worry about the logistics. We just need you two to prep the volunteers," Frank states.

He turns his attention away from us. I give Bodin a worried look.

Bodin shrugs. "You heard the man. Not our problem."

"But Bodin, this is a suicide mission," I protest.

"We got out," he states.

"We had help, and we didn't sabotage anything. As far as we know, we weren't on their most wanted list. We know their surveillance systems. How can they possibly think there's a chance to succeed here?"

Bodin's tone is sharp and dismissive. "It's not our problem, Ava. Frank knows more than we do, and they still have their inside man. Stop freaking out about it."

I huff and turn away from Bodin. The sounds of multiple muffled side conversations converge into unintelligible noise. Plus, the blood is pounding in my ears, hot from the rebuff from Bodin.

Finally, Sam quiets the group and says, "We'll be asking for volunteers tomorrow evening at supper. We'll take three days to prepare them before transporting them to Salt Lake for the next Army recruit pickup." I swallow. Sam adds, "And God bless their souls."

CHAPTER 27

Carrie

November 15, 2025

I wake up and stretch out before opening my eyes, letting out a groan of satisfaction.

"Sleep well?"

I jump. "Christ, Pax!" I pull the sleeping bag up reflexively before I remember I'm fully clothed, still wearing my coat even.

He waggles a finger at me and makes a tsk-tsk sound. "Don't use the Lord's name in vain," he teases.

"I didn't peg you for a Christian boy," I respond as I unzip the sleeping bag. The cold immediately sinks into my skin through my pants. I take in a deep breath and rub my fingers through my hair.

"Catholic, actually. You're cute when you sleep."

I groan. "How long were you standing there?"

"Five minutes, maybe."

I give him a pointed look. "Creepy."

"I didn't want to wake you. It seemed like you could use the sleep. Your bunkmates probably left an hour ago."

I sit up straighter. "Oh my god, I overslept. How could I have overslept? I never oversleep."

Pax shrugs. "Ready to go now?" he asks.

"Give me a minute," I say.

"Ok," he says, unmoving.

"Alone!" I say.

"Oh, right." He folds back the animal hide that covers our naked doorway and steps out.

I suck in a breath. First, I use the chamber pot. I'm acutely aware of the sound of my pee this morning as it hits the bottom of the near-empty chamber. I change my underwear but pull on the same pants and socks. Funny enough, I've been neglecting my own laundry while I wash everyone else's. Then, I brush my teeth and my hair, pulling it back in my signature ponytail. I peek in the small handheld mirror we keep hanging on a hook. I look tired even though I've just slept probably ten hours. I pinch my cheeks to give them some color. I debate putting on some mascara, but I don't want to look like I'm trying too hard, and wearing makeup in the Colony is a dead giveaway that you're trying to impress someone. I snort. I'm not trying to impress Pax. *Then why bother looking in the mirror?* a small voice inside of my head asks me. I silence it and tie my boots.

When I exit the hut, Pax is standing dutifully outside. His hands are folded in front of him. I notice a backpack he's carrying and figure he's thought of our provisions for the day. He gives me a wide, victory smile showing a row of perfect white teeth with bicuspids that look slightly vampirish. I swallow.

"I have to go tell Marlene where I'm going." I begin heading in that direction.

"I'll come with. It'll look more official that way since I'm on the recon crew." I look at him, wondering if he really believes Marlene will look at two attractive people around relatively the same age, leaving the Colony alone as nothing but business. I shake it off. *Who cares?*

As expected, Marlene looked at us with suspicion written all over her face before she nodded her approval. What would she have done anyway? And, more importantly, if she had said no, what would I have done? Everyone just seemed to fall into some kind of ranking here naturally. I don't remember anyone appointing Marlene as boss. She was just the one who took charge of the laundry first. That hardly makes her my superior, I think. However, I did just "report" to her.

"What are you thinking about?" Pax asks as we reach the top of Dynamite Hill to descend onto the road on the other side. They call that the large chunk of earth moved with dynamite to block the ranch's only obvious entrance in the early days. The hill gives them a good vantage point of who is coming up the road through the gully towards the ranch.

"Nothing," I mutter. Once we've gone about a half mile down the shaded road, it opens up more, and the sun hits my skin, warming me instantly.

"It's a nice day," Pax says.

I nod, though I wish I'd had the foresight to wear gloves this morning. My day was thrown off by waking up to Pax. I blame him. I blow into my hands. "Yeah, still damn cold though."

Pax stops in front of me and removes his gloves. He tucks them beneath his arm and takes my fingers, rubbing them between his large, warm hands. I don't stop him. "This is the worst of it," he says. "If we can make it through this winter, things will get better."

"What makes you say that?" I ask.

"We'll have time to plant decent crops and build better structures," he says. It's the same line we've been fed by the council before as they attempted to lift our spirits in the face of our dwindling food supply.

"I hope you're right," I say, looking away from him. He stops rubbing my hands but grips them tighter, willing me to look at him. I find his brown eyes staring intently at me.

"It will. I promise," he says. He lets go of my hands and holds out his gloves. "Here, wear these for a while."

"Thank you," I say, feeling the warm, soft fabric as I slip my fingers in. We walk in silence for another mile. The birdsong is loud this morning. The dirt road we're walking down is littered with curled, dried leaves. Some are still yellow, holding onto the last remnants of fall. The skeletons of aspen trees litter the roadside. Some evergreens poke through here or there, but they become fewer as we descend into the valley. The Salmon River snakes along the valley floor before us. It emits a soft mist. It's beautiful here. With gloves warming my hands, the sun on my face, a substantial meal in my future, and Pax next to me, I feel content for the first time in a long time.

"Your turn," I say as I return his gloves.

"No, you keep them. My hands are fine," he says. I think about refusing, but then I slip my hands back into them.

"What kind of name is Pax?" I ask.

"Short for Paxton," he says. I snort in laughter before I can catch myself.

"Ok, what kind of name is *Paxton*?" I ask.

"You'd have to ask my parents."

My tone changes. The birds seem to pause their song. "Where are your parents?"

"They moved this last summer. A couple of months before doomsday. To Florida. Couldn't take the long cold winters of Salmon anymore."

"Aw," I say. "Good timing."

"Maybe," he says. "I've come to realize that during hard times, your relationships with others hold the most value. They barely know anyone there. Mom knows how to garden, but they're both slowing down in their old age." He kicks at the dried leaves as he walks.

I think of reaching out and grabbing his hand but offer a shallow bit of solace instead. "At least it's warm there."

"The heat can be just as much of a threat as the cold," he says. "Maybe more. At least you can guard yourself against the cold. Things can be done. But the heat? After you've removed all your clothes and fanned yourself, what else is there?"

"Go for a dip, maybe. Did they move by the ocean?" I ask.

"Yeah," he says without sounding cheered by it. I let him sit with his thoughts. We've all lost people. People whose fates may be forever unknown to us. It's a scar we all must wear, and we're all way past platitudes like "I'm sure they'll be fine" or "You'll see them again one day." So, I don't offer him one. Instead, I change the subject.

"So, why did you move back?" I ask. "If your parents were leaving."

"That was always the plan. I was working in the oil fields in North Dakota. I'd saved up enough to come back and open my own business."

"The gym?" I ask, remembering when we stopped by his office/apartment hybrid home.

"Yeah. The town didn't really have one. Not a good one, anyway."

"A gym seems fitting," I say as my eyes travel over Pax's body.

He shrugs.

Once the road turns to pavement, I know we're close to our secret stash of survival food. My stomach growls in anticipation. We cross over the Shoupe Bridge. At least half a dozen people are spread along its banks with a line in the water. Pax and I exchange a knowing look. We have to be careful not to be spotted. We don't want to share. We turn down the highway and into the campground near the bridge.

"Stay here," he warns. "I'll grab us something from the bucket. Warn me if you see anyone."

"Got it," I say, looking around. "Coast is clear."

Pax takes off to the closest outhouse. The backside is surrounded by thick brush. We stashed the five-gallon bucket behind the outhouse in the thicket. Pax used a dirty brown t-shirt to put over it to hide the glaring white and red packaging. Then he threw some dirt on it for good measure. The bushes are thorny, a good deterrent. Plus, the package was so heavy-duty no animal would smell anything resembling food in there. I feel confident it's still there. I hear Pax lift the lid from the bucket. I look around. No one is nearby, and with the sound of the river muting us, we should be good.

I hear the lid being replaced. Pax emerges a few minutes later, zipping his backpack up. He smiles brightly.

"Come on," he says. "I know a place."

"Of course you do," I say, failing to prevent a smile.

We walk down the highway in the opposite direction from town. After a few minutes, Pax hops over a gate that leads away from the river on the other side of the road. Once on the other side of the gate, he holds out a hand for me, but I don't take it. I swing my leg over and jump to the other side. There's barely any indication of a road save for two thin dirt lines. A thicket of trees lines the road, but I can see it doesn't last long before it opens up in front of us. Pax stops once we enter the clearing. The road keeps going up and over a hillside, but Pax walks perpendicularly along the tree line, dodging sagebrush before deciding he's found a good spot.

"Here," he says. "The tree cover should shield us from anyone on the road, and there's nothing behind us." He gestures at the hills.

"How do you know?"

"Used to come up here with a friend to shoot rabbits," he says as he opens his backpack. He pulls out a small silver box that unfolds, revealing a single, small burner. Then he removes a small green tank and screws it into the stovetop.

"A stovetop with gas? How fancy," I say.

He beams at me. "Oh, you think this is fancy? Wait until you see what comes next." He pulls out a checkered blanket and flaps it in the air until it unfolds, and he pulls it down to the ground as a perfect square. Then he tosses two water bottles on the blanket and pulls out two silver packages. "What'll it be, my lady? Savory Stroganoff or Cheesy Chicken Rice?"

"Oh, that *is* fancy. I'll have the chicken, kind sir."

"Good choice. I've also got mashed potatoes for us to share. Here, have a seat." He gestures towards the blanket. I oblige and watch as he pulls a small tin cup from the bag and lights the stove. He boils water and then pours it into my chicken pouch. He reseals it and gives it a good shake before handing it to me. "Just have to give it a few minutes."

I nod and watch him boil more water for his meal. He pulls two forks from his bag and hands me one.

It's tough, but I wait for him to eat. He starts the water for the mashed potatoes. "Let's eat," he says, rubbing his hands together. I open the bag. The smell is intoxicating. I take a bite and close my eyes. The chicken, the cheese, and the rice are heavenly, but the cheese really does me in. I know it's highly processed powdered cheese, but right now, this feels like a dinner at the Ritz. Pax holds a fork of Stroganoff out to me. "Try this," he says.

I take a bite. It's good, but mine is better. "Mmm, try mine," I say as I dig in and hold a heaping fork to him.

"Oh, this is better," he says through a full mouth. We both laugh.

We finish our entrees and then alternate bites of the mashed potato. They're smooth like satin with a buttery taste. They're almost as good as my cheesy chicken rice was. I lean back with my face to the sky and sigh, satisfied.

"But wait, there's more," he says. I look over at him with my eyebrows arched. "I brought dessert." My eyes widen as he reaches into the backpack and pulls out another silver bag. "Maple Brown Sugar Oatmeal," he says.

I groan. "Oh my god, I think I love you," I say in jest, but he's looking at me seriously. I reach over and slap his arm. "You know what I mean."

He sighs, disappointed. "I know."

"Oh, come on, don't pout," I tease.

"Carrie, when will you give me a real chance?"

"I'm here, aren't I?" We stare at each other for a moment. He gives me a crooked smile and gets to work making the oatmeal.

When we've finished, we lay on our backs staring at the clouds above us, our hands interlocked. We talk about so many things. We talk until the sun moves behind the trees and the temperature drops. We pack up reluctantly and leave for home where another watered-down bowl of soup is calling my name. When Pax takes my hand during the walk home, I feel them fuse together.

A town meeting is starting when we return to the ranch.

Ava finds me through the gathering crowd. "Where have you been?!" she hisses. "I've been looking for you all day!"

"Sorry, I went with Pax. What's up?"

"I wanted to warn you about the meeting tonight," she says through the loud booming voice of Tom, who has begun the meeting.

"Warn me about what?" I whisper. I'm shushed by people nearby.

Ava crosses her arms and turns her attention to Tom, who stands atop a picnic table. Other council members are standing on tables, too. They look like messiahs, looking out at all of us gathered around. "Guess you're about to find out," she says.

What we learn at the meeting has me worried. As the crowd disperses, Pax looks at me without turning to leave, and I know immediately what the look in his eyes is telling me.

"No," I say in disbelief. "You can't possibly be thinking about volunteering."

Pax frowns. "I think I'll show up in the morning just to hear them out and see what other candidates they have to choose from."

"Why?" I ask.

Pax's eyes close. He pushes a breath out through his nose, "I know people in this community, good people, who have died or are going to die. My parents might be some of those people. I have a chance to make a difference here. To make my life mean something." He opens his eyes and looks at me, willing me to understand. Tears fall from my eyes silently, and I don't even care.

Ava interrupts us. "You have no idea what you're signing up for, Pax. They're brutal. They're heartless. They won't hesitate to kill you. This is a suicide mission."

He regards her and says, "Maybe so." He looks back at me. I shake my head with disbelief. I feel as if my world is imploding.

"I need to get some sleep," I say as I release his hand and take a step back.

He frowns at me and then nods.

Ava and I leave Pax standing alone behind us.

"I can't believe him," Ava says. I stay silent, the tears still falling down my face. Ava takes my hand. "I'm so sorry, Carrie," she says. I can't say anything. We walk together until we reach my hut. She hugs me goodbye. I climb up to the top bunk and flop down, staring at the ceiling while the wheels inside my head turn. The way I see it, I have two options: I can go with him or stay here and hope he returns. The fact that two options have presented themselves at all is a sign that I already know what I'm going to do.

CHAPTER 28

Sam

November 15, 2023

"It has to be you, Sam," Tom had said, and everyone had agreed. I sigh deeply with the weight of this announcement I've been tasked with as we approach the fire to address the community. Lately, we've been making announcements around the fire instead of from the deck to be close to the fire and the warmth. Though, again, I feel the privilege of my last name because those in the back are too far away to feel the fire and shiver, huddled together in the dark and the cold of the night anyway.

The council stands on picnic tables to address the colony. I stay on the ground.

"Thank you all for coming. We have some important announcements tonight," Tom projects as loud as he can. The people fall silent. It's like we can all feel it tonight, the shift in the air. "First up, we'll be delivering some of the heaviest news. We've asked Sam to give the announcement." He nods down at me. I look around and realize I'll have to elevate myself for everyone to hear and see me. I reluctantly climb to the bench, not mounting the top of the table. When I turn around, all eyes are on me.

I clear my throat and remove my hat, holding it to my chest. "We are at capacity," I state. Someone in the back shouts something.

Tom leans down and says, "Louder, Dad. They can't hear you in the back." He pats my good shoulder as he stands back up.

"We are at capacity," I repeat, much louder. I continue, feeling my confidence grow. "We cannot sustain another person. We have beefed up our security measures, and we will be turning away any newcomers." I look around and see people exchange glances. They know this might mean turning away friends—people we've all known as a part of this small community for ages. "We cannot save them all," I say, not as booming as before, but regardless, everyone seems to hear. There are some solemn nods. Others glare. "If this decision weighs as heavily on you as it does for me, we have provided an option." I pause before continuing. "We will not shoot to kill newcomers unless threatened. We will provide a trial for each person attempting to join the Colony if possible. The point of this trial is not to pass judgment or to deem anyone worthy but to provide us all with the opportunity to trade places with them." With this, a loud hum of chatter erupts from the crowd. "What this means..." I try to continue, but they're not quieting down. I stick my fingers into my mouth and let out a loud whistle. This gets their attention. "What this means is that you will have the chance to leave the Colony in exchange for another person entering."

The crowd erupts again. There are shouts directed at me, though I can't make out the words. My head swims, and my shoulder throbs. I need to refocus. I take a deep breath and wait for the crowd to settle.

As my eyes scan the crowd, I spot a familiar face. It's the boy who shot me. Despite the sun's absence, he's wearing the same wide-brimmed hat. I was right. Judging by his patchwork beard, he must be around sixteen. His Adam's apple bobs as our eyes meet. His shoulders hunch, and he steps back, attempting to shrink away. There's a man beside him with a hand on his shoulder who notices his change in posture and looks up to see what the boy has seen. I wonder briefly if I should tell this man what his son has done and, evidently, not reported. The man's expression changes to one of consternation at the attention I've given the boy. I decide it's not my place, that God can take over this one. I look away.

"Let us pray now." I lower my head and pray for forgiveness and guidance through these difficult times. I pray for understanding, and, with the most emphasis, I pray for a miracle. "Amen." Echoes of *Amen* reach my ears. I get down from the bench and sit on it, feeling exhausted. The chatter picks back up immediately. My shoulder begins throbbing like someone has poked their finger in the bullet hole. My body starts to sweat despite the cold.

"Our second and final important matter for the evening is that of utmost importance," Tom bellows. His voice carries more than mine. It's his words, the hint at more bad news to come, or the range with which he can project that causes the crowd to fall silent in eager anticipation. "We've all suffered in some way, sacrificed in some way. We've all been forced to live a life far below what we had before. Before, our way of life was ripped from us, and we were forced to fight amongst ourselves for survival."

I wonder how long Tom spent coming up with this speech. I know Tom, and it seems scripted, but looking out at the faces staring up at Tom, it seems to have the desired effect.

He continues, "If given the chance, who would seek revenge? Who would like to see them suffer as we have suffered?" His voice gets even louder towards the end—most of the crowd cheers. When Tom speaks again, his voice is quieter, but it doesn't matter because they're all hanging on to his every word. "Well, we have that opportunity. It'll be dangerous. But it'll be worth it. We are seeking a few brave souls to infiltrate their city by posing as army volunteers."

To my surprise, there were already shouts of "hell yeah!" and "I'll do it!" from the crowd. Tom uses his arms to indicate for the crowd to settle down. They obey.

"It can't be just anyone," he says. "They'll only take the young and the healthy. If you're over forty-five, you're out. If you have a health condition you can't fake your way out of, you're out. And... listen," Tom strains to regain control of the amped-up group. "Listen! Take the night to think about this. Talk it over with your loved ones. Do not take this decision lightly. There's a good chance you won't be coming back."

That shuts them up. Frank takes a small step forward to be beside Tom on the table and says, "Volunteers meet tomorrow morning at sunup at the big house for further instruction. You're dismissed." With that, the crowd disperses. I find Rose and take her hand. We walk back to the house together.

"Will anyone volunteer?" she asks.

"Let's hope," I answer. Rose loops her arm through my good side.

When we return to our room, Rose lights a candle and puts on her nightgown. I don't change. It hurts too much. I'm beginning to stink. Especially in the armpit of my bad shoulder, which I can't raise high enough to clean out. Rose sits beside me on the bed when she's finished and leans over to blow out the precious candle. She finds my hand in the dark. Her hands are cold and soft. They feel as delicate as a rose petal.

"We have provisions back in Stanley," I say. Rose sighs as if she knew this was coming. "We're old," I say in my defense.

"I know, but our family is here, and we're pulling our weight," she argues.

I scoff. "I'm useless now."

"Don't say that. They look up to you. They listen to you—the Colony. The kids need you," she counters.

"They're grown adults; they don't need me, and Frank and Tom can lead together."

"I don't want to leave the grandkids." Rose's voice cracks.

We sit in the silence. "Then, stay," I say quietly.

She sniffs. "Not without you."

"I can't let it weigh on my conscience, Rose," I reply, louder than I had intended. The impossibility of our situation is getting to me. I don't want to be without Rose, but I also don't want to pull her from her kids and grandkids. I can't stay, though. I know I'll swap places with the first woman or child's face that I see. I won't be in the Colony for much longer. I know this with absolute certainty. I just don't know where Rose will be.

***

Today is the day the volunteers leave for Salt Lake. I haven't slept well in the three days since we made the announcement around the fire. The pain in my arm tortures me. It runs up my neck into my head, and across my shoulders. Every hand movement is agony. I can't say it to Rose, but sometimes, I wish that bullet would have hit a better mark.

Of all the volunteers, we whittled it down to four people. Four viable candidates brave enough to infiltrate Eyth and carry out dangerous espionage tasks. And for one of those volunteers, murder. Our hopes are particularly pitted on two of them—Carrie, who may have enough experience in the corporate/city world to pull off her guise as a Software Engineer, and Phillip, the only one willing to take on the task of killing another human being—a woman no less.

Fueled by anger, Phillip may be motivated enough to see this through. He lost his son a few weeks ago to an asthma attack after his albuterol ran out. His wife he lost the first day when her car veered into the river. His grief has been spoon-feeding him resentment since. He's full of it. He needs an outlet—somewhere to direct it—someone to blame. We've given him that, and like a starving dog who's been thrown a steak, he's eager to devour it. Still, I know that Phillip wouldn't be the first to lose his nerve when faced with the reality of what he's agreed to.

These two hold the keys to our success.

The group is leaving today after sunrise. I'm waiting for that moment, but it's still too early. The morning outside is still black as tar. I attempt to breathe deeply to try to relax myself into sleep, but even that hurts. I give up. Instead, I form a speech as I listen to Rose sleep. I've never been one for deep, meaningful talk. If I try to talk about something relating to *feelings,* I freeze up. I don't have the tools to express myself, but this is different. I have to get this right so Rose understands. I'm not choosing to leave her to join the volunteers, but I am choosing when it's my time to meet God. I want to make my life meaningful. I won't throw it away attempting to be a recruit. That's futile. But I can help from the outside. I can plant the bomb we've pulled from the weapons cache to target the intake system. Still, a war rages within me. I try to remind myself of the Ten Commandments, in particular, Thou Shall Not Murder. But the injustice of this. *Can't we defend ourselves, God?* I've heard of too many horror stories. Children who have died without access to insulin. Children slowly starving to death. *Your children, God.* Enslavement, countless murders, and rape at the hands of those people sitting comfortably under their dome. Is it so wrong to want to put a stop to it? To avenge ourselves even? I don't have the answers to these questions. It's easiest if I follow the others. Go along with it.

I sigh deeply, pain throbbing anew. *Is this my punishment?* I sigh. I look up to the heavens. *We'll talk when all of this is over. Face to face, perhaps.*

Finally, the first signs of dawn cast themselves in the milky shadows that wash over the valley. I look at the mountain tops and watch the first golden tips appear. I watch as movement begins to descend on the valley floor. The large community fire is rekindled, still smoking from last night. It now blazes with strength. I see the first purposeful movement as a young man weaves his way through the settlement on his way up to the house. I can't tell from here, but that must be Hammer, with his tall, lean frame moving languidly. He's one of the boys I brought from Stanley. I feel proud knowing two of the four viable volunteers are here partly because of me. Hammer I brought from Stanley. Carrie is the young working professional we picked up from Salt Lake. I'm most hopeful about her, in particular, but she also has the biggest responsibility. She's been in the corporate world and lived in the city. She'll be the most at home there. She was perfect for the Software Engineer role. Despite the immense pressure of this particular role, she didn't hesitate, eager to please and earn respect in the Colony.

Then there's Phillip. The fourth volunteer is someone I'm also proud of. I've known him and his parents since he was a boy. His folks would buy a cow from us every year for butchering. While Paxton may have fallen in with the wrong crowd at one point in high school, he also dug himself out. He came back to this small town after working in the oil fields in North Dakota, like so many do, but he stayed clean, and he made something of himself. I see Paxton, who has managed to hold onto considerable muscle mass, move across the valley perpendicular to the house. I watch with interest. A second figure emerges, and the two join hands. Carrie and Paxton? I suck in a breath. Maybe I was wrong about her motivations. This could complicate things.

I scan the Colony and spot Phillip. All four of our volunteers are now heading to the big house for a rendezvous before hiking to Ron's Cessna for takeoff. We've always kept gas in a 250-gallon tank on the ranch. We've had to ration it considerably. The Cessna is a gas guzzler. We've secured more by siphoning it from abandoned cars in the surrounding areas, but it's in precious supply, and the clock is ticking. Even with the fuel stabilizers Tom has added, after six months, the combustion becomes so poor it'll begin destroying the engines. We'll have a warning before that happens—sputtering of the engine and poor vehicle performance. Yet another reason why it's now or never. Frank is also concerned about the life of the motorcycles. They'll run off solar power fine, but the battery life in past models has not been a promising indicator. Three years with good performance, hopefully. Then what, we're back to horse and buggy?

I turn away from the window at the sound of Rose stirring awake. She's stretching her thin arms above her head, a big yawn spreads across her face. I plod over and sit on the bed next to her. She smiles at me, and I almost change my mind. Pinpricks sting my eyes. I blink them away, surprised by their appearance.

"Rose." I clear my throat. "Rose," I say more clearly. She seems to notice my tone and sits up, alarmed.

"What is it?" she asks.

I had a speech worked out, but it leaves me. "I'm going with them," I say.

Her eyebrows draw together, confused, and then understanding strikes her features as her eyes widen. "Why?"

"I'm in pain. Excruciating pain," I explain, unable to elaborate further while a lump builds in my throat. I just need her to understand what I'm saying.

"I know, but it'll get better, Sam." She puts her hand on my thigh, her eyes boring into mine.

"I don't know," I say. My gaze drifts around the bare room before turning back to her. "I'm tired. Real tired."

She nods slightly, but I deflate when she decides she won't let it go. "What are you trying to say, Sam?"

I swallow and look at the floor. "It's my time, Rose. Soon. I want to go make something of these last days."

Rose shifts. "You can't be serious. You have plenty of time. Your shoulder will heal." Her voice is heavy, and I know the sound. She's about to cry.

"It's not just my shoulder." I breathe in. "I feel as if my heart is failing me. Before the bullet wound, I felt it. Like it was getting weaker, beating irregularly, and now, with the stress of this pain, I know it won't be long."

Tears run down Rose's cheeks. Her eyes are rimmed in red. My hope that Rose would make this easy on me has been swept away. She's going to fight. I've known Rose for a long time. Her strong will, thick skin, and gentle nature were never going to roll over and let her say goodbye without trying to change my mind. I feel exhausted already at the prospect, coupled with the lack of sleep from previous nights, and I wonder if I'll drop dead right here and now.

That wouldn't be so bad.

"I can tell you're tired, Sam," she pleads. "Let me take care of you. Stay here so that I can take care of you."

"Rose." Finally, a rogue tear escapes. I try to swallow away any other escape attempts. "You're the best. I couldn't have asked for better." I pat her leg, hating myself for crying and then doubly hating myself for being too preoccupied with my distressing show of emotions to express what I want to say properly. Rose falls into me. Pain, like a branding iron, seers into my shoulder, but for once, I'm glad for the pain. Pain, I understand. I grit my teeth and let Rose cry into my shoulder while I stroke the back of her head.

"Promise you'll try to come back," she says through sobs. I think about this. I won't throw my life away carelessly. This isn't a suicide mission, but I also know the odds aren't favorable. Should the opportunity come, I'll take it. And death is always nearby, waiting for its moment. We are looking for each other, and the chance that we don't collide is infinitesimally slight. Still, there's a chance.

"I'll try, sweetheart." I plant a kiss on the top of her head. It's easier to talk to her now that she isn't looking at me with those doe eyes. "You are the best thing that ever happened to me," I whisper. Rose cries harder, recognizing the goodbye. I get up and walk out the door, unable to look behind me as I do.

"Absolutely not," Frank says when I join the group and express my desire to join them. I plead my case, but Frank won't hear of it. They walk away from me as I kick the dirt after them in frustration.

I hadn't counted on this. I never imagined Frank would turn me down, but he did. I watch their backs as they begin the hike to the field where the Cessna is located. This doesn't change one fact: I can't live with this pain. Then, it comes to me. I have another option.

I go to the Med Shed and find Marie, the lead nurse there. She's well aware of my case. She had been the advocate to remove the bullet.

"Marie," I say.

"Sam," she says. "What's going on?"

I steel myself for what I'm about to ask. "Can you take it out? The bullet."

Her brow furrows. "Sam, it's been weeks. There will be new tissue to cut through. Why now?"

"Because I can't live with the pain. I can't sleep," I say.

She nods as if she understands, but I still feel she isn't grasping the situation and will likely refuse.

"I want to die," I add.

"What?" she asks like she didn't hear me.

"I said, I want to die. And I mean it. I'll take death over this pain. You're my last hope, Marie. Try to get it out, even if it kills me. I'll write a letter to exonerate you. Anything. Anything that could help, I have to try."

Marie walks over to me and looks into my eyes. "You don't look good," she confirms. "But Sam, this will hurt worse than whatever you're feeling now. A hundred times worse. And it's likely you've got a fractured shoulder. I can't repair the damage. I'm not a surgeon. This might not fix you."

"But there's a chance it'll improve after we remove it, right?" I ask.

"Yeah... A small chance," she concedes.

I grit my teeth with anticipation. "Then let's do this," I say with finality.

CHAPTER 29

Carrie

November 16, 2023

Tonight, with my nerves singing, I toss and turn, unable to sleep. There is only one other person I suspect is in a similar state at this hour. Or, at least, he wouldn't be too bothered by my intrusion if he was sleeping. I imagine all four of us are high-strung tonight. Pax, two others, and I are confirmed volunteers as of this morning. The briefing we got and the job I've been assigned are nauseating to think about.

I tiptoe quietly from my hut, hoping not to wake the other inhabitants. I can still smell the hair dye I washed out of my hair earlier as I repaired my roots and restored my hair back to blonde. Outside, the cool night air fuels my anxiety further. I walk hastily to find Pax, using the moon's light to guide me. Pax sleeps alone in the loft in the barn most nights when he's on Med Shed guard duty. Which, from what I understand, is every other night. When it's not Pax, it's John. I hope tonight is an on-duty night since I don't know where Pax sleeps on the other nights.

Ava is furious with me. She said I look like a Green. She told me more about being paraded around the Trade Party my first night, like the prize pig at the fair. I'd heard it all before, but she had to remind me that I'd be inches from the faces of the people responsible for all of this, and if I couldn't hide my disgust, they'd kill me. She made it clear she thought they'd do that anyway. I had argued that we had a plan that would keep me out of Green. I was going to be a Software Engineer. This only fueled her anger. I thought the vein on her forehead would pop. I eventually had to just walk away. We were at a stalemate. I wonder if we'll ever repair our relationship. She called me stupid as I walked away. It still stings. I know she was there, but her anger only pushed me farther from her and closer to Pax.

As I lift the latch and push the barn door in, I call out in a hushed tone, "Pax?" The barn smells of hay, mildew, and manure. I wonder how he sleeps in here.

He answers immediately, his shape appearing like an ink stain as he peers over the loft's edge, "Carrie?"

"Can I come up?" I ask.

"Of course," he answers. If he is surprised by my appearance, he's playing it cool.

I climb up the rough wooden ladder to the loft. Pax holds his hand out to me once I've reached the top. I take it because my eyes are still adjusted to the pitch-black interior of the barn.

We pad along until we reach his bed. It's a mattress on a low, metal frame. The moon seeping in from a small oval window nearby illuminates the outline of the bed.

"Ouch!" I hiss as my shin bangs against the bedframe.

"Shoot, you ok?" Pax asks as he flops down on the bed. I sit on the edge of the bed, still rubbing my shin. We're silent for a moment. After the pain in my shin subsides, I lie back and stretch my legs out.

"Here, get under the covers," Pax says as he tosses a soft, heavy blanket over me. I get comfortable and rest my head on the pillow next to his.

"I could get used to this," I say.

"You're always welcome anytime I'm here," he responds. "I'm sure you'd be welcome when John's here too, but then I'd have to punch his teeth out." I chuckle and smack him playfully. He pulls me into him. I don't protest. I soak up the heat from his body and let my hand rest on his chest, feeling him breathe. His fingers absently trail along my neck.

"What did we do?" I ask, breaking the trance. He pauses his caress.

"What we had to do," he answers before asking, "do you regret volunteering?"

"Sort of?"

"You could back out, you know? I think you should." He resumes his caress and then adds in a quieter voice, "It's safer here."

I don't respond immediately as I try to sort out my feelings. Somewhere in the forest outside, an owl hoots.

"It's just..." I begin. "I finally feel like I'm starting to fit in. Like I'm coming to terms with my life here. It's so... simple. I think I like that."

"So then, why'd you volunteer?" he asks, even though I know he knows the answer to that.

I answer him anyway. "Because you did. You were a big part of why this life started appealing to me."

He finds my hand and squeezes. "The funny thing is, I might not have if I'd have known we could have been happy here. I just thought you'd always be somewhere else. Mentally. Longing for some different kind of life. I didn't want to always be some consolation prize or something you pursued out of options or boredom."

I open my mouth, shocked. I thought the message I was sending yesterday at our picnic was loud and clear, but somewhere along the way, our lines got crossed.

"Pax..." I begin, but he cuts me off.

"But now, because you volunteered after me, I see this crack, this... *possibility* for us. But ironically, now we're stuck volunteering. Going down a different path."

"Are we really, though? Stuck?" I ask.

Pax sighs deeply. "You know the pool they had to choose from. The four of us are the best chance we've got. Besides, what better cause than to try to get back at the bastards that fucked up our lives?"

I cluck my tongue, teasing him for his use of language. "And here I thought you were perfectly content out here playing Johnny Appleseed," I say.

"Psh, hell no. Without you, there'd be no silver lining." We're quiet for a few minutes, and then Pax says, "I used to wonder why men would agree to fight on the front lines in a battle. They would literally step up knowing there was a good chance they'd take a bullet."

"You don't wonder anymore?" I ask.

"I think I get it now. But it's like it's partly just ingrained in us. Genetic maybe. This drive to join a cause. To make a difference. Even if it's small." He pauses now and then says, "I think you feel it too—that drive. When faced with a life-altering decision, it's like, for just a moment, I can step outside of myself and make a decision that isn't about me."

I don't know what Pax is going on about, but I let him talk it out. When he's finished, I reach up and trail my fingers along the stubble on his jaw. "Guess we're stuck with it then," I say with a loud yawn, feeling the pressure of sleep begin to creep in. "I have a hell of a lot to learn about software engineering. I felt like I was drinking from a firehose today when I was handed that book."

"You're a bright, attractive woman. I agree with Sam that you're the best fit for the role. Though, I don't like to think about it too much. When all else fails, don't forget how much power you hold as a woman," he says.

"Ah, yes. My womanly charms," I say, trailing off.

"We'll be alright," he whispers into the night, turning his head to kiss me on the forehead. "We'll do this and come back to live out our days here as Mr. and Mrs. Johnny Appleseed."

I feel the comfort of his promise wrap around me. I smile and drift off to sleep.

***

Five days later.

Getting here was not uneventful, but the anxiety I'm feeling now as I watch the sand-colored Army caravan trucks pull up to the volunteer pick-up location is unbridled. I didn't expect so many people to be here, waiting. This is not how Bodin and Ava described their recruitment day. Word must have spread to the farthest corners, drawing out the increasingly desperate people. I find Pax in the crowd, standing in the parking lot, but he isn't looking at me. We thought it would be best if we pretended we didn't know each other. That way, if one of us gets caught, we don't all go down. Hopefully, anyway.

When the trucks pull up, people begin to crowd closer, pushing and shoving. I do my best to remain calm. When the army doors slam shut, at least four soldiers dismount from each of the three vehicles. A couple of them stand on the hoods of the trucks and shoot their weapons into the air. The piercing sound stills the crowd.

"Line up, single file. Starting here," a soldier with a buzz cut bellows from atop the hood of a vehicle. A shot rings out again from a different soldier, and there are screams from the crowd, who start pushing again. Another shot rings out to demand our attention. "If we see a weapon on you, we'll shoot. No questions asked. Now line up!" We scramble to do as we're told, and as the crowd conforms to a line, I see the source of the earlier scream and gunshot. The body of a man is folded over itself, a pool of blood seeping into the pavement of the parking lot. I swallow, trying to control my fear.

"If we say you're a no-go, we mean it. Anyone who causes trouble will be shot," a booming male voice informs us. A no-go? I hadn't expected there to be a selection process but looking around and knowing that Ava and Bodin had been among only a few, I assume they can be more selective up front now, giving themselves better odds that they're transporting green door people. I'm in the middle of the line. I can peer around the people in the line and see three officers looking people over. Some people are asked to jump or do pushups. I watch as an officer tells an elderly woman, "No."

Two people in front of her who had already been selected begin to protest at her rejection. A gun is put to the elderly woman's head. I squeeze my eyes shut. I hear more shouting and crying but, thankfully, no gunshot. I open my eyes and see all three walking away with their arms around the old lady. I breathe a sigh of relief.

By the time it's my turn, I already know I have a good chance of being selected. Some people are nothing more than walking skeletons. Weak from starvation. These are the ones that are being weeded out. It's a death sentence, and everyone knows it.

I come to the front of the line. A man looks at me without expression and says, "Push-ups." I drop to the ground and do my best to crank out three pushups. I'm weak, but many couldn't even do one. "Up!" he commands. I hop to my feet, trying to exude energy and youth. He studies my face for a second and then instructs with a jerk of his head, "Truck three." I breathe a sigh of relief as I go to stand near truck three. I peek over at Pax, who looks relieved, too. His turn is coming up. He makes it. I throw my head back, grateful, and then turn my back, not wanting to watch the rest of the proceeding.

There are some scuffles, and I expect that a couple of people have provoked the officers on purpose after they were rejected, taking the option of a quick death. A bullet to the head is better than a slow death from starvation. My eyes leak with tears. There are at least three more shots. Three more bodies.

I attempt to distract myself by reviewing software engineering terms in my head. I studied as much as I could, given I only had a few days. My nose was in a book twelve hours a day. I practically read them in my sleep. I'm nervous as hell that I won't be able to pull off this facade. My legs itch to run as we mount the steps into the back of the truck. There are sixteen of us in each truck. Unfortunately, Pax is in truck one, and I'm in three. Hammer and Phillip make it also. I don't know which trucks, only that they're not mine.

The ride goes as expected, thanks to Bodin and Ava's recounts. We're in the truck most of the day, stopping for only two bathroom breaks. One of which consists of small sips of water. It must be around four or five in the afternoon now as the truck backs up and comes to a stop.

Once we've dismounted and entered the sorting area, I recognize the green door Ava told me about. My eyes glance at the yellow door. None of us should be going through this door since we've all been prepped to present ourselves as healthy and robust—which is mostly true and only over-embellished to provide us with a safety net that casts far away from that yellow door. However, given the preliminary screening process in Salt Lake, fewer people should be going through that door overall.

As my number is called, I walk up to a table and sit across a bored-looking man in a gray uniform. A lanyard hangs from his neck, though it's turned, so I can't see his name. He asks me basic questions, all of which I expected. I answer honestly, not wanting to complicate things with a fake name. Plus, Frank warned us that it wasn't out of the realm of possibility for them to have facial recognition software that would give them my real name anyway. I pray that it doesn't contain information on my previous job occupation, which is not Software Engineer. It's a risk we had to take.

Finally, the questions to which I have more scripted answers come up. "What skills do you have?"

I wring my hands beneath the table. "Oh, not much, I'm afraid. I was a Software Engineer before all this. Not much use now, I'm sure," I say, finishing with a rehearsed, nervous chuckle.

He raises his eyebrow, interested. "What kind of Software Engineer?"

"Machine learning," I state. "I designed advanced algorithms and models using generative AI to solve industry problems. Boring stuff." I flash my best smile.

He taps his pen on the table before deciding on something. He stands. "Would you mind waiting here, please?"

"Oh, sure." Nervous toe tapping has joined my incessant hand wringing beneath the table as I wait.

The man returns with a woman in the same boring uniform. He stands while she takes his place and peppers me with questions. This is an interview, I realize.

The woman stands and tells me, "You may proceed through the green door. A woman named Sheila will meet you on the other side." She nods to the man to reclaim his seat as she stands.

"Thank you," I mutter as I approach the door, wiping my damp palms on my pants. I push open the door using the bar and see who must be Sheila already waiting on the other side.

"Congratulations, Carrie," she says. She's dressed professionally in a black pantsuit with a polka-dotted blouse underneath. Shiny, black, pointed pumps poke out from under her pants. She's wearing moderate makeup with thick black liner. Her curled brown hair falls past her shoulders. She's a woman in her forties trying to appear to be in her thirties. She smiles confidently. She's precisely the executive-type I'd encounter at my old job.

"For what?" I ask.

She continues, "You've joined the ranks of essential workers here in Eyth. It's a coveted position, I assure you."

I smile at her, hoping it passes for proud and not scared shitless.

"Let's walk and talk," she says as she turns down the hallway. "I'm Sheila. I'll be your liaison, showing you the ropes until you're settled. Our first stop will be your quarters, where you'll be given time to shower and eat before reporting to your work assignment in the tower."

I gulp. "Tonight? I'm pretty tired. Do I have to start tonight?"

Sheila looks at me sideways. "Of course you are, but I'm afraid our situation necessitates a hasty commencement."

To my surprise, we walk past the branding machine Ava and Bodin had described for me when they showed me the numbers tattooed on their wrists. When the double doors beyond it open, I forget about my nerves for a moment and gasp. The city is gorgeous. I feel giddy, like a kid who just got to Magic Kingdom for the first time.

"It's marvelous," I say.

"Isn't it?" Sheila beams with evident pride. "It never gets old seeing that look on new recruits' faces." Her smile is broad, and then she seems to return to herself. "This way." She turns on her heels again. No guards escort me, as they did with Ava and Bodin. I'm beginning to feel like I've entered entirely new territory. For which I'm woefully unprepared. My earlier confidence came from placing too much emphasis on knowing what to expect. I follow just steps behind her.

We walk through a dizzying maze of sidewalks until Sheila stops in front of a waiting car. It lights up at her approach. The door opens without her having to touch it.

"Neat, huh?" she says. "We're going to building twelve, by the way. It's where all essential workers are housed."

I pull one question from the myriad swimming in my head. "How'd you do that?" I ask as she gets in and scoots to the passenger-side bucket seat. I look down at the driver's seat she left vacant for me.

She ignores my question, reading my confusion. "It's self-driving," she says with a giggle. She's enjoying herself. I must look like an idiot to her. I get in and sink down into the plush leather bucket seat. The door slides closed. The car glides away smoothly, hardly making a sound. I stare out the long window that runs like a stripe from the front to the back of the car. There are four other seats behind us, all empty. Looking up at the towering buildings and seemingly floating along, it all seems so surreal. It's like I've entered an alternate universe.

"Metalink," she says, picking up on the threat of our earlier conversation. I look at her. She's smiling as she taps behind her right ear. "With this, just thoughts turn into real actions. You'll have one soon, too."

I freeze. She mistakes my horror and continues, "The procedure doesn't hurt, and you'll love it. It's sooo convenient. I don't know how I ever lived without it, to be honest."

"Oh," I manage. I swallow. "When will I get mine?"

"Day after tomorrow, we have you scheduled for two o'clock. Don't worry. I'll walk you through everything you can expect. I'll put it on your calendar and arrange the transportation."

"Ok," I say, trying to mask the panic rising. Ava told me about Metalink. I'm so wholly fucked if they install that thing in me. My thoughts will betray me instantly. I thought it was a choice, but it's not being presented that way. I don't want to draw any more suspicion to myself as the mysterious outsider. So, I don't ask this. Besides, it's clearly not a choice. With me, they won't be taking any chances. I have less than two days to accomplish what I came here for. A horrifying thought occurs to me: it's not just me. My thoughts will give away Pax and the others, too. I wonder if they'll have to get the implant. I slump further down into the car's seat.

I entered this city less than an hour ago, and already we are so fucked.

CHAPTER 30
Carrie

November 21, 2025

My housing arrangements aren't what I expected either. The space is probably around 600 square feet with a bedroom, living room, and kitchenette area. It feels a little like a stay at the Residence Inn. Everything about it is so... normal. The electronics work. The shower is hot. The bed is comfortable. There's toilet paper next to a flushable toilet. The sheets smell clean. There's bottled water in the fridge. As I stand on the glistening marbled tile of the shower with the water rushing over me in indulgent, hot rivers, I shuffle through all of the recent living arrangements I've had: the office, Cal's house, and the tent on the ranch. This feels positively dreamlike in comparison. It makes me think of Ed. Like, for just a second, I can imagine that nothing bad ever happened. There was no EMP. It was all just a nightmare, and here I am, in a hotel room away on a business meeting. *I'll be home soon, honey.* The thought makes my throat constrict. I turn my face into the stream of water and allow myself to cry. I don't even care that this shower has become the longest one I may have ever taken. I let myself enjoy it. I shave. I allow the water to wash away my tears, whisking them down the drain.

I turn the shower off and step out, wrapping a warm towel around my body. I look at the clothes hung for me on the backside of the bathroom door: khaki trousers and a dark blue blouse with a v-neckline size small. I dress. I stand in front of the mirror and swipe the condensation away with my hand. I stare at myself for a moment. It's me. Carrie. But it's also not me. This Carrie has shed a layer of skin and stepped out in a new skin—a stronger one. *You can do this*, I tell myself.

I poke around in the bathroom drawers and find a packaged toothbrush, hairbrush, hair dryer, and some makeup. I get ready as I try to keep my nervous energy from consuming me. When I emerge, Sheila looks annoyed. She gets up from the couch and walks over to a small, metallic square on the wall. She proceeds to explain to me that it's where the food comes from. She shows me how to use it and then encourages me to order food before we leave.

"So, we don't have to pay for it?" I ask as I browse through the menu options.

She laughs. "There's no money here. We all work and pull our weight, and we get what we need in return. You get three meals per day and unlimited coffee."

I raise my eyebrows.

"This is what a civilized, advanced society can accomplish." She says it flatly, and I can't help but feel like that was an intentional poke. Something has recently caused a shift in her attitude towards me. I shake it off and return my attention to the menu on the digital display. The ease of all this at my fingertips strikes me. It's ludicrous. I think back to the picnic I had with Pax just days ago and how all of that seemed so luxurious. What is this in comparison? Heaven? Pax has to be feeling giddy over this feature. I wonder what his first meal will be. Or will it be a meal bar like what Bodin told us about? Guilt falls like a rock in my stomach. Of course, he won't be an essential worker like me. He's eating a meal bar tonight, if anything.

Pax. There's a name I never thought would coexist alongside technology like this. I had Pax and Ed on two sides of a firm line: post-technological blackout and pre. But now, Pax is mingling with the other side. Should I feel guilty? I feel as if my life with Ed was eons ago. If I'm being honest with myself, I'm not even sure Ed and I would fit anymore. If I could have Ed back, but that meant giving up Pax, would I choose that? I don't know anymore. Even though Pax is my post-blackout prospect, he feels safe. Right, almost. Who am I kidding? I'm only torturing myself with the illusion of choice. Ed is not here. I'll never see him again, and I may have all but sealed my fate with Pax. My hand goes to my abdomen. Still no period.

It could still be due to a nutrient deficiency. I've heard of women who were too skinny to get their periods. But it was so regular before. You'd think it would sputter out and end slowly if it were a calorie-deficit thing. I sigh deeply. And then there's the way I've been feeling lately. More tired than usual. More emotional. It could be anything.

I think back to a scene from my favorite childhood movie, *Finding Nemo*. "Denial," the sharks had said during that AA meeting. Movies. There's another interesting thought. I punch in my order for pizza and sides. "Are there movies here?" I ask.

"Oh, sure. There's a theater, or you could watch just about anything right here during your time off." She sweeps her arm over the window I have that looks across the street at another building. My confusion must be evident because she says, "It's a voice-activated interactive display when you're using it. It's a window when you're not." She smiles impatiently. I'm ready to be out of her company, too. My food arrives. I thought I'd enjoy the fresh fruit salad, breadsticks, and pizza, but my stomach is in knots, and it's hard to choke down.

Before I finish chewing my last bite, Sheila stands to escort me to the engineering tower. We're quiet almost the entire way. Sheila attempts small talk once, but she clearly can't converse politely without me making a remark or referencing the outside world and what I'd been through.

"So, it's just you? No family?" She'd asked and then winced when she noticed my face harden. She doesn't want to know. Not really. She wants to keep her fantasy world neatly bottled and unadulterated to keep herself distanced from the sticky business of logistics and what it took for this fantasy land to exist.

Sheila shows me the nineteenth floor. At least twenty people sit behind computer screens. "You'll mainly be working here, but I want to show you the upper level, too. That's where most of the hardware and processors are housed, and the real important work is done. Not that your work isn't important." She blushes. "Oh, before I forget..." She digs around in the pocket of her navy-lined trousers and pulls out a lanyard. "This is your temporary security badge to use until you get Metalink. It'll grant you access to your apartment and the nineteenth floor only." I nod.

I take the lanyard with the dangling white card encased in plastic and place it around my neck. We take the elevator up one flight. The doors slide open before us without instruction. A wave of warmth washes over me as we enter the room. The hum of equipment and the blinking lights make it feel like I've entered a spaceship. To top it off, the ceiling is sloped with dark glass and sweeping 360 views of the city below.

"Wow," I say. Just then, three men who sit in roller chairs turn from their screens to see who's arrived. Like dominos, I watch as their faces change upon my acknowledgment. I can't help but feel flattered by the apparent impact of my presence. One has a hand frozen midair with a donut waiting outside a gaping mouth. Another has wide eyes, and another looks scared, gulping audibly.

"Boys, you can all roll your tongues up off the floor now. This is Carrie. She's a new tech downstairs," Sheila says. The boys snap to attention, waving off the shock of an attractive, novel female presence. I shake each of their soft, chubby hands. It takes me a minute to pinpoint the source of my rising anger. They seem nice enough, but their presence irritates me. Then it hits me. It's the donuts in their hands. It's their fat, round cheeks, and bellies. It's their regular clothes and brushed hair. It's their paper cups of half-drank coffee. I hate them for these displays of normalcy and glutton.

There are so many people out there starving, and they're in here, fattening themselves up. I grit my teeth through the introductions. Their names are Carlos, Phil, and Duncan. I'm asked about my work history. I keep it vague. I notice one has a lanyard around his neck, like me. They're identical. This means two things to me. One, not everyone is required to get Metalink around here, and two, his badge has access to this floor.

I feel the adrenaline pulse as I realize I have to seize this moment. I scan the room, and a plan is devised, but before I enact it, I have to ask, "What's that?" I point to a hatchet encased in glass on the wall.

The guys look around at one another, and then a brave one says, "Oh, it's mostly a joke. Break in case of emergency kind of thing." I stare at him, not getting it. "You know, because there are no stairs," he adds.

"No stairs?" I ask.

"Naw, don't need 'em," he replies. "We keep this place running smooth as a whistle. Stairs are archaic, now."

"So, what's the joke?" I ask. "That if there's an emergency, you'll use that thing to break a window and jump to your deaths?" I deadpan. The guys look at each other, unsure. I give a fake laugh. "You guys are so uptight," I say, but in my head, I think: *you guys are so lame.* Then, it's time to make my move.

I target the lanyard guy. I step closer to him. "So, what is it that you do up here?" I ask. As I expected, he's flustered by my attention. I glance at Sheila. "Is there any way I could get one of these?" I point to Phil's coffee, but I'm clumsy and knock it into his lap. He jumps back.

"Oh my god. I'm so sorry!" I stride over to a paper towel dispenser on the wall and pull a few away. When I come back, I begin patting the brown liquid on his crotch, saying "sorry" repeatedly. I'm blotting at the coffee in his lap. It's driving him crazy. I can see it. I turn back to Sheila. "Can you get him another coffee?" I ask sheepishly. She narrows her eyes at me, unmoving.

"No, it's fine. It's fine." He's backing away from me now, embarrassed by the situation and the growing bulge in his pants from all the contact.

"Why don't you practice using the food panel some more?" Sheila says, eyeing Phil's pants. "You can order Phil a new coffee yourself."

"Oh, ok," I respond, hoping to sound meek and embarrassed. She looms over me as I fumble with the panel. She informs me that outside of my place, I have to scan my card to order anything so they can keep track of who's ordering what. She reminds me that once I have Metalink, I won't have to bother with the card.

Once the door slides up and a steaming coffee is presented, I walk it over to Phil. When I place it before him, I bend down and whisper in his ear. "Come see me downstairs, Phil." He stiffens, but I'm sure no one else heard. Sheila and I leave. Phil better show up. I need that lanyard.

Sheila introduces me to my direct report, Dan, and leaves me there with him. The evening is a blur. Dan is not affected by my presence like the others upstairs were. I can feel my armpits begin to sweat, and my cheeks blaze as he asks me questions. My uptake is slow. My inadequacies are evident after just thirty minutes with Dan. I can't believe we thought I could read a few books and slip in here. I only had to pose as a Software Engineer for a few days. Already, I can tell he is questioning my legitimacy with his disapproving looks and scrutinizing eyes. It doesn't help my case that I'm exhausted. At one point, Dan gets up from his computer. He locks it and steps away.

I put my head into my arms. I'm nearly asleep before I catch myself and dart upright, looking around guiltily. Then, I see Dan standing behind the glass paneling of an office. My blood freezes. He's talking with another man, and they're looking at me. Dan does not look happy, and the other man looks concerned, with his eyebrows drawn together. I can't pretend I don't know what they're talking about, and I can't let this get out of hand. I know men like these. I've dealt with them my entire finance career. They get uncomfortable around women and emotions, and if there is any Human Resource presence here, I can use that to my advantage.

I can see the looks of surprise cross their faces as I stride over to them and knock on the closed office door. Dan opens the door, and I step through.

"Hi, I'm Carrie," I say, outstretching my hand to the man beside Dan, who introduces himself as Naveed. He looks at Dan and then takes my hand. His face is firm. I sigh.

"Look, fellas, I can't even begin to explain to you what I've been through recently, and I'll spare you, but the truth is, I'm exhausted, and my life as a Software Engineer feels like it was a lifetime ago. I know I'm sucking out there right now, but I assure you, I just need a good night's sleep. I haven't had one of those in months."

The men exchange looks.

"Can we just start fresh tomorrow?" I ask, giving my best smile.

Naveed nods his head. "Of course, Carrie. We understand." I can tell by Dan's expression that he doesn't understand, but Naveed is in charge here, not Dan. "Why don't you go home and get some sleep, and we'll reassess after tomorrow's meeting?"

"That sounds great. Thank you for understanding," I respond. I don't know what meeting he's referring to, but I don't want to remind the men of my incompetence by asking about it. Having been dismissed, I leave the office and breath in relief, but then I realize I'm not sure I know the way back home.

I stand in front of the elevator. I'm just about to suck up my pride and walk back to Naveed to ask for his assistance when the elevator door slides open, and my knight in shining lanyard stands there, his hands in his pocket and a look of surprise on his face when I'm there in front of him. I blink at him. "You came," I say.

"I came," he replies. His forehead glistens.

"Good," I say as I rock back on my heels. "I'm supposed to go home now, but I'm not sure how to get there."

He eyes me. I hold up my hands. "I'm not trying to pick you up, promise. But could you show me the way?"

"Ok," he agrees.

I enter the elevator, and we make a very awkward, silent descent together.

Once out on the street, he approaches a screen on the side of a building with a prominent white border. He stares at it and says, "I could just call you a car and punch in the destination as tower twelve."

"Oh," I say, wondering why he hasn't done it yet. Then, my brain catches up. "Or you could come with me?" I pose it as a half question.

"Or that," he confirms, diverting his eyes. His cheeks glow brightly even in the dimming light.

"Ok," I say. "Would you mind doing that tonight? Coming with me?"

He taps at the screen and turns around, keeping his hands in his pockets. His face is boyishly giddy. His round belly protrudes past his pants like that of a pregnant person. He is, to put it lightly, not my type.

"Sure thing," he responds.

The car comes, and we climb inside. We're silent. The air of expectation hangs heavy. We exit and go through the entrance to the building I remember from earlier.

As we enter the elevator, Phil says, "Just scan your badge, and it'll take you to the right floor."

"Got it," I say, wishing I'd paid more attention earlier. However, Phil seems to be getting a rise from helping me. I'm like his damsel in distress right now. This is probably his fantasy playing out.

Once we've exited the elevator, I go straight to my room, 443. At least I remembered that. I scan my badge and open the door to my home sweet home.

"Why don't you have a seat on the couch," I say. "Make yourself comfortable. I'll make tea." He takes off his jacket. I turn towards the kitchen and pause. The couch groans as he sits on it. I have no idea if there's tea. I open the cupboards and close them. There are neatly stacked dishes and glasses in a couple of them. The rest are empty.

Phil tries to make small talk, oblivious to my flailing. "Are you going to the meeting tomorrow morning? What am I saying? Of course, you are. It's for the whole software/tech department."

"I heard about it briefly. Remind me, what is it?" I ask.

"First thing tomorrow morning, we'll go to the Vivent Center to listen to a lecture and begin a round table discussion. It's always the third Tuesday of the month."

"Huh," I say as I try one last cabinet. "Could I follow you there?"

He perks up at this. "Of course," he says.

"Uh," I say awkwardly, turning towards the living area. "I guess I don't have tea."

"Let me help," he says as he gets up from the couch and walks towards the food panel.

"Oh, right," I say and blush. My eyes watch him. It's then that I notice his lanyard is not around his neck. I eye his coat on the back of a barstool just a few feet away. The lanyard is hanging from a pocket.

"What kind of tea do you like?" he asks, startling me. I force my eyes away from his coat.

"Any kind of herbal, I guess." I let out a steady breath and remove my lanyard from around my neck.

"There's hibiscus rose, peppermint, chamomile..." As he's listing off the teas, I walk lightly towards his coat, pausing when it's just behind me. I pretend to get a better view of the options on the screen before him. He pauses and turns his head to me, smiling. I smile back. When he returns his eyes to the screen, I keep my eyes trained on him as my hands switch out the lanyards behind my back.

"Peppermint is fine," I say, leaning closer to him. "Be right back." I slip into the bathroom. When I close the door behind me, I press my back to it and let out a long breath. I did it. I put my hand on my chest over my heart. I feel it thudding rapidly beneath my sternum. This is all happening so quickly. I thought I'd have more time to adjust here to develop a well-thought-out plan. Instead, things unfold before me almost faster than I can mindfully react. I feel as if I'm walking a tightrope suspended hundreds of feet into the air over a void, and twice now, I've nearly fallen to my death. But still, I did it. I clutch the lanyard between my clenched fist, feeling the edges biting into my flesh. I allow myself a few seconds of celebratory thinking before a thought stops me dead. He'll need his lanyard to get into his own house tonight. *Oh, fuck me.*

When I return to the living room, I make words come out of my mouth that make me want to vomit, but they're portrayed outwardly as vulnerable and desperate. "Phil, I have a request." He looks up at me from his position on the couch. His lips are large, and his eyes seem too small for his large head. "Can you stay with me tonight? Not in a sexual way? I just want someone sleeping next to me. It's just that I'm feeling so alone right now."

Phil looks disappointed for a split second and then says, "Yeah, sure. Whatever."

"Great," I say. "I'm exhausted. Can we turn in now?"

"Now?" he asks. I give him a pout. "Uh, sure," he agrees reluctantly.

We're finally in bed, lying beside each other, crammed on the full-size bed with his large body. Phil doesn't try anything. I get the sense he's just happy to be here, thinking he's playing it cool by "taking it slow." I don't think I'll tell Pax about this. I fake being asleep immediately, but my mind is running too wild to sleep. In the morning, I'll find a way to have him go on to the meeting without me. That's my window to sneak back into the engineering tower. What will I do? I need to damage their systems somehow, but then what? I sleep fitfully, knowing that tomorrow will either be a day of victory or a day that ends badly for me. Very badly.

CHAPTER 31

Carrie

November 22, 2025

P hil and I walk to the Vivent Center for the meeting. I suggested this as a way to see the city more instead of hopping in a car. I plan to say I forgot something in my apartment—a tampon, maybe. I want to be far enough away that he's less likely to suggest he comes with me. As we walk, I take in the city. The faint outline of the dome gives the city a futuristic look. Glimmers of shiny buildings peek out from the vegetation coating so much of the vertical surface area. Everything is immaculately clean. What they've done here is incredible. We pass shops and restaurants. As I glimpse through the window and see all the people doing everyday things, I have a hard time reconciling the evil I've assigned to them. The woman holding up the purple dress and pressing it against herself as she considers her appearance in the mirror doesn't look evil. The man bringing a fork up to his mouth as he dines with his two children doesn't look evil.

"Wait until you see the city park," Phil says. "It's right around the corner."

When we round the corner, a large, flat circular chunk of land is before us. It has various sculptures and massive trees encompassing the space. We walk towards the center. As we go, there are patches of grass for picnicking or lounging, and there are concrete structures that dip and twist in exciting ways. I watch as two kids laugh and chase each other through tunnels. Parents sit on benches, books in their hands. Some talk to no one in particular, and I wonder if they are using Metalink to connect to others. I'm so focused on these normal displays of human behavior that when Phil says, "Not another one" in a petulant way, I don't see what he's referring to at first.

He stops, and I follow his gaze. Hanging from what look like lampposts are two lifeless bodies strung up by their necks side by side. A sign hangs around each of their necks. "Traitor," the signs read. One appears to be older. The coloring on his body is a mottled purple. His face is badly swollen, but the fresher one... he looks... I stare in disbelief at him. I stop breathing. He's wearing gray coveralls with a green patch around the bicep. His curly brown hair falls across his face. His mouth is slightly agape. A swollen tongue hangs out of his mouth. His eyes are open. The world seems to spin around me, but I'm frozen in place. The familiar milky brown of Pax's eyes look as if they've been painted over with bright red. I gasp. Fall to my knees. My body starts to shake. I feel like a house has collapsed on top of me. I'm aware of nothing else, only suffocating beneath the weight of it.

"Are you ok?" Phil asks with alarm.

It takes me so long to try to work through the chaos of my emotions. Intellectually, I know I should play it cool and not give any indication that I know Pax. Emotionally, I am raging. I can hear those children playing. They're *playing,* and Pax is dead. But worse, they're playing around his strung-up body. Like it's nothing. Any compassion I felt for these people only moments ago is wiped away in one cold rush. They're barbaric. I swallow back vomit.

Just for a minute, I have to pretend that I did not just see Pax and some other man hanging in the public square. If I want revenge, I have to do this. I slowly release my clenched fists and get to my feet. The nausea subsides.

"I've never seen a dead body before," I say quietly, not looking up. It's a lie, but Phil could never know that.

"Well, if it makes you feel any better, they deserved it," Phil says. "This one helped two recruits leave the city. I don't know what this guy did, but

I'm sure we'll hear the story soon." I can't look at either one of them. This does not make me feel better. Instead, I resist the urge to strangle Phil. The temptation to reach out and wrap my hands around his thick throat is so strong that the only thing keeping me from doing this is knowing that I could potentially do more damage if I act unaffected by this. I swallow it down.

"Yeah, I'm sure you're right. It's also that time of the month for me. I don't think that's helping." I try to make an abashed grin with all my might. I hope I succeed. "Oh, crap. That reminds me. I have to run back to my place and grab a tampon."

Phil looks uneasy. "You might miss the meeting," he says.

"No," I say. "I'll run. I'm fast. I'll meet you there." I'm already turning to go. I pick up the pace to a jog. Before I disappear from view, I turn back to see if Phil has carried on. He's walking away with his hands in his pockets. I go even faster, sprinting now for the engineering tower. The comforting thwap of Phil's lanyard bouncing off my chest propels me forward. I catch my breath as I enter the lobby and walk to the elevator. I scan Phil's badge at the elevator entrance and walk through its opened doors, hitting the twentieth-floor option. The doors shut, and the elevator responds. I'm too much of a wreck to celebrate this fact, and maybe it's my conscience, but I feel watched in this elevator. I exercise every ounce of control I have to remain composed.

I swallow saliva and bile for the hundredth time as the elevator ascends to the engineer's bay. It's making me sick to hold my feelings in. I fight the urge to vomit. The weekly meeting I was on my way to is about to commence. Will they wonder where I am? Will they wonder why Phil is scanning into the tower right now? How soon before someone comes looking for me? As the elevator slows and the doors open, I step out onto the twentieth floor. I'm calm, my face unreadable, until I hear the elevator doors shut behind me. I can't hold it in any longer.

I unleash. Rage rips through me. I pick up a rolling office chair and slam it down on the control center. This accomplishes little. I walk over, remove the hatchet from the glass case, and let loose. I smash the security camera in the corner of the room first, though they'll know it was me by now anyway. I'm not thinking straight. I'm thinking in color—red, specifically. I raise the hatchet behind my head and bring it down, again and again, on the control panels. I hear the satisfying crunch of contact. I pry it free each time and repeat the motion. Sparks fly. The computer monitors go wild.

I know only one thing right now: damage the servers.

I'm exhausted. I open my hand and release the hatchet, hearing it *thunk* onto the floor beside me. I fall to my knees, which barely hit the floor before my tears. Torrents of them spill from me. I hate these people. I hate them so much. I wish I could unsee Pax. His swollen tongue hanging from his mouth, his bloodshot, bulging eyes staring lifelessly ahead of him. I don't want to remember him this way. The hate and the rage return. They've taken everything from me. I bang my fists on the floor. My job. My promising future. My security. My comfort and, now, Pax. A guttural cry rips from my throat. I place my hand on my stomach, coming back to myself. Maybe not everything. I look up at the destruction I've caused, suddenly feeling stupid. I keep my hand like this for over a minute, as if my hand were a shield, providing an extra layer of protection for the tiny human I've been denying inside me. It won't matter that I'm pregnant. They'll kill us both. String us up like Pax and the other man. From what Phil said, the other man had to be Mark, Frank's inside contact.

I walk over and call the elevator. There's no sound. The button doesn't light up. I hit it several more times. It doesn't come. I turn back around and scan the room. Sparks fly from gashes in the metal equipment. If it catches fire, I'm trapped here. But wait, there's the fire extinguisher. I consider it momentarily when my eyes fall on the nearby food delivery chute. It's a rectangular opening, about three feet wide and two feet deep. I retrieve the hatchet and wedge it beneath the bottom lip of the hatch's vertically sliding door and use the axe as a lever to pull the door open a couple of inches. The hatchet wedged beneath the door creates a gap. I curl my fingers around the bottom and lift. It's heavy. I'm pulling against some kind of mechanism. It grinds and screeches as I move it up, inch by inch, but I manage to open it all the way. I put my head into the long, dark chute. It's pitch black. I stride over and grab a pen from a nearby desk. I bring it back and drop it down the chute, listening for the landing. One one thousand, Two one thousand... It's taking so long that I think I must have missed the sound until it comes as a soft, echoing ping. Eight one thousand. It's a long way down, and that might not even be the bottom. That is wherever the food cart is.

I look at the elevator again and frown. Of course, there are no stairs. No backup escape routes in the tower. I'm not sure if there are any anywhere, just as I'm not sure if it's only my elevator that has been halted to keep me from escaping or if the damage I inflicted on the servers keeps it immobile. Either way, I should act fast. I can't assume I have time—that they haven't figured out what's happening here. This is a smart city, after all. They must know. I grab three more pens and fold them into the elastic waistband of my pants. Before I commit, I try the food panel on the wall. The screen doesn't light up at my touch. Well, that's one less thing to worry about—being taken out by an incoming food cart. Unless, of course, it's just this floor. I listen for a few minutes for sounds from within the chute that would signify the food cart is functional. There's nothing.

I take a deep breath to steel myself. "Here goes nothing," I mumble as I climb awkwardly through the hatch door and into the cramped chute. With my feet bracing on the wall out in front of me and my back to the wall opposite, I've managed to wedge myself into the chute. The tension I've created from the opposing force of my body and the added traction from my rubber-soled shoes and my hands down below me, palms against the cool metal, are keeping me from falling. I'm lucky the two opposing walls are smooth. The sharp, metal tracks the food cart runs up is located at the wall to the back—the one opposite the hatch door. I stare into the engineer's room and wonder if this is the right choice. *It's the* only *choice*, I reassure myself.

I inch up and use one foot to kick at the door. If I can close it behind me, I can conceal my escape route and maybe buy myself some time. The portal door slams shut. I'm engulfed in pitch blackness. I'm committed. No turning back. My heart hammers in my chest. I can't do this. I breathe in deep breaths. Pax flashes back to the forefront of my mind. Pax hanging. If I'm carrying his baby, I should do whatever I can to get us out of here. To preserve a part of him. Tears spill over and down my face again.

"What happened?" I whisper into the dark. "What went wrong?" My voice is strained.

I have to move. I'll die if I don't. This is the only option that gives me a chance to live. I could also die a painful death if I fall. My god, I have to think of other things.

Inch by inch, I begin my descent. I play songs in my head. I breathe. I picture Pax as he was at our picnic. I imagine a little boy who looks like him and maybe a little like me. I do whatever I can to keep from thinking about falling. My palms are beginning to sweat already. It's warm in the chute. I begin to move more fluidly, my movements more confident.

After a while, I drop another pen and count. Six one-thousand. *Fuck.* It's getting hot in here; my muscles threaten me with cramps, and I've made it a sad 25% of the way. I have to push against the back, using the opposing force to remove my hands and wipe them on my shirt, more and more. I have to move faster. My ears are acutely trained for the whir of the food cart moving to its next destination, but so far, there has been silence. Beautiful silence. This could mean the whole building is out of service. Did I do that?

After a while, I drop another pen—three one-thousand. I keep moving, using my mind to distract me as much as possible. A joke Ed used to tell me. The baby I've imagined growing inside me. An electric beat in a crowded concert. A proposal I pitched to my corporate superiors on doomsday that fell flat. Finally, I feel my butt hit something solid beneath me. I tentatively test my weight, barely able to keep myself wedged here anymore. My muscles are shaking with fatigue. I think it'll hold. It has to hold. I release my weight and sink against it. Sweet relief floods me. I sit for a few minutes as I attempt to gather my strength. What now? I'm exhausted. I stand and feel along the walls of my prison. There isn't an outline of a portal door anywhere that I can reach. That means the food box below me must be stopped at one. I crouch back down, curling into a tight fetal position. With my body now resting, the dark and the warmth begin to settle in my bones, pushing me into sleep. I feel safe tucked away here. My weight is being held, no one knows I'm in here, and the food service is clearly nonoperational. I can close my eyes, I think.

I open my eyes and blink several times. Where am I? My body aches. I attempt to stretch and find that I'm confined to a small space. Then, it all comes back to me in a rush of anxiety. I'm in the meal chute. Holy fuck, I must have nodded off. The box is still holding my weight beneath me. Sweat trickles down my forehead. That's why I woke. I was dreaming of a refreshing pool of water I could dip into and drink from. I have to get out of here. Panic creeps into every one of my pores. I stand up tall. My body aches as the contortions of my sleep are unwound. I brace myself as best I can with my arms out wide, hands pressing against the walls of the chute I'm confined to, and I jump. The meal delivery box below me doesn't budge. I jump on it again. Nothing. I let out a guttural, deep cry as I jump even higher and slam down on the box. It produces a loud, screeching sound and drops a couple of inches. My heart thuds wildly in my chest as I brace myself to fall. It doesn't happen. I return to my crawling position, braced with my back to the wall and my feet on the opposite wall. Then I take one leg and donkey-kick the box below me. I kick. And kick. The box moves centimeters at a time. I stop to catch my breath and wipe the sweat from my brow. I can't sustain this.

I take a moment to collect myself. All I can hear in this cramped space is the beating of my own heart and my labored breathing. I stand back up and jump on the box again, tentatively at first. It moves like it did the first time: an inch or two. As I gain more confidence, I jump higher and down with more force on the box. It moves one screeching inch at a time until it doesn't. The box gives way below my feet, and I'm freefalling. I reached out. There's nothing to grab. My hands and feet attempt to slow my descent. My hands gain contact, and then my feet. My sweaty palms make sounds like a squeegee as they try to stop me. I'm slowing, and then, I succeed, thanks to the rubber on my shoes. I'm splayed out like I'm doing a jumping jack. It's uncomfortable, and I can't hold it for long. I'll have to move. I push off with one hand while kicking my feet together on the wall opposite the one I aim to place my back on. My back slides below my feet. I'm wedged, but it was almost a disastrous plunge backward, head first. I use my hands against the wall below me to push myself into a horizontal position.

"Holy fuck," I say out loud. My heart is pounding in my chest. When I feel like I've regained command of my senses, I take a pen from my pocket and drop it—one one-thousand, two one-thousand—the pen clatters. I let out a victory 'woop' and begin crawling down the wall, one baby step at a time until I feel the box below me again. This has to be it. I have to be on the bottom floor. I stand on the box. I use my hands to feel the wall. My fingers trace the outline of a slat opening. It's above my head. The bottom lip of the slat is in line with my forehead. However, there isn't even a tiny sliver of light that would give me enough leverage to sneak a pen beneath it or a finger to pry it up. Pressing my hands flat on the door, I push up using the surface area of my hands to create friction. It moves just enough to see a sliver of light appear in a long line at the bottom before it slams shut again.

I take a deep breath. "I can do this." I try again—the same result. Then, I use one hand and attempt to jab the pen through the opening with the other, but I can't get it high enough. I want to cry. With each passing second, this seems more hopeless. In frustration, I bang my fists against the door and hang my head between my arms.

An answering, *BANG! BANG! BANG*! I look up, startled. It came from the other side. I respond with another *bang, bang, bang* of my own.

"Hello?!" I scream.

There's a muffled response on the other side. I start to cry. Big, fat tears roll down my cheeks. "Help me!" I shout, banging again. There are more muffled voices behind the wall and then a glorious, screeching noise as the slat is forced up—light floods into the space. A head sticks through the opening. It's a man.

"Holy shit," the guy says. "How'd you get in here?" But I can't respond. I just cry. "Come on," he says, extending his arm to me. "Let's get you out." I take his hand gratefully and make a clumsy, exhausted stumble into the familiar lobby.

CHAPTER 32

Carrie

"I did it," I say, bewildered. And then, the room spins. I double over my knees and make a terrible retching noise as my breakfast is expelled all over the floor in front of me. The three men in the lobby who witnessed my emergence from the shaft scatter. When I'm finished, I sit back and slump against the wall. I wipe my mouth with the back of my sleeve.

"Ugh," I say. "I'm sorry."

A man comes into view. He holds a half-drank clear bottle of water in front of me. "Here," he says. "If you want it."

"I do," I say, reaching for it. I drink a couple of gulps and lean back against the wall with my eyes closed, allowing my stomach to settle.

"What floor did you come down from?" one of them asks.

I open my eyes. I think for a moment and tell a small lie. "The tech floor," I say.

He turns away from me. "Guys! Guys! She came from nineteen stories up. This is it! This is how we can get them down!" He turns back to me, "How'd you do it?"

"I..." I stumble for the right words. "What do you mean this is how we can get them down?"

"Oh, honey, it's not just you that was stuck up there. Everyone is stuck. None of the elevators work."

"Oh my god," I say. "None of them? Anywhere?"

"None of them," he says, looking at me curiously. "How come it's just you? Where's the rest of the floor?"

"At a meeting," I say. "I was late. Bad time to be late."

The man shakes his head. "You're telling me."

"I crawled down by putting my back to one wall and my feet to the other," I say, answering his earlier question.

The man looks thoughtful. "Alright," he says. He turns back to the other two milling about in the lobby and begins talking with them, but I'm not listening. I stand and take stilted steps toward the exit, my body already sore but becoming more fluid as I move.

Once onto the street, my heart leaps as a woman wearing an army uniform approaches me. But then she passes me, evidently going somewhere else. I look around. The streets are crawling with army personnel and other civilians. Ladders are being moved, and ropes are being tied. Broken glass crunches beneath my feet, and as I survey the buildings above me, I see a lot of windows have been broken.

This was me, I think. *I did this.* Some of the lower windows have ladders propped against them. I see people descending a ladder. The ladders aren't high enough to reach the upper floors, though. How will they get down? I can't think about that right now. I have to get out of here. I walk through the streets, unaware of where I'm going exactly, except that I'm moving away from the black tower I left just moments ago that represents the city's center.

I could have trapped Hammer and Phillip in one of these buildings. I shake my head. A headache begins to bloom at my right temple. I look around. It's chaotic with army personnel and citizens all trying to make themselves useful. With my badge and my essential worker attire, no one questions me. I feel invisible.

Wandering the streets reminds me of this morning and what I stumbled upon. I walk with trepidation now. Hatred blooms inside of me. I look around me at the chaos. *You deserve it. You all deserve it.*

I keep walking. I want out of here. Then, I see a strange sight in front of me. It looks like a lidless blue dumpster being pushed down the street by a recruit. The person pushing it has the patch of a Brown. His head is down.

"Meal bars!" he shouts out. Why would anyone want a meal bar? There's something about his voice, though. I trail behind him, watching him. There are no takers for meal bars. There are some curious glances, but mainly, everyone is preoccupied with rescuing those trapped in the higher-up floors. I've closed in on him. He's only a few feet in front of me. I touch his shoulder. When he looks up at me, I see that it's Hammer. It takes everything I have to keep from reacting in a way that involves me throwing my arms around him in relief.

"Carrie," he says. "Have you seen the others?" I try to swallow back my tears. I try to stay collected, but I can't. It bursts from me.

"He... he... Pax..." I can't complete the sentence.

Hammer puts his hand on my shoulder, and I'm grateful he doesn't make me say it. "He knew the risks, Carrie. Let's focus on getting us outta here now. He'd want that."

I still can't talk. We walk together for a few minutes, not speaking. Hammer calls out for meal bars occasionally, putting on the rouse that he's been tasked with delivering food to the people now that their food transport systems are down. There isn't one taker. When there isn't anyone in our direct vicinity, he asks, "Do you know what's going on?"

"Oh," I say despondently. "Yeah, I think I did it." His eyes go wide.

"How?" he asks.

"Took a hatchet to the servers in the command center," I say.

"Damn," he says.

"What's the plan now?" I ask.

"To get the hell outta dodge," he replies. "With these bad boys." He nods to the large container he's pushing in front of him. "I got assigned factory duty yesterday," he says. "They make these things out of *bugs*." Ava had told me that, but I don't care right now. Still, I can appreciate that Hammer is trying to distract me.

We approach a massive rectangular opening in the dome's wall that blows air from two of the biggest fans I've ever seen. The force of the air is enough that we have to turn back rather than try to pass it.

"That must be the intake system," Hammer says. "It's still working."

I nod. That makes sense. I'm sure there are backup system for some of the city's most essential features. Guess they didn't think the elevator situation through.

Having to backtrack, Hammer looks as anxious as I feel. We have to get the fuck out of here before someone suspects us.

"Do you have the generators?" I ask. Hammer frowns.

"That was Phillip's department," he responds.

"But I thought he was the assassin?"

"The three of us came up with a plan in private," he regards me. "I'm sorry, Carrie. We just didn't know who would get what work assignment. We did our best to give answers that would nudge their decisions, but it was never a sure thing. Whichever one of us had the opportunity, they'd be the one to do it."

Anger floods me. Pax had to have known he had a good chance of being a Green and Greens go to the Trade Party their first night. I clench my fists, digging my nails into my palms until the anger turns to despair and squeezes the tears from me. "Do you think...was presented with that opportunity?" I can't say his name.

"Probably," he concludes. "If it was him, let's hope he succeeded."

"Do you know where you're going?" I ask. The city center stands tall behind us like looming defenders of Eyth.

"Not really," he admits. "I just figure we'll continue along the edge of the dome and look for an exit."

I nod.

A reverberation follows a loud boom. Hammer and I duck instinctively and cover our ears. There's heat at our backs. We turn around to see a plume of smoke curl along the dome's interior as it snakes its way up.

"Christ, what the hell was that?" Hammer exclaims.

We exchange worried glances. "The intake," we say in unison as we turn the large rolling container around and head back towards the source of the explosion.

We drop our casual walk and clip along the fastest the factory bin will allow. It's heavy, so we push together. There's a gaping hole in the wall. Smoking remains litter the surrounding area. Only a few blades from one of the massive fans remain intact, but they're not spinning. This is it. This is our opening, but there's still so much heat from the area. We glance around nervously.

"Won't be long before the army is here," Hammer says.

"But there isn't a clear path for this cart," I say. "There's too much debris." We could leap and climb without the cart, but we've come so far that we're both reluctant to leave it. Then, we see a beautiful sight standing on the other side through the smoldering area. *Our guys.* Frank, Crowly and Miller. They're attaching a rope to a large piece of a fan blade. We watch as they connect it to a motorcycle and pull. The motorcycle spins out, unable to pull the weight.

"Come on, come on," Hammer says quietly through gritted teeth.

Finally, the bike gains traction, and the blade trails along behind it, opening up an aisle that may just be big enough.

"Come on!" Crowly is screaming at us as he runs towards us to help, covering his mouth with his arm. We spring into action. Miller and I kick small pieces of debris out of the way while Crowly and Hammer push the cart. I'm trying to hold my breath. The air is hot and still hangs heavy with smoke. Just as Frank returns, we've cleared the hole and stepped onto the dirt on the other side. I gasp for fresh air and cough.

My eyebrows feel singed, and my cheeks throb from the heat. Crowly and Frank are trying to secure the rope around the meal bar bin. They're stressed—their fingers fumble. I've never seen them like this. And then, looking behind us through the smoke, I see what they do—a large crowd of uniformed soldiers running towards us or the hole that was blown into their wall.

"We have to go!" I shout with an infused pitch.

"Working on it," Frank says tightly. The world seems to move in slow motion.

"Now!" he yells. "Let's go! Let's go!"

We scramble to get on the bikes. Hammer goes for the back of Miller's bike. I run and throw my leg over behind Crowly just before he peels out. Frank is a lot slower with the heavy bin behind him. I keep watching behind me. He's considerably farther behind, but he's coming. After about thirty minutes, I lose sight of him completely.

"Where are we going?!" I yell against the wind.

"There's a rendezvous spot about an hour away. Frank will meet us there."

An hour later, we stop at an outcropping of rock. When we get off, Crowly and Miller remove the seats of their motorcycles, exposing the charging panels to the sun. I keep my eyes trained on the way from which we came.

"Will he come?" I ask when he stands beside me.

"He'll come," Crowly responds.

We wait. And then, finally, there's a trail of dust in the distance. Crowly takes a breath and places his hands behind his head as he turns away. His reaction tells me that he wasn't confident he'd come.

When Frank pulls up, Crowly and Miller approach him, and they do a quick handshake with bumps and slaps.

"The wheels on this thing will not make it home," Frank says as he removes the motorcycle seat and exposes the panels to the sun. "And it's draining the juice."

"Were you pursued?" Miller asks.

"I don't think so," Frank says. "They've got bigger problems now. The city will need to be evacuated."

"What about Phillip?" Hammer asks.

"I can go back to our stakeout and watch for him," Crowly offers. Frank considers this.

"We can't move for a few hours anyway until this thing charges enough to get us to the Boeing, but we need to put more distance between us and them. Tonight. You've got four hours, Crowly," Franks says.

Crowly gives a salute and goes to retrieve his bike. We watch as he drives away, and I notice Hammer touch his forehead, chest, and each shoulder in the sign of the cross. I walk away to find a comfortable place to pass the time.

Miller approaches and lowers himself beside me in the shade of the rock I claimed. "She'll be ecstatic when you return," he says. I know he means Ava. "She didn't mean what she said, you know."

I look down at the sand remembering her harsh words after I volunteered. She avoided me the days after that.

"She was pissed but she never meant for you to leave without saying goodbye. She was torn up about it," he says. I feel tears spring to my eyes. "And I'm sorry about Pax," he adds.

I nod numbly.

"I hope you know you've still got her when you return," he says, patting my back.

I fold my legs and hang my head as I watch tears darken the dirt below me. "Thanks Miller," I say.

"You can call me Landon too. If you want."

I attempt a weak smile and sniff. We sit in silence, listening to the noises of the desert.

Crowly returns two and a half hours later—earlier than expected. Frank and Miller trade knowing looks. They jump up to begin preparing their bikes before Crowly comes to a stop. Alone.

"Sorry, mate," he says to Hammer. "No sign of Phillip, but they're on the move. The army is using transport vehicles to move supplies from the city. They'll be looking for a place to set up camp. No telling how long they'll be able to stay under that dome, but they're preparing to evacuate. No doubt about that."

Frank gives a nod. "Let's get moving then."

But before making a move, Frank looks curiously at Crowly. I look, too. Crowly has a wide grin spread across his face.

Frank mirrors his smile, shaking his head in disbelief. "We did it," he says.

"We did it," Crowly repeats.

CHAPTER 33

Sam

June 1, 2026 Six Months Later

T he heart problems were likely harmless palpitations caused by stress and exemplified by nutrient deficiencies, the family doctor told me when Rose and I returned to the town of Stanley. It didn't feel harmless when my heart sputtered, and my stomach dropped with the feeling of falling, but it has improved since the stress of winter and the threat of Eyth has been eliminated. Plus, I've been eating better since Rose, and I returned to Stanley shortly after the Eyth crew returned with Carrie and Hammer. The rest of our original nineteen rag-tag crew from Stanely remained on the ranch. Well, those who are still living anyway.

I say a silent prayer for those who have lost their lives and for Phillip, who could still be out there somewhere. But Rose and I finally agreed—we couldn't be another mouth to feed on that ranch. We calculated what remained in the food shed and the meal bars, and they'd barely get by. If the hunters were lucky, that would be gravy on top. We left so more children could enter. I know of others who did the same—mostly elderly people.

Frank came to see us about two months ago on his way out of town on a recon mission with Crowly. He came as soon as the snow melted and the roads were passable. He said they wanted to see what had become of Eyth and the inhabitants. He brought letters from Tom and Lilly and drawings from the grandkids. That's how we found out they did it. They made it through the winter without anyone having to starve. However, Frank was no longer "Frank the Tank," as they used to call him in high school. He carried that body image with him his whole life (just about) until last winter stole it from him. His head looks too boxy now. I'm not sure lean is a good look on him, but I'm not about to tell him that. He didn't have much say in the matter. Frank informed us that calving season was underway and that we had managed to hold on to twenty-three head of cattle. One cow lost her baby, and they used her milk to serve fresh milk daily. She produces six gallons a day. They get a little extra from the other heifers but don't want to take too much away from the babies. It's enough to make sure everyone gets a decent portion daily. I remind him that while the babies are young, they won't go through six gallons, but as they get older, they'll need to scale back and leave more milk for them. Frank told me they've started a milk ration system where they pass out cards. Once your card is used up, no more milk for the day. Everyone gets handed a new card in the morning. Of course, the cards have made it into the monetary system, and they're often traded or given as gifts. After he completed his report to us, he left eager to see what he could find out about the country after Eyth's fall.

After Frank left that day, Rose looked at me. Her eyes danced with excitement. "You know what this means, right?"

"What?" I asked.

"We can go back," she said with animation. When my facial expressions didn't match hers, she cozied up beside me and took my hand. "Oh, please, Sam. They made it through the worst of it, and so did we. They'll be self-sustaining soon, and we could help." I chewed on that for a moment. "Oh, please, Sam. I want to be with our children and our grandchildren. We're too old to live in isolation."

"We're not alone," I said, and she knew I meant the other residents here. The Stanley community pulled together and put up a hell of a fight this last winter. We all felt like kin now—one big family.

"I know, but it's not the same, Sam." I turned and stared into her pleading eyes. I sighed.

"Yeah, alright. We'll run it by Frank next time he comes by and make sure he doesn't have any reservations," I said. Rose jumped with giddiness and kissed me on the cheek.

Rose and I have been living off the food stored in the cellar. Digging it out was an impossible task with my shoulder being out of commission. So, we had to ask for help. We agreed to share the food with Sheriff Wilson, his wife, and their new baby girl for their help. We also offered to help feed Ron, who returned to Stanely with his Cessna but he said he didn't need it. He was well prepared. A 'prepper' he called himself. Between Ron and me, we had enough to dole out rations to sustain the community. There isn't much left, but we have a decent spring crop started, and more wild animals have started to appear. We'll be alright. The cellar food served its purpose and got us through the worst of it. My shoulder is mostly healed now. I still have to baby it, but I can move it without pain most days.

For now, we've got Rose's Cadillac to help connect people and do pickups in the morning to get people to work. We've all come together to construct a community garden that should bear enough food to feed us this year and store enough for next winter. Eventually, the gas will run out, and vehicles will be caput. Talks about community planning (moving folks closer to the garden and each other) have started. Eventually, they'll all live around the garden.

I see the dust coming up the long stretch of dirt road that leads to our house. The motor is quiet, nearly imperceptible. It has to be Frank. Back after two months of scouting or whatever he was doing. I sit on a chair on the front porch and watch as he parks the bike and throws his leg over as he dismounts. We nod at each other in acknowledgment, but I can tell immediately from his facial expression that something has happened. I stand up.

"What is it?" I ask.

"There's power," he says as he approaches the porch.

"Power?"

"Electricity," he clarifies.

My eyebrows shoot up. "Where?"

"All the cities that were slotted for Act Two of the Era Unveiling: Salt Lake and Portland. And I assume Cleveland, Austin, and New York, but we didn't venture out that far."

"What does it mean?" I ask.

"It means someone who knew how to flip that switch has done that."

"An elite or an old government official?" I ask.

"Has to be, but here's the interesting part. The army is occupying all of those cities, but they're not acting in a strategic, defensive manner." I draw my eyebrows together. "They're helping the citizens. *Actually* helping them," he says. We stay looking at each other for a long moment. Frank rests his dusty boot on the top step leading up to the porch.

"Let's have a seat," I say. We sit side by side on the wicker porch chairs. Rose is out at the moment. She went to bring Sheriff Wilson and his wife, Ann, some ground-up oats for the baby. Ann hasn't been producing enough milk to feed the baby despite being given extra rations to aid in lactation. Luckily, the baby is old enough now to supplement with solids.

"So, that's where you've been? Out scouting all these cities?" I ask.

"Yep," Frank replies. "Crowly was with me, but he's headed back to the ranch to spread the news."

"What's he going to tell them, exactly?"

"That we've been extended an invitation." I look at Frank, shocked. "I know," he says. "I was skeptical at first, but I don't think I am anymore. Well, cautiously optimistic is what I'd call it. With the power up, the city's water systems work in certain areas. The army has begun handing out water and rigging systems to water crops. They've built large hydroponic systems to kickstart their growing efforts."

"Could this be a trap?" I ask.

Frank scratches his head. "We're going to continue to monitor them, but from what I've seen, their actions don't suggest anything other than a willingness to help and restore some kind of normalcy for the people."

"Why?" I ask.

"Genevieve is dead. We succeeded. Without her to listen to, they've fallen back on their captain's orders and their sworn oaths of enlistment." I know the oath. I remember seeing it in Frank's enlistment paperwork that he left on his bed in his room the day he signed his papers without telling Rose or me. He left after his high school graduation ceremony a few days later to begin basic training. After four years, he went to college, completing a bachelor's in engineering in just three years. From there, he enlisted again and went to Officer Candidate School. He worked his way up from Second Lieutenant to Captain and finally to Deputy Lieutenant Colonel at the Office of Personnel to the Army in the Pentagon. The oath is a promise by the new servicemember upon enlistment that states they will defend the Constitution and obey the orders of the President of the United States and the officers appointed over them.

"How do you know she's dead?" I ask.

"I talked to them," he says.

"You what?"

"They seem like my old buddies. I told them who I was and my position in the old government, and they told me what they were doing. What their plans were," he states.

"Even if the army is back to protecting the citizens and defending this country as a whole, someone told them how to return power to those cities," I say.

"Yeah, but Crowly watched them crawl out from their hole. We knew most would survive. They still had the army transport vehicles. With the dome being uninhabitable, it makes sense that they'd want to turn the power on in those other cities. Their sinister act two of the Era Unveiling became their Plan B," he says.

"So, the army isn't a threat anymore. Do you believe that?" I ask.

"Elites are still out there, but without Genevieve, the army is upholding their fiduciary responsibilities to our country and its citizens."

"How can you be sure?" I ask.

"They're acting differently, for starters. Of course, I can't be 100% sure, but if they are back to protecting the people and this country, we've just won the lottery. We might have a chance of defending this country. Of course, we won't be able to do it alone in this state, but with so many other countries signed up to be part of the One World Order, their populations have also been drastically reduced. Right now, Canada stands neutral against them and China. I was told we've already started negotiations to enter into a strategic alliance. With Canada's population being intact and our people being mad as hell, we might stand a chance."

"Will there be war?" I ask.

"Maybe, if we can't manage to make ourselves look like enough of a threat to deter that. But Canada wants to avoid those scenarios as much as we do. We still have a strong military presence in this country. After all, it was never their intention to weaken the military, just the people. They're strong."

I sit with this, digesting it. This means five cities throughout the country can provide water, light, heat, air conditioning, and flushing toilets to a small percentage of the population. These cities will be like magnets, attracting everyone.

"How long before those cities are overrun?" I ask.

Frank lets out a long, drawn-out sigh. "People will flock to these spots, no doubt. I've watched the army move around, actively looking to take survivors back. But here's the sad part, Dad. I can't be sure of the exact figures, but I'd say 75-90% of the population has been pruned." I look over at him and search his face. He's serious. "And those that have survived, some by the skin of their teeth, and others because they were prepared, some of them won't come back to city living because they don't trust other people anymore. If they've figured out a way to survive without the aid of outsiders by now, as you guys have here and as the Colony has, why move to the congested city? Naw, it'll just be the desperate ones."

"So, who's in power now? Who's calling the shots?" I ask.

"Army Colonels, from what I gather. Seems like a coordinated effort to lead with no single head," he says before adding, "Yet."

"But if there are elites and legacy government officials out there still, how can we be sure they won't find a way to regain power? To negotiate our way back into the One World Order and continue with plans for this so-called Era Unveiling?" I ask.

"We can't," he says quietly, adding, "That's why I'm putting together a team while we still have transportation options that don't involve horse-back."

"A team for what?" I ask.

He looks at me, his expression intense. "We're going to hunt them, Dad. Every last one of them."

CHAPTER 34

Carrie

June 1, 2026 Six Months Later

I place my hand on the tight skin stretched across my rotund belly and press lightly. There's an answering pressure that pushes from within. The spot takes the shape of a tiny foot. I put my hand on the foot. I still haven't gotten used to it—the feeling of a tiny human growing inside me. It quickens my pulse when the baby flips. It hurts my ribs when the baby kicks up high. I'm out of breath easily, and just about everything I eat gives me heartburn. Ava tells me that means the baby will have a full head of hair, according to an old wives' tale.

I can't help it. When I picture my baby, I imagine a boy with wispy brown hair and kind eyes like Pax. It still hurts to think about him. The threat of tears pricks my eyes any time he comes into my thoughts. Hormones can't be helping.

I may not have Pax, but I do have a community now. People. Support. Upon my return, I became somewhat of a local celebrity. I was rewarded for my bravery with one of the more built-out log cabins that I share with Ava, complete with a fireplace. Though, she's not home much. For most of the winter, it felt like my own private digs—a luxury. Ava and Miller have gotten quite close, but Ava has started staying with me more recently, saying she wants to be there in case the baby comes. Ava might be more excited about the baby than I am. Though, I know my reservations come largely from the prospect of unmedicated childbirth. It seems like every woman in the Colony has offered some advice on the topic. While I'm not ungrateful, it also isn't particularly helpful. I have to go through this—just me. Women used to die in childbirth. Ava assures me that this was primarily because we weren't aware of sanitization factors back then, but we are now. I won't die, she has promised me.

The winter was not without its trials, but we made it. The love I felt when people, noticing my growing belly, offered me their portion of food is a feeling I will always hold onto. It's the feeling of acceptance and belonging, and it's a treasure to be stored and taken out to marvel at when I'm feeling low. This is my place. These are my people. For the first time since this EMP business, I feel deep satisfaction with my life and circumstances. Once I'm holding that happy, healthy baby in my arms, I'll have everything.

It's funny how Bodin, Ava, Hammer, and I have been grouped into a little club. They're not people I would have normally chosen to associate with, aside from Ava, but we often find ourselves in each other's company. People seek us out around the fire to ask questions. The children beg for stories, which we're happy to tell with only the slightest embellishment. Even Caroline has tried to make amends with me. For now, I'm keeping her at a distance. It's too hard to think about the reasons why she feels sorry for me and why she no longer needs to hate me.

Even without her Eyth-survivor status, Ava would have turned into somewhat of a darling here in the Colony. Her physician assistant training has translated into something useful. She makes house calls for illnesses and aids the nurses who work the complex cases in the Med Shed. I'm envious of her for this. She got to take a part of her identity from before with her. I've had to recreate myself. Or find myself depending on how I look at it. It was a grueling process. Bodin finally gave up hope of ever having a romantic relationship with her once he saw that she and Landon were unbreakable.

Bodin is on the recon crew. He gets to make trips into town periodically. The Colony exchanges books with the local library, which has established an exchange policy—a book in allows you to take a book out.

The recon crew brings things to trade when their business takes them into town. Fresh milk is a local favorite. They carry back salves, tinctures, alcohol for sterilization, needles, fishing bait, etc, in exchange for the milk. Frank is stingy with his guns and won't allow us to trade ammo or weapons, although we have those aplenty. He says they're our strategic edge; we want to maintain that position to secure the Colony's safety. I get it. He's still operating from a military perspective.

Bodin tells us stories about his trips to town. There's an outdoor market that's popped up on Main Street in the center of town. It's the place to go if you're looking for something and have something to trade. It all sounds exciting to me since I've been grounded in the Colony until the baby is born and strong. But Bodin says it's not enjoyable. He says the people in town have a hardness to them now and a cynicism that makes doing business hard and, at times, dangerous. Even so, I'm glad he goes. He brings back treasures for Ava and me sometimes. I have him to thank for my most treasured possession—a picture of Pax. I told him where Pax lived and asked him to go there to see what he could recover. The gym was ransacked, probably in worse shape than when we were there, but a framed picture of Pax with his parents was left behind as it was of little value to anyone else. There isn't a day that goes by that I don't touch the smooth glass over his face in that picture.

There's a midwife in the Colony. She's old, and with the exception of one delivery a few months ago, she's out of practice. Still, the baby and the mom lived, and she has a confidence about her that's hard to question. She's delivered hundreds of babies in her lifetime. She's training Ava to become the next midwife. Ava is thrilled but hasn't received much education, aside from lectures, due to the lack of baby action around here. I wonder if she's so excited about my baby because she gets to help deliver it or because it's my baby—maybe both.

Ava bursts through our door. "Crowly is back. He has news. Everyone is gathering." She's out of breath. I prop myself up on the bed with some effort. My belly is a constant obstacle these days. The easiest things can be challenging, like bending down to pick something up. One of my old bunkmates, Clara's mom, returned to her house, taking Bodin and another guy from the recon crew with her. She retrieved her old maternity clothes to bring back for me. Two boxes were placed on the floor of my cabin that day. Clara's mom looked at the boxes in my living room with yearning and said, "I always thought I'd have more babies." Then, she was gone before I could adequately thank her. Retrieving those boxes was no small feat in early March, with the snow and ice still crusting the earth and mud holes pocked throughout the sunny places.

As Ava and I walk toward the community gathering place below the ranch house, Ava slips her arm through mine. It's a habit we'd started over the winter months when snow and ice made dangerous slipping hazards for pregnant women, i.e., me. Ava and I pick a spot on the edge of the gathering crowd. I look around. I spot Bodin standing with Evie and Ted. Evie is on his shoulders. He notices me watching and waves. I smile and wave back just as Alex arrives with his adopted mom, and Evie squirms to get down from Bodin's shoulders so she can play. I wave to Corrin, Alex's mom. She lost a child a few years ago to Leukemia, and she was thrilled to take Alex in. She hasn't seen her husband since he went out of town on doomsday. It's just her and Alex now. She isn't the only adult who's had to take in other people's children. The Colony is littered with them after so many desperate parents left them at our doorstep. Very few of those parents have returned to claim their kids. Despite the exchange rule established last fall, I sense a disproportionate number of children were allowed to enter the

Colony compared to adults who volunteered to leave. I like them having them around. They're little reminders of the goodness of humanity.

I turn my attention back to the deck. There's an excited energy infused throughout the crowd today. We all want to know what is important enough to interrupt a workday. Well, nap for me. I look up onto the deck and see the council members plus Landon, Crowly, Lilly, and Tom. Ava smiles sweetly as her eyes meet Landon's. I squeeze my friend's arm. I love seeing her like this—lovesick. Crowly sees me and breaks from his entourage, taking the stairs off the deck two at a time. I give Ava a questioning look. She makes a "dunno" sound. He reaches me and places a hand on my shoulder.

"I want you to know first," he says, trying to catch his breath. "Pax did it. Pax got her."

"Thank you," I whisper. My eyes brim with tears. He gives me a single nod and turns to bound back up the stairs. "He did it," I repeat as the tears spill over. Ava pulls me in close and puts her head on my shoulder. I squeeze my eyes shut, letting the information settle. I'm glad he didn't say her name. I know Pax did what he had to, but I'd still rather not think of Pax as a woman killer.

The announcement is made. An infectious buzz spreads throughout the Colony. Electricity in some cities? It's almost too much to fathom. To top it off, we were all given the option to leave. They will transport anyone who wants to move to Salt Lake City in a few days.

As Ava and I walk back to our cabin, she says, "There's a hospital there, Carrie. A *functioning* hospital."

"I heard," I respond.

"You could have your baby there," she says.

I sigh, knowing this was where she was going.

"Will you go back?" I ask. Ava has to be tempted. She'd get a position at an actual hospital again. She could live a life that resembles what she had before. Or, at least, it'll get there.

She hesitates. "I don't think so."

"That seems like a maybe," I point out.

"Depends on what you and Landon want to do," she replies.

The water begins to well in my eyes again. "Same goes for me. We decide together." Then, I ask, "Do you think the hospital has epidurals?"

Ava frowns. "Doubt it."

"That's what I thought," I say.

"But they will have trained personnel from the army medical team, a clean environment, air conditioning, monitoring equipment, running water, and proper tools," she adds.

We reach the door to our cabin. I know Ava intends to leave me here so she can return to work. I lean against the door. "Before you go," I begin. She raises her eyebrows expectantly. "If it's fine by you, I'd rather stay here." Ava's face breaks into a smile.

"I was hoping you'd say that," she says. "This is our home."

I smile. "This is our home," I repeat.

The static of old man Kirk's radio comes into focus as he's passing by Ava and me. The radio snags on something. He stops and tunes it until it comes in loud and clear. It's a song. He looks at us, elated. I know the song. It's *See You Again* by Charlie Puth. I stop breathing for a moment as the lyrics wash over me.

Old man Kirk scampers off, eager to show off his discovery, but I can't move. I'm frozen in place with tears streaming down my face. I can't help but think of it as a message from Pax. Ava blinks at me, disbelieving. Then she nods at me and smiles in understanding. We both think it. She squeezes my hand. I feel the tiny human inside of me flip.

About the Author

Hailey lives in Park City, Utah, with her husband, two daughters, and two dogs. Thrilling fiction stories with real-world takeaways are her thing. When not writing, she's reading, focusing on a healthy lifestyle, and spending time with her family.

Connect with Hailey on Facebook or on haileygosack.com

Also By Hailey Gosack

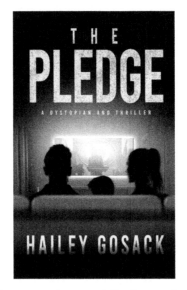

A novella set in Dystopian America. A family struggles to survive under an oppressive regime, their lives dictated by scarcity and surveillance. In a sinister bid to sustain a crumbling food system, the government demands citizens pledge their lives for the greater good. The family faces a harrowing choice—secure pledges to ensure the survival of at least one parent and both children or succumb to the ruthless consequences of an unforgiving regime.

Printed in Great Britain
by Amazon